THE BLOOD DESCENT SERIES

WHEN VENGEANCE BLEEDS ROYAL

L.Z. CATHCART

Visit my website at:
www.lzcathcart.com
Cover Design & Map: Miblart
Editor: Jessica McKelden
For inquiries or licensing requests, please contact:
lz@lzcathcart.com

PRONUNCIATION GUIDE

PEOPLE

Alaric Vhalryn (AL-ah-rick) (VAL-rin)

Arabella Kyrvayne (air-ah-BELL-ah) (KY-ruh-vayn)

Aviah Kyrvayne (ah-VEE-ah) (KY-ruh-vayn)

Avner Cadmius (AV-nur) (CAD-mee-us)

Azrix Thaelorn (AZ-ricks) (THAY-lorn)

Bramble Starling (BRAM-bull) (STAR-ling)

Calista Auroran (kah-LISS-tah) (ah-ROAR-un)

Cyrus Nyvelis (SIGH-russ) (NYE-vel-is)

Dom Frostholm (DAHM) (FROST-holm)

Elowen Rothewen (EL-oh-wen) (ROTH-eh-wen)

Emberly Kyrvayne (EM-ber-lee) (KY-ruh-vayn)

Evren Rothewen (EV-ren) (ROTH-eh-wen)

Florietta (floor-ee-ETT-ah)

Granite Morenai (GRAN-it) (MOR-en-eye)

Hadralis (hah-DRAY-is)

Hugo Auroran (HYOO-go) (ah-ROAR-un)

Ilyan Frostholm (ILL-ee-an) (FROST-holm)

Ilara Rothewen (ih-LAR-ah) (ROTH-eh-wen)

Jaggard Kyrvayne (JAG-erd) (KY-ruh-vayn)

Jexi (JEK-see)

Kalum (KAL-um)

Korrigan Cadmius (CORE-ih-gan) (CAD-mee-us)

Lumira Kyrvayne (loo-MEER-ah) (KY-ruh-vayn)

Lysander Meridian (LIH-san-der) (MEH-rih-dee-an)

Marnox Kyrvayne (MAR-nocks) (KY-ruh-vayn)

Nerissa Thaelorn (nuh-RISS-uh) (THAY-lorn)

Nikolai Frostholm (NICK-oh-lie) (FROST-holm)

Orielle Vhalryn (OR-ee-ell) (VAL-rin)

Pyraxus Kyrvayne (pie-RACKS-us) (KY-ruh-vayn)

Quinn (KWIN)

Samir (sah-MEER)

Solarin (so-LAR-in)

Tavern Orren (TAV-ern) (OR-en)

Thara Kyrvayne (THAR-ah) (KY-ruh-vayn)

Thornley Blackbriar (THORN-lee) (BLACK-bry-er)

Wrenna Teravale (WREN-ah) (TARE-ah-vail)

Yasmin Predaxia (YAZ-min) (pre-DAX-ee-ah)

Zedriel (ZAY-dree-el)

Zylven Meridian (ZIL-ven) (MEH-rih-dee-an)

LOCATIONS

Aelric Bridge (EHL-rick) (BRIJ)

Aethervoid (EE-thur-voyd)

Altareth (AL-tuh-reth)

Crimsun (KRIM-sun)

Cyrathea (SEER-uh-thee-uh)

Vesper (VES-per)

Bravara (bruh-VAR-ah)

Grovenar (GROVE-eh-nar)

Naiad (NIGH-ad)

Shadowspire (SHAD-oh-spire)

Terravox (TERR-ah-vox)

Zestria (ZESS-tree-ah)

Rimefall (RIME-fall)

Aurova (ah-ROH-vah)

Regale (reh-GALE)

Tigran (TIE-gran)

A NOTE BEFORE YOU BEGIN

This book contains blood, betrayal, and bedroom scenes, not necessarily in that order. Expect graphic violence, morally gray choices, dead bodies (plural), political backstabbing, language that would horrify my grandmother, and intimacy that is raw, sharp, and not meant for the faint of heart. Also: trauma, power struggles, questionable coping mechanisms, and a fair amount of alcohol (some of it deserved). All led by one woman who doesn't ask for forgiveness—or permission.

If that sounds like too much, no judgment. Close the book.

If not—*great*. Step inside. She's dealt with worse.

For the girls with quiet rage and clever hands, who were told independence was a flaw—may the world learn to fear your silence.

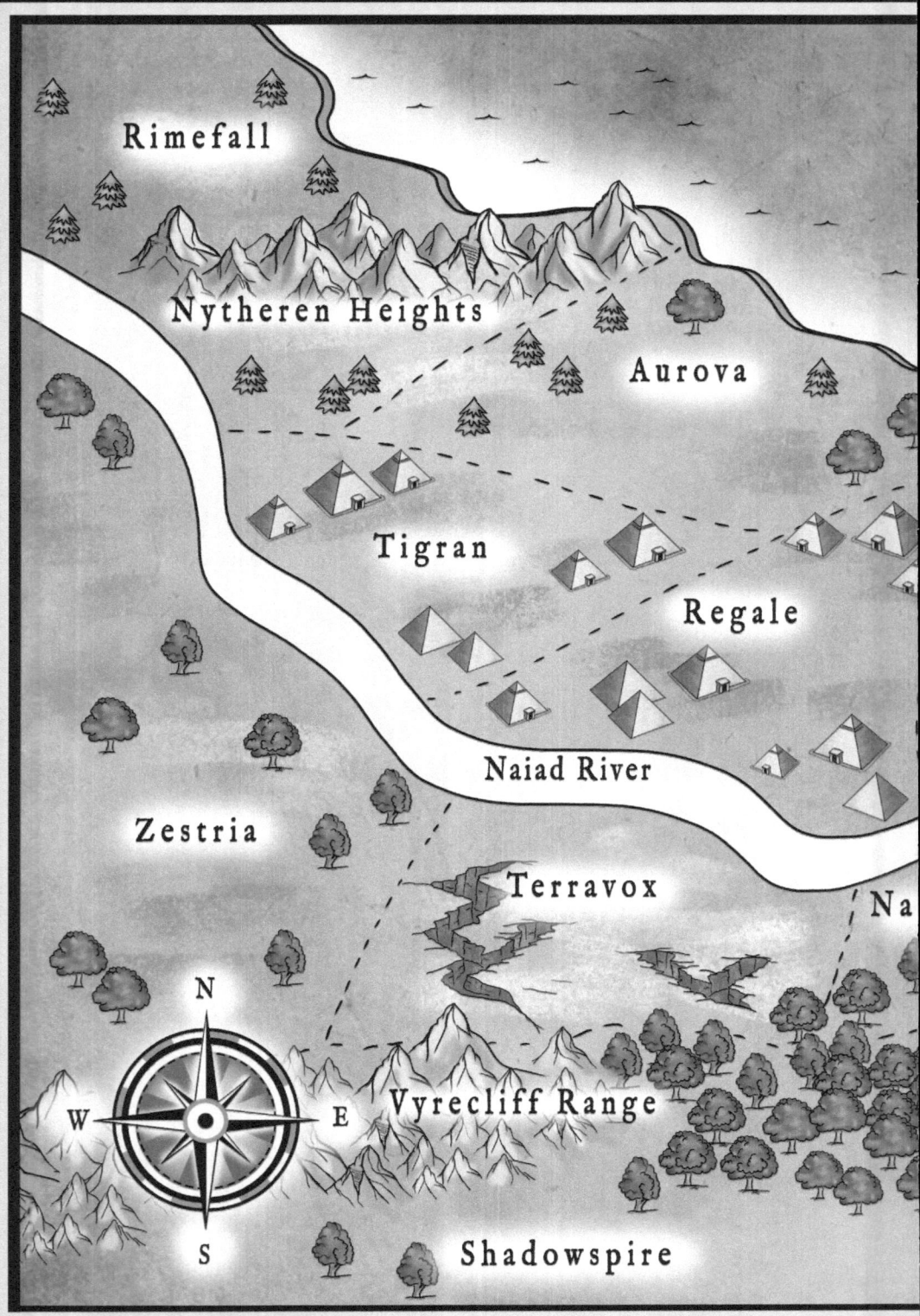

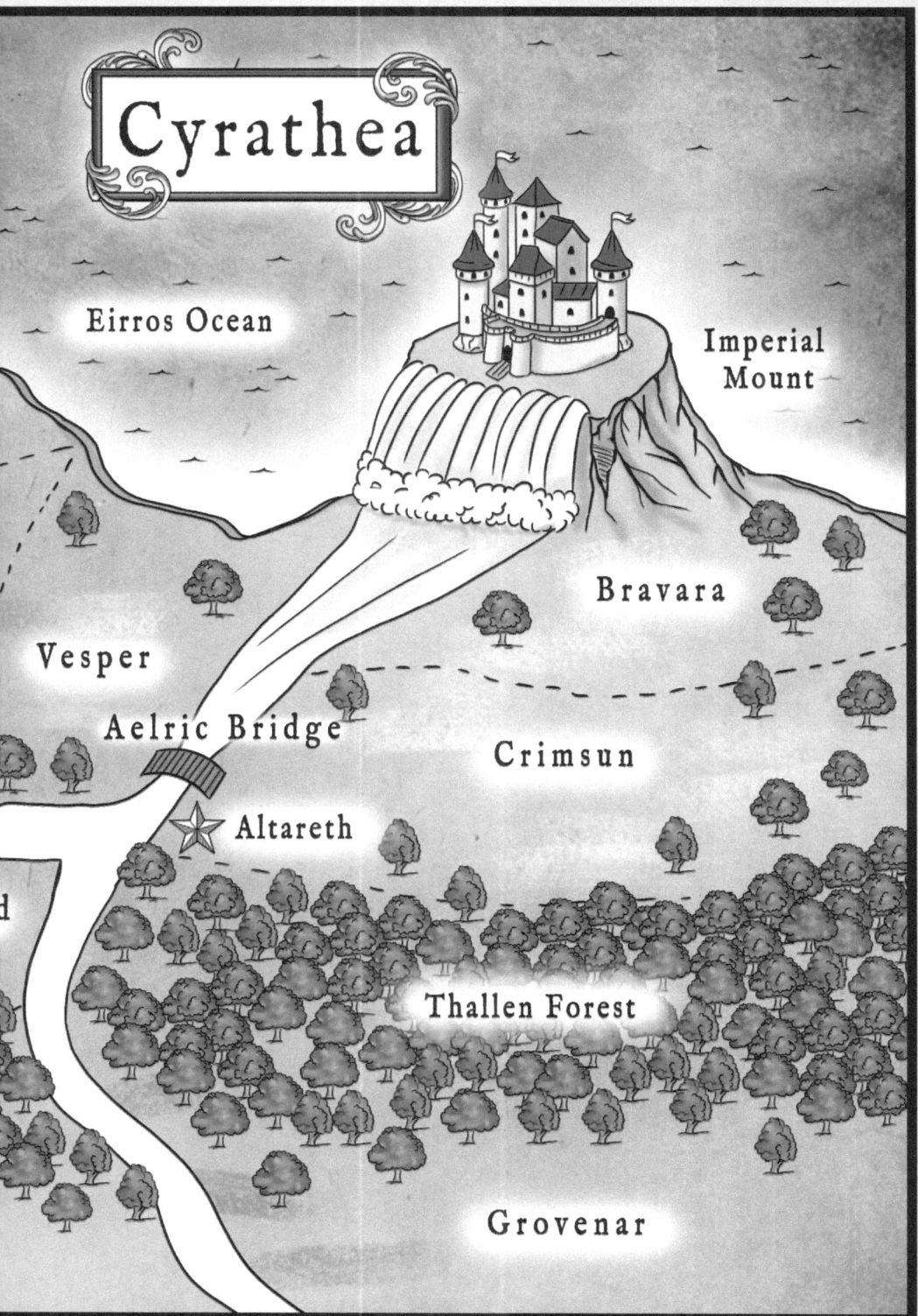

1

THEY ARE HERE

The palace in Crimsun Territory rises from the heart of Altareth, a city built on ruthless power and blood-soaked secrets that don't just kill—they erase entire bloodlines with the same efficiency the royal gardeners use to prune unsightly branches.

Some mysteries slither through velvet-draped corridors, traded like exotic currency. Others become ammunition—political, legal, or personal—depending on who whispers them and when.

Then there are the truths buried so deep beneath the palace foundations that even the High Sovereigness wakes clawing at her throat, pretending they're not devouring the silk of her sanity like ravenous moths. But Lumira Kyrvayne is done letting them feast unseen.

Even Emberly's room is no exception—another carefully guarded haven, hidden in plain sight among the palace's countless chambers. Lumira pauses at her sister's doors, motion halting inches from the gilded handle—as if touching it might summon the past.

She hasn't been back since the funeral. Not because it hurts—more because the moment she steps inside, pretending to be patient becomes impossible.

But now, her fingers hover—then land. It gleams coldly beneath her fingertips—a deceptively ordinary barrier. Matching the palace's countless deceptions, simplicity is its first lie.

Her free hand drifts to the dagger at her hip. Ceremonial in name only, forged for function, not flair. She didn't come to grieve. She came prepared.

The hallways behind her appear emptied of sound, but the palace never truly sleeps. Under its opulent façade, it hums with tension—every gesture rehearsed, every silence a strategy.

She steadies herself, then turns the knob and steps into the shadowed room. The air is thick and stale, like time decayed here and never moved on. Dust coats each surface, though she suspects servants intentionally maintain this neglected state, preserving the delicate illusion of perpetual grief. One balcony window stands ajar, the heavy curtain swaying enough to stir the settled film near her boots. A cool breeze, nothing more, she tells herself, ignoring the prickle at her spine. She swears she can almost catch a trace of warmth in the sheets—a ghost of memory more than presence.

It's a shrine and a warning all at once, prompting Lumira's lips to curl in bitter recognition. Her mother refuses to speak Emberly's name, yet the room remains untouched. The door stays closed—not forgotten—emptiness preserved like a memorial, forcing Emberly to linger at the edges of Lumira's vision.

She exhales slowly through her nose, shoulders tense.

Of course.

Bury the daughter. Worship the absence.

Let her mother have the performance.

Her fingers drift over the desk, tracing the fine grit left behind by time. She pauses at the corner where Emberly always kept her favorite paint tin, the one with swirling blues and violets they'd used for secret midnight sky paintings. Her hand reaches before logic catches up. Lumira shifts the tin slightly, revealing a small cleared space beneath. The wood feels rough and uneven. Carved.

Stillness seizes her for a beat.

Leaning in, she brushes away more dust. The marks are shallow and hurried but controlled. Not words—a symbol.

A jagged crown, split down the center.

Her stomach tightens. Emberly tucked away a truth too dangerous to speak—etched into their childhood hiding spot, where only Lumira would think to look. They'd used the paint tin as code since they were children—nudged three inches left to signal a message. Lumira hadn't noticed the subtle displacement until now.

Movement stirs behind her. Intent without sound.

Her muscles coil, instinct overriding thought. She spins—dagger raised—as a figure steps from the heavy shadows near the curtains.

Steel meets steel, the clash sharp and jarring, ricocheting off the chamber walls.

Lumira throws herself sideways. Her hip slams into the bedpost with a crack of bone against wood, and pain sears through her spine. The second strike comes fast. She blocks it, blades locking in a brutal jolt that rattles her bones and forces her backward.

Hazy bursts rise around them, caught in fractured light. The scent of sandalwood, old cloth, and adrenaline thickens the air.

Her attacker advances with predatory grace—no wasted steps, no room for doubt. Towering above her, a living wall of shadow—massive and unbreakable, the air itself folding around him. Inevitable.

He doesn't walk. He glides—ancient and wrong, a hunter buried inside his bones, patient as a void that's been watching her from the dark. Shadows don't follow him; they expect him. The light recoils in his wake, skimming past him like it knows better than to stay.

He's not here to kill her, but to stop her.

The realization sparks a bitter edge, almost tipping into amusement.

Gods, do people ever tire of underestimating her?

She lunges, forcing him back against the desk. The edge digs into his side, and for the first time, his motion falters.

His sleeve slips. A glimpse of skin above his left wrist, inside his forearm—inked with a jagged crown split by a blade. The same symbol carved beneath Emberly's paint tin.

Air abandons her lungs. Not coincidence—confirmation.

The Brotherhood of the Eternal Shadow isn't a myth. They're here in the palace. And whoever he is—he's one of them.

She feints, pivots, drives upward with her blade—but he's faster, not with brute strength, but far more dangerous: restraint.

In a single, fluid motion, he catches her wrist mid-swing. Not violently or urgently—enough to stop her with infuriating ease.

They are close. Closer than they should be. She's forced to tilt her chin to meet the hollow dark where his eyes should be. He dips his head slightly, that impossible height folding down to hers, hood nearly brushing her cheek—like the shadows want to mark her as well.

For one suspended moment, her body halts—not in fear, but with an ache that never left. That awful, treacherous pull that starts beneath the ribs and dares to suggest: you've felt this before.

She should wrench free. Should drive her dagger through his chest. Should do anything but stand there like she's waiting for him to speak.

But she doesn't.

And neither does he.

Only tension weaves the space between them, quiet and tempered, heavy with weight. Like he's done this before—slipped close, stolen the surrounding space, dared her to push back.

And then—he's gone.

Not a retreat. Not a step. As if reality tilted—and took him with it.

Lumira stiffens.

Her heart crashes inside her, sudden and savage. She forces her grip to loosen, feels the throb where her blade had been braced for impact.

No time to dwell.

Emberly didn't just know. She marked it—intentionally, in their old hiding spot. It wasn't a message. It was a warning.

The Brotherhood of the Eternal Shadow is real.

And they are here.

So, no—Lumira isn't waiting anymore. She'll hunt the truth the way he hunts her.

2

SPARE HEIR

A nobleman's son hits the training yard stones with a satisfying thud—a reminder that gravity doesn't give a damn about lineage.

The courtyard crouches in the shadow of the eastern tower, a rare pocket untouched by the palace's stifling grandeur. Marble columns, imported at an obscene expense to showcase Crimsun's reach, stand witness without ever betraying a word. Mist curls between the pillars as the first rays of daylight slice through the yard, casting long, fractured shadows—perfect cover for things that shouldn't exist.

Across Cyrathea's twelve territories, bloodlines are measured like wealth, and each royal line bears its distinctive title, which means Crimsun's Blood Descent, Lumira Kyrvayne, shouldn't be spending her mornings teaching merchants' children how to break noble noses. But she does—every morning, without fail. These lessons are hers to lead. Titles be damned. Then again, adding "Blood Descent" to hers is meant to make being a spare heir more palatable—like tying a silk bow on a battle axe.

She alters her weight, restraining the urge to sigh. "And that," Lumira announces, as the noble boy peels himself off the ground, "is why we don't get cocky because we were born with the right surname."

The assembled group meets her cutting green gaze—some smirking beneath a veneer of calm, others absorbing the moment with reluctant understanding. Merchants' children, disgraced nobles, and palace staff stand before her—exactly the sort her mother would prefer to ignore. Most are tangled in petty concerns, missing the real lesson. They come for bruises and leave with a rarer prize: the skill to survive one more day in a palace built to devour.

"But I had the proper form—" he starts, precisely the kind of stupidity that gets people killed these days.

"Proper form?" Lumira's laugh holds all the warmth of her mother's affection. "Tell that to the last poor bastard who thought proper form would save his ass. Oh wait, you can't—his 'proper form' didn't stop that tragic accident after he questioned the wrong trade policies."

She lets the moment stretch, sweat dampening the braids of her mahogany hair as she studies the gathered students. Some look uneasy. Good. Others hesitate, clinging to the belief that skill alone makes them untouchable.

"Strange, isn't it? How many accidents seem to happen to people who ask inconvenient questions."

A shadow flickers along the far wall—smooth, unhurried. Every instinct screams run.

Hadralis, Crimsun's Master at Arms, and her mentor, has drilled awareness into her bones.

If it's too perfect, it's planned.

Her grip tightens around the practice blade's hilt as she guides her students into their final forms, disguising readiness as routine. The real weapons—twin daggers, curved for speed and close work—remain strapped under her cloak, always within reach, always ready. Not ceremonial. Not polite. Entirely effective.

Watch everything. Show nothing. The warning replays in her mind, stripped of tenderness, etched in discipline.

She catalogs the anomaly and commits it to memory while a certainty settles coldly in her gut—someone is observing.

"Enough for today." She lets it fall lightly, though her mind races beneath the surface. Her students scatter into their usual routines—noble-born sons and daughters drifting back to their chambers, merchant children melting into servant corridors, and the overlooked staff folding into the palace's hush like they never existed at all.

To any observer, it's the palace repositioning in practiced rhythm—another morning of Crimsun's carefully managed order and hidden rot. But she sees them for what they are. Building an army was never the plan. But standing by while her mother ground them down for sport? Unthinkable.

They totaled a few dozen spies and informants now, threaded through kitchens, corridors, and trade stalls—woven so tightly into the palace's bones that the High Sovereigness can't catch them all. Lumira had built them to protect each other. But Emberly's mark changed that—they're meant for more than survival. They'll listen for her, slip secrets through doors that shouldn't open, and whisper her truth back through the walls when the Brotherhood no doubt comes hunting for her again.

Three clipped footsteps sound behind her, then—Hadralis's signature pause.

He stands like a weapon at rest—lean, built for precision over power. The silver in his black hair is no longer just a streak, and though it's cropped short in the Crimsun style, age has only made him more lethal. His pallor—pale in a territory known for sun-warmed skin—catches the light in a way that raises questions no one dares ask.

"You're tense." His voice is as flat as ever. No inquiry, pure observation.

Unimpressed, Lumira offers a glance that lands between boredom and disdain. "Must be the invigorating morning air."

Hadralis ignores her. "Orders came through last night. The High Sovereigness wants Emberly's chambers cleared. You're overseeing it."

The practice blade nearly slips from her hold.

They must be reacting to her earlier intrusion.

Two weeks they'd waited after Emberly's so-called illness, and now—suddenly—there's a rush to strip the room bare. Like vultures picking a carcass clean.

Someone wants to make sure nothing is left behind.

Or maybe they want to see what she finds.

Of fucking course it would be today.

She'd noticed the small variations over the last week, guard rotations adjusting, new faces in old positions. Subtle enough to pass for coincidence, unless you knew the signs.

"By sunset," Hadralis adds—because, apparently, the universe is feeling especially cruel this morning. "Her orders were explicit."

Lumira flows into her cool-down forms—suppressed fury woven into each exacting movement. If Hadralis had a sentimental streak, he might ramble about form and focus.

If he had emotions at all, he might be proud.

The practice sword thrums in her grip—an extension of the rage she refuses to unleash. Two weeks since they buried her sister, and already, the palace speculates about her replacement.

As if Emberly was nothing more than an ornamental vase to be swapped out.

Footsteps echo through the courtyard—each one placed with intention, each one meant to be heard.

The answer's behind her. She sighs, loudly. Jaggard strides as though the world exists to step aside, each footfall a statement, his presence a demand. He's always been that way. One of her older brothers, though not the eldest—the loudest.

Her voice is casual, too casual. "Hadralis, how much trouble would I be in if my dear brother had an unfortunate accident?"

He doesn't answer. Instead, Hadralis levels her with a stare—flat and unreadable—then turns and walks away, boots muted against the stone.

She rolls her eyes at his dramatic exit but doesn't bother to stop him.

It isn't dismissal or disapproval. It's the space only a man like Hadralis offers when he knows a storm is coming—and trusts her to be the one who survives it.

Her blade arcs through the air as Jaggard steps into the courtyard, radiating unearned confidence. Not a step out of place, each one meant to be seen.

His dark-auburn hair—almost black in the morning light—is swept back with artful ease that betrays hours of effort. His olive skin carries a colder undertone than Lumira's, and his angular features would be handsome if not for the smugness etched into them. He notes the bruise on her arm before settling back on her face.

She doesn't flinch. If he wants to see, let him. Let him report, twist, use it—whatever suits him today.

It's balance. Fury, refined.

"Still playing at swordcraft, sister?" he asks smoothly. "You're twenty-two, not some eager page. Or do you truly believe these strays would stand with you, should circumstances demand it?"

Lumira smiles, dangerous enough to have wiser people edging away—if any were present. She almost laughs. They'd stand. Because no one else gives them this, the chance to fight back. "Jaggard." She spits the name like it tastes wrong—disdain that could turn milk on command. "I see Mother's least consequential progeny has descended from his lofty perch. Did you require something, or are you merely here to remind everyone of how insufferable you are?"

His cheeks flush. "You really should learn to mind your tongue, sister. Someone might think you weren't properly bred."

"Whereas you, dear brother, are so impeccably bred, you make prize horses seem positively provincial." She shifts her stance to make him flinch. "Didn't you try to report me to Mother once? That went well, didn't it?"

She remembers his outrage, the dramatic accusation, and her counter: a group of noble girls arranged in perfect formation, fans in hand, executing dance steps that concealed fighting stances. His sputtering temper. Her mock innocence.

He remembers it too. She sees it in how his fist clenches.

"Mother wants Emberly's chambers cleared by sunset." He struggles to recover, tone hitching as he adds, "Try not to turn it into another one of your dramatic performances."

"I wouldn't dream of it, dear brother. That's clearly your specialty." She turns back to her practice forms. "Do take your leave. Your presence is upsetting my balance."

Jaggard smirks, but it's brittle at the edges. "Enjoy playing at rebellion while it lasts. The moment you actually become a threat, you won't get to play anymore."

Lumira turns her focus, then smiles—wicked and unbothered. Let him think what he wants. He'll learn soon enough.

She dismisses him with a curt slash through the air, but his certainty lingers, gnawing at the edges of her thoughts. As if he already knows what she can't yet name—but should.

The light catches on a miniature portrait of Emberly, half-tucked behind the rack of practice swords—as if someone meant to hide it, but not forget it. Her sister's smile—preserved in oil and careful brushstrokes—used to mean more. Now it feels like a warning she failed to understand in time.

Emberly had their mother's beauty: amber eyes, burnished complexion, a grace that didn't need to be declared. Everything about her was effortless. Expected.

Lumira had always been the contrast—angles where Emberly was softness, restraint where there should've been charm. Harder to categorize. Harder to control.

She doesn't touch the frame. Can't.

The ache under her ribs isn't grief. It's colder and laced with teeth.

Only when Jaggard's footsteps fade does she let her mask slip slightly.

Sunset. They're giving her less than a day to pick through the remnants of Emberly's life before they strip it bare. One day to find whatever her sister left behind.

How generous.

Her mind drifts back to this morning's confrontation. She has no proof—only a symbol, a presence that shouldn't exist, a stillness that moved like it had purpose.

Emberly knew more than she was meant to. And someone spilled blood to keep it buried.

Now, with her mother's "official blessing" to clear the chambers, scrutiny will follow her every choice—servants, guards, all of them another pair of eyes trained to report back.

By sunset, Emberly's chambers will be bare.

But before that, she will tear through every lie they buried in silk.

Let them bear witness. Let them run to their masters.

And her strays—her people—will know where to sink the blade when the time comes.

She won't stop until the breaking point strikes back.

And gods help whoever stands in her way.

3

WHAT LIES BENEATH

She hesitates at the threshold, palm braced against the doorframe like it's the only thing keeping her from splintering. This morning, she hunted shadows—tense and ready to strike. Now, daylight bleeds across the floor. The room isn't smaller or different—quiet in a way that demands attention. The mystery of Emberly's death hangs in the air, a puzzle waiting to be solved.

For half a breath, Emberly is there—hunched over her easel, humming absently, copper paint smudged along her knuckles. The hit of memory punches Lumira in the chest. It clings to the scattered brushes, the half-finished sketches, the faint scent of pigment no one thought to clear away.

The illusion doesn't shatter so much as it fades.

Books lie open to their last pages. The teacup on the windowsill remains untouched, its contents dried to dust.

Nothing's changed, and yet the air feels misaligned.

Lumira steps inside, pressing the door shut with a muted snap. Final and unmistakable. Her touch drifts over the desk—then stops at the raised groove of the carving.

She loosens her grip, scanning the room with fresh eyes.

"Let's see what you left for me, dear sister."

Lumira starts with the places anyone else would have checked first. The desk drawers yield nothing but scattered brushes, crushed charcoal, and half the palace's supply of copper paint—as if Emberly had been preparing to paint the fall of empires in startling metallic detail. The bookshelf holds the usual selection of poetry and history. Even now, Emberly had arranged them with a familiar, defiant touch—if one looked closely, the first letter of each spine spelled out *Begone, wretches*.

A smirk tugs at Lumira's lips. Her sister's rebellions had always been more elegant than her own.

The bedchambers prove equally fruitless. Until—

She pauses.

Among the half-finished sketches strewn across Emberly's worktable, one is different—a noblewoman in the rose garden. At first glance, nothing seems unusual—until Lumira notices the clear crystal shot through with topaz pinning it down. Emberly had been many things, but careless with her art wasn't one of them.

"That's odd," she murmurs, lifting the crystal. It's heavier than it looks, its jagged facets catching the light in ways that don't match the palace's usual cut glass. Unease prickles down her spine. The feeling is familiar, unshakable—but she doesn't know why.

It was placed off-center, a marker left to be noticed. As she tilts it, her grip slips—no, it jerks free, landing with a hollow thunk and a faint chime. The paperweight rolls back to her feet, as if summoned.

Intrigued, she picks up the crystal again, turning it in the light. Through its facets, she notices how the refracted patterns line up with the natural whorls of the wood-paneled wall. "Clever," she utters. "Very clever, sister."

She tucks the crystal into her utility pocket in her leathers, unease prickling her neck. Emberly never left things out by accident—and Lumira has no doubt this was meant for her to find.

Naturally, Emberly tucked her resistance into the most offensively ornate part of the wall—a grotesque flourish that practically begged to be ignored out of sheer aesthetic protest. Or pure, godsdamned spite. She mutters a curse as she tests each ridiculous curl, half expecting none to give—until one does. The panel swings open without a sound—no creak, no scrape, just seamless movement. The hinges are oiled to perfection. Trust Emberly to make secrecy an art form.

Inside lie two items: a leather-bound journal and a folded slip of paper—a receipt, perhaps. She hovers, palm outstretched but not touching, tension strung tight with unease, drawn by a pull dangerously close to longing.

The journal's leather is worn smooth, edges darkened by the restless motion of Emberly's fingers. How many times had she glimpsed her sister hunched over these pages, tongue caught between her teeth in deep concentration? She remembers teasing Emberly about secret admirer notes, not knowing those pages hid far deadlier intentions.

A memory stirs—Emberly dragging her into an alcove at last Mabon's ball, expression raw with an emotion Lumira couldn't name. Mabon was meant to honor the turning season, or so the stories claimed—but the court had polished it into another excuse for silk and spectacle. Emberly had always seen through it. "Not everything beautiful is harmless, Lumi," she'd whispered, using the childhood name only she was allowed. "Remember that." The words hadn't made sense then, but now they slam back into her, a door thrown open—unwelcome and useless.

She lifts the journal, and below, a glint of metal catches the lamplight. She tucks the journal under her left arm, freeing her right hand.

The folded paper sits tucked tight against the wood. She snatches it up, thumb smearing a line of ink she'll puzzle over later, then tucks it into her pocket with the crystal.

Her focus snaps back to the metal, tension tightening just beneath the surface. It's a key, but unlike any she's ever seen: forged from a burnished alloy that changes color in the light, iridescent as oil on water. Intricate filigree winds around the bow, ending in thorn-like curls that look both ornamental and defensive. Along the shaft, grooves run like veins—old, etched with unnerving precision.

Heart thudding, she reaches in for the key. The moment she makes contact, the crescent-shaped mark over her collarbone flares—burning like it remembers why it exists. A jolt of warmth rushes up her arm, settling deep in her bones. The sensation is so sudden and wrong that she almost drops it, but it hums in her palm, pulsing with the rhythm of a second heartbeat. A chill dances along her neck—the unmistakable pressure of unseen eyes.

At the edge of her mind, a thought slithers—the shape of intent without language, circling, waiting. As if the key is listening… or testing her.

Air lodges in her throat. Did Emberly know? Did she leave this for her alone?

Lumira stares at the hidden compartment, now shut tight behind its elaborate carving. Its secrets—Emberly's secrets—are hers now. But the sense of being watched lingers, the key's unnaturalness seeping into her, an unspoken promise.

A knock at the door. Not the hesitant tap of a servant—this one is firm.

Lumira barely has time to tuck the journal and the key into the inner pocket of her tunic before the door swings open, revealing one of her mother's guards. He doesn't react to her presence, but his gaze drags over the spot where the items press against her chest—not her face, never her face. The unnatural calm in him feels off—another subtle crack she files away for later.

"The High Sovereigness requests your presence," he announces. His tone is neutral, the care in it twisted into threat.

She touches her collarbone, where the birthmark tingles. "Of course," she replies, matching his tone. "We wouldn't want to keep Mother waiting."

But as she speaks, the air thickens—weighted, disturbed, a held breath sinking into gravity. Lumira stays rooted, willing herself to ignore it. It's nothing. A trick of the light. Her own paranoia.

She resists the urge to glance over her shoulder, although there is a sense of unseen attention. Whatever it is—*who*ever it is—will reveal itself in time. They always do.

At first, Lumira follows the guard—measured steps, spine straight. But at the corridor's split, she veers left without a word. A minor detour he'll report. Let him. Sweat and dust aren't part of the plan, no matter how much her mother deserves it—and Emberly's secrets won't be left where the palace staff might stumble across them first.

Minutes later, she wipes the worst of the training yard from her skin and slides into a formal dress—a token nod to the High Sovereigness's endless appetite for appearances. Underneath, she leaves the combat leathers and holsters strapped tight, the hidden weight pressing reassuring warmth into her ribs. Let her mother choke on the compromise. The secrets stay with her, exactly where they belong.

Her mother's private study is a room that announces its importance through sheer overwhelming pretension. Every surface gleams with carefully curated symbols of power—ancestral weapons untouched by battle, ancient texts too hallowed to open, and gold leaf gilded thick enough to plate a small army. Lumira has always thought it resembles a treasury vault arranged by someone with more wealth than taste.

High Sovereigness Thara Kyrvayne sits at her massive desk, a spider presiding over its web—elegant and deadly in equal measure. Her flawless sunlit aura glows with barely contained fury, and the inner fire that makes her so terrifying to courtiers suffuses the space between them, an invisible threat coiling around her defiant daughter. She keeps reading—because to acknowledge Lumira would be to concede importance, and Thara yields nothing.

Lumira remains standing and composed.

"You've been in your sister's chambers." Thara delivers it as though passing judgment for treason, each word steeped in disappointment honed over years.

"Yes, Mother dearest. Following your orders, as any dutiful daughter would." Lumira keeps her tone just shy of insolent, posture relaxed but subtly angled toward where the key presses against her ribs. She stands with perfect alignment, the leather elements of her attire—distinctly outside her mother's taste—intentionally visible beneath the expected courtly layers. Unlike the women of the court, she wears fitted pants under her formal robes, the outlines of concealed holsters noticeable only to those trained to look.

Thara's quill pauses mid-stroke, the only ripple in her otherwise perfect composure. Her chin lifts, expression already sharpened—daggers aimed without needing a source. "Have you found anything… interesting?"

And there it is—the real reason for this summons.

Lumira allows herself a small, bitter smile. "Nothing that would interest you, Mother. Just art supplies and half-finished sketches." She keeps her face placid, a perfect courtly mask revealing nothing about the carved mark or the items now tucked close, hidden in folds of cloth and leather. Her touch drifts unconsciously to the spot where her birthmark tingles with residual warmth. "Though someone appears to have visited the room before me today," Lumira says lightly, listening for the hitch in her mother's breath. "Your guards, perhaps?"

She doesn't expect an answer. They're not guards—Brotherhood wolves, fattened in her mother's den.

Her mother's expression hardens, but Lumira's mouth tilts in a ghost of amusement.

The moment you actually become a threat, you won't get to play anymore.

She pushes the thought aside. Jaggard is always full of theatrics. But still…

"You'd do well to keep such thoughts to yourself." Thara sets down her quill with unsettling care. "And I trust you'll handle such personal items appropriately?"

"Oh, absolutely." Lumira layers on the innocence like frosting. "I wouldn't dream of doing anything that might reflect poorly on the family."

The temperature in the room drops several degrees. "You will finish clearing your sister's chambers by sunset. You will maintain appropriate decorum. And you will remember your place in this family."

"Of course, Mother." Lumira dips into a curtsy that borders on parody. "Is there anything else? I have so little time to do it properly."

Thara's amber eyes narrow slightly, which is the only indication that she recognizes the mockery. She gestures over a stack of papers, the wax seals of three different territories pressed into the parchment like voiceless sentinels. "You fancy yourself clever, daughter. But you've failed to understand that true power isn't found in training sessions or building little networks of misfits." She leans in, intimate and lethal. "True power," Thara murmurs, locking on to Lumira with sudden, fire-lit focus, "is knowing which pieces to sacrifice… and remembering you're not above it."

The words brush against Lumira's mind, soft and insidious, unlike any ordinary persuasion. This is magic—her mother's Compulsion, subtle and sinister in its cruelty, sliding effortlessly through Lumira's mental barriers as though they aren't there. A faint deep-scarlet shimmer gathers in the air around Thara's outstretched fingers, coiling and darting like living threads. The glow flickers through the lamplight, unmistakable to anyone paying attention—power made visible, a blade pointed straight at Lumira.

"Be a good little pawn, Lumi," Thara coos, lips curling into a feigned pout. "Do as you're told." The nickname drips like poison—Emberly's ghost warped into a cruel joke.

A strange pressure blooms at the back of Lumira's skull, delicate yet insistent, coaxing obedience, insisting that compliance would be so much easier than defiance. A tremor ripples through her, pulse quickening as scarlet threads slither closer, weaving into her thoughts like barbed silk. She grits her teeth, nails digging into her palms, and mentally shoves against her mother's hold. Thara's magic has always been more potent—perfected by decades of ruthless practice—and no matter how often Lumira resists, it never gets easier.

A chill slithers down Lumira's spine at her mother's words. Not for the first time, she wonders if Emberly's so-called illness had been another sacrifice.

With a careless flick of her wrist—as if she's slicing the air between them—Thara snaps, scattering the last threads of her magic. "Go."

Lumira turns to leave, then stops at the door—because why miss the chance for one last jab? "Oh—and Mother? Do give my regards to your new watchdogs." She cuts a glance toward the corridor where she knows they're listening. "The sneaky fuckers almost passed."

She shuts the door on the sound of her mother's barely contained temper and lets a grim smile curl at her lips. The key hums faintly against her chest—somewhere between shadow and command.

Whatever it is, it's hers now.

And she has work to do.

For the next few hours, she plays her part as the devoted daughter and grieving sister. She moves with steady precision through Emberly's belongings, sorting what stays, what gets archived, and what she'll keep tucked away in memory alone.

At the desk, she keeps her actions deliberate, careful—another daughter in mourning putting her sister's things in order. She reaches for the place Emberly carved, fingers moving along the rough lines with certain intent.

A jagged crown split by a blade. The Brotherhood's mark.

Even children know that symbol—a name hissed in the dark, a threat traded over too-loud cups of ale. A secret society that claims to protect the continent from chaos, some say. A cabal of spies and blades for hire, others maintain. They manipulate courts, broker alliances, and vanish entire bloodlines when it suits them.

Officially, they don't exist. Unofficially, they turn territories like gears in a clock.

But no one ever sees them—not openly. No one bears that mark in plain sight. And yet Emberly found proof worth carving— right into her desk.

She frowns. Emberly hadn't done it for drama. It was a warning and a name. Whatever she'd uncovered, it ended her before the truth did.

No other clue remains—no hidden compartments or cryptic notes. If Emberly meant to tell her more, someone else got here first.

With steady focus, Lumira searches the room, inspecting sketches and drawers, cataloging everything exactly as her mother demands. The servants receive crisp instructions, her grief clipped down to something her mother might actually approve of. She scans their faces for her morning intruder—or anyone bold enough to bear that same mark in plain sight.

By sunset, Emberly's chambers are stripped of everything that once made them hers. Each trace of her vibrant life has been boxed and labeled, destined for the family archive. A few items, however, won't make it that far. But Lumira carries the pieces that matter—and the questions that refuse to rest.

Later that evening, behind a locked door, she goes through her chambers with the ease of routine. Trusted allies stand stationed nearby, the official explanation being that she's "overcome with grief" and wishes to be alone—a story Jaggard won't bother to question. Pretending to care about emotions isn't his strength.

Lumira carefully removes the items she's kept hidden since Emberly's chambers—the crystal and folded slip of paper from her pocket; the journal and the key, pulsing with unnatural warmth, from inside her tunic. She spreads them across the bed, each one a question she's not yet ready to answer.

Her gaze settles on the slip of paper. In the clearer light of her chambers, she smooths it flat, thumb brushing over the faint ink. At the corner, the paper bears a tidy merchant stamp: Pigments & Pints—and below it, a quick flourish of a name: Wrenna.

She's heard of Pigments & Pints—a small artist's café in the merchant district. Emberly mentioned it once, nearly in jest, but Emberly never joked about art.

The receipt is short—pigments, brushes, a stretch of canvas, merchant-style script lined with prices, and a note of thanks. It looks harmless, but there's nothing that explains why Emberly would hide it so carefully. The truth remains maddeningly out of reach.

She turns to the journal and lets it rest on the bed for a moment. The leather binding is worn smooth, corners bent from constant handling—Emberly's nervous habit of thumbing pages whenever she was deep in thought.

Lumira runs her palm over the cover, then slips her fingers under the flap, easing it open. The pages part with a faint sigh, releasing the scent of charcoal and dried pigments—close enough to feel.

Each page is filled with Emberly's looping scrawl—so familiar that, for a heartbeat, Lumira almost expects to hear her sister beside her, explaining half-finished thoughts no one else is allowed to see.

She flips through slowly, thumb brushing each margin, cataloging the sketches and odd annotations. An unease begins to stir—subtle, but persistent. Several sections appear to be written in code, strange symbols hidden in the swirl of ordinary lines—tucked in like they're meant to be missed.

A memory clicks into place. The peculiar patterns in Emberly's paintings, the oddly placed copper flecks—they aren't artistic flourishes. Of course they aren't. That was Emberly all over: turning beauty into camouflage.

She can almost see Emberly now: hunched over her worktable, brush held like a blade, secrets blooming inside every swirl of copper paint.

Lumira flips deeper, careful not to smudge the brittle pages. Near the back, a line stops her cold.

They say the artifacts are cursed—that they drive you mad or make you see things that aren't there. But I don't believe that. It's not a curse. It's something deeper. The key doesn't respond to just anyone. It chooses, for reasons I'm trying to understand. And it only chooses those who are... whole.

Her fingers hover over the page. *Whole?*

The next lines trail off, half-erased—like Emberly was interrupted or changed her mind at the last moment.

Amusement flickers in Lumira's eyes as a quiet laugh slips free. Trust Emberly to bury the truth where suspicion wouldn't wander.

She makes contact with the key. A breath of hesitation—then she gathers it in one smooth motion.

The sensation is immediate. Every thought flees her mind.

Heavy in her palm, the key catches the lamplight in impossible ways, as if the metal holds its own fire. Her birthmark flares with sudden heat, sending a shiver down her spine.

It pulses in rhythm with the key's energy. Recognition. Connection. The feeling is deep, primal, almost alive in her bones. The warmth fades quickly, leaving only a faint impression, like the whisper of someone brushing past in a crowded room. The timing and reaction are precise enough to raise suspicion. Maybe Emberly hadn't buried it for protection—maybe she'd left it, a breadcrumb meant to be found.

The key's heat fades to a hum, or so she tells herself. It's metal, nothing more. Another relic from a sister who left many secrets behind.

A soft knock cuts through her thoughts—three taps, a pause, then two more. Her shoulders relax slightly as she recognizes the familiar rhythm. It's her network's signal.

"A message regarding tonight's social arrangements." The words slip through the door, soft and nondescript—the familiar code for a guard shift. Curious, how it comes after she cleared Emberly's rooms.

"Thank you," she replies, matching their casual tone while embedding her own coded response. "I'd prefer not to be disturbed while I sort through these memories."

After the footsteps retreat down the hallway, Lumira considers in silence. The timing is too neat to be a coincidence—but that's a problem for later.

She returns to the objects spread across her bed, each one a piece of a puzzle she's only beginning to understand. The key is clearly more than ornate metalwork—somehow, she knows it's only the first thread in whatever dangerous web Emberly began to unravel. Did her sister know about the key's strange reaction to her birthmark? Had Emberly hidden it specifically for her to find?

More importantly, who else knows about its existence?

She crosses to her vanity, tracing the ornate trim with her fingertips. Along the underside of the tabletop, she finds the hidden catch and presses. It gives with a soft click. The panel slides open, revealing the narrow compartment she installed herself. She slips the journal and receipt inside, pressing them into the shadows with care.

Without thinking, she pulls the strange crystal from her pouch, fingers running over its uneven surface. Clear as glass, veined with burnished topaz, it's heavier than it appears, the light catching on its jagged facets in a way that doesn't quite sit right. She turns it once, then shrugs. Whatever purpose it served, it isn't hers to decipher—not now.

She tucks the crystal beside the journal, letting it settle among the folded paper. Only then does she slide the panel shut, pausing to smooth every edge until it disappears—Emberly's unfinished story sealed in one final, hidden place.

But the key stays. Too many onlookers and chances for it to vanish if she blinks.

She threads it onto a chain around her neck, the weight settling against her collarbone. The metal isn't as warm now, but not cold either—a faint pulse flickers through it as she fastens the clasp.

"What were you mixed up in, sister?" she exhales into the empty room. "And what in the void is this thing?"

The metal presses gently against her as she moves, and for a fleeting moment, it seems almost alive—neither comforting nor threatening, simply aware. Then the sensation vanishes, leaving only a mess of unanswered questions.

She crosses the room to the far wall, where her mother's portrait hangs prominently above a small marble-topped side table, positioned exactly as Thara requires of all her children. Behind the heavy gilt frame, Lumira finds the hidden latch—right where it's always waited, etched into ornate curves.

The portrait eases outward on concealed hinges, revealing a small cavity behind. She retrieves her network ledger from its shadowed recess, lips curling into a faint, ironic smile. After all, what better place to conceal rebellion than behind her mother's carefully composed mask?

Lumira quickly sketches the jagged crown split by a blade into her ledger, ink smearing under urgency. Emberly hadn't known them in passing—she'd hidden their mark in the foundation of their childhood keepsake, a betrayal buried until now.

Tomorrow, she'll visit Pigments & Pints. After all, what better way to honor Emberly's memory than to suddenly cultivate a passion for art? If Emberly hid messages with paint tins, who's to say there aren't more—layered in brushstrokes and canvas. Clearly, someone thought so—someone willing to send an armed agent to keep Lumira from finding them.

The Brotherhood of the Eternal Shadow—a bedtime threat to keep children from wandering into the dark. No one spoke of them in daylight, not as anything that still existed.

But they did. And they were worth bleeding for.

Veiled architects manipulating Cyrathea's tangled web. Secrets they'd kill to keep buried.

A shadow slips across the windowpane, pulling her upward with it. A Blood Raven perches on the sill, cloaked in dusk, its feathers shimmering like ink by candlelight. It doesn't fixate on her face. That disturbingly sharp awareness drops—narrowing on where the key pulses beyond layers meant to hide it.

The raven stills—ancient intent rising along the surface, unreadable. It studies her, not with curiosity, but with cold calculation. As if weighing her worth on a scale before bloodlines ever formed. The air thickens, dense with meaning she can't yet name.

Then, without sound, the raven dips its head. It settles like recognition, more knowing than reflex. An acknowledgment perhaps, or warning. Its wings unfurl, capturing the honeyed light's final gleam before shadow claims it entirely.

And what follows isn't absence.

It stirs at the edge of hearing.

Not from the bird, but from the space it leaves behind. A murmur curls at the edge of her mind—that same strange cadence the key stirs when a force wants to break through. Not words exactly, but older. A will straining to be heard or emotion shaped into thought.

She exhales slowly, hand pressing the key flat against her chest. Questions can wait. For now, she has a family dinner to survive—one wrapped in silk and smiling teeth, and far more treacherous than it pretends to be.

4

BLOOD AND BREEDING

The sinking sun slants through the window, its light a blade, as Lumira transforms from fierce combatant to refined aristocrat. Midnight-blue fabric glides over lingering bruises, earned in training and slow to fade. The corset comes next—laced tight to crush lungs and apparently reason. Each tug carves her into elegance—an imitation that feels painfully untrue. She arranges every fold to hide the calluses that betray labor, the scars on her shoulders, and the damning truth pulsing against her. The high neckline masks the crescent-shaped birthmark at her collarbone, the same mark that burned when she touched Emberly's key.

Her mother's idea of proper dinner attire is clearly designed to discourage concealed weapons. Lumira takes it as a challenge. She's particularly proud of the sheath hidden in her sleeve seam, perfectly positioned to drop a blade into her palm with a flick of her wrist.

She sits while Quinn, her childhood handmaiden and closest ally, begins the tedious ritual of formal styling. Few would guess how many "mere servants" Lumira has folded into her private network. Even fewer would guess how many weapons and escape routes Quinn has helped her map into the palace itself.

Gentle fingers work through her hair. Lumira allows it. Outwardly, she plays the obedient daughter. Inwardly, she prepares for war.

"Lumira?" The soft question brushes against her thoughts. "You're stiff as a statue. Everything alright?"

"Yes, of course," Lumira murmurs, her hand withdrawing from her birthmark, startled by the unconscious touch. A sensation creeps in—unwelcome. She pulls back, forcing herself into the moment. Right. Hair. Another ridiculous ritual of nobility—the more elaborate the style, the more supposedly refined the breeding.

Moments later, she stands before her chamber mirror, methodically destroying everything Quinn spent so long arranging. She tugs a few strategic strands loose, letting them fall in artfully disheveled waves. A few subtle adjustments ensure wrinkles in the right places—exactly where they'll make her mother twitch. Small victories, but she'll take what she can get on a day like this.

The staccato rhythm of her heels rings out against polished marble, echoing through corridors designed to impress and intimidate in equal measure. The grand dining hall looms ahead—less a room, more a stage draped in gold and expectation. The room's opulence, like the palace itself, offers no comfort—only a reminder of power, each gold-veined wall and precision-polished corner weaponized for political advantage. Servants rush to open the towering doors, every gesture rehearsed. Mistakes here aren't corrected—they're punished. At the High Sovereigness's table, even what's unsaid follows protocol. As always in this palace, beauty is a weapon honed to a mirror sheen.

Her mother is already seated at the far end of the table, beneath the ancient Blood Raven crest, where candlelight makes the metalwork gleam like freshly spilled blood—details meticulously arranged for maximum intimidation. High Sovereigness Thara Kyrvayne sits as if she were built from the room itself, the living centerpiece of a performance no one dares upstage.

As if the gods couldn't help themselves, they gave her skin the gleam of sun-warmed bronze—richer than Lumira's, practically gloating. Dark-brown hair, threaded with faint auburn undertones, is twisted into an elaborate court style meant to impress and subtly strangle, much like her approach to motherhood. Golden-flecked scrutiny rakes the room, cataloging flaws with merciless finesse—judging who to correct or cast aside.

Tonight's gown flows like smoke, its deep red skirting the edge of almost sinister. The bodice dips scandalously low for a family dinner—cut to display cleavage and dominance. Glinting runes spiral down sheer sleeves like veiled threats, magic humming within the silk. There's no softness left—only intent in her posture, Compulsion in her tone, and power lurking in her smile.

The arrangement, as always, is strategic. Disapproval radiates from Thara in steady waves from where she is seated, coiled tighter than the platinum around her wrists. At the opposite end sits Pyraxus—the golden son, the firstborn and presumed Blood

Heir, groomed and sculpted into the palace's ideal of Crimsun nobility. The chandelier's glow catches on him like polished bronze, his posture flawless, his restraint exhausting to witness. He doesn't bristle under the palace's expectations anymore; he's been sculpted hollow by them. His sleek brown hair, streaked with auburn like Thara's, lies perfectly in place—no doubt trained into obedience, like him.

Beside him, his wife Arabella embodies every insufferable trait imaginable—fashioned into a Crimsun masterpiece. She carries the bloodline's amber intensity, the golden polish of Thara and Pyraxus—only sharpened into something smug. Not a strand of her dark hair dares fall out of place. Even her posture feels accusatory, like everyone else is slouching on purpose.

Emberly's empty chair sits between Arabella and Aviah, carefully set but heartbreakingly undisturbed. For a moment, ridiculous and involuntary, Lumira almost turns to catch her sister's smirk, expecting a wry jab aimed at their mother's latest theatrical sigh. A subtle roll of the eyes. A quirked brow.

But there's no teasing murmur. No muttered quip tucked amongst the clink of silverware. Only the ache of what wasn't said. The chair is just a chair, and Emberly is gone. But gods, she would have hated the table looking this obedient.

The ache rises before she can stop it—thick, hollow, all Emberly. But she buries it fast. The table's already full of vultures, and they feed on weakness.

Instead, she fixes her gaze to Aviah, the sister who remains.

Twelve-year-old Aviah, with her father's sterling-silver hair softened by threads of her mother's darkness, creates an effect like moonlight rippling on water. She's artfully mastered the starlit façade—innocence worn like silk—while missing nothing. This trait would be concerning if Lumira hadn't caught her using it primarily to sneak extra desserts and cover for servants' mistakes.

Lumira takes her assigned seat beside Jaggard because, apparently, her mother's idea of punishment is forcing her to endure an entire meal next to someone whose voice makes her consider turning a soup spoon into an creative fucking weapon.

On her brother's other side, young Marnox fidgets with his napkin, barely old enough to grasp the tension crackling through the air. He leans around Jaggard's shoulder, eyes bright and unguarded. She returns it with the only real smile she's likely to offer all evening.

At ten, he remains untouched by the family's political machinations and believes wholeheartedly in the fairytale version of nobility. He'd spent the previous morning showing her his latest sword practice moves in the garden, wooden training blade whirling with more enthusiasm than accuracy while his dark, silver-streaked hair fell in messy waves. She'd praised his form, carefully neglecting to mention that she'd been simultaneously teaching far more lethal techniques to her own students.

The illusion fades. It always does.

"Lumira," Thara begins, in the tone that always precedes some new fresh hell of social obligation, "regarding your future… We must find you a match with a strong bloodline and impeccable abilities. Someone who won't dilute our legacy with mediocrity."

She doesn't need to lift a finger to command the room. That measured calm? It's the one Thara uses when she's about to turn her children into bargaining chips.

Annoyance surges through Lumira as the servants begin the first course. Metallic cloches lift in perfect sync, revealing roast pheasant with glazed citrus roots and firefruit compote—an opulent spread no one seems interested in.

She knows what's coming—the same conversation they've repeated a hundred times in the last few months, each repetition more grating than the last.

Lumira bites back a reaction that would scorch the air. Not that anyone seriously considers her heir material—but that doesn't stop her mother from dressing her up as a prize mare for potential political breeders. Or, as Thara so delicately puts it, *accommodating suitors to ensure a worthy extension of the bloodline.*

"It'll just result in another eligible match wasted," Jaggard mumbles, aiming for dutiful son delusions but landing closer to insufferable prick. He speaks louder this time. "Lord Thornley Blackbriar's bloodline is exceptionally pure, sister. His life force manipulation abilities alone—"

The name strikes like a match—fuck, she hates that little creep—igniting a memory Lumira has savored on particularly tedious days at court.

She leans back in her chair, lips curling into a slow, dangerous smile.

Oh yes, she thinks. *Let's talk about Lord Thornley.* She wonders if he still walks with a limp.

5

A TASTE OF POWER

Her mother's expression tightens, sensing the shift in her attention, but it's too late—she's already slipping into the delicious recollection of Lord Thornley Blackbriar, a man of excellent lineage, great power... and absolutely no survival instincts.

The memory rises—sharp-edged and satisfying. At the Ostara celebration—an ancient rite the court barely pretends to understand—Thornley's meticulously oiled, kelly-green hair was slicked back in a style meant to impress. It only emphasized the hollow ambition in his eyes, a snake sizing up its next meal. He might have been one of the most sought-after bachelors between Grovenar and Crimsun—*gods help us all*—but Lumira would have rather hurled herself off a fucking cliff than be shackled to him for eternity.

Fortunately, she had a much more entertaining solution in mind. She played him, master hunter in every motion, each designed to draw him closer. Her touch skimmed his arm, fleeting, but its absence burned more than the contact. The way her focus dipped to his lips, slipped away with practiced shyness, then returned with slow, simmering promise—it was all deliberate. His throat worked as she leaned in close for him to catch the oversweet floral of her perfume, close enough that her breath ghosted across his ear.

The alcove had been chosen carefully—secluded so to invite scandal, but not so hidden that discovery would be impossible. Thornley was the type who found risk arousing, especially when he thought he had the upper hand. The thrill of almost being caught unraveled him—pupils blown wide as she retreated into the shadows, each step silently summoning him closer.

His beauty came from money, not nature—symmetry so precise it bordered on dull, the sort of face made for portraits and men who paused to admire their reflection in polished armor. He had that pale-birch coloring found in some Grovenar lines, the faint bark markings across his collarbone wasted on someone so thoroughly unimpressive.

He thought it was a game. She thought it was practice.

The scent of jasmine—intentionally overused—hung between them as she slowly gathered her skirts. His shoulders heaved, fingers twitching at his sides. So this was the threat he fancied himself? A coward draped in borrowed power, still clinging to a reputation he'd never earned.

She could almost admire how easy it always was—men like Thornley stumbling right into the snare, all hunger and entitlement. That heat wasn't about her—it was the thrill of conquest. About pursuing a force rare, powerful, and wholly disinterested in being possessed.

But there was no time for nausea. Not yet. The game wasn't over, and she wouldn't play to lose.

She moved with poised grace—the whisper of silk on silk—first her calf, then her knee, then the slow reveal of olive skin sun-warmed and gleaming under the nearby candlelight. He watched the hem like it revealed a secret, lips parting at the thought of the marks he'd leave behind.

"My lord," she cooed, dropping to that throaty register that men somehow always associated with bedroom promises, "would you kneel for me? I have something… special in mind."

The Compulsion unfurled at the back of her throat—a faint scarlet thread curling through the shadows of the alcove, swift and evading Thornley's notice. The magic drove in, a barbed thread that met only silence. He was already so drunk on the fantasy he didn't see how easily he'd given himself up.

She didn't need to use it—not really. He would've crawled for her anyway. But she did it because there could be no mistakes. No loose ends. She'd learned that much from her mother.

The hunger on his face was almost comedic—Lord Thornley Blackbriar, momentarily forgetting every ounce of self-preservation in favor of a lie that made him feel powerful. He dropped so quickly she wondered if he'd split the seams of his trousers.

Pathetic. Desire blurred his vision—easy, when the blood rushes south. Another soft-hearted tyrant, hard in all the wrong places.

She leaned down, the heat of her mouth brushing his ear. "I heard"—each word honeyed steel—"that you like it rough." Court secrets always rotted their way to the surface.

Then—contact. She wove into his hair, clutching near the scalp like she could anchor herself there. He didn't resist. He leaned in.

Of course he did.

His face hovered inches from the part of her body he assumed was the prize, warmth brushing against the thin strip of silk she'd let him believe was an invitation. Glazed and ravenous, he fixated on the shadow between her thighs like salvation waited there.

Then he latched on to her thighs—greedy, bruising—nails biting in as he tried to spread her wider. She let him get high and close enough to taste what he'd never earn. When his fingertips grazed the heat of her through that fragile layer, he whimpered—a pitiful, animal sound that soured the air.

Then his tongue darted out, desperate and uninvited.

A wet bloom darkened the expensive fabric at his crotch— clear as any confession: she owned him. She couldn't have posed him better if she'd sculpted him herself.

"That's the trouble with men like you," she murmured, lifting his chin with a single finger.

He followed the touch, eager—a puppet begging for its strings. "It doesn't even cross your mind, does it? That you're not the one in control."

And that's when she struck.

Her fist connected with the bridge of his nose in one clean, devastating strike. The crack of cartilage shattering was sudden and wet, the sound vibrating all the way through her bones. His head jerked back with the impact, blood spurting in a bright arc. His whole being flared open—confusion tangled with agony and disbelief, green depths awash in sudden, perfect clarity.

She smiled.

Lumira didn't give him time to process the betrayal. Her steel-tipped boot landed with merciless precision—cruel, and likely fatal to future generations. Satisfaction flooded her veins—not pleasure, but dominance. This moment belonged to her. He was hers. But there was no thrill, no forbidden tension—only the intense relief as he crumbled at her feet.

His sound was glorious, somewhere between a wheeze and a soprano's highest note, cut off halfway as the air evacuated his lungs. The color drained from his face to the sickly pallor of defeat, his body seconds from collapse.

"Was that rough enough for you, my lord?" she purred, malice threading each word, as he writhed on the ground clutching his precious jewels. Blood from his nose soaked into his pompous excuse for formalwear. "I do hope I haven't disappointed. Mother insists I should put more effort into these courtship rituals."

His spittle-filled rage was absolutely worth the political fallout. He tried to curse at her between pained gasps, managing only to spray a fine mist of blood and saliva onto her boots. She admired its pattern—a constellation of his humiliation.

Lumira crouched beside him, close so that only he could hear what came next. The jasmine that lured him moments ago now mingled with the metallic tang of his blood.

"Let me be crystal clear, Lord Blackbriar. If you ever regard me like a delicacy again, I'll make sure your bloodline ends in disappointment."

The memory fades, and Lumira finds herself back at the dining table, her lips curved into a ghost of a smile. The same satisfaction she'd felt then ripples through her now—a private victory her family wouldn't understand.

"What are you smirking about?" her mother snaps, dragging Lumira back into the moment. Thara's tone cuts soft but lethal, the kind that makes courtiers lose sleep. The same heat that bends rooms to her will lashes her daughter, unrelenting. Every movement is a display of power, from the angle of her chin to the way her grip rests against the wineglass—contemplating violence. She wears her rage like her court attire, each element crafted to remind everyone exactly who holds power in Crimsun Territory, a skill honed through decades of dissecting her children down to their finest flaws.

"Nothing of concern, Mother dearest." Lumira takes particular pleasure in how Thara's jaw clenches at the pet name. "Just reflecting on previous entanglements and the... educational experiences we've shared. I'm sure Lord Blackbriar thinks of me fondly whenever air wheezes past his slightly crooked nose."

A few forks pause midair. No one laughs.

Young Aviah, who is learning the exhausting intricacies of palace table etiquette, reaches for her dessert fork with all the careful concentration of disarming an explosive. "Bella, is this right?" she asks hesitantly.

"It's Air-ah-BELL-ah, darling," Pyraxus's wife trills. Each syllable falls from her lips with the same elegance she uses to correct others' table manners. "And one simply must hold the dessert fork at precisely this angle. The fourth finger should never—I repeat, never—touch the stem."

Lumira maintains her placid smile while contemplating how many of Arabella's precious table settings could be repurposed as impromptu weapons. The sauceboat alone offers some tempting possibilities: the heavy porcelain cracking like bone, the hush that would follow. *It would be so easy.* A single slip of the wrist, and Arabella's careful performance would spill out red across her mother's fine linen.

Lumira's grip tightens briefly around her fork. She doesn't do it—not tonight. But the thought warms her more than the wine.

Gods, if only she could scrape the court clean of women like Arabella—trade their brittle perfection for Ilara's quiet roots. Now there's a woman who wouldn't bite her tongue to soothe fragile egos. Where Arabella smooths the edges of every word, Ilara lets hers settle like stone, every syllable anchored in truth.

Grove Descent Ilara Rothewen of Grovenar Territory—Crimsun's southern neighbor and ruled by its own High Sovereign—refuses to pretend court life makes sense. She carries herself with a confidence that turns performance into irrelevance. Ilara doesn't fit. Doesn't bend. And Lumira has always admired her for it—perhaps more than she should.

And yet, the court fumbles to know what to do with women like Ilara.

The palace rose garden, her refuge after the Thornley incident, blooms again in her thoughts. She'd been sitting among the moonblossoms, thrumming from the aftermath and adrenaline, when Ilara had discovered her there.

Ilara had looked at Lumira's bloodied knuckles and disheveled appearance and burst out laughing. Grace came naturally to her—tall, willowy, somehow both refined and untamed. When she settled beside Lumira, it felt like being seen by a vast, steady witness—

like the moon watching the tides. Deep-green hair, streaked with earthy brown, tumbled past her shoulders in wild waves. Bark-like markings flexed faintly along her arms as she crossed them, alive in the dim garden light, moving in rhythm with her. Amusement curled at the corners of her mouth, rich and old as forest soil.

"Let me guess," Ilara had said, settling beside her on the marble bench, "teaching another suitor about the dangers of overconfidence?" She arched a brow. "Please don't tell me it was Thornley Blackbriar. I've dodged him at our seasonal gatherings for the last three years." The amusement in her gaze was unmistakable—keen, knowing, tinged with the kind of bitterness only other daughters of power ever truly understand. "At the very least"—a sly edge woven through—"tell me you made it unforgettable."

Lumira demonstrated how askew Thornley's nose was post-impact, complete with the theatrical spray of blood onto his precious silk cravat. Ilara's delighted cackle drew frowns from passing courtiers, which only made them laugh harder.

"Oh, that's magnificent," she rasped, brushing moisture from her lashes. "Almost as good as the time I convinced half the court I had a flesh-eating illness. You should have seen how fast the nobles scattered!"

That had been the beginning. Their shared hatred of arranged marriages and court fakery had blossomed into a genuine friendship amid the artificial garden of noble alliances. Ilara understood what it meant to be a daughter whose value was measured in bloodline potential, whose every move was monitored for signs of rebellion. She'd taught Lumira to hide slender tools in her elaborate hairstyles and read the subtle signs of court intrigue in seemingly innocent conversations.

More importantly, Ilara had warned her about strange changes back in Grovenar—guard rotations, closed-door meetings, and her father growing more paranoid by the week. "The balance is unraveling." She'd said it at their last meeting—strained, almost swallowed by the sound of the garden fountain. "He keeps muttering about ancient bloodlines and threats in the shadows. He won't name it, but whatever it is... he's terrified."

At the time, Lumira had brushed it off as another Grovenar superstition—cryptic warnings from a paranoid ruler. But now the memory coils tighter around her ribs. Her own father had seemed the same, in the end—restless, hunted by shadows. Whatever he feared... it might not have been paranoia after all.

"That reminds me," Thara says, all effortless charm—so perfectly placed it sets every nerve in Lumira on edge. "The Annual Territory Summit approaches. While attendance will be more... selective this year, all principal heirs and eligible children of suitable age are required to attend—and participate in all formal functions." She pins Lumira with a fleeting glance. "The High Sovereigns have agreed to a more intimate gathering. Fewer distractions, more distilled discussions."

It's Crimsun's turn this year—her mother's territory, her rules. The summit always circles like a vulture, but this time, the carrion came straight to their door.

The emphasis on "all" and "formal" strikes home with lethal intent. The summit echoes in her mind, wrenching memories from the depths.

Shadowspire. Last year. The last time she saw her father.

Images flash through her mind: her father moving through the rites of the summit, each gesture steeped in the haze of a borrowed dream—present, but only just. The warmth she'd once known in him had vanished, replaced by a restless tension that never quite left his shoulders. His awareness kept sliding toward the shadows between the pillars—restless, taut, as if he could feel the threat gathering just beyond reach.

The memory strikes clear. She sees herself finding him alone in one of Shadowspire's lower libraries, deep in the ceremonial halls, surrounded by ancient texts on bloodline inheritance and life force manipulation—the same subjects Lord Thornley publicly champions. The same topics that keep surfacing wherever the Brotherhood leaves a shadow.

"Papa?" she said, halting inside the archway.

He startled like someone expecting a blade, not a daughter.

"What are you doing down here? Hunting ghosts?"

He tried to smile. It didn't stick. "Just some research. Territory matters."

"Research that involves ancient bloodline rituals and inheritance magic?" She stepped closer, scanning the open texts before he could shut them. "Sounds less like politics and more like prophecy."

His hand trembled as he reached up to touch her cheek—subtle, but she saw it. "You always saw what others missed," he murmured. Then, the shelves drew his notice. "Promise me this. If anything ever happens with your birthmark—if it shifts or changes…"

A sound in the stacks.

He spun, every line of him drawn taut, reacting on instinct. "Never mind," he said quickly, pulling away. "Be careful, Lumira. Not everyone at court is what they seem."

And that was it—his last words.

By morning, he was gone—no note, no trail. A library of closed books and unasked questions was all he left behind.

Only now does she understand what he might have been trying to keep hidden—and what that key would wake up in her.

Her mother hadn't wept. Of course not. He hadn't been her latest conquest in bloodline strategy, just the inconvenient father of her least predictable child. Lumira—their only shared creation—had become little more than a reminder of whatever that union had once been. Or what it had threatened to become.

Lumira leans into the chair's carved back, its pressure anchoring her in the present. There's no room for ghosts at this table—only obligations draped in formality and sharpened with etiquette.

"Several prominent families have expressed… interest." Thara doesn't smile, but the words do. "Naturally, I've begun coordinating introductions."

The return to court reality hits fast and without grace—no warning, no breath between past and present. This time, Lumira doesn't bother hiding her eye roll, muttering into her wine, "Fantastic. A week of dick-measuring in embroidered nonsense."

"What was that, dear?" Thara's tone could freeze boiling water.

"I said, *how fascinating*, Mother dearest." Lumira offers her a saccharine smile, edged with contempt. "Please, do tell me more about the proper way to accommodate potential suitors. I find your advice ever so… enlightening."

"Your attitude does you no credit," Thara replies, each word crisp enough to shatter. "Your bloodline is a gift to be wielded for the territory's advancement. A sacred duty that requires—"

"—that I spread my legs for whatever entitled lordling you've decided has the right lineage?" She lifts her glass with a mocking flourish. "To duty, Mother. And to all the noble cocks it demands."

Marnox's fork clatters against his plate. She feels a flicker of guilt, quickly smothered by the twitch in her mother's jaw.

That twitch says it all: Thara's still deciding.

None of them—Aviah, Marnox, Jaggard, Pyraxus, or Lumira herself—have been named Blood Heir. Not yet. Until Thara chooses, they remain Blood Descents: technically equal, unofficially ranked, and all enduring the same performance—smiling, courting—just to appear worthy.

Lumira didn't volunteer for the pageant. But calculated smiles, strategic matches, and dinners like this one tighten the noose just the same. Whether anyone admits it or not.

So she leans in. Lets the venom steep. "Your suitor selection is truly remarkable," she purrs. "The last one cried in under three minutes." A sip. A smile. "Though, in fairness, he never said which sword he'd mastered. I'm guessing neither."

The temperature drops. A subtle dip in air pressure, the palace itself holding its breath.

"Your persistent refusal of suitable matches grows tiresome, Lumira. The bloodlines must be maintained. The strength of Crimsun relies on—"

"—breeding," Lumira finishes, swirling her wine. "Yes, we've all heard the sermon. If bloodlines are so important, pick someone who doesn't crumple from a single boot. Blackbriar's genetics hit the floor faster than he did." She pauses. "Though I must admit"—she met her mother's stare without flinching—"his crooked nose does add a bit of character."

Thara remains perfectly motionless. Then she lifts her glass, slow and deliberate, candlelight glittering across rings that announce her reach to anyone foolish enough to forget. "You've always had a flair for turning dinner into performance," she says, setting her glass down with a single crisp tap. "But don't mistake spectacle for strategy. One of them will outmaneuver you. What will you do then?"

The words land soft as perfume, lethal as poison. And for the briefest moment, Lumira feels that familiar whisper at the edge of her mind—*a pressure, a curl of intention*—like Thara might reach for Compulsion again. Might tighten the leash.

But it fades. Not mercy. A warning.

"You will maintain proper decorum at the summit," Thara continues, a refined finality that renders protest pointless. "You will attend the scheduled introductions. And you will remember your place in this family."

The words are deceptively soft, but they land with the weight of a closed door, of a verdict already decided. A reminder that, no matter how venomous Lumira's words are, she is expected to play her role. Thara fixes on her—unblinking—an iron collar pressing down.

The key cools. No panic, no alarm—only a swift alteration in temperature, as if in recognition. Not the message, but the messenger. It's reacting to Thara herself.

At the opposite end of the table, Pyraxus sits in measured silence, the verbal skirmish unfolding as a play he's long since memorized. Words aren't necessary—his blade glides through pheasant with practiced precision, but the food remains largely untouched. Unlike Jaggard, who swings words like a dull axe, Pyraxus says less and means more—poised and far more cutting. His marriage to Arabella was pure strategy—another of Thara's neatly brokered alliances, securing land, leverage, and another pawn on the board. A tidy exchange, even if it condemned him to a lifetime of her dinner table corrections.

He meets Lumira's eye then, a faint twitch at the corner of his mouth—almost amusement. Of all her siblings, he's never tried to change her, maybe because he knows what it costs to pretend.

The thought barely finishes before the dining room doors swing open.

Conversation stutters. Chairs still. And then—

Zylven Meridian, High Sovereign of Vesper Territory, arrives with the kind of energy that turns heads without trying—magnetic, self-assured, and entirely at ease in a room that seems to loosen its shoulders when he enters.

His sterling hair, streaked with platinum, catches the light like liquid mercury—radiant, not showy, a natural reflection of his Vesper heritage. He's tall, his movements smooth and unhurried, someone with nothing to prove and no need to rush.

There's easy affection in the way he scans the table, his warmth almost at odds with the rest of him—layered, unreadable, until he smiles and the corners of his face crease with sincerity. Even his coloring, silver-hinted and dusk-touched, holds a subtle glow—less a show of power than a seamless echo of his territory's restrained luxury: refined, understated, impossible to ignore.

His jacket, flawlessly tailored in soft charcoal and pearl, outclasses every other outfit at the table without trying. This isn't about standing out—it's about becoming what the moment demands.

And somehow, it works. It always does.

"Father!" Marnox and Aviah's delighted cries shatter what remains of the dinner's rigid formality. They half rise from their chairs before Arabella's withering glare pins them back in place.

Lumira observes the performance unfold with detachment. Zylven was never Thara's husband—merely a convenient storm she let sweep through her bed when it suited her. He'd given her offspring, yes, but had no claim on her power. Rumors claimed they shared more than children and polite smiles, that Thara liked her men like her politics—volatile for as long as they amused her, discarded the moment they didn't.

The younger ones adored him, unable to see how he drifted in and out like mist—dazzling but gone before they could hold him to anything real.

"My darlings." Zylven's smile lights up his already-too-handsome face as he spreads his arms in greeting. "I do hope I'm not interrupting. I've arrived early for the summit and couldn't stomach the idea of dining alone in my chambers." He steps into the glow of the chandelier, presence effortlessly commanding without demanding. "Alone—for now, of course. The rest of my party will join me once they finish final arrangements." He marks Emberly's empty chair, and a slight unreadable flicker—swift beyond naming—crosses his face. "Might I...?" he asks gently, nodding toward the empty seat. His manners are immaculate despite the familiarity.

"Of course," Thara begins, ready to accommodate charm and status.

"Why not?" Lumira drawls before she can stop herself. "Though I do hope you brought your own cushion. These chairs don't care how important you think your ass is."

A few shocked gasps around the table only fuel her satisfaction.

Zylven, to his credit, lets out a rich laugh. "Ah, Lumira. Your wit continues to... entertain. Though perhaps we could save the commentary on my posterior for after dinner?"

"And miss the chance to critique it while you're actually sitting? Where's the fun in that?"

Marnox barely contains his giggle, though he tries to hide it behind his napkin. Then, as Zylven lowers himself into Emberly's chair, the key responds—not a warning, not colder... attentive. As if it is studying him the same way she is.

A server quietly replaces his plate with a fresh dish, but Zylven doesn't spare it a second thought.

"Now then," he announces with practiced charm, "I've only just arrived and already feel I've missed half the drama. Someone catch me up—have any insults been traded yet? Or are we saving those for dessert?"

Lumira ignores Zylven and holds her position, a single loose strand of hair brushing her cheek, her expression unreadable. "More wine, anyone?" she purrs, sweet enough to rot. "It pairs beautifully with thinly veiled threats and generational trauma."

Jaggard snorts into his goblet, muttering what sounds suspiciously like, "Here we go again."

At the far end of the table, Zylven sits in Emberly's old seat—an absence made visible. He looks perfectly at ease—charming, effortless, a man who belongs in any room he enters.

For now, Lumira smiles, the expression of a woman with nothing to lose.

And watches the game unfold—with teeth bared, patience stretched thin, and a war brewing behind every toast.

6

SHADOWS AND SECRETS

The taste of yesterday's politics lingers—bitter on her tongue—as Pigments & Pints hums with creativity and the soft clink of glassware. The scent is layered—lavender oil, citrus zest, and the faint trace of varnish clinging to open canvases. Lumira steps inside as if she's done it a hundred times, though the space couldn't be less familiar.

Here, the chaos is curated: sketches taped along exposed brick, brushes resting in old wine bottles, and patrons tucked into velvet-backed chairs like they're part of the décor. She doesn't know where to stand, so she keeps moving. The atmosphere is warm, but she stains the scene, ink marring a delicate painting.

She doesn't let it show.

The massive fireplace beside her radiates a gentle heat, but Lumira doesn't let herself settle. She perches on the narrow ledge of a low-set bench, back straight, every angle precise. Her legs cross at the ankle, composed in the shadow of her hood.

The performance isn't a façade, but a crafted one—just arrogant enough to pass for boredom, calculated to keep them guessing. Each act she performs is a testament to her control, a reminder that she sees more than she reveals.

And gods, there's plenty to notice. The ceiling rises like a cathedral, wooden beams arching in elegant defiance. Shelves stretch from floor to rafter, packed with books—real, weighty volumes. Not the leather-bound props in her family's collection, chosen more for the gilding on the cover than the content within. These resonate with substance—ink, parchment, raw magic buried in echoes of forbidden knowledge and half-forgotten truths. Not history. Power too, hidden so deep most pretend it never existed. A slow pass of her gloved hand drifts along the spine, the impulse to vanish into the book nearly overwhelming. These are dangerous books—her favorite kind.

The sunken hearth area forms a natural focal point, though calling it a "gathering space" feels like calling her mother *mildly selective about bloodlines*. Polished beams curve between columns, forming alcoves tailored for secrets. The bar glows in invitation, lantern light glinting across its lacquered wood. Stools line its edge—refined in form, uncomfortable by design, the kind that discourages lingering without purpose.

Everything here feels intentional, from the lighting to the ambient murmur of conversation—masking meaning without revealing content.

A woman in russets and warm golds moves through the space with authority—adjusting a lamp here, straightening a chair there. Her motions are purposeful. Measured. Every gesture carries the weight of choreographed perfection, setting Lumira's instincts bristling.

Near the bar, a harried server calls out, "Wrenna—need you for this order!" The woman immediately pivots to handle it.

Wrenna. The name on the receipt. The owner, then. Has to be. Her influence clings to the composition like perfume: unmistakable, enduring, and hard to place.

The aroma of fresh-baked pastries drifts from a glass case near the bar, mingling with the richer notes of coffee and the sting of fresh paint. Rows of exquisitely crafted desserts gleam beneath the glass, each more ostentatious than the last. The honeyed pastries catch her attention—golden, flaky, their folds gleaming with glaze and spiced almond filling. Tiny masterpieces meant to be devoured, another indulgence dressed as subtlety. The case is positioned so that even the haughtiest noble must stand shoulder to shoulder with common merchants to retrieve their confections. A cluster of elegant ladies does that now, their practiced indifference cracking as they assess the pastries.

Croissants flake and charcoal drifts as artists sketch, smudges blooming across parchment and napkin without pause. The "merchants" loitering near the poetry stage nibble cream-filled delicacies with the kind of guilt that suggests espionage—spies or smugglers, most likely, but mortal enough to fall for pastry.

A small stage occupies the far wall, framed by curtains in a weathered rust hue, soft and heavy as dusk. It currently hosts a painfully earnest young man midway through what appears to be a heartfelt ode to his beloved's tragically misunderstood elbow. Lumira holds fast, unblinking. A little horrified, but not retreating. She flags him for investigation. Anyone who commits to that level of artistic agony is either hiding secrets or should be barred from public speaking to preserve civilized society.

She can almost see Emberly here, moving between easels with that unshaken rhythm of someone at home in their craft, a rhythm that turned Lumira into a drunken bear during their ill-fated drawing lessons. The recollection breaks through without warning, her sister's patient instruction met with Lumira's mounting frustration as every line came out wrong. Eventually, Emberly had laughed—not unkindly—and said, *"Well, if you ever need to unsettle someone with bold, unpredictable shapes… you may have a gift."*

The ache flares—quick, unwelcome. She buries it.

Her gaze drifts outward, snagging on the absurdity of the scene around her.

The café's patrons are a tableau of barely concealed comedy. Merchants shout their deals with the volume of people who think secrecy is a suggestion, while the wealthy try—and fail—to blend in under layers of silk and embellishment that scream otherwise. Artists hurry past, noses buried in sketchbooks, colliding with chairs and tabletops like the next masterpiece might vanish if they dare lift their heads.

But it's Wrenna who pulls Lumira in, not by charm but by undeniable command. Her bearing is purposeful, each step exact. Used to scrutiny, she doesn't endure it—she anticipates it. No Crimsun native treads like that, and Lumira would bet her favorite stabbing knife that she's not from the neighboring territory of Grovenar either. A steadiness in her bearing suggests training, discipline shaped somewhere far less refined than polite society.

Their paths intersect long enough for Lumira to recognize the telltale sting, examined and logged, a threat to revisit.

Wrenna's silver-white hair catches the lantern light, revealing blue undertones that shimmer like shallow water—an unmistakable sign of Naiad Territory blood. The sharp chin-length cut sways as she crosses the room, but her presence tells another story. There's weight in it, grounded in fluid grace. Her skin holds that same blue-silver sheen, but in the shadows, a warmer, earthen note surfaces—almost metallic, like buried ore—a shift Lumira doesn't recognize.

That's what unsettles her most. The traits don't add up. The combination shouldn't work, and yet Wrenna wears it like armor. Lumira learned to place bloodlines in moments, but Wrenna refuses to be placed.

Wrenna's constant motion feels like clockwork wound tight, her fingers conducting invisible symphonies that make Lumira's teeth ache.

The performance isn't limited to Wrenna, the entire café plays along. Conversations flow and falter with deliberate rhythm, laughter fading on cue.

Each table hosts its own quiet act: gesturing merchants, dramatic artists, nobles cloaked in understated wealth, pretending not to be noticed. One woman sketches the room with remarkable precision; her neighbor, far less talented, delivers a monologue about his creative process with such conviction that a nearby lord nods, solemn and enthralled.

By the bar, seasoned traders toe a careful line—loud to appear open, vague to obscure intent. Their voices, like their clothes, are muted and measured.

But it's the group near the poetry stage that draws Lumira's focus. Three men, supposedly discussing manifests, move in eerie harmony. Their relaxed poses are too perfect. One catches a falling cup midair—a fluid motion born of habit, not chance.

That kind of reflex isn't learned by hauling crates.

Her instincts flare—a prickle at the edge of awareness. The stillness of trained muscles pretending to be at ease. She scans again. They aren't gathered—they're spaced. One lingers at the stage, another leans against the bar, a third browses near the art supplies.

Strategic placement. Maximum coverage. A triangle of surveillance clicks into place—suspiciously clean, perfectly exact.

She'd thought the Brotherhood might skulk in palace shadows, not tuck themselves into back rooms in the city. Yet no one here seems surprised. The thought settles cold in her gut:

How many more are hiding in plain sight?

And then there are the nobles—the obvious ones in jewel-toned silks trying not to complain about the furniture, and the quieter kind, in unremarkable tailoring, who avoid direct eye contact. Lumira notes them all.

This place was built for concealment.

The stage is perfectly angled to monitor the rear exit. The alcoves catch and redirect sound. Mirrors hang purposefully, creating blind spots that swallow the slightest motion. Sunlight splinters through stained glass in restless patterns—coded signals in color and cast, gliding like whispers across the floor. She notices the staff accommodating the light without hesitation. That kind of choreography doesn't happen by chance.

Behind the bar, a server slides a drink to a flushed noblewoman—Wrenna's latest creation. She takes one sip and stares at the glass like it confessed her sins.

"How does she *do* that?" another woman murmurs, cradling a pale-amber cocktail. "It's like she knew I'd fought with my husband. Tastes like guilt—with a bitter finish."

Her companion leans in, glancing around. "Wrenna always does it. She reads people—mixes whatever you're hiding into the drink. Like she knows exactly what you deserve to taste."

Lumira arches a brow. So that's the story: Wrenna can read a person's secrets and pour them into a glass. Ridiculous. Probably. But... she files it away.

The brilliance of Pigments & Pints lies in how it uses beauty to camouflage intent. A noble gives the impression of a curious patron rather than a courtier. Three merchants tucked in a corner seem like critics, not conspirators. A heavy purse sliding below a table could easily be a payment for art, not intelligence. Here, the questionable is hidden behind beauty.

Even the gnomes know how to play their part. Small but composed, they command their corner with steady control. Their earthy-toned clothing is practical, but they all wear a gleaming piece of metalwork, too refined for mere decoration. Their braided beards and intricate hairstyles appear ornamental, but Lumira suspects they're more like sigils than fashion. Identifiers. Or warnings.

Wrenna's art class steers Lumira toward a different track. She walks through her students easily, correcting one with kindness and reprimanding another with calm precision—one boy flushes, chastened by her critique. She never stops moving—adjusting a brush here, repositioning a canvas there—small reminders that this is her space as much as theirs. Remaining stationary doesn't seem to suit her.

Interesting. Very interesting.

The memory presses in before she can block it: Emberly observing her during one of their long afternoons in the palace garden studio—an ill-fated attempt at bonding through art. Her paper looked more like a battlefield than a canvas, and Emberly, ever diplomatic, had murmured, *"Maybe your talents lie elsewhere,"* with a grin that softened the blow.

The ache fades as Lumira spots Wrenna drifting toward the bar—class forgotten, smile polite, every line of her threaded with intent. A drink suddenly tips over a man asking persistent questions. A flinch, an apology, a distraction. The timing screams intention.

Lumira has seen that maneuver before.

A year ago, a visiting lord from another territory leaned uncomfortably close during a formal banquet, each pass by Lumira's chair marked by a bolder reach. He hadn't touched her— not quite—but he was testing boundaries she wasn't allowed to defend in public. One adverse reaction from her and everything she'd trained for could be jeopardized. Emberly had swept past him and tripped. Perfectly. The wine, the noise, the indignation—it was distraction enough.

Later, Lumira asked, "That wasn't an accident, was it?"

Emberly's smile was soft but sure. "Sometimes, the best defense is misdirection."

Now, Lumira follows Wrenna's pacing the way she once did Emberly's—and the recognition stings.

How many lessons had her sister wrapped in laughter and offered without explanation?

This place isn't a café. It's a blueprint. A network. A message.

Wrenna pauses at a landscape painting tucked into a secluded alcove. The way she touches the frame—light, reverent—halts Lumira mid-step. The style is unmistakable. Emberly's early work.

Wrenna's expression flickers—there and gone. Grief is quickly hidden under the professional mask. But Lumira sees it. She *knows* it.

They shared something.

Wrenna steps back, murmuring something to a staff member. Her stride stays fluid, composed—but the purpose behind them sharpens. She's leaving.

Curious.

Lumira watches her slip out into the deepening dusk and decides it's time for her to vanish too. She's learned more from one day at Pigments & Pints than from a week of drills. She won't say it aloud, but Emberly might've had a point about observational skills. Her network needs more than fighters. What it needs are listeners, infiltrators, and ghosts.

She rises and strides for the door, slipping a coin onto the edge of a table—she's planning treason, sure, but she's not a savage.

The key pulses against her—not soft, but wild, electric. Like the charge before lightning splits the sky. It doesn't feel like warmth, but a warning—sharp and wordless, pressed into her bones.

Or maybe a promise. With her luck, it's both.

She steps into the evening air as Wrenna disappears into the crowd. If Emberly left a trail here, Lumira would hunt it down—every trace, every breadcrumb.

After all, what kind of sister would she be if she didn't take an interest in Emberly's favorite artistic haunt? And if she uncovers a few intelligence networks along the way, that's being efficient. Mother always said she should develop more refined hobbies.

She probably didn't mean espionage and mild treason over espresso.

But here we fucking are.

Though really, that's entirely her own fault for not being more specific.

7

FOREST WHISPERS

Wrenna moves through the merchant district, a noble slumming without the courtesy of disguise. Lumira squints. She'd hoped the woman would have some sense—some instinct for caution—but apparently not. She handles fruit like a street-market seductress while half-heartedly checking for a tail. Sloppy. Insultingly so.

Blending in takes zero effort. Lumira lets the crowd swallow her, slipping through the churn of merchants packing up and nobles pretending they belong. The air reeks of salt, rot, and desperation baked into every coin.

Wrenna isn't wandering—she's guiding, probing.

Of course she is. Gods forbid anything be simple.

Lumira collects herself, the adjustment subtle but unmistakable. So that's how this is going to go. She follows. Not because she trusts her. Not out of curiosity. Wrenna retreats like she's carrying a secret—and if it has anything to do with Emberly, she'd better start talking. Now.

The key hangs close, smug in its silence—aware. Like it's in a joke she hasn't heard. And gods, does she hate that.

Wrenna's pace carries unnatural evenness, disturbing deliberation. A performance dressed up as casual meandering.

Lumira brushes the hilt of her blade. If this is a trap, it isn't good. She almost turns back.

Almost.

But where is the fun in that?

The silver-haired woman cuts through another alley, probably thinking she is being clever. Lumira keeps her distance, noting the tempo of her stride and the too-long pauses at corners, the fractional turns of her head. Tactical missteps, every one of them—and Lumira counts them like debts, small and stacking.

Wrenna adjusts her satchel strap—precise, practiced—and a chill settles in Lumira's core.

Not because it's suspicious. Because it's familiar.

Emberly did that, too, only visible to those who know where to find it. Years of moving through noble courts, always navigating without being seen, had etched that reflex into her. Lumira used to tease her for it, calling it her "paranoia tic." Emberly would arch a brow and say that nobility never noticed anything unless it wore silk and smiled.

Now, that same ghost of a gesture echoes in Wrenna, an uninvited memory stirring.

She clenches her jaw, willing the thought away. This isn't the time. Grief is selfish—slinking in, dragging reminders into spaces she's fought to keep clean. Emberly would have recognized the setup and known precisely how to turn it to her advantage.

But Emberly isn't here.

She's dead.

She chokes on the shape of the word.

There was a time—long before she started training—when Lumira believed in justice. Justice for the beggars beaten by the Blood Legion, Crimsun Territory's elite enforcers, loyal only to her mother. For the merchants taxed into ruin. For the servants discarded like spoiled wine. Maybe even for Emberly.

But that was a child's fantasy, shattered long before her sister's death.

She remembers the first time she decided the system wasn't enough. A disgraced noble, stripped of title and tossed onto Crimsun's streets for offending the High Sovereigness's pride. She'd stayed in the shadows, bearing witness as a Blood Legion guard broke the man's ribs near the marble gates. The next night, she found the noble battered and bleeding behind the wine shops, discarded into the gutter like he belonged there.

Lumira didn't give him pity. She gave him poison—a neat little vial, easy to slip into the guard's ale at a dockside tavern where the brutes liked to drink themselves stupid. She taught him how to wait. How to smile when they called him worthless. How to stand back and let the bastard choke on his own tongue.

When it was done, she gave the noble coin, a new name, and a look no one would recognize. A chance to vanish before the Blood Legion noticed the pattern. He became one of hers—loyal not because she asked for it, but because she showed him what his rage was worth.

That was the real beginning of her network—not a band of spies or rebels, but a gathering of the broken, the cast-off, the ones with debts no court would honor but her.

Justice doesn't bring people back. It doesn't explain why they're gone, or who decided their life was worth less than theirs. Emberly had risked everything for the truth.

So Lumira will too.

Not because she believes it will fix anything. But someone has to drag that truth into the light and make them choke on it. And if Wrenna holds a fragment of it, Lumira will follow—no matter how tangled or theatrical the path becomes.

When Wrenna finally seems satisfied she's alone—she isn't—she picks up her pace, drawn to Thallen Forest. Because apparently, they're doing the whole mysterious-meeting-in-the-haunted-woods routine. How delightfully cliché.

The moment she steps into the trees, the air turns sharp and cold, Altareth's warmth retreating like a held breath. Thallen Forest stretches west from the eastern coast of Grovenar, past the Naiad River, and into the veiled edges of Shadowspire and Terravox Territories—far enough to make deniability plausible and legality questionable. To the east, the cliffs give way to the Eirros Ocean, though locals call it the Eirros Deep, as if renaming it might make it less likely to devour them whole.

The scent of pine and damp earth clings to her senses—thick, grounding, laced with an older presence. Above, the canopy shifts against the stagnant air, branches stirring as if brushed by an unseen will. Massive roots arch along the path, their bark lined with markings not made by time—and far older than names. The gnarled wood pulses faintly, not with light, but with an ancient presence. Noticing.

A group of Dusk Deer emerge between the trees, their bioluminescent antlers casting fractured light through the mist. They glide with otherworldly grace, barely disturbing the underbrush—creatures born of the forest's oldest hush.

The air thickens, old magic curling through the trees, wrapping around her as if memory had taken shape.

From the deeper shadows, a silhouette detaches—smoke-bodied, lightless. An Umbra Wraith. It drifts at the edge of sight, rippling like breath exhaled by the forest.

The Wraith glides with a bird's eerie grace, drawn to some quiet rhythm threaded through her skin.

Beneath her boots, the ground quakes. A low, subterranean groan—far below the roots—probably one of the Terran Gnome tunnels. Their underground networks run the length of Grovenar and beyond, carving out a second world below the surface. She doesn't know why they built their halls so vast. Too big for gnomes. Maybe it was for dragons. Or perhaps the earth stopped saying no.

Above her, a force stirs—and stays.

Grove Dragons.

They move through the canopy like living branches—scaled in lichen, bark, and emerald shadow, their bodies long and sinuous, camouflaged by centuries of evolution. Their wings stretch like leaf-veined sails—so thin they shimmer with moonlight, but powerful enough to shake the trees when unfurled. They don't descend. They don't speak. But they notice. Not enemies, not allies, but older than either.

A voice cuts through the trees—confident and irritatingly familiar. "I was wondering how long you'd follow before getting caught."

Lumira doesn't startle. She turns slowly, her balance tilting, already cataloging escape routes out of habit.

Ilara stands a few paces in front of her, arms crossed, her expression unreadable but not unkind. Behind her, Wrenna waits, a silver-ringed shadow—poised and watchful, catching far more than she pretends.

They aren't surprised to see her.

But Ilara? Here? Her chest tightens. This isn't Wrenna's game—it never was.

"How thoughtful." Lumira's delivery is composed, but tension threads through the last word. "You left a trail just subtle enough to insult me."

Ilara huffs, almost a laugh. Almost.

"You planned this?" Lumira snaps, glancing between them. "Since when is she part of it?"

Wrenna steps forward, curious. "You came for answers."

"I came for Emberly," she shoots back. "Not… this. Not you," she adds, fixing Ilara with a glare. "What are you doing here? What did you do?"

Another glance passes between them. Familiar on Ilara's part. Calculating on Wrenna's.

"Come with us," Wrenna says, like this isn't already a secret meeting in a forest thick with ghosts.

Lumira hesitates. A heartbeat. No more. Then she turns.

The clearing they've led her to is small—confined, and far from accidental.

In the center, a slab of stone rests against the moss, cracked with age. An altar, though to what gods, Lumira can't begin to guess. No names remain. Maybe they were meant to vanish.

But it's what is carved into the stone that halts her in place.

Copper-flecked etchings shimmer faintly in the low light, inked into ancient rock with impossible precision. They are not paintings or sketches. The symbols were positioned with purpose and rhythm, their placement too exacting to be arbitrary. She doesn't recognize the language, but the style is unmistakable.

Emberly's hand.

Of course she'd find a way to make the stone look elegant. Show-off.

"She was mapping something." Wrenna keeps it quiet, but the words sink in and stay. "Not recording. Tracking."

Lumira doesn't answer right away. She pauses over the carved symbols, near enough to sense their gravity, yet not quite touching. "Tracking what?" The evenness in her tone is practiced—careful.

"Artifacts," Wrenna replies. "The ones tied to the old gods."

The words hit harder than she expects. Lumira's focus locks on the stone while her thoughts fracture, then reassemble. The ache along her collarbone flares to life—searing and alive.

"She found one." The words leave Lumira in a whisper: statement, not inquiry.

But a different number nags at the back of her mind—twelve. The old stories about artifacts bloom in her mind. Scattered across

Cyrathea, buried deep enough that even the High Sovereigns pretend they're myths. It's said they're not relics of power: prison shards, each anchoring a piece of the old gods that couldn't be killed, only sealed away. Emberly never let it go—murmuring twelve like a prayer while sketching maps by candlelight, as if saying it out loud would make it real.

Wrenna nods once. "She found the Blood Key."

The key pulses with heat as Wrenna speaks, as if recognizing its own name.

The pause that follows doesn't settle—it lands. Heavy. Final.

The Blood Key was supposed to be a myth: a tale spun to keep restless children from chasing the wrong kind of treasure. And yet here it is, thrumming with restless life, daring her to obey the pull.

But Emberly hadn't been chasing legends. She'd been chasing the truth.

And she'd found it.

Lumira snorts. "Oh, she found it, all right—and buried it behind a hidden panel like it was one more secret to choke on when she was gone." Frost clings to every word she utters, cut glass meant to wound. "So unless that counts as discovery, I'd say it was planted."

Wrenna and Ilara stop in unison, tension rippling between them.

Not shocked. Just… measuring.

"You have it." Wrenna keeps her tone carefully neutral. "Right now."

"She didn't tell you where she hid it, either," Lumira mutters. "Guess I'm not the only one she kept in the dark."

"Show us," Ilara says, softening as Lumira raises a brow. "Please. We need to be sure."

She reaches with intention, drawing the key into the open.

The clearing relaxes—or hesitates, as if uncertain what comes next.

The metal doesn't glow. It breathes, drawing ambient light inward until it gleams with a deeper resonance—vibrant, alive. Faint pulses of heat rise from it, syncing with a faint tempo she hadn't noticed until now.

Wrenna inhales quickly. "It's responding to your blood—like Emberly suspected."

A familiar warmth, gentle and insistent, stirs against her collarbone. The crescent-shaped birthmark burns like it did the first time she touched the key, an echo of power older than blood. She doesn't flinch. But she registers it.

"Suspected?" The word tastes wrong. Understanding clicks into place. "She knew. That's why she left it for me to find."

Ilara nods slowly. "She had theories. Those artifacts respond to complex bloodlines. People with ties across multiple territories. But she never got to test it."

"Because someone killed her first." Lumira is calm, but only on the surface. "And you didn't tell me."

Silence.

They don't deny it. What passes between them isn't surprise—it's confirmation. And something darker, laid bare in its vileness.

Pity.

"Don't." Her low, lethal voice slices through the clearing. "Don't do that thing where you decide what to tell me. I've had enough of people deciding what I get to know."

"Lumira—" Ilara begins, but she's not finished. Not even close.

"My sister is dead." The words hit like a lash. "Emberly's gone, and apparently, she trusted both of you more than she trusted me. So tell me—what made you so special? What made you so worthy while I got left to rot in the dark?" Her stare pins Ilara, the sting deeper than anything Wrenna could ever cut her with. "And you—my friend. I trusted you. You stood at my side, all while keeping her secrets buried. You chose her over me."

No fear. No falter.

Ilara's posture angles toward Wrenna, the weight of guilt settling in the space between. "She introduced us." Calm, composed, like she's accepted the consequences. "Said we'd need each other. That if anything happened to her—"

"We'd be the only ones left who *know how to finish it*," Wrenna finishes, tone flat. Not remorseful—just matter-of-fact, like she's reasoned it through a hundred times. Then a silver edge flashes through her expression. "Because you react exactly like this," Wrenna adds, cutting clean. "With anger. Accusations. You want someone to blame? Fine. Blame us. But she didn't tell you because she couldn't trust what you'd do."

It hits Lumira hard—air vanishing from her lungs in an instant. "Excuse me?"

"She was scared, Lumira. Of what you'd do." Wrenna doesn't soften. Doesn't flinch. "Scared you'd charge in blind, chasing vengeance like it owed you something."

Lumira's throat tightens. "She was my sister." The words crack under everything she's held back. "And she trusted you, an artist she barely knew. And you, a forest noble so busy playing politics in the shadows you couldn't be bothered to tell me the truth. But me? The one person who's bled for her, lied for her, would've gone to war for her—" Her voice splinters. "And you all just… what? Left me out?"

Ilara remains calm, but it cuts deep. "Because war is exactly what you would've brought."

Lumira stiffens. She curls her fingers into fists, knuckles white. "And maybe that's what she needed."

"No." Wrenna's tone is brittle now. "She needed someone who would keep her alive."

"Well, you *fucked* that up too," Lumira bites out.

The clearing contracts as if the very air fears breaking.

She turns away, jaw clenching. Wrenna's steps follow—soft as ashfall, but full of threat.

"That's what you do, Lumira." Wrenna's words are ice-edged and unforgiving. "You escalate. And that's exactly what got her killed."

The hit doesn't bleed—it fractures.

She staggers back a step. "You think I *killed* her?"

"*We* think she was trying to protect you." Ilara's tone drops lower. "The Brotherhood was waiting. One misstep—one burst of temper—and they'd know. She couldn't risk it."

"So instead, she just—what? Died alone? While I stood there, lying to her face, telling her she'd be fine?" The word *fine* shatters in her mouth. She hates how it sounds—how it shakes. Grief rises, but she bites down, tasting blood to anchor herself.

The forest hushes around them. Even the trees seem to lean back, unwilling to interfere.

"She wasn't alone," Wrenna murmurs.

Lumira turns toward her slowly.

Wrenna doesn't meet her gaze. She remains locked on the markings Emberly left behind, fingertips tracing the copper-flecked lines like she's afraid they might vanish.

The possessiveness in it makes Lumira's stomach twist. "You speak like you know. But you weren't there. You didn't see her."

Wrenna holds her tongue.

Lumira laughs—a jagged sound that barely resembles humor. "Right. You weren't there. And somehow, you ended up with all the answers." She doesn't turn away this time—lets the fury burn a little longer before speaking. "And neither of you thought I deserved to know that either."

Ilara cuts in, soft but steady, impossible to ignore. "What would you have done differently, Lumira? If she told you what she found—if you knew someone was willing to kill to keep it hidden? Would you have waited? Or set the city ablaze chasing the truth?"

Lumira stiffens, jaw clenched, everything else falling away. "I wouldn't have waited." Not a confession. A truth without apology. "I wouldn't have sat idle while the walls closed around her."

A Grove Dragon stirs above, its leafy scales rustling in warning or approval.

"I would've protected her."

Wrenna's composure doesn't break, though a chill edges in. "No." The words slice, calm and clear. "You would've bled the realm dry. And she knew it."

Lumira's lips curl, not into a smile, but colder. "You're damn right I would have." She turns toward them, no longer hiding the fury. "And now that she's gone, tell me—what do your secrets buy us? What good did it do?"

The clearing tightens. More Umbra Wraiths emerge between trees and shadows, as if drawn to the ancient humming in her blood. They move like smoke given thought, soundless and knowing, as if they understand more than they should.

The key warms where it touches her—not angry, not afraid. Ready.

Ilara steps forward. "We finish what she started. But we do it her way. Discreetly. No trails. No bodies."

"Adorable. Really. You two are precious with your no-bodies plan." Lumira snorts in disbelief.

The forest air thrums with pressure before lightning splits the sky.

She could compel them. The thought rises, slick and uninvited. That part of her—the one she hates admitting exists—knows exactly how to unravel a will with nothing but a tilt of her chin and a few words. The Compulsion sits coiled within her, a blade she's used before but vowed to wield only when there's no other choice.

But that's a lie, isn't it? She doesn't like using it, though sometimes she does. Sometimes the cleanest cut leaves no trace— only the aftermath it doesn't explain. She prefers her truths bloodied and earned, not dropped in her lap like pity. But the fact that the urge even surfaces now? That's all the clarity she gets. She swallows it, the taste of iron rising in her throat.

Lumira takes them in: the artist her sister trusted, the noble she's confided in, and the ancient forest curling tighter around their gathering like it, too, is listening.

"We know patience isn't your strength." Ilara's comment is light, edged in old affection. "That's why there are three of us."

There's a shift in Lumira, subtle but unmistakable—the kind that says she's willing, for now, to try words instead of weapons. "Your artist circle," she tells Wrenna, "they see what my combat network misses."

"Artists are invisible to nobles," Wrenna replies, the corners of her smile carrying more bite than comfort. "They see us as part of the décor. And merchants? No one guards their tongue around a trader."

"And your forest allies?" Lumira asks, glancing toward the clearing's edge, where mist thickens and shadows bend. "The ones most forget exist?"

Ilara's expression transforms into something deeper, older. "Thallen has its own rhythm. Grove Dragons guard what the sun can see. The Terran Gnomes dwell underground, keeping secrets in stone. And the Umbra Wraiths... They dwell in the places beyond our reach."

Lumira follows her line of sight.

The Umbra Wraiths are there—barely. Fleeting forms at the edge of perception, shadows shimmering like oil over water. They do not approach. They do not stir. But they are fixed on her—mute and feminine, like forgotten goddesses made of mist.

A rarity.

"They've been waiting." Ilara meets Lumira's eyes, the weight of ages stirring in her expression. "The old powers haven't forgotten. They only went dormant."

"Good." The single word leaves Lumira's lips—cold enough to burn. "We use all of it. My combat network. Your artists. The forest. No one expects nobles to conspire with merchants or to scheme with your dragons."

Wrenna nods. "We'll need a way to pass messages. Safe meeting points. Neutral go-betweens."

Ilara folds her arms, thoughtful. "We'll need more than that. Layers. Backup. People who pass as harmless—right up until they're inside."

Emberly risked everything to prove the artifacts are real and the Brotherhood killed her for it. If they bury the truth again, it's like she never existed. Lumira won't let that happen.

"Then we build it." Lumira doesn't blink. "Not a network. A web so fine they won't see it until it's already strangling them."

The pieces begin to slot into place. Combat-trained nobles. Merchant spies. Thallen's unseen network of runners and listeners—elusive as mist and twice as deadly. The beginning was Emberly's, carried out in wordless defiance. Now Lumira has no choice but to finish it.

The trees tremble as a Grove Dragon eases forward, its breath rolling out in a slow, earthy rumble that feels older than the forest itself. The Umbra Wraiths shimmer once more before vanishing back into the mist. They are not gone. They are... unseen.

"Fine." Lumira rises, shoulders squared. "We do this together. But when we find the one who killed her..." Her tone turns to steel. "They're mine."

Calm on the surface, Wrenna offers a clipped, "Agreed." But danger simmers underneath.

"Agreed," Ilara echoes, a crackle of magic dancing at the edge of her control. The pact settles like a storm cloud pressed low against the earth—three women bound by grief, fury, and a promise no one dares break.

The forest listens, motionless.

And Lumira—descended from secrets older than any throne— lets the rage root itself deep.

Some powers are worth dying for. Others are worth killing for. This one? It's always been both.

8

TEETH BEHIND CROWNS

The Crimsun Palace has been stripped of its warmth—polished to a gleam. It doesn't welcome; it tolerates. The marble floors shine bone-white under torchlight, the banners hang in unnerving symmetry, and the air is thick with ceremonial incense, masking tension within sanctified smoke. For the Annual Territory Summit, the palace has shed its skin as a fortress and dressed itself as a theater of power—details sharpened to intimidate.

Lumira leans against a pillar at the fringes of the gathering, arms crossed, brooding and sulking, though she'd never admit it aloud. A bad habit, she knows—haunting the periphery like a Wraith—but it keeps her out of the immediate line of fire. She's here because she has to be. Not out of duty. Not out of loyalty, but obligation laced up in velvet, scented with ceremony, and no less binding. It's been only a day since that meeting in Thallen's shadows, and her mind drifts to Wrenna's vow, Ilara's promise—the fragile plan they stitched together while the branches listened.

It makes this room feel smaller. Riskier. Every smile, every heir another variable she can't predict.

Across the gathering hall, her brothers—Pyraxus and Jaggard—stand with many of the other heirs and descents, a curated portrait of power-drunk children, polished and posed like glass blades. They're positioned with calculated elegance: each close to their territory's delegation to assert allegiance but arranged together like prized pieces on a polished board. They are decoration—strategic, but replaceable.

Unlike them, Lumira chose her vantage point for its shadow, not its spotlight. As always, she assesses the would-be leaders—their heirs apparent, their confidence carefully bred—unnoticed.

Most of the power players are already in place: beasts, banners, bored heirs pretending their attention isn't fixed on the doors. The hall is cavernous by design: vaulted to house dragons, wide to let entire delegations posture without colliding, every echo sharpened by marble and intent.

The Annual Territory Summit comes once a year, Cyrathea's twelve ruling territories drag their monsters and grudges into one gilded cage. This year, that cage belongs to Crimsun. They posture, bargain, and pretend at civility—part alliance, part threat display, all teeth behind pretty words.

But not everything in this room moves as it should. A servant's steps are deliberate. A scribe pauses at the dais, hesitation stretched thin. Her network—unseen, their awareness buried in plain sight—remains intact. Listening. Waiting.

She finds the hidden Blood Key inside her bodice. It neither warms nor chills—only pulses once, steady and unreadable. Not a threat, but a crossroads. A subtle warning that the unseen is paying attention.

Memory flickers—Emberly, hunched over her sketchbook during last year's summit in Shadowspire, capturing the sweeping arches and storm-lit balconies while everyone else schemed. "The architecture may be the only honest thing in this room," she whispered when Lumira leaned over her shoulder. Now Emberly is gone, and Lumira remains, clutching what was left unsaid and pretending not to drown in it.

Two ornate thrones sit conspicuously empty atop the platform meant for King Azrix and Queen Nerissa Thaelorn of Cyrathea, who rule from their palace on Imperial Mount. Their absence isn't unexpected, but it hums, a void too well-placed to be harmless.

Lumira doesn't look. No one does.

They've missed the last three summits. The excuses change. The silence lingers longer.

She's never seen the queen in person. The last time she heard the king speak, she was ten.

What kind of rulers govern by absence? No one says *abdication* or utters *illness* or *treason*.

The truth, whatever it is, has been buried too long to matter now.

Above, the Blood Ravens resettle in the rafters, her mother's chosen power piece in this elaborate display of pageantry and menace. They seem carved from shadow and metal, feathers gleaming copper and blood-red as they fold themselves into stillness. Not creatures of nature, but weapons forged in magic—hulking and aware.

They cling to the beams like living relics, talons gouging wood as they resettle—waiting for a signal only they will recognize. Trained to kill in the space between thought and action, they scan the hall with unblinking focus. Torchlight dances across their feathers as they track each new arrival. Each potential threat.

One raven, in particular, seems fixed on her. The air distorts, molten and directed, drawn straight to the key pressed against her chest. A coincidence, surely. The artifact remains still—neither warning nor welcoming—but the bird's stare prickles down her spine. She resists the urge to check her clothing. The raven's focus is unnervingly calm, disturbingly knowing. Watching.

As if summoned by the thought, Thara makes her entrance. She doesn't sweep into the hall—sweeping is for those who crave the spotlight. Thara arrives, and the room realigns, recalibrating around her gravity.

Her gown is black silk with scarlet trim, cut to flatter without apology, clinging to curves she wields like weapons. Protective sigils shimmer faintly across the fabric, stitched in forgotten languages—ancient arcana disguised as an ornament. The neckline dips to provoke, the slit rises to challenge, yet every line of her remains immaculate. Every detail is part of the performance. Grace clings to her like instinct, sharpened by a lifetime of taking power instead of asking for it. She doesn't command; she consumes.

"We shall commence despite the absence of our imperial guests," Thara announces, merciless in melody. Her mother's gaze lingers on certain territory leaders, measuring reactions, cataloging weaknesses, deciding where to press next. It's a brand of scrutiny

Lumira knows intimately, having been slowly unraveled by it more times than she cares to count.

Near the grand entrance, Hadralis stands among the Blood Legion guard, his expression impassive behind the dark armor. But the briefest acknowledgment of Lumira draws a flash of awareness—keen, vanishing as quickly as it came. Not concern, not yet. Understanding passes in the space of a heartbeat, before it vanishes like smoke the moment Thara resumes.

Lumira exhales slowly, arms tightening around herself. The summit has always been theater, but the script feels rigged this year, like the actors already know who's meant to die. Her mother is poised. The Blood Ravens are circling. And every player in this gilded charade seems primed to strike first.

A breathless pause grips the chamber—three heartbeats of unreadable restraint. Talons rasp softly against timber beams as wings settle in anticipation, the rustle of feathers barely audible. From the shadows, a copper gleam cuts through the dark—fixed on the ripple of unease.

Then the spell breaks. Thara's words hang in the air as the veneer fractures.

The doors burst open—not politely, but with the chaotic force of a Light Dragon skidding across polished marble. Torchlight shatters across its scales, the chandelier sways wildly, glass trembling like it knows what's coming, and a painstakingly arranged orchid display is obliterated without apology.

High Sovereign Bramble Starling of Aurova has arrived.

Of course—the cocky bastard never could resist a scene.

A second dragon follows: elegant, assured, prancing with theatrical grace. Her scales shimmer like a fresh sunrise, and with the haughty entitlement of youth, she coils herself onto one of the ceremonial thrones as if it were meant for her.

They are young. That much is clear in their untempered energy—wild, unbothered, and utterly untrained. It explains everything.

Bramble enters a beat later, rose-gold robes rippling with light that seems to follow him willingly. He glows with a warm bronze underpinned by a soft, sunlit luminescence that brightens as he moves through the torchlight. Pale-magenta hair shimmers like dawn breaking, and a spark of fuchsia mischief lights his eyes, curling at the edges of his grin. His Blushwardens—guardians clad in petal-hued steel—fan out behind him, armor catching flame and scattering it in prisms. He surveys the room with the self-satisfaction of a man convinced the party was thrown in his honor.

"Ah." His voice drips with mock sympathy. "I see that Mr. Whiskers got a little excited."

A gasp escapes near the entryway, a Blood Legion guard struggling not to laugh.

He gestures toward the occupied throne. "And look—Lady Fluffy Pants has chosen her seat. A monarch in the making."

The dragons preen with exaggerated pride. Somewhere near the rear of the chamber, a servant knocks over a tray in an effort not to snort.

Lumira bites back a laugh—absurd as he is, Bramble's chaos has a way of slicing clean through tension. Enough to make the others flinch.

Across the room, High Sovereign Alaric Vhalryn of Regale releases an exaggerated sigh that could salt a field, head tipping back in weary resignation. His silver-streaked hair frames a face of deep bronze, dusted with freckles that catch the light like fine gold.

Effortless, he claims a glass of wine from a passing tray and drinks as if it appeared on cue. Time draws thin as gray eyes anchor to hers, heavy as fog and twice as difficult to outrun. His navy-and-gold coat sits crisp as a blade, not a single fold out of place.

Beside him, his current wife, Lady Orielle—the fourth to hold the title—embroiders. Her slender fingers, marked with freckles that gleam like scattered gold leaf, guide the pale-pink thread through a delicate linen hoop with excruciating precision. A rose, perhaps. Or a dagger disguised as one. She stays as she is, impervious.

Alaric drinks deeper.

Crown Eagles glide along the vaulted ceiling, wings casting blade-like shadows across the marble, while his Truth Mages fan out in perfect formation, midnight robes fluid and seamless—a wall of hush and iron.

Tension seals the room quiet, all eyes on Thara to see if she'll reclaim control. Instead, she smiles, calm and unbothered, as though the throne occupied by a sun-scaled dragon is little more than a passing inconvenience. That serene, composed smile is the warning—the restraint. She notes the dragon: arrogant, comfortable, exactly where it shouldn't be.

"Fortunate indeed," she murmurs, "that I have other chairs."

The ripple of disruption settles like dust caught in a shaft of sunlight, and with it, Thara's authority reclaims the space—absolute and inevitable.

The territory leaders begin to take their places. Most arrived throughout the morning, including High Sovereign Cyrus Nyvelis of the Naiad Territory, who slipped in with his delegation during the early lull, his composure hiding more than it revealed. Some sink into their chairs with the grace of long-practiced formality; others remain standing at ease beside their trusted seconds, each measuring the others through the ancient lens of alliances, rivalries, debts, and grudges.

The political dance has begun.

Then—

"THARA!"

Not "High Sovereigness." Just "Thara." He always has preferred thunder to titles.

High Sovereign Korrigan Cadmius of Bravara bursts into the chamber like a battering ram with opinions. His deep-ebony complexion with rich purple undertones is carved with ritual scars, each line a promise of old victories. Warrior braids of deep plum fall past his broad shoulders down to his waist, framing dark eyes shot through with glints of lavender that miss nothing despite his theatrical roar. His grin sparkles brighter—a threat and delight rolled into one.

"YOUR HOSPITALITY CONTINUES TO RIVAL THE SPLENDOR OF VICTORY ITSELF!"

The chandeliers tremble. At his heel, one of the War Wolves—massive and charcoal-dark, its fixed glare cutting through the tension—lets out a low, rumbling groan that echoes like distant thunder.

His Battle Guard follows in perfect formation, each suit of weathered bronze armor etched with ceremonial sigils and burnished by real war—not a single plate left untested. Behind them walks Avner, the Iron Heir—broad-shouldered and battle-scarred, with a sword across his back and the steady gait of someone who's led more charges than councils. He remains wordless, his presence a challenge in itself.

And then comes Jexi, Korrigan's latest lover, armed to the teeth—blades glinting from every surface, probably a few sheathed in bloodier places. She winks at one of the Truth Mages near the door, and the poor fool flushes so hard he might as well be on fire.

Korrigan spots the throne situation and stops dead—

"BY THE GODS, I LOVE IT!" He turns to Bramble, wild with delight. "TELL ME, STARLING—IS THIS A DECLARATION OF WAR, OR YOUR VERSION OF FOREPLAY?"

Bramble places a hand over his heart. "Can't it be both?"

Korrigan roars with glee and claps Jexi on the back. She doesn't blink. The wolves sigh again—louder this time, their exasperation bordering on performance art.

Then, like a candle snuffed mid-laughter, everything halts.

Cold seeps into the room as High Sovereign Dom Frostholm of Rimefall glides into the hall, the air frosting at his feet. Each step exudes with otherworldly grace, leaving a thin sheen of ice in his wake. His Frost Dragons exhale long streams of mist that curl across the marble like smoke. One snorts near a silver tray, instantly freezing its contents. A goblet shatters.

No one in his line of sight dares speak.

Dom offers a smile as thin as an icicle. "How dreadfully warm in here."

Beside him walks Lord Ilyan, his expression unreadable through a sheer veil of frost. Their son, Nikolai, trails them, only breaking formation to slip away and join the other heirs—all false laughter and smirking secrets like they haven't schemed together in ages.

Across the hall, High Sovereigness Calista Auroran of Zestria observes the frost spread with the faintest arch of an eyebrow. Her son, Hugo—the Amber Heir—lounges beside her, only half listening, as if political frostbite is a seasonal inconvenience. Calista scans the room before landing on Alaric, her nose wrinkling faintly, then flicking to Korrigan nearby—an irritation she makes no effort to hide.

Behind them, the Season Shifters—her guard—hold position, their forms blending between sun-drenched bloom and snow-laced chill. At their feet, a pair of Time Foxes curl and uncurl, tails ticking like pendulums as they slip in and out of sync, locked in a magical argument no one dares to interrupt.

"Careful, Dom." The smile Calista gives is all honey and mischief. "You'll make the spring spirits cry."

The room becomes a clash of bloom and blizzard, serenity and fury.

At the edge of it all, High Sovereign Tavern Orren of Terravox pauses mid-entrance, one palm pressed thoughtfully to a nearby column. "Fascinating," he murmurs. "This load-bearing curve suggests early artifact shielding—certainly never meant for gatherings of fragile, emotional delegates." He appears to be speaking to the stone itself. He brought no other guards—only the Earth Elementals, massive with menace radiating from every stone-set limb. Tavern, as ever, seems completely alone, even when surrounded by stone that would kill for him.

Already seated, High Sovereign Granite Morenai of Shadowspire remains unmoved by the commotion. He picks at his cuticles with bored ease, already dismissing the entire affair as pointless—and might be right. A small contingent of his guards stands nearby, unremarkable and unnamed by tradition or necessity. They exist simply because protocol demands it.

The real threat coils closer.

His Nightmare Stalkers drift around his chair in slow, predatory spirals, phasing lazily through stone like the marble has forgotten how to resist them. One wavers beside a servant, its outline warping the air before vanishing again. The servant turns three shades paler and wisely holds still.

And finally, High Sovereign Evren Rothewen of Grovenar enters, flanked by his daughter Ilara and his wife, Lady Elowen. The air shifts around them—not cold, not hot, but unmistakably alive. Elowen walks with the slow, rooted grace of growing things, her crown of woven vines glowing faintly with a living green light. Forest Sprites trail behind them, glow-winged and murmuring with the rustle of leaves in a summer breeze. His Rangers follow in perfect formation, their living wood armor pulsing faintly with the rhythm of ancient heartwood.

Evren turns toward Thara, when he finally speaks. "May this gathering find its balance."

Elowen's nod follows—subtle, but laced with steel.

Leaders, heirs, and descents settle into their places. The room is full, the stage ready and stretched to snapping.

As Lumira steps away from her pillar, the space around her reacts—not with drama, but tension so taut it hums. Conversations falter mid-word. Eyes trail her path, catching and holding a beat longer than comfort before sliding away. The magical creatures ripple as well—Season Shifters and Forest Sprites leaning forward, curious; Crown Eagles and War Wolves pulling back, instinctively wary. The Blood Ravens adjust in soundless unison, their burning copper orbs fixed on her—omens etched in flesh.

The Blood Key throbs against her skin, swinging from searing to ice-cold as she passes each gaze. Her fingers make a casual adjustment, masking the discomfort—and the way one raven's stare lingers.

She reaches the table, and the temperature of the room warps again.

High Sovereigns known for stillness now lean toward her, their bodies aligning like compass needles finding true north. They don't assess with sight alone. They're weighing her. Their entourages mirror them in unnatural calm.

Zylven leans closer to Dom Frostholm, his Dream Walkers rippling like dark water behind him. In their wake, two of his Shadow Cats slip between columns with feline grace, their velvety forms nearly indistinguishable from the shadows they inhabit— seen only when they choose to be. Lysander, the Dream Heir of Vesper, crosses to Zylven's side without a ripple of fuss, silver-streaked hair catching a hint of torchlight as he takes his seat. Every choice is polished, intentional—the perfect heir completing the picture while the room's attention stays fixed on Lumira.

Korrigan's laughter cuts through the tension, but his War Wolves' stare remains on her. Even Thara keeps hold of the ceremonial scroll—graceful in appearance, though her posture hums with barely contained strain.

Hadralis tracks Lumira from his post along the wall, his expression unreadable. His demeanor holds a warning she can't cleanly decipher.

But before she can piece it together, a voice cuts through—her name.

"Lumira."

High Sovereigness Yasmin Predaxia of Tigran lounges at the table like a predator at rest, molten gold flickering behind her composed exterior. Her Crystal Basilisks coil at her feet, their jagged scales catching the torchlight with diamond-like brilliance. Each twist of their bodies makes a soft chiming sound as if gemstones are grinding against one another. "I was wondering when you'd grace us with your presence."

Lumira slides into her seat without haste. She takes the goblet in front of her, the stem cool—steadying in its weight, her chosen shield. Her knuckles tighten around it. "I wasn't aware my timing was of such interest to you."

"Oh, everything about this summit is of interest to me." Yasmin's lips curl into a smile designed to cut as she swirls her wine. "Especially those who operate from the shadows."

The words hit harder than they should. A trap laid in front of the realm's most powerful.

A smirk tugs at Lumira's lips before she lifts the goblet in a gesture edged with thorns.

"Well then—what secrets do you want to drag into the light?"

Yasmin's grin deepens, all poison-lined teeth. "Darling, I thought you'd never ask."

All around them, the air remains charged. Conversations falter. Creatures tense in their places—attentive, aware.

The summit doesn't react. It waits.

And the stage, at last, begins to burn.

9

PAWNS AND PLAYERS

"Perhaps Blood Descent Lumira would prefer a moment to compose herself before we proceed with more pressing matters." High Sovereign Cyrus Nyvelis of Naiad speaks with the pressure of deep water, every word honed to draw blood. Light catches on his silver-white hair, tinged with blue, and his pale cerulean eyes, rimmed in silver, assess the room with calculated patience. His deep-blue skin shimmers with an azure sheen as he moves, as though part of him remains forever under water. They say he rules from within the Naiad itself—from a palace carved into the river's stone heart, where light and lies both go to drown.

His mouth curves, but the chill behind it never thaws. Around him, the Water Nymphs flow with mirrored grace, reflections breaking and reforming in their wake. Beside them, the River Wardens stand unmoving, spears tipped with river-forged steel.

The opening gambit lands.

And Lumira—who had hoped to skirt the edges of this summit unnoticed—now shoulders the full brunt of court interest. The moment between her and Yasmin fractures as Cyrus clears his throat again, his Water Nymphs gliding into a tighter, more attentive formation.

"Since formality seems to be concluded"—his tone remains silken—"perhaps we might discuss the matter of excessive vessels violating Naiad Territory." A pause. "Some of us forget that the Naiad River is not a shared resource. It is a territory—inhabited and defended by those who have lived within its depths far longer than most here have ruled." A shimmer ripples around his sleeves, as if the river answers him—old power hidden in plain sight, waiting for someone to remember how to use it.

Korrigan's laugh slices through. "AH, YES, THE SACRED RIVER SPEECH. I WAS WONDERING WHEN WE'D GET THERE. IT'S BEEN—WHAT? A FULL MONTH SINCE YOUR NYMPHS DRAGGED A BRAVARA SHIP UNDER?"

Cyrus doesn't blink. "A vessel armed with six crossbows and carrying contraband."

"TWELVE CRATES OF WINTER GRAIN," Korrigan snaps. "WHICH YOUR PEOPLE WERE HAPPY TO REDISTRIBUTE."

The air stretches taut.

The Blood Key pulses with unstable heat, caught between warmth and chill—uncertain, like it's listening a little closer than it should. Lumira lays a steadying touch over her bodice, hoping it settles.

Across the room, Tavern's Earth Elementals align in slow, deliberate symmetry, briefly illuminating ancient sigils etched into the marble floor. One of them catches Lumira's attention—a symbol she recognizes from Emberly's journal.

Before the tension can tip further, a cool interruption slips between them.

"Trade and territory are distractions." Evren's tone is soft but grounded. "The real concern is Shadowspire—and the creeping shape its influence has begun to spread. Guards with falsified allegiances. Servants who answer to no one. Advisers whose loyalties bend with shadows. These aren't accidents. They're patterns. And they're pressing against all our borders." He pauses, his gaze sweeping the room. "Seventeen disappearances in the past month alone. A scholar vanished mid-lecture. A baker's daughter never made it to market. All gone. All mixed bloodlines. This is not a coincidence, and we all know it." He surveys the room, collected but sharpened at the edges. The message is clear: something is moving in the depths, unseen by most.

Granite doesn't look up. He studies a ring on his finger with exaggerated interest, as though the entire exchange is a performance he's already seen—and discarded. Then he sighs. Not loudly, but with enough weight to make his opinion known.

His indifference is so complete it drains the air from the room.

Evren doesn't rush. His cadence stays calm, but there's a sharpened weight behind it. "And I find it curious that these patterns echo those that surfaced before Lord Solarin's... unfortunate disappearance." A thin vine creeps along the marble near his boots, tiny leaves unfurling as if listening to his words.

He keeps his distance, but the words strike deep. Her father's name tears straight through. She grips the table's edge, keeping her expression unreadable, as memory claws upward—his final warnings, sudden absence, the official lie she never believed.

Warmth stirs where the key rests—measured, unhurried, like a hidden scale tipping before returning to rest.

That's when she notices him.

A Shadowspire guard lingers near the entrance—massive, armored, half swallowed by the stone and torchlight. The high-collared cloak and deep hood turn him into less a man than a silhouette carved from the dark. The long sword strapped across his back catches the firelight, a burning implication that he could cross the room in two steps—and cut it in half.

But the shiver on her neck tells her he was there long before she noticed.

The heavy, layered armor glints darkly, ancient and scarred, overlapping plates that shouldn't glide as they do. Shadows mask most of his face, revealing only the chiseled line of a jaw beneath the hood and the faint curve of a mouth, patient and predatory. His posture is neither slack nor alert; it's something worse. Intentional.

He doesn't scan the room like the others; he doesn't pretend.

His focus is on her—not with curiosity, not with strategy, but with a force that doesn't pursue. It only waits. People don't usually regard her that way; they're cautious, speculative, eager to guess but never to understand. This is different. Somehow older, colder. As if he's not seeing her, but the imprint she left behind—carved so deep it refuses to fade.

A flicker of air brushes her cheek, a phantom touch that feels like him, even from yards away. The sword on his back catches the firelight again, a threat and a promise, the steel as unreadable as the man wearing it.

At its core, a twitch, small and almost imagined. The corner of his mouth quirks—not a smile, not quite, and out of place on a soldier's face.

It pulls at her mind, wrongness with edges, a dream that isn't hers. She doesn't move or flinch. Her instincts, dulled by court formalities and forced smiles, ignite with a clarity that carves straight through pretense. The torchlight sputters. The shadows cling to his armor like loyal hounds, waiting for his word.

And then—he's gone.

No sound, no trace, gone without warning. And the world feels thinner for it. But the space he leaves behind is hollow. The air itself clings, tasting her name and finding it pleasing.

A flutter of memory coils in her ribs, unfinished and unwelcome—the curve of his mouth under the hood, the flash of blackened armor, the way he vanished. It hovers like smoke after a fire, impossible to breathe away. Worse is the sense he's still here, only hidden, watching from somewhere she can't reach.

The Blood Key stirs.

It doesn't hum. It seizes—alive and certain, as if responding to a call she didn't issue. This isn't passive magic. It's an answer or a reaction.

She freezes.

The tension winding through her is focused and impossible to dismiss. The key doesn't resist. It aligns. As if it recognizes what she can't yet name.

Which means the guard didn't simply appear.

He allowed her to see him. Or worse—he planned for her not to. Either way, whatever game he's begun, she's already on the board.

He's been waiting. And he's not finished.

Dom picks up on her reaction across the table, subtle but not lost on him. "How fascinating," he murmurs, voice scarcely more than a breath—yet somehow it carries. "What did you see... a ghost, Lumira?" He draws a silent arc along the rim of his glass, an echo of thought or threat. "Or a truth you weren't ready to name?"

A muscle twitches in her jaw. She smooths it away, tucking the instinct behind her mask.

Around her, the summit chatters on: empty, gilded noise, a flock of jeweled birds too busy preening to notice the hawk in their midst. How exquisitely appropriate.

Lumira's mind drifts back to the intentional way the guard disappeared. Not the crisp efficiency of a well-trained soldier—but a grace that felt rehearsed. Like he vanished not to be seen, but to provoke.

And she'd taken the bait.

"Bloodlines built our empires," Yasmin declares, her regal scrutiny sweeping the table, hunting for soft places to sink. She pauses on Tavern first—Terravox, a territory whose recent generations have favored compatibility over legacy—before turning to Calista, whose Zestria line has allowed more than one marriage for love over strategy. "And yet it seems certain territories have... diluted theirs in recent years."

Zylven's usual smirk briefly falters before returning, now edged with a darker glint behind it. "A fair point," he concedes, but his tone hardens, as if she's forced him to reconsider what he once believed was settled.

Alaric lifts his goblet with practiced ease. "My dear Yasmin, surely you're not suggesting that certain lines have… diminished? Though I suppose someone of your particular breeding would be uniquely qualified to recognize weakness in others." A pale-gold gleam flickers across him, the rim bending candlelight into fractured prisms.

Yasmin smirks, exposing the slender line of her throat—an arrogant display equal parts drama and defiance. Sunlit and unblinking, her awareness slides from Tavern's glimmering Earth Elementals to Calista's uneasy Season Shifters. "I merely suggest that strength should be preserved. Some of us remember what that means."

Tavern refuses the lure. Instead, he adjusts his spectacles and murmurs, "Actually, mixed crystalline resonance patterns create stronger structural integrity than pure ones. The varied frequencies reinforce rather than deplete potential energy." Hints of rippling light flow beneath his rich terracotta skin as he rests a broad hand on the stone column beside him. Veins of muted color ripple outward through the marble, a gemstone waking at his touch. Light glints off the bronze flecks within and his chestnut hair, practical waves streaked with copper, gleaming with the same quiet certainty as his scientific assertion.

Lumira registers the slight change in Thara's grip on the goblet, a twitch that betrays more than words ever could. Her mother's mask rarely slips, but Tavern's correction lands deeper than expected.

Thara rises with unhurried grace, a faint scarlet glimmer unfurling across her iris—a ripple of Compulsion that rolls through the table, stilling conversation mid-breath, snuffing it out as cleanly as a candle pressed between fingers. "We speak of strength and tradition." Her voice carries with a steadiness that feels unforced. "Yet our houses remain… disconnected. Perhaps it's time we began weaving stronger bonds between our territories." The Blood Ravens above move in sync as she marks each place at the table. "And what better place to begin than with my daughter?"

A ripple shudders through the room.

Evren cuts through, calm but effective. "And you suggest Lumira, I assume?"

Thara inclines her head. "My daughter is unwed. Your sons— surely among them stands a match worthy of Crimsun blood." She singles out Lumira. "The time has come to secure her future."

Lumira stiffens, the words landing like shackles, delicately gilded but shackles all the same. She strangles the goblet stem, the wine inside gleaming like fresh blood. Her mother hadn't planned this; she'd choreographed every fucking beat. Concern, weaponized as theater.

The room tenses.

Bramble, of course, is the first to speak. "Oh, how exciting," he hums, delighted. His Light Dragons freeze mid-tumble, golden scales catching torchlight. "Shall we all take turns declaring our bloodline's worth? Perhaps keep score?"

A few polite chuckles ripple across the table, but the air grows heavier—thick with restraint. Because under his playful proposition runs the truth: this is a power play.

And Lumira is the piece on the table, served up by her mother. The offer lands exactly as intended.

Calista lifts her chin, warm golden tones shifting through honeyed hues. Her hair falls in a curtain of burnished amber waves, framing the fine lines of her face. Her citrus-bright eyes darken with resolve, sliding toward sunset as she makes her offer. "My son, Hugo, is strong, disciplined, and trained in governance and war. A bond between Zestria and Crimsun would be… formidable." She lets the word linger, honeyed at the edge yet carrying a hidden sting. "And, of course, our northern ports would remain open to Crimsun interests."

Korrigan scoffs, folding his arms across his broad chest with a flourish of impatience. "HE'S A DIPLOMAT." The words land flat, stripped of emotion. "BRAVARA OFFERS AVNER. HE LEADS FROM THE FRONT, NOT HOLED UP WITH LEDGERS." His grin feral, teeth flashing. "OUR ALLIANCE WOULD SEND A MESSAGE NO ONE COULD MISTAKE." A beat. "AND WE CONTROL THE RIDGE TRAILS YOUR ARMIES RELY ON."

Calista's goblet hovers just shy of her lips, her face unreadable except for the dead stare she levels at Korrigan when he crows about Avner's so-called "valor"—projecting the exact energy of someone two seconds from biting through the rim rather than enduring another gulp of his posturing.

Dom uncrosses his legs slowly, the temperature around him dropping a few degrees. His Frost Dragons unfurl in a soundless arc behind him, fixing on the scene with glacier intensity. "How brutish," he murmurs, frost crystals blooming along his sleeve hem, misting the air around his wrist in pale, wavering patterns. "My son, Nikolai, handles problems before they become visible." He taps the goblet once against the table, the wine chilling instantly. "A union with Rimefall offers not strength, but subtlety. Why waste armies when a whisper will suffice?"

Granite lifts his head at last, a small but telling motion—he's listening now. Not speaking. Not yet. His obsidian-black hair absorbs light, not reflecting but devouring it, framing pale features tinged with that faint translucence only Shadowspire bloodlines bear. Unstable form distorts him—starlight flecks drift within the voids of his eyes, as if reality refuses to map cleanly onto his shape. His Nightmare Stalkers linger at the edges of his space, their smoky forms threading through the stone like they've already claimed it. A thin wash of darkness slides around his shoulders, carrying the suggestion of a doorway he could step through at any moment—though he seems far too uninterested to leave.

"Charming," he murmurs, dry as ash. "I've seen slave pits with subtler bidding." A pause. "But I suppose"—his eyes land on Lumira with unsettling clarity—"a girl with blood like hers— muddy enough to stain any legacy, pretty enough to be sold—was always meant for the auction block." And then, as if the matter no longer holds his interest, he returns his attention to the cuff of his sleeve.

Bitter revulsion rises in Lumira's throat. She wills her face to be expressionless, but the words cling like oil—a girl with blood like hers. Her pulse pounds against the key, a futile warning she forces back down.

The offers mount, each weighted heavier with intent—trade routes, military support, exclusive contracts—each more elaborate than the last. Lumira's worth is weighed in gold and armies, measured in territorial leverage and political gain.

Across the table, Hadralis leans subtly, instinct pulling him closer to his weapon as the marriage proposals curdle into threats.

Zylven leans back in his chair, wine swirling in his goblet. "A match should be more than strategic." His voice is smooth as lacquered steel. "It should be fated." His Shadow Cats creep forward, slipping through patches of darkness as if the shadows themselves part for them. "And fate," he adds, casting a look at the line of heirs, "has not spoken yet." He settles on Lysander, his Dream Heir, who straightens with unforced poise, pale strands glinting like polished metal. The young man's lips curl into a smirk, his eyes catching Lumira's—entitlement sparking, a claim already made, though it leaves his features untouched.

Zylven redirects back to her without a word, expression deceptively mild. "Unless the woman in question has a preference. Or shall we keep trading her like a luxury spice?" In a blink, the space around him seems to ripple—light bending at the edges, shadows stretching and shortening like reality forgot its shape.

Across the room, Jaggard tracks the exchange with undisguised amusement, confiding some quip to a nearby heir that earns a shared smirk in Lumira's direction. He enjoys her predicament as a potential bargaining chip.

Sound flees, leaving nothing but judgment.

And the room turns to her as one.

She forces herself to remain unreadable, her pulse a battle march pounding in her ears, waiting to break loose. Her mother is playing her. Every beat of this has been laid out like a trap. A strategic marriage to secure Crimsun's power. A bloodline match to tighten their hold. Emberly had warned of this exact thing, tracing old family trees in paint-stained fingers, showing her the patterns that had existed for generations. And now, Lumira is staring down the barrel of one.

And Thara drinks in the moment, satisfaction gleaming. This isn't about securing an alliance; it's about ensuring her rebellious daughter can no longer slip through her grasp.

Lumira's stomach clenches so hard it feels like it is tearing. The thought of being shackled to any of them—her freedom gutted, her future bartered like cattle—makes her vision blur. Rage claws at the inside of her ribs, raw and biting, begging for a way out. She swallows it down, tasting blood at the back of her teeth.

"Perhaps," Zylven suggests smoothly, "we might find a more… equitable solution? After all, arrangements like these shouldn't feel like chains, but opportunities."

"Chains?" Alaric's smile could cut glass. "How charmingly barbaric of you to equate marriage with imprisonment. Given Vesper's recent border disputes, perhaps chains are often on your mind?"

Korrigan's grin turns wolfish. "WHY ALARIC, YOU BEAUTIFUL BASTARD. CHAINS TEND TO FEATURE IN MY PRIVATE NEGOTIATIONS ALL THE TIME. SO DOES MY BIG-ASS SWORD."

Alaric's perfect poise cracks for a moment. "How grotesquely predictable of you to turn statecraft into a brothel story."

"JEALOUS?" Korrigan's laugh rattles the chandelier. "I'D BE HAPPY TO DEMONSTRATE MY TECHNIQUES. THOUGH I DOUBT YOU COULD HANDLE MY… AGGRESSIVE NEGOTIATION STYLE!"

Dom exhales frost from his nose. "Spare us."

The room resets. Its focus returns to Lumira—the final piece on the table.

Lady Orielle glances up from her embroidery, coolly assessing the room's evolving alliances. Her gaze drops back to the needlework, but her fingers are rigid, the thread pulled taut, the hoop straining.

Heat spikes through Lumira, the Blood Key pulsing with a warning deep inside her. The coolness of it draws the chaos from her rage, leaving only the aim. She rises slowly. "Such generous offers." The sweetness in her voice is laced with venom. "How touching to learn my bloodline is suddenly worth so many… benefits."

She lets the glass rise just enough to pass for courtesy, their hunger only deepening her contempt. Thara's features tighten—a quiet promise of payback. Lumira savors with her wine.

"Though I wonder," she continues, letting the key's heat guide her, "whether these proposals might have anything to do with what Evren mentioned earlier—these mysterious disappearances along our borders?"

She looks directly at Evren, whose earlier comment about Shadowspire's influence and the seventeen vanished people had been conveniently forgotten in the marriage frenzy.

Evren meets her eyes, a flicker of surprise giving way to cautious recognition.

"All with mixed bloodlines," she echoes his words. "Rather curious timing for everyone to suddenly be interested in who marries whom."

It happens then, a turn so subtle most would miss it. The magical creatures begin to move.

They drift toward one side of the hall—Crown Eagles, War Wolves, Shadow Cats, and Crystal Basilisks—predatory. Opposite them, Forest Sprites, Time Foxes, Water Nymphs, and Earth Elementals form a mirrored cluster. Between them, the Frost Dragons, Light Dragons, and Nightmare Stalkers prowl—uncommitted, but watchful. Above them all, the Blood Ravens continue their slow, ominous arcs, observing.

The creatures aren't responding to politics. They're reacting to what came before, to power long buried.

Alaric drags his focus nervously to the Crown Eagles. Even Granite acknowledges his Nightmare Stalkers with the faintest twitch, his indifferent demeanor thinned by the scent of awareness.

Thara rises, her face a perfect mask of maternal concern—convincing, if not for the hollowness behind it. "My daughter forgets herself—"

"I'm remembering quite clearly," Lumira cuts in, noting how her mother's composure instantly fractures. "Though I wonder which facts others are choosing to forget?"

Evren steps forward, seizing the opening she's provided. "The girl speaks the truth. These disappearances are not coincidental."

Lady Elowen settles in her seat, vines creeping briefly up her wrists before a calming gesture reins them in. She doesn't need to speak. Evren already understands.

Cyrus follows, cold as the depths of his waters: "Some knowledge was buried for a reason. Our ancestors sealed some doors because what lay behind them threatened everything." He locks on Lumira, the intensity catching her off guard. "Perhaps the real question is not who will marry whom, but who is collecting bloodlines, and why."

Thara's face hardens to marble. The Blood Ravens above rustle in unison, their wings catching torchlight in ripples of copper and crimson.

"This summit will stand as it is." The words come unshaken. "If anyone wishes to challenge that—bring proof, not panic."

But Lumira catches the flash of calculation in her mother's eyes, less dismissal than judgment.

Lumira's been circling a threat she never saw until now. It weaves through the secrets traded in shadow, linking to the papers Emberly held in her cold grasp.

And now, they're seeing her through a different lens: no longer certain whether she's a bride, a pawn, or a problem they didn't plan for.

The Blood Key settles—a slow, searing promise.

Let them wonder.

She'll end the game by flipping the board.

10

CHOOSING SIDES

Thara doesn't speak right away. She lets the silence thicken like smoke from a slow-burning fuse, heavy and deliberate, ready to ignite. "Since some of you are eager to act." Her tone carries the chill of command. "Then we'll speak of survival—nothing less." She takes her seat slowly, the motion precise, almost ceremonial. A body held in check. A blade not yet drawn.

That's all the opening Cyrus needs. He leans forward, diplomatic as ever, though the silver embroidery at his sleeves flares in the torchlight. "There have been troubling reports of unauthorized movement between territories." His tone remains formal, careful. "Along the northern trade routes, specifically."

The tension tightens—not eased, merely redirected.

The room sways in tidal rhythm, though several faces angle toward Lumira with unreadable interest. She exhales, tension slipping from her shoulders as the weight lifts, no longer on her worth, but on the age-old dance of Cyrus and Korrigan. Same script, different crisis. Cyrus needled, Korrigan roared—some observed, others took sides, all waiting to see which would bleed first.

"Unauthorized activity?" Korrigan's voice drops to what, for him, constitutes a near-whisper, which means only the nearest chandeliers tremble. "You mean theft. Let's call it what it is." He rises again with sudden fury. "THE NORTHERN ROUTES BELONG TO BRAVARA!" He slams his fist on the table, and his War Wolves surge forward, hackles raised.

The Crystal Basilisks at Yasmin's feet respond instantly, uncoiling with liquid grace, their scales flashing like cut diamonds, scattering torchlight in a spray of cold fire as they rise to meet the perceived threat. Yasmin leans forward with predatory intent, sun-bronzed features glowing warm under the flickering light. Her blonde hair spills forward, black streaks framing the molten, ancient force behind slitted golden eyes.

Lord Ilyan leans toward Dom, mouthing a phrase that briefly ices the air between them before dissolving. Dom's eyes harden, the frost-dusted goblet creaking faintly under his tightening grip as he weighs the words.

From her position against a pillar, Jexi casually slides a blade into her hand, the weapon dancing across her knuckles. Though her posture drips with nonchalance, she doesn't miss a thing—and when a guard stares too long, she runs her tongue along the blade's edge, a slow, wicked smile unfurling, a threat in full.

Above, the Blood Ravens stir on their perches, wings half-spread, responding to some subtle signal from Thara that Lumira can't quite catch. Competing magics churn, the Frost Dragons exhaling plumes of winter-white breath that solidifies in elaborate patterns. Lady Fluffy Pants, draped on her velvet throne, bats at a falling ice crystal with idle grace, scattering rainbow light without ever rising.

"Belong?" Cyrus remains calm, but his Water Nymphs hover like storm clouds ready to break. "How fascinating that you believe trade routes can be owned like baubles. Tell me, do you also claim ownership of the wind? The tides?"

"THE TIDES DON'T STEAL MY FUCKING MERCHANTS' GOLD!" Korrigan bellows, his restraint evaporating completely.

"No," Dom interjects, frost crackling along his goblet as his fingers tighten. "But they do seem to keep washing up rather interesting debris lately. Wreckage from ships that never existed, carrying cargo that was never officially declared." His Frost Dragons prowl closer, their presence visibly dropping the temperature. "How unfortunate."

Mr. Whiskers chooses this moment to pounce on a particularly elaborate ice crystal, sending it spinning across the marble floor. Not to be outdone, Lady Fluffy Pants rolls onto her side and stretches a lazy claw to claim the largest fragment, dragging it possessively toward her throne.

"My goodness," Bramble murmurs, "they get so excited about shiny things." His smile stays fixed, but he follows the division forming across the room with surprising shrewdness.

A Blood Raven flies directly at Lumira but veers away at the last moment, seemingly repelled by the key's energy, which pulses in an almost defensive rhythm against her. The bird circles back, rejoining the formation as if reluctant to obey.

Territory leaders push back from the table as the argument escalates, rising to their feet and subtly positioning themselves across the chamber. Unconsciously, they form two opposing factions, drifting to opposite sides. The once-theoretical divide becomes physical—bodies aligning like compass needles to true north.

Ilara stays seated beside her mother, but the sympathy she sends Lumira's way is brief and unmistakable, a small signal that wouldn't escape anyone paying close attention.

Tavern studies from the sidelines. "Curious," he remarks to no one in particular. "Crystal resonance patterns, once disturbed, can never return to their original configuration." He gestures vaguely to the alliances forming across the room. "A rather apt metaphor, wouldn't you say?"

The ceremonial bell rings out—a clear note that slices through the chaos. Lumira jerks up to see Thara at the bell, her expression a perfect mask of controlled authority, as if the gesture were incidental.

"Enough." The word slices through the room with the unwavering finality only Thara can wield.

The tension doesn't fade—it congeals. Lines have been drawn. Retreat is no longer an option.

The immediate crisis passes, but the damage is done. The room has been divided, and alliances have been declared: some spoken, others merely implied. Whatever game unfolds, the first moves have been made, and there's no turning back.

Several leaders share unreadable expressions and muted gestures as the tension gradually dissipates, quiet negotiations for "more private discussions" later in the evening.

Cyrus and Evren draw close, their conversation hidden behind a careful arrangement of Water Nymphs and Forest Sprites. Their voices don't carry, but their expressions speak of preparations and precautions. When they part, both are grimmer than before.

Thara rises once more with the fluid grace of a viper preparing to strike. "We will reconvene tomorrow," she announces, her words edged with cold finality. "I expect all territories to reflect carefully on today's... revelations." She scans the chamber, lingering on each threat in turn until even the boldest start to fidget. "The evening grows late, and some discussions require proper preparation."

The dismissal in her tone is unmistakable—not a suggestion—a command. Several leaders still, the message settling among them.

Granite rises with exaggerated effort, surveying the divided factions with apparent boredom. He doesn't speak, he lets the air curdle in his wake. Whatever he's thinking, it's darker than words could weaponize. He lets the contempt show, for a breath, before turning and walking away—Nightmare Stalkers phasing through reality behind him. The chill they leave behind speaks for them, a reminder of Shadowspire's unsettling power.

Evren departs with quiet authority, his Rangers closing in like roots around an ancient tree. He says nothing—only a nod, sealed with the finality of an oath. His forest-green hair stirs faintly, bark-patterned skin rippling with steady resolve. A few subtle cues pass between him and select leaders, weaving an unseen net through the formalities.

The summit ends in a haze of unfinished business. Leaders depart in small groups, careful about who they're seen walking with, while their magical companions remain locked in a wary standoff.

The heirs and descents file out in proper formation, Jaggard's satisfied expression telling Lumira everything she needs to know about how he views her predicament. Unlike her brother, Pyraxus maintains careful neutrality. However, the tightness in his shoulders betrays his awareness of how the political landscape has shifted, with his sister now at its center.

Then Hadralis approaches with a scroll bearing Thara's unmistakable seal. He leans in as he passes it to her, muttering, "Your sister saw too much. Don't make the same mistake."

Before she can respond, he's gone, returning to his post with an unnatural swiftness that strips the exchange from reality. The warning settles cold in her stomach, confirmation of what she's long suspected about Emberly's death.

Lumira withdraws to her familiar place by the pillar, tracking the slow unravel of the room. She notes who leaves together, who avoids each other, and whose expressions say more than words ever could. The hidden alliances bleed into view—veins of meaning running under palace decorum. The shadows peel back around her, obedient as if to a presence they already serve. Before she can turn, his voice brushes her ear like velvet over steel, amusement edged in danger.

"You're losing your touch, little fox. I counted at least three openings where I could have killed you."

Little fox. Two words, and the world lurches beneath her. She doesn't startle—she calcifies, refusing to give him the satisfaction of seeing her pulse jump. But that name pries open a memory she'd locked away.

Her body remembers before her mind can catch up—heat pinned under bruising hands, a mouth that bit down just to hear her gasp. A night she'd buried deep, on purpose.

But the warmth dies fast. Cold slithers up her spine as it clicks into place: the shadows at the market, the weight on her back, the rooms she only *thought* were empty.

Her heartbeat spikes, then funnels into cold precision.

She hits him with a glare that turns every ember to ice. "Funny." She lets the word curl like smoke. "I counted four where I could have killed you first. And yet—you're here."

His laugh scrapes low, a sound closer to a purr than a laugh. "Sharp claws, little fox. Quick, clever, always slipping past the traps meant to hold you."

He steps out of the dark, hood low—the same Shadowspire guard who tracked her earlier, the one who never really left. She sees only his mouth, half-hidden—the mouth that left bruises on her collarbone, the one she woke up reaching for before she realized he'd vanished. Cruel and generous all at once, that mouth coaxed sounds from her she doesn't let anyone hear. Her pulse hitches, heat spilling through her—wicked and wrong.

And now he's here again, every word a slow drag across her gut, impossible to forget. Each syllable lands with intent, a scrape of teeth where no one else can reach. She swallows the tell, but she knows he hears it.

He moves like she does, a predator who knows how many ways to end a life and how to leave you wanting it.

"Though, as I recall, you have... other talents." He doesn't smile—not quite. His words are steady, unapologetic—meant to land without volume. "I've killed for less than the memory of you."

"How long?" The words slip out before she can stop them. "How long have you been following me?"

His mouth twitches like he's tasting the word before letting it loose. "Watching," he corrects, the word rolling slowly off his tongue. "Every night you thought you were alone. Every room. Every moment of air you claimed that hadn't already been stolen. *Mine to watch.*"

A shiver breaks down her back, not fear exactly, but not clean want either.

"You're stalking me."

He smiles, finally, a flash of teeth meant for her alone. "Always have, little fox." A ghost of a laugh. "Always will."

The memory crystallizes—Samhain night, a few years back, the local tavern, The Crimsun Flask, where she'd started a brawl. Then, following him to his lodging at The Shadow's Rest, fully aware of every choice she was making. His fingers tangled in her hair, murmuring "little fox" against her neck. She'd never asked his name, never cared to know. A single night of indulgence in a life ruled by restraint.

"Careful," she warns, unsure whether she's warning him or herself. "Stalkers bleed too."

His mouth curves under the hood, a laugh barely audible, weighted more with promise than threat. "You'd enjoy making me bleed, wouldn't you?" His voice drips slow as poison.

Shadows cling to his face, but she sees enough—that mouth, all promise and threat, a smile that tastes like it already knows her secrets.

The same command curls through each word—and she can feel those storm-gray eyes, steady as they were that night.

No mercy. No distance.

Nothing like most men. He's the mistake she wants to make again.

Instead of addressing the heat building between them, she meets him head-on. "You're part of Granite's guard. Interesting choice of allegiance."

"Is it?" His smile shows teeth. "And here I thought you'd appreciate someone else who knows how to play both sides."

She stops. "What exactly are you implying?"

"Only that some of us understand the value of keeping our options open." He steps closer, heat rolling off him in slow, inevitable waves, until it tightens between them—*not a touch, but a claiming all the same.* "When the territories choose sides, which mask will you wear?"

Before she can answer, he's gone, fading into shadow, certain he'll be remembered. But his words linger, heavy with promise and threat.

11

TORN PROMISES

The ceremonial scroll—her mother's demand—lies on the floor in two torn halves, ripped apart by her own trembling grip moments ago. A sealed promise to bind her to Lysander Meridian, destroyed before the ink could stain her name. Hadralis had pressed it into her grip, his warning echoing in her head. She hadn't planned to destroy it, only to silence the future coiled inside its words before it could claim her. The golden Kyrvayne crest that once gleamed at its center now flakes apart, gold leaf falling like dust. Ink seeps into the fibers, bleeding into the parchment's seams as if mourning what's been lost. She stares at the pieces, heart pounding, certain there's no way to take it back.

Lumira's breath stutters, but her poise remains perfectly intact. The storm in her chest—days, weeks, years of being measured, traded, ignored—finally breaks through. All that remains is ruined parchment and a release she hadn't meant to give, tainted with vicious relief.

The Blood Key pulses warm where it rests, an unsettling counterpoint to the cold knot tightening in her stomach, as if it approves of the ruin she's made.

"You would," Lumira mutters to the key. Talking to enchanted heirlooms—new low. Even for her. She's starting to sound like Tavern, who reportedly holds lengthy philosophical debates with his breakfast pastries.

She paces her chambers, fingers threading through her hair as she considers her options, each more ruinous than the last. The torn scroll isn't defiance but swallowed fury, rage tamped down, a smile worn like armor while men debated her future like livestock.

The summit's first day unfolded with the well-rehearsed pageantry she'd come to expect. The factions formed quickly—predictably. But Thara? She tossed her daughter onto the bargaining table, a valuable chess piece, a ruthless move for a woman who wears the title of mother in an ill-fitting crown: ornamental, yet unearned.

A soft knock pulls her from her downward spiral. Her spine snaps straight, the habit of centuries of Kyrvaynes shoving fury behind a mask of composure before she registers the sound.

"Enter," she calls, quickly kicking the torn scroll under her bed—practiced in hiding evidence of insubordination since childhood.

Quinn slips inside, the crystal pitcher held close against her chest. A harmless servant's posture, but Lumira catches the subtle tremor beneath the calm. The alertness threaded through it. One of her own.

"The network's been… reduced," she murmurs, eyes cast down, tone unwavering. "Half of our usual contacts are denied entry for tomorrow. Several reassigned to outer posts."

Lumira's throat tightens. "How many are left?"

"Seven," Quinn begins. "Three in the kitchens. Two guards on the outer eastern wall. One with the musicians. And me." A pause. "The musicians' rotation have changed too. We're under surveillance."

Seven left, from nearly twenty once trusted to see what others missed and keep silent. Thara began this purge long before the scroll hit the floor; every tactic Lumira deploys, every precaution she takes, has already been seen and undone.

"Where did they station the new guard posts?" Her words crack. "Any pattern?"

Quinn's focus jumps to the window, then snaps back to meet hers. "Most replacements rotate on a tight loop, but one stayed fixed. They stationed him at the northern hall, direct line of sight to your chambers. No blind spots."

No escape. That isn't a precaution. It's a message—*I see you.*

She doesn't need to see his face; his shape is carved into memory. The Shadowspire guard—half-shadow, half-threat—always near, never there.

And gods, what if he was the same figure who stepped out of the shadows in Emberly's room that dawn? The silence that traveled with him. The way the darkness seemed to bend around him, reluctant to let him go. The thought curdles in her gut. What if she's always known?

The Blood Key doesn't flare in warning at the thought of him. It pulses once, heavy with inevitability.

"Do you think he's Brotherhood?" Quinn's voice drops.

Lumira offers the ghost of a shake, the lie thick on her tongue. "If he is, he doesn't act like it. They take orders. His bearing is that of someone who gives them."

That's what makes him dangerous.

And what's worse—some part of her wants him dangerous. Wants to see if the man who bows to no one would kneel for her.

She buries that thought deep, where it won't stir.

"Go," she murmurs. "Don't draw attention. Tell the others to do the same."

Quinn hesitates. "We're with you, Blood Descent."

That loyalty—that undying, blade-edged thing—cuts deeper than any betrayal ever could. It will be the death of them.

Of all of them.

Lumira doesn't respond. She stands there as the door swings shut behind Quinn, the stillness that follows stretching long and taut, brimming with truths she refuses to unpack.

Alone again, she crouches and scoops the torn halves of the betrothal scroll. The parchment feels thinner now, fragile beneath her fingers, as if it has always known it wouldn't survive her. Her name, inked beside Lysander Meridian's, sits there—undeniable. A sealed promise, not a match but an official alliance, cold and binding as iron. A ledger of what her body is worth to the empire.

Lysander Meridian. Dream Heir of Vesper.

She's known that name her whole life. Now, it feels like a verdict.

"Bloodlines are the key," Emberly whispered once, paint smudging the page as she traced worn family trees. "They'll pair you like breeding stock if they think it'll awaken old power."

And here it is. The proof. The price. The cost of what she is. Dread curdles in her stomach.

The Blood Key stirs against her skin—deliberate. Comfort doesn't touch it. Warning doesn't cover it. It's the echo of a force older than empires and far less patient.

It's been more reactive lately, around certain High Sovereigns, around the Shadowspire guard. And always when she most wants to feel nothing at all. It doesn't just respond. It remembers. What, she isn't sure. And she's not ready to know.

The thought makes her jaw tighten.

"I get it," she mutters, curling her grip around the chain. "You made your point."

The key, mercifully, remains mute.

If it ever speaks, she'd have no choice but to leap out the nearest window, and the garden spikes below aren't nearly dramatic enough to make that a satisfying exit.

She rises and unlatches the window, the cold night air brushing past, a blade drawn soft and slow. Below, the gardens stretch in symmetrical elegance: hedges trimmed, paths lined with menace. More guards now. More scrutiny. The palace tightens around her, a crown of roses cinched too tight—ornament turned weapon. They strip away her options, seal off her exits, and redefine her freedom into a version that is clean, contained, and gilded. But they spare her.

And as long as she lives, the choice remains hers. Her grip on the windowsill tightens.

That's their first mistake.

12

THE PRICE OF OBEDIENCE

Morning light filters through the stained-glass windows, casting shadows of red and gold on the floor. The air is heavy from yesterday, thick with smoke residue and unspoken words. Her hearth has gone cold. The gown she discarded the night before lies crumpled on the floor.

The mattress carries the weight of unrest—half-slept hours and bitter regrets—while the torn scroll hides underneath it, out of sight but not out of mind. Her desk is in disarray, cluttered with maps, coded messages, and a goblet of wine she poured but never touched.

A moment later, she realizes she forgot to shift the wardrobe back in front of the old service passage. She used it during the night, one more bottle of wine she didn't need, and hadn't bothered to seal it again. The gap is there, narrow but visible, a wound reopened in the stone.

When Hadralis steps through it, she doesn't startle.

"The passage was left unsealed." His gaze sweeps the room. "No sleep. And whatever that is in the mirror—I hope it wasn't a plan."

She doesn't rise from the edge of the bed. "You must be truly bored if you've come to assess my chaos."

"If I could walk in, so could someone with a dagger."

"Maybe I was hoping for an assassin." Her tone is bone-dry. "Would've saved me the trouble."

He doesn't smile. He never does when it counts. "You know better than to leave your back exposed," he replies. "Don't start slipping now." Hadralis crosses to her desk, lifting a piece of parchment stained with wine and scanning it like it personally offends him. Everything he does is intentional: every glance, pause, and breath held too long. It's maddening.

"Quinn said we lost most of our positioning." She watches him, mind already moving three steps ahead.

"We didn't lose them. They were taken. Efficiently. Your mother's been culling your network node by node. What's left is barely functional. Quinn's overtasked. The rest are pinned, compromised, or feeding back falsified reports."

"Faster than I expected," she mutters.

"She's had time. So have the ones working in the shadows."

A faint tremor stirs at her knee. "The Shadowspire guard."

Hadralis doesn't hesitate. "He hasn't looked away from you since yesterday."

"And you've been tracking him," she says coolly.

"I keep tabs on everyone," he replies. "But he's different."

She knows better than to ask. Truth from him always comes at a price. Besides, she's not in the mood to be lied to—or worse, told the truth.

"Is there anything left worth salvaging?"

"The creatures." The words hang heavy. "They don't follow orders anymore. They follow power. And they've already begun to realign."

She doesn't reply, but he continues anyway, voice low. "Monitor them closely. You won't have long. Your mother will summon you soon." He moves toward the wardrobe, halfway into the shadows of the old passage, when she speaks again.

"You sound certain."

"I am." He doesn't turn. "Because I assured her you'd refuse. Vehemently."

And then he's gone, as he arrived, without apology or pause, leaving nothing behind but the echo of his presence and the bitter taste of being outmaneuvered.

Lumira closes her lids tight, as if that could hold back the storm. She wants to scream. Wants to shatter a vase against the wall or hate him entirely.

But she can't. Not yet—because he's right.

And that makes it worse.

Thara's private study hasn't changed; it never does. Timeless and immaculate in its perfection, gilded surfaces, gold-threaded tapestries, and stained glass spill sunlight across ancestral weapons—polished past purpose. Everything about it invites admiration before the jaws snap shut.

Outside, Blood Ravens cluster on the ledges, their copper glint surveying her through the glass. They've seen her fall before—and likely expect to see it again.

Lumira drops the torn betrothal scroll on Thara's desk. Split cleanly—a verdict passed.

"Sit." It comes out wrapped in civility, but Lumira hears the warning underneath.

Lumira holds her ground.

"*Sit.*"

The word lands harder—weighted, coiled, and winding through her like smoke with teeth. The temperature drops. A Blood Raven flares its wings in warning. Her limbs obey before her mind can resist. She sits.

Thara gestures to the torn parchment. "Explain."

"It's the marriage proposal." Lumira's tone is cool. "Or it was. I thought it deserved a more honest presentation."

Thara's smile is a scalpel. "Curious. I thought it was your latest attempt to draw blood from your future." She circles the desk, all slow, predatory grace. "Did you imagine it would change anything?"

Lumira's chin lifts, her tone dry. "I thought clarity was preferable to passive aggression. But perhaps that's not your style."

Thara's laugh is soft—humorless and sharp at the edges. She leans in close, a slow smile curling like she knows how this ends, and who's left standing. "My sweet, naïve child. When did you start believing your life was ever your own?"

Lumira doesn't flinch. "You don't get to decide what I become."

"Oh, but I do," Thara replies, sugar-dipped and venomous. "And you will marry Lysander Meridian."

For a moment, the room spins.

Thara steps in closer, the air tightening between them. "You are a Kyrvayne. Your blood is not a birthright—it's a bargaining chip. And I will spend it how I see fit."

"I won't be your pawn." Lumira's voice is brittle with fury, every syllable honed to cut. "Not now. Not ever."

Thara's lips part wider, all cold hunger. "Who said pawns get to choose?"

The ravens beat their wings above them.

Rage burns, but Lumira stays flat, almost detached. "Is that all?"

"For now." Thara waves her off, already turning away. "Oh— and Lumira? That defiance you carry? I stripped it from my face a lifetime ago. Don't think I won't do the same to you."

Lumira turns on her heel, spine rigid, chin lifted in unspoken challenge.

Behind her, Thara remains in her golden lair, convinced she holds the strings. Let her. Lumira has no intention of dancing.

13

A DANCE OF BLOODLINES

Morning breaks over day two of the summit, bright enough to blind. Security forces line the chamber in formations that parade as pageantry but exist to control. Slate-gray uniforms stand interspersed with the Blood Legion's oxblood ranks, their insignia discreet. But Lumira feels it, a prickle along her spine, a metallic bite in the air. She sees it in the way they hold their weight, the way their presence scans the room. A threat half-realized. Not Crimsun. Not hers. Vesper's dogs—on the Brotherhood's leash. Embedded already.

Territory leaders enter with carefully choreographed grace, each entourage settling into position with the practiced subtlety of diplomats who know exactly which rival to face and which ally to flank. Even the magical creatures seem to remember yesterday's divides, falling into mirrored patterns around their masters.

Lumira stands near Thara's throne, posed in ornamental stillness. Her gown almost appears prudish beside Thara's customary plunging neckline—high collar, long sleeves, crisp lines—but the velvet is midnight, not Crimsun's blood-red hue—a silent rebellion stitched in shadow. Storm-silver embroidery slashes through the fabric like a promise. No loyal Crimsun tailor would dare suggest such patterns. She chose them herself, every stiff fold and hidden seam made for concealment. Her hands rest briefly on each sleek handle, the surety of steel grounding her, the severity of her attire its own kind of armor—modesty turned weapon. The Blood Key rests warm where it lies hidden. The only thing in this room that feels honest.

She scans the space. Quinn is already in place, part of the background until it matters. Invisible to everyone but her. Two loyal guards remain on duty, though posted far enough to intervene in anything meaningful. The minstrel is in place, posture docile, awareness anything but. Listening.

Seven. Seven threads in a net stretched thin—set against operatives shaped by shadows, against Thara, and whatever force now commands the Blood Ravens.

And then there's Hadralis, stationed near the entrance, posture precise. He doesn't turn toward her—he's already mapped the scene. From that vantage, he sees everything: her, the security detail, the exits. Protection or surveillance, she can't tell.

The Shadowspire guard haunts the periphery of her senses—real, but always beyond reach. Every time she tries to fix him in her sightline, he's somewhere else, visible only to prove he can disappear whenever he pleases. A phantom, not hiding—choosing.

Thara enters with imperial grace, the Blood Ravens circling above her, a crown of wings and shadow. She takes her seat with the effortless confidence of someone who has never questioned her authority. Before the chamber has fully settled, Thara lifts her chin and gestures. "Before we resume, I have a joyous announcement."

Lumira keeps her face composed, though her stomach tightens into a fist.

"It is my great pleasure," Thara begins, smooth and resonant, "to announce the betrothal of my daughter, Blood Descent Lumira Kyrvayne, to Dream Heir Lysander Meridian of Vesper."

A ripple moves through the assembly: some startled, others already prepared for this inevitable maneuver.

Zylven Meridian steps forward, his Dream Walkers gliding behind him like smoke. "Vesper is honored by this alliance," Zylven says, his tone warm, meant to smooth ruffled edges in the room. "Together, our bloodlines will shape a future brighter than we could craft alone."

Lumira scans the chamber, taking in each detail. Yasmin, Korrigan, and Alaric don't need to speak—their alignment with Zylven is written in the pleasing flickers Crimsun's reinforcement draws from them. Dom remains expressionless, but the thin rim of frost creeping along his goblet speaks louder than words.

On the opposing side, Calista's expression flickers—concern, quickly buried under courtly pleasantness. Tavern appears distracted, muttering about the "harmonic convergence of bloodline frequencies" to no one in particular. Tension sharpens between Evren and Cyrus, wariness stretched thin across the space between them, neither impressed.

Bramble, predictably, is delighted by the spectacle, while Lady Fluffy Pants yawns at his feet, tail flicking, wholly unmoved by mortal mating rituals.

Above them, the Blood Ravens reform—subtle, like muscle memory honed to instinct. Lumira stills. The shape they create matches one of Emberly's old drawings, which she used to sketch in the margins of her journals when she believed no one noticed. Once dismissed as artistic nonsense, that strange sigil now strikes her with unsettling familiarity. Emberly once scrawled a note beside it: *bound by blood, broken by blood*. The chill that runs through Lumira is immediate. This isn't politics—it's older, maybe even a ritual. And Emberly had tried to warn her.

Lysander steps forward with practiced elegance, offering her a technically flawless and subtly patronizing bow. "My heart is overcome with joy at this union," he declares, polished for performance.

Lumira notes, with detached amusement, that he hasn't spoken to her, only to the room. A small omission. A telling one.

The Blood Key doesn't warm. Doesn't chill. It waits. Poised, as if perceiving—judging a mystery it was never meant to comprehend. Not approval or rejection, but a decision unspoken in between.

Thara gestures for Lumira to join her betrothed. Her smile is a flawless display of maternal pride, fooling no one who knows her.

Lumira advances like someone navigating a minefield, taking Lysander's extended hand with the enthusiasm one might offer a dead fish. His grip is firmer than expected—reassurance or possibly a warning.

"Smile, beloved," he murmurs. "We have an audience."

She bares her teeth in what barely qualifies as a smile. "Touch me again without permission, and I'll take those fingers as a souvenir."

His laugh is low—and unexpectedly genuine. "There she is. I was beginning to worry they'd broken your spirit already."

Before she can respond, Thara rises, reclaiming the room with effortless dominance. "Now, let us return to the matters before us." She discards the betrothal charade with a dismissive wave. "Yesterday's discussions on territory disputes and trade routes remain unresolved."

Lysander offers Lumira his arm again, this time less for spectacle than function. He guides her toward the table as the murmurs fade and order reasserts itself. They settle side by side among the other dignitaries, courtly decorum snapping back into place. The summit resumes with practiced formality, polished words and measured tones, diplomatic pleasantries layered over barely veiled threats.

Lysander leans in, his breath warm against her ear. "Meet me in the eastern corridor at dusk. I have a proposition that might interest us both."

She draws back smoothly, leaning far enough to make the rejection unmistakable. "What makes you think I'd be interested in anything you have to offer?"

His smile tightens with shared understanding. "Because, my reluctant bride, neither of us wants this marriage. But we both understand the value of maintaining appearances while pursuing… alternate goals."

The admission lands harder than it should. She's always assumed Zylven wanted this alliance—that bedding Thara and fathering Aviah and Marnox was calculated, another way to keep Crimsun close. But maybe it was not that clean. He made no claim here, wore none of Thara's colors, and stayed only as long as she allowed.

And now here's Lysander, following the same script: appearances held tight, freedom traded in the margins. Maybe he hates it as much as she does. Maybe even Zylven did. It isn't cruelty. It's Thara, driven by a ruthless kind of practicality. She knows Lumira won't bend easily, so she binds her instead. That's how power survives. That's how blood stays useful.

The Blood Key pulses once, deliberate. An echo of the truth she's no longer willing to outrun.

She's not sure which thought unsettles her more.

Lysander Meridian isn't trying to own her. He's offering her a part to play—on her terms.

At some point during the exchange, Hadralis has drawn closer, a barrier between her and whatever danger he senses. His attention stays fixed on Lysander, not suspicious, but carrying the measured interest of someone calculating the cost of intervention.

The weight of Lysander's offer lingers while she decides whether to entertain it or dismiss it. Then another sharp sensation threads through, prickling along her spine. She follows it, and finds the Shadowspire guard in the archway, watching her. Not studying—marking. As if memorizing what's his before stealing it back.

She refuses to yield, even as the Blood Key hammers steady against her ribs—a pulse not her own, older than her bloodline. Older than her name.

He tilts his head slightly, as if to remind her: let them make their plans. He has his own.

Lumira presses her heel into the floor, tapping once, twice, the rhythm sharp under the table. She bites the inside of her cheek hard enough to taste copper. He doesn't have to disappear to prove his point, just leans back, watching her in a way that says she'll never be out of reach. Never free.

And that promise scrapes at her more than any chain Thara could forge.

As the summit resumes, Lumira settles beside Thara, her expression composed, her patience fraying. The debate circles the same territory disputes and trade routes without resolution, while alliances reshape themselves in the margins. Whatever game is being played, the rules are mutating faster than she can track—and she has far better things to do.

Yesterday, she had the luxury of staying hidden.

Today, she's already on the board.

What passes for formal diplomacy grinds on, slow and joyless. They settle around the table like players in a rigged game, positions chosen for advantage, glances traded like wagers. The official topics—trade routes and border disputes—are nothing more than cover for older tensions, unspoken betrayals, ancient rivalries, and quiet threats dressed up as civility.

Thara keeps Lumira close, seated between herself and Lysander. Not the words—but the patterns.

The magical companions shift as subtly as their masters speak, arranging themselves in formations that often contradict the politics being performed. They answer to nothing written in treaties or spoken in titles, only to the older, truer bonds that decide where they stand.

The War Wolves, Crystal Basilisks, Crown Eagles, and Shadow Cats gather around Korrigan, Yasmin, Alaric, and Zylven—a protective arc disguised as loose independence. Like their masters, they move in separate directions with a shared destination.

Across the chamber, the Water Nymphs, Forest Sprites, Time Foxes, and Earth Elementals draw closer, forming a mirrored opposition. Lumira recognizes the tension—coiled and building. Cyrus, Evren, Calista, and Tavern don't speak in unison, but their points converge.

Dom's Frost Dragons and Granite's Nightmare Stalkers prowl between factions, claimed by neither. The unrest they carry hangs heavy, offering no promise of resolution.

High above, the Blood Ravens keep their perch, talons curled in patient ownership of the room below.

Bramble's Light Dragons—chaotic as ever—flutter through the chamber, chasing dust motes and lunging at flickering reflections. Yet their disorder is a mask. Each sudden burst of motion draws instinctive reactions from the leaders: a stiffened spine, a tightening jaw, a flash of unease. The creatures reveal what words hide.

Lumira keeps her expression calm, though instinct screams. And whatever Emberly saw starting to rise... it hasn't stopped.

The few network members present exchange predetermined signals—a goblet placed just so, a guard's deliberate repositioning, a lingering note in an otherwise forgettable melody. Each threads into the reports they managed to slip through before the summit:

a High Sovereign's envoy entering a sealed corridor before dawn, a hidden guard rotation outside a chamber that should be empty. None of it gives her the full picture, but it's enough to remind her the real bargains happen far from this table.

Hadralis stands within reach—close enough to fray her nerves, steady enough to keep her anchored. He tracks her and the rotating guard patterns with that unreadable stillness she's never cracked, his earlier smirk replaced by a soldier carved for battles not his own. She hasn't forgotten his betrayal, or that his warning bought her time to armor herself.

Cyrus picks up the thread of discussion. "The northern trade routes have seen seventeen incidents in the past month alone—ships disappearing, crews found dead, strange symbols carved so deep they've split the hull." His Water Nymphs drift into watchful alignments, their bodies holding the same quiet as the tally in his voice.

Evren follows, grounding the report with forest border violations. "We've seen similar signs along Grovenar's eastern edge—missing patrols, trees marked with unfamiliar sigils, ritual remnants left in sacred groves."

Calista and Tavern offer supporting accounts, their testimonies weaving a cohesive picture of coordinated events across multiple territories. The threat grows clearer and more disturbing with each voice added. The opposing faction, meanwhile, shows little concern.

Yasmin, Korrigan, Alaric, and Zylven stand as a unified front. Their rebuttals are smooth, practiced, and dismissive—"isolated incidents," "exaggerations," and "nothing that stronger bloodline protections can't prevent."

Korrigan slams his fist on the table, voice booming. "BORDER SECURITY BEGINS WITH STRENGTH FROM WITHIN! PURE BLOODLINES ARE THE FOUNDATION OF OUR TERRITORIES' STRENGTH!"

The words land like a war drumbeat—loud, crude, and meant to rattle the room.

Evren rises slowly. His Forest Sprites bristle at his side, sensing the disturbance. "Then explain this," he remarks, low and unwavering. "Seventeen nobles with mixed heritage have vanished. All of them last seen in the company of individuals bearing those same hidden marks."

The temperature in the chamber drops. The War Wolves growl low, hackles rising as one, mirroring Korrigan's fury. A faint crackle sparks at his fingertips, electric lavender dancing, a threat held back by sheer force of will.

Yasmin intervenes smoothly. "What my esteemed colleague means is that our strongest bloodlines have always served as a bulwark—one that protects the vulnerable as well as the worthy. If there are gaps, perhaps the question is whether these families failed to maintain what once kept them safe."

"How remarkably convenient," Calista notes, her Season Shifters stirring miniature weather systems at her feet, "that those disappearing happen to be mixed-bloods, while the pure remain untouched."

"Correlation is not causation," Alaric counters, ever the diplomat. "We merely argue that ancient protections are worth preserving."

Granite hasn't spoken a word all day. He's reclined, a spectator to the slow collapse of diplomacy with the cool disinterest of someone waiting for the final act of a play he's already seen. But when he finally speaks, his voice slices through the chamber—laced with contempt.

"Truly, I'm on the edge of my seat," he deadpans, fixed on an invisible flaw in his cuticle. "You're all dancing around the obvious question." Only then does he look up—brutal and unbothered. "Which of you is performing blood rituals on the missing mixed-bloods—and what, exactly, are you hoping to awaken with such amateur sacrifices?"

The silence is immediate. Complete. Even Bramble's Light Dragons freeze mid-pounce.

Thara doesn't speak. Her knuckles pale where they press against the table, an undeniable tell he struck a nerve.

Above them, the Blood Ravens break their circle. One brakes midair with a hard backbeat of wings, another tilts into a slow, spiraling descent, talons flexing as if testing their grip. Shadows lengthen over the table.

Granite's words slam into Lumira like a blow to the chest. She wants to deny it, to laugh it off as a provocation but she can't. The truth sits heavy and sour at the base of her throat. Ritual sacrifice. Blood magic. She feels it in her marrow: they're taking blood, binding it, twisting it into power they can't control and don't understand. The key answers her horror with a cold pulse of agreement. Her stomach turns. She swallows it down, but the taste of it clings like rot.

The magical creatures continue to prowl, instinct pulling them into uneasy order. Their formation feels choreographed, but something else arranges the pieces that is far more insidious.

This isn't instinct. It's design wearing instinct's skin. It scratches at the edge of Lumira's memory, an old composition, a diagram Emberly once sketched in the margins of her notes. She can't place it. Only knows that the symmetry is wrong. Unnatural.

But the thought slips as Korrigan surges to his feet—scarred fists slamming into the table, voice booming. "PURE BLOODLINES ARE THE FOUNDATION OF OUR TERRITORIES' STRENGTH!"

His War Wolves lurch forward, snarling, muscles taut and ready. Light skims across Korrigan's dark stare, lavender sparks flickering like coals about to ignite.

Cyrus.

No longer the calm presence he was yesterday, he stands tall, Water Nymphs protectively circling him. "And what happens"—the words cut through the air, clear and unwavering—"when that foundation turns on the rest of us? When purity becomes permission to erase those who don't fit your mold?"

A thin trickle of water slips from under Cyrus's boots, cold as if it could bite through leather and steel alike. It hangs in the air as Korrigan growls deep in his throat. Yasmin lifts a brow, her unreadable poise giving way to a razor-thin thread of intent. Alaric straightens beside her, his gaze narrowing as the tension finally snaps.

The hall detonates—sound, motion, fury erupting all at once.

Shadow Cats vanish into the gloom, slipping soundless between bodies until they're at Zylven's flanks, already in position. The War Wolves snarl and surge forward, hackles bristling as they clash with the Forest Sprites' line in a blur of fur and thorns. A Crystal Basilisk hisses, tail lashing marble into dust as it barrels into the waiting Earth Elementals, sending cracked stone skidding across the floor. Crown Eagles dive from above, talons flashing, driving back the Water Nymphs and Forest Sprites with shrieking precision.

Across the room, sprites slip forward, thorned branches cracking like whips as they lash out at the wolves' exposed flanks. The elementals roar as they slam fists into the polished floor, splitting stone beneath rival paws and claws. The Water Nymphs spiral brine and steam at the advancing Basilisks' flanks, drenching diamond scales and forcing them to recoil. A Time Fox darts between the chaos, weaving in phantom motion, its vision pinned to the weakest breach, waiting.

At their vantage above the chamber, the Blood Ravens arrange themselves in formation—aloof but bristling. One Frost Dragon drifts low, ice swirling around its jaws. A Crown Eagle clips its wing, sparks and snow bursting in a shriek of feathers and frost. Light Dragons circle at the edges, teeth bared but movements precise, only striking when a stray wolf's jaw snaps close. The Nightmare Stalkers slip along the walls, darkness clinging to fur and scale. They don't choose sides—just victims.

Noise. Teeth. Claws. Magic. The chamber shakes with it—no sides breaking yet, but the lines bleed all the same.

Hadralis shouts to the guards, placing them with ruthless precision. The usual glint of arrogance is gone—only steel and calculation remain. He pointedly avoids Lumira. The barked orders make his meaning clear.

As blood begins to spill—

"Enough."

Thara threads just enough Compulsion into the word to reach every corner of the chamber, the effort tightening her jaw. A faint red haze creeps across the room, blurring the edges of faces as the command settles.

The Blood Ravens descend in formation, wings slamming the air into walls. They carve space between warring creatures. Guards flood the chamber, dragging factions apart by force if necessary.

The temperature stabilizes. Storms fade. Elementals retreat a step, though the vibration underfoot lingers.

Thara stands motionless at the center, in a throne of undisputed power. "This Annual Territory Summit has concluded. All delegations will return to their territories by morning." The words fall cold. "We will reconvene when civility returns to our table."

Time falters inside the walls. They retreat in disorder, tension thick.

Granite rises with an exaggerated sigh, Nightmare Stalkers slipping across the floor like ink in water. "Utterly predictable," he mutters. "Next time, let's skip the speeches." He doesn't bother with a backward glance—merely steps into the darkness, the stalkers folding into the shadows behind him.

Bramble whistles to his Light Dragons. "Well," he chirps, patting Lady Fluffy Pants as she swats at a passing Shadow Cat. "That was dreadful. Someone should really host a proper afterparty next time. Preferably with snacks." With a practiced spring, he lands on her back, giving her neck an affectionate scratch before she lumbers toward the exit.

As the gathering hall empties, the exits themselves tell the story—spaced just so, companions falling into step in measured unison, some pairs breaking away on silent cue. It scratches at a place in her mind she'd rather keep closed.

A painting. The memory sharpens—Emberly painted it last year, once dismissed as whimsy. She can almost see it now: rows of women at a long tea table, postures echoing old alliances and buried grudges, porcelain cups lifted at angles too deliberate to ignore.

The Ladies' Tea Party.

But now… Now, it feels like a code she hasn't cracked.

Hadralis appears beside her, voice low. "Security's changed. Territory leaders and their entourages only—no hidden corners, no shadows to hide in. Every step traced."

Lumira avoids him, not out of uncertainty but because the terms leave no room for doubt: no secret meetings, no private messages—only favors traded in plain sight.

Someone brushes past, a familiar face from Wrenna's circle, an artist's apprentice who once worked with Emberly. "Wrenna sent word," she murmurs. "Same place you first met. After dusk."

Lumira doesn't ask which place. There was only ever one.

But escaping tonight would be reckless. Eyes track the halls. Guards block each turn. She wouldn't make it back unseen.

"No." She says it soft, but with finality. "Tell her to come to the Conservatory Hall. At first light."

The apprentice nods once and vanishes into the crowd.

Her mind drifts to the painting—*The Ladies' Tea Party*—hanging in the Conservatory Hall. The same symmetry tonight: creatures mirroring one another, alliances tightening, old rivalries locking into place as neatly as the seated women and their cups. She knows Emberly saw it. She knows it's still there.

Lumira reorients herself toward the doors, the day's weight settling on her shoulders, a shroud she cannot shrug off. Her betrothal is a noose. The summit is fractured. An ancient hunger stirs below them, vast in its patience, unrelenting in its need.

She slips from the gathering hall, already planning for the next day. Whatever Emberly saw, it's been left out in the open.

This time, Lumira won't dismiss the signs. This time, she'll see the whole picture—and tear it wide open.

14

THE LADIES' TEA PARTY

It hasn't even been a full day since the summit cracked wide open—allegiances shattered, magical creatures turned, and the Blood Key turned cold in Lumira's grasp with urgent intensity. And now she's in the Conservatory Hall, trying to make sense of a painting that might be a warning, a map, or both.

Morning light spills through the arched windows, bending through dew-laced prisms and ivy-draped glass. Rainbows scatter across the marble floor, catching on the oil painting Emberly insisted belongs on the far wall.

Twelve noblewomen sit mid-sip, porcelain cups poised between gloved fingers with practiced grace. Hats tipped, backs straight— details impeccable. And above them, the Blood Ravens perch in shadowed corners, watching like sentries.

The Blood Key pulses once. Not with heat or fear but with rhythm. Steady. Intentional.

Moving forward, she follows a pull she can't explain. Emberly never painted to pass the time. Every brushstroke was a message. Every detail, a warning.

"You painted the whole fucking summit," Lumira spits under her breath. "Before any of us saw it coming. Of course you did, Emberly." The territories. The creatures. The unraveling of it all, woven into brushstrokes and bone china. Her voice drops, edged with bitter disbelief. "And none of us pieced it together."

The Blood Key pulses again—stronger this time. Urgent.

Memory claws its way forward: Emberly, pale and glassy-eyed, whispering, "They speak beneath the caws," before the physicians dosed her into silence. Everyone had dismissed it as another flare-up.

Lumira's jaw tightens. "She knew, and tried to warn us."

Crisp, unhurried footsteps close in and halt. Hadralis crosses the threshold, wind and cold in his wake. The gusts cling to his coat, the chill trailing him like a shadow. He carries a linen-wrapped bundle no larger than a curled fist, bound with a twist of Vesper silver that catches the hall's lantern light.

"You're alone," Hadralis observes across the hall, studying the space the way others study a weapon.

"I prefer it that way." Lumira stays locked on the painting, unmoved.

He leans closer, speaking low. "The terrace is sealed, and patrols are changing routes—no pattern, tighter coverage. Not my order."

She doesn't bother turning. "Then someone's panicking. Desperation makes people sloppy."

He lifts the bundle slightly, holding it between them in a careful manner. "Your betrothed had this delivered before his delegation withdrew. Impressive, considering the lockdown."

Lumira surveys the bundle, suspicion simmering behind her calm. "And you offered to deliver this out of the goodness of your heart?"

"Obviously," Hadralis replies, tone flat. "My compassion knows no limits." He lays the bundle on the table beside her, grip slow to loosen, hesitation etched in the pause before he speaks. "You skipped your meeting with Lysander."

She doesn't deny it.

"Smart," he adds. "The eastern corridor sweep came later, hours after your exchange. Someone was paying attention."

The bundle rests between them, the pale fabric streaked with shifting tones of silver and shadow. The wax seal bears the Meridian crest—precise and untouched.

"If he meant to kill me, he'd have chosen a more elegant method," Lumira mutters, reaching for the gift. She unwraps the cloth slowly, each fold revealing intent rather than ornament. Inside: a small wooden box and a single folded note, sealed not with the Meridian crest but Lysander's signet. Absent are the emblems of house or seal. What remains is his mark, a boundary drawn in wax.

She breaks it.

The corridor wasn't safe. You were right not to come. This will be of use eventually. Tell no one—especially not her.

The message lands clean—pared down, designed to cut between the lines.

She reads it twice, then slides it into the hidden pocket of her tunic with the practiced control of someone used to hiding blades in plain sight.

Hadralis studies her—a pause stretched thin, heavy with things unsaid. "What did the Dream Heir send?" he asks, tone unreadable.

Lumira doesn't answer. Not directly.

She opens the lid of the box.

Nestled in black velvet, a single crystal rests—small, polished, and cool as ice—deep blue, cut to catch the light without flashing. At first, it seems like decoration, a harmless bauble. But the weight of it in her palm tells a different story.

She lifts it carefully, turning it slowly within her hold. She flinches, jaw clenched, but clamps down on the urge to move. It feels suspended, waiting for the moment to matter in a way she hasn't recognized.

"A lover's token?" Hadralis asks, though his dry tone makes it clear he doesn't believe it.

"It's too calculated," she responds, flipping it as if it were a secret intended to be overheard. "It's crafted to seem sentimental—enough to divert suspicion." She repositions it once more, but it yields no insights: no flicker, no indication. Whatever it holds remains concealed at this moment.

Hadralis offers nothing more. But the way he lingers on the crystal speaks louder than any admission. He knows exactly what it is. And he's choosing not to tell her.

"Should I be concerned that your Vesper fiancé is sending you sealed gifts with unclear intent?" Hadralis speaks instead, his expression flat.

Lumira tucks the crystal away with the note, lifting a brow. "Only if Lysander's hoping for a heartfelt poem in return," she says, then flicks to the note again. "Or he's withholding on purpose. The treaty's nearly finalized. He wouldn't risk this without a reason." She shoots him a look over her shoulder, voice clipped and barbed. "You always know exactly where I am, Hadralis. Should I be flattered or worried?"

He folds his arms, unbothered. "It's my job to know where you are, Lumira. Especially when you're collecting riddles from fools who think they're poets."

She scowls but doesn't argue.

He nods at the painting. "Concentrate on what's here. Not his theatrics."

Lumira exhales, rolling the tension from her shoulders. The crystal and whatever it truly is—can wait. There are more immediate threats pressing in.

She returns to the massive painting, where twelve noble ladies sip tea with deceptive tranquility. A hidden thread winds through the scene, waiting for the right eyes to pull it loose.

"Twelve territory ladies," she murmurs. "They mirror the summit factions—but that's not all they're hiding…" She trails off.

She traces the canvas methodically, taking in each woman in turn. The porcelain teacups catch her first, some raised high, glinting below the fractured prism light. Others are nestled close, partially obscured by lace cuffs and draped sleeves.

"The cups…" She squints. "Some displayed, others tucked away. That's interesting."

Hadralis positions himself behind her, arms folding. "Or it's just aesthetics. Emberly liked balance."

She crosses to the far end of the painting, reviewing the positioning again. Her brows knit. The differences aren't random—they echo a pattern. Her pulse ticks faster. "They're not painted that way for visual variety." A beat passes. "They're sending us a message." Her reach stalls over the half-hidden cup, poised but unmoving.

Her stare skims the line of painted women, each frozen mid-sip, frozen in secrets. *What did Emberly want her to see?*

An old lesson uncoils like smoke: the cold scrape of Mother's words. *"You will never mistake an enemy's colors—not even in the dark."*

She huffs out a bitter laugh. "She drilled each territory's colors into me before I could read my own name," she mutters, half to Hadralis, half to herself. "Every crest, every dye, every ceremony." As she traces the elegant brushstrokes, the truth clicks into place—she recognizes each of the territories now. "Bravara. Regale. Vesper. Tigran. And Zestria…" Her mouth twists. "All hidden cups…"

Lumira squints at the painting, the edges of her voice softening, thoughtful. An itch stirs deep within, a crack she can't smooth over yet.

She then scowls at the bold orange threads half swallowed by painted shadow. "Zestria doesn't belong there if this is about alliances. Calista hates them—she'd never pretend otherwise. This isn't about loyalty."

Hadralis draws near, eyes narrowing in quiet study. He doesn't interrupt.

Lumira shakes her head. "So… not alliances or loyalty. What then? Leverage?" The word leaves a metallic tang on her tongue.

"Secrets buried under courtly smiles? The Brotherhood's reach? Emberly wouldn't paint this to gossip about petty feuds." She glances over her shoulder. "This has to be about the Brotherhood, right? Emberly knew they'd be monitoring; she wanted me to see who's already compromised. Who they're choking from the inside."

She returns to the painted women, cups held high: Grovenar in deep greens, Naiad in flowing blue, Shadowspire wrapped in black silk, Rimefall shimmering with frost. Terravox. Aurova. Each one bright under the fractured prism light.

"They are so exposed," she exhales. "So confident. But that doesn't mean anything, does it? Not if they're next."

Lumira's pulse stutters when she reaches the twelfth figure. Auburn hair swept high, that sharp, familiar chin exposed at a perfect angle—the Crimsun lady, Emberly's mirror, teacup lifted in a mocking, knowing toast. The brushwork seems to catch the angled light, making each painted face shimmer—half-smile, half-warning.

She examines the pendant at Emberly's throat, a painted key of copper alloy that shimmers subtly, equal parts decoration and defense.

It's the Blood Key. *Her* Blood Key. The real one presses warm where it rests: answering the sight with a subtle, low pulse that flickers between her breasts. Not to soothe her, but to promise there's no slipping this snare.

Lumira's mind races, each thought tripping over the next. *If Emberly painted herself wearing the Blood Key—an artifact—maybe every lady hides one too. Secrets buried beyond finding.*

She lingers on Emberly's painted toast—cup held aloft, mouth curled in a knowing twist that speaks louder than words. "She made herself the toast. The bait." Her throat tightens, the weight of it pressing against her ribs. "And with her gone…" The words slip out like a confession, raw and certain. "It's me now. I'm the one left holding the cup."

Lumira inches forward, searching the canvas as though Emberly left more than pigment behind. Her fingertip hovers over the first lady on the right—purple silks, a stiff, martial sash, the blade peeking out where it shouldn't. "Bravara," she mutters. "Military pride, but they'd never flaunt what they've lost… or what they surrendered." Her gaze flicks to the cup, half-buried in a gloved grip. "Probably already in the Brotherhood's jaws."

Moving counterclockwise around the table is Vesper. Pale-silver threads shimmer where a small mirror remains tucked slyly at this lady's waist. Lumira lets out a humorless laugh. "The mask and the lie. They'd swear they're untouched, but the Brotherhood's in their veins."

She slides to the next. Heavy silk drapes the painted lady, a faint crown motif nestled discreetly against her hip. "Regale," she mutters. "Gold vaults, old priesthood. All that wealth's a chain when the Brotherhood gets its hooks in. Of course it's gone."

One by one, the pattern locks. Tigran's ceremonial chalice. Zestria's scepter half swallowed in shadow, the contradictions Emberly painted clear enough to see if you knew where to search.

Her throat tightens. "She didn't paint a court scene." The words rasp from Lumira—strained, tight, the truth aching with every syllable. "She marked which pieces they've already stripped away, and what's hidden."

The room goes still.

Hadralis's voice, low and controlled, settles beside her ear. "It's a cipher." No sarcasm this time, only that too-certain edge she hates. He gestures toward the lady draped in layered greens. "There. Grovenar. Her lap—do you see it?"

Lumira squints, the faint outline of a branch, painted like it's being cradled. Her pulse ticks up.

Hadralis's tone is smooth. "That's the Living Branch."

She pivots toward him, suspicion sparking cold under her ribs. "*The Living Branch?*" Not a branch, or a symbol. A name. Specific enough to cut past coincidence.

He stays rooted, offering no reply. The truth lingers between them, unsheathed and undeniable.

Lumira brings herself back to the table: the ladies, the delicate porcelain cups, the arrangement that feels almost ceremonial. It hits her all at once: the spacing, the way each figure angles toward another, how the gaps match old maps she's memorized since she was small.

"The way they're seated…" She swallows, the words tasting like rust. "It's geographic. Territory layout. This isn't a painting. It's a map."

Hadralis doesn't respond, but his agreement lingers between them.

Her voice slips as the pieces slot into place. "If that's true… then this marriage isn't politics. Mother's positioning me. She's putting me in Vesper for a reason."

Before he can answer, a soft knock echoes from the corridor. Hadralis moves—finding his vantage point, a predator at the door.

Lumira straightens, mask slipping back into place, the bored distance of a woman inspecting her sister's art. But inside, her thoughts burn, a fuse catching flame.

She's already moving toward the door, steps measured. "Enter," she calls, layering the words with enough annoyance to sound convincingly interrupted.

The door opens to reveal Wrenna—composed, purposeful, with paint streaks marring the grace she wears, a second skin. Her beauty doesn't ask to be acknowledged; it owns every inch it touches.

"Pardon the interruption, Blood Descent." Wrenna offers a formal bow, wearing the court-perfect calm they've both learned to master. "I've been sent to clean the painting's frame."

"I'm sure the painting appreciates the admiration." Lumira holds the door partially open, blocking Hadralis's view with her shoulder as she leans closer to Wrenna.

The crystal digs cold against her ribs, tucked deep inside her tunic. She could keep it close, pry out what Hadralis is still holding back tonight. But she's tired of waiting. And if they're being watched… better it's not on her.

She slips the crystal to Wrenna, quick and discreet.

Wrenna's composure dips, then returns—guarded, but trusting. "Should I know where it came from?"

"It's from Lysander," Lumira murmurs. "Diplomatic pretense."

Wrenna snatches up the crystal and slips it into her coat without hesitation. "You trust me with this?"

"I trust you more than I trust him." The rest stays unspoken: Hadralis doesn't lie—he fractures the truth, offering pieces honed to make her question everything.

A shadow crosses Wrenna's face, unreadable, but she nods. "Then I'll protect it."

She steps inside, posture smoothing back into place as she stands before the canvas with the reverence of revisiting sacred ground. Her focus lifts to the crystal prisms strung along the windows. "These weren't Thara's idea," she murmurs, the name slipping out like an insult. "Emberly requested them. Said the painting only revealed itself when the light struck it a certain way."

A ray of morning sun catches one of the prisms, bending through the glass and scattering faint rainbow streaks across the canvas.

Wrenna adjusts it by a hair's width, refining the fractured light into clean lines that slice across painted silk and porcelain cups. "There," she murmurs. "Now we're seeing what Emberly wanted us to."

Under the refracted light, the painting comes alive. What once seemed like faint wisps of steam rising from each painted teacup now shimmer and unfurl—no longer soft curls, but delicate lines that twist into shapes, faint script nested inside.

"Special varnish." Wrenna skims the edge of the frame with delicate care. "She blended copper into it, the prisms catching it and drawing out layers you'd never notice otherwise."

"Copper?" Lumira straightens, startled.

"The steam." Wrenna slots the final prism into place. "It isn't decorative."

Lumira leans closer, studying the strands twisting and weaving.

Some steam lines bend and flow freely, curling like smoke. Others hold rigid, pinned unnaturally straight. But within the haze, a flicker: subtle markings, half-formed characters that seem to breathe.

"It's not the shape," Lumira leans closer. "It's a script. Or a trail?"

Wrenna nods once. "She called them 'fractured whispers.' Coordinates. Said they weren't symbols so much as echoes, translations of an older language, hidden under all we believe is true."

Hadralis's voice cuts in. "Old language. Old paths. I've seen these markings before." He steps closer, eyes narrowing as he examines the steam script. "Fragments—etched into ruin walls, boundary stones, relics that predate the territories."

Heat builds in Lumira's sternum, impossible to ignore, as a Blood Raven perches on the windowsill, feathers stirring in the splintered shimmer of morning with unshaken certainty.

Wrenna's voice threads into the moment, low enough to almost miss. "She'd enter these... trances while painting. Muttering in languages I didn't recognize, languages she shouldn't have known."

Lumira addresses them coolly. "What exactly are you saying?"

Hadralis's answer comes low, steady. "Those echoes—the script—they're not coordinates. They're remnants of the old gods' language. The ones who were tricked and bound."

Lumira spins on her heel. "And how would you know that?"

"Because the Brotherhood's been hunting these artifacts for centuries," Hadralis says, expression unwavering. "And not to set anything free." The certainty in his voice rings clean. Not a guess. Not an educated theory. A confession, dressed as information.

The Blood Key gives a single, warm pulse. Of course he knows.

A tightness clamps down in her chest. "You're Brotherhood, aren't you?"

The words land, each one a strike stripped of courtesy.

He doesn't flinch. "I know them well enough to see how deep they've buried themselves. They're in every territory—every court, even the Crown's inner circle—every bed of power." He lets that hang, offering no more. The rest stays unsaid: *He's theirs. Or was. Or both.*

Lumira's attention snaps back to the painting, to the steam unfurling in the prism light. "It's worse than I thought," she mutters. "They don't take what they want and leave, they settle in. Wait. Search out the next weakness."

"And yet." Hadralis gestures to the raised cups. "Grovenar, Naiad, Aurova, Rimefall, Terravox, Shadowspire—they're untouched. Their artifacts haven't been taken. Not yet."

She leans in, eyeing the concealed cup in the Zestrian lady's grip. "Whatever they lost, it hollowed them out. You can see it in the way they hold on, desperate." The threads knot together. "The disappearances. Mixed-blood nobles. It's not random, it's part of the pattern." A jolt of cold clarity cuts through her. "Granite warned us. Might as well have screamed it." Her expression twists. "But ignoring good advice is practically tradition."

"He wasn't guessing." There's a hum in Hadralis's voice, certain and laced with truth. "There is a ritual—twelve artifacts bound through blood. Not one willing line. One marked to bear them all."

It cuts deeper than she wants to admit. A *sacrifice*. Not taken—hunted.

The Blood Key pulses warm and steady against her ribs, a truth that won't stay buried.

Stirring behind her, the Blood Raven's feathers settle with a soft scrape. Its copper eyes catch the fractured light—fixed, unblinking, a silent dare to see what's hidden.

Its unspoken pull drags her back to the canvas. She scans the rippling steam, the buried symbols, and then sees them: Blood Ravens, half swallowed by painted shadows, wings spread behind the ladies, a second layer of sentinels.

"And the ravens?" she asks, though the shape of the answer is already waiting in her mind—an itch behind her ribs.

"Conduits," Wrenna speaks softly. "Witnesses. Translators for voices that were never meant to be understood."

Hadralis fixes on the painted birds. "The gods spoke through them. Through her." He doesn't say the rest but Lumira feels it settle anyway, heavy as stone.

"She wasn't meant to bear what they poured into her," Wrenna adds, barely audible.

And for a beat, the air itself feels occupied, like the room is listening.

Lumira senses a subtle tilt in how Wrenna regards the painting now—not reverence or grief—quieter. Deeper. "You knew her better than anyone," Lumira murmurs, the words more statement than a question.

Wrenna's grasp tightens on the frame. "I thought I did." There's an ache beyond her words—not for a person, but for a future that never came.

"She came to you during the episodes, didn't she?" Lumira presses, gentler now. "When the voices overwhelmed her."

Wrenna hesitates, then nods. "She'd show up at odd hours. Shaking. Barely standing. I'd close early, bring her upstairs..." She trails off as if realizing how much she's already said.

The unspoken lands hard.

Lumira remembers Emberly insisting her quarters be moved to the east side of the palace, claiming the morning light helped her symptoms. But from that vantage point, the merchant path to Pigments & Pints was obvious.

"She wasn't your protégé," Lumira says, certain. "You loved her."

Wrenna's composure cracks—for a moment—and pain flickers across her face before she pulls it back into place. "Three years." A fragile admission. "We were careful. Your mother would have—"

"Destroyed you both," Lumira finishes. "Yes. I know her brand of maternal devotion."

She doesn't say it cruelly. Just plainly. The weight of it is heavy enough.

Surprise flickers through her—at how deeply Emberly had hidden it—followed by a sharp ache for what her sister endured, and a sliver of relief that she hadn't been alone.

"She tried to spare you from it." Wrenna's voice tightens. "She thought it would protect you." Tension creeps into her grasp on the frame. "But she made sure you'd be the one to finish it."

Lumira exhales through her teeth. "Fucking useless—for both of us. I'm neck-deep in whatever killed her, with half the answers and twice the enemies."

Wrenna's expression softens. "You have more than you realize." She gestures toward the painting. "This isn't only information, it's a weapon. A map. A guide to what comes next."

Hadralis steps in, scanning the canvas. "Based on what we've uncovered, the Brotherhood has five artifacts. And they're positioning to take the rest. They're actively hunting the one in your possession." His gaze lingers long enough to make clear he already knows. "Emberly's death wasn't the end of their search. It was the beginning. Look at the steam," he adds, pointing to a delicate sequence connecting several teacups. "Your sister didn't catalog the artifacts. She mapped their course. The disrupted steam patterns form a sequence. The next in line"—he taps the Grovenar lady's raised cup, where the steam curls into a delicate forest rune—"is the Living Branch. Thallen Forest."

Lumira studies the painting, her mind stitching the fragments into a shape that finally makes sense. "Then we go first. We take the Living Branch before they do. We're not letting that fall if that's the next artifact."

Hadralis huffs once, not quite amusement, more the edge of disbelief. "Into Thallen Forest? Brotherhood patrols at every pass. And you think Emberly's cipher alone tells you what waits for you in there?" He locks on to the rune, then to her, his gaze measured, grim. "It's a clue—not a shield. You'll need more than a painted map to walk out with it alive."

Lumira offers him nothing. She runs her thumb along the edge of the canvas, tracing the forest rune as if she can feel her sister's presence pressing through the varnish. "We have this. Her notes. Her allies. My network. The paths she marked." She lets the words hang in the space between them like a blade. "It's enough."

"And your birthmark," Wrenna adds. "She believed it would respond when you neared the artifacts. She wrote about it and said it wasn't symbolic. It's how they'll find you. Or how you'll find them, she wasn't sure which."

Lumira doesn't speak. But the heat buried within responds. It flared when she neared the Blood Key. It wasn't the key reacting—it was her.

A signal is written into her very body. Into her blood.

Outside, the raven tilts into motion, light glinting off its feathers in acknowledgment.

"There's more." Wrenna approaches the frame, tracing a sequence of nearly invisible notches. A soft click echoes as a narrow panel slides open—a secret hidden in plain sight. Inside the hollow frame waits a tightly rolled parchment, its edges worn, the ink faded, thinned by waiting.

Lumira observes her closely, suspicion coiling in her chest. "You knew this was here. Why didn't you say anything sooner?"

Wrenna runs her thumb across the delicate seam, tracing Emberly's careful marks, a promise etched in paint. "I knew parts of it, the mechanism and the failsafe. But it wasn't meant to be traded over like a coin. Emberly designed it to be found here, not in corridors. You needed to see it for yourself."

She lifts the parchment from its hidden cradle and places it into Lumira's palm—not Hadralis's. The old paper feels lighter than it should be. A blueprint written in lines so fine they seem ready to vanish at the slightest touch.

Lumira unrolls it with care, taking in each inked detail: patrol rotations, hidden entry points, safe houses tucked along the old forest paths. Each faded mark settles into her ribs like iron. A failsafe spun between madness and myth—a weapon.

Hadralis leans closer but doesn't touch it, only reads over her shoulder, his delivery flat. "This isn't a map. It's a battle plan."

"In her final weeks, she worked through everything." Wrenna drifts, voice steady despite the memory. "Even when the pain was unbearable. She said there wasn't time to rest."

All those court rumors—fragile things, elegant but empty. They hadn't seen what Emberly was really building. But Lumira sees it now. Not weakness. Not madness. A blueprint hidden in plain sight.

"We find the Living Branch." Each word lands—a strike driven deep. "We trace the pattern. And we drag her killer into the light."

"Ilara knows the forest," Wrenna adds. "Her ties to the old paths run deeper than the Brotherhood's reach."

Lumira turns back to the painting, settling on Emberly—the Crimsun lady—forever caught mid-toast, the Blood Key gleaming at her painted throat. The real one warms steady against her ribs, alive and unignorable. Plans begin to align in her mind, the path forward slicing into view with cold precision.

But beneath it all, one truth clings, a shadow at her heels.

Hadralis knows things he has no right to. And if he isn't Brotherhood, then he's another blade pointed at her back. A man with perfect aim, and no one seeing where he's pointing.

Outside, the raven lifts from the sill. It holds her suspended for a moment, then takes flight, wings slicing east toward Thallen Forest.

"She did trust you." Wrenna's words carry no doubt. "Even when it cost her everything."

Lumira's grip tightens around the fragile parchment. "And I won't waste it. I'll use every breath to make them bleed."

15

TRAINING GROUNDS

rost grips the stones, edges biting in the hush of early light. Yesterday's revelations still cling, sharp as the steam and paint that delivered them. Now, from the shadow of a stone pillar flanking the training grounds, Lumira lingers, observing her network, her creation, stretching and sparring under the watch of the Blood Ravens. For a moment, they resemble dancers in a violent masquerade until a noble daughter drops a footman with clean precision, or a merchant's son shatters a practice shield like bark. They are raw, imperfect, and learning.

But they are hers.

The pieces she's carefully positioned for what comes next— not the retrieval itself, but the orchestration required to make it possible.

"Good morning, Blood Descent," they chorus, voices pitching somewhere between reverence and rigid obedience as she approaches, boots crunching over frost.

"Punctual. How charming." Her tone is clipped. "Let's see if your reflexes are equally disciplined."

Blood Ravens gather along the rooftops, their presence less decorative than usual. They've always flocked to morning training—an unsettling tradition often attributed to a taste for Crimsun blood spilling before breakfast. But today, their numbers are more significant.

"Today's exercise is urban terrain diversion," she announces. "Close-quarters movement and unpredictable obstacles."

Hadralis steps from the shadows, as if summoned by the gods themselves. Morning light rests on his shoulders, another reminder he's too at ease with holding the upper hand. Predictable. Utterly insufferable. "Blood Descent." He offers a bow precisely engineered to convey respect without performing it. "I see our eager students await enlightenment."

"More likely they await breakfast," Lumira replies. "But we'll postpone basic mortal necessities in favor of violence and cryptic instruction."

Hadralis's mouth curves, enough to suggest he's amused. Or lying. He steps into the center of the training ground as a raven passes by. His body shifts with it, the subtlest brace—like someone preparing for a blow. Or a reckoning.

"We'll start with technique drills—Grovenar's defensive forms adapted for close-quarters work," he says, easing into a stance that halts Lumira mid-motion.

Refined. Familiar. And neither by accident.

The angle of the feet. The arc of motion. Every detail has a quality of familiarity that strikes her as wrong. These aren't common forms. They're specialized techniques that shouldn't be in the repertoire of Crimsun's Master at Arms.

"Curious," Lumira murmurs, mirroring his form with continuous grace. "You've never been quite so... specific with Grovenar technique before."

Hadralis doesn't blink. "Perhaps I underestimated its relevance to controlled environments." He adjusts the stance slightly and gestures to the outer ring. "Maintain spacing. Redirect pressure— don't absorb it. Let the pressure bend, don't break. Redirect it inward and preserve the formation."

And there it is.

The final word lands with practiced force, clipped and disciplined in a way Crimsun doesn't teach. Grovenar, maybe, but carrying a colder precision. It rings of Shadowspire, unmistakable in the way it edges each syllable with authority.

Of course. Why stop at the Brotherhood when you can stack Shadowspire secrets on top?

The Brotherhood takes you apart in the dark, but Shadowspire knows how to make you thank them for the blade.

She pins this lie to the growing tally—another fracture waiting to split when she needs it to.

The Blood Key warms, but she doesn't need its verdict. She knows the shape of betrayal by now: posture, breath, slip of the tongue.

How exquisite, she thinks, *that betrayal unfolds so neatly—before breakfast is even served.*

"You seem distracted, Blood Descent," Hadralis chides, his tone smooth as ever, before easing into a sequence of forms that feel foreign: Grovenar forms, all fluid steps and weightless turns that would never belong in Crimsun's rigid drills.

She's only seen these techniques drawn in old forest-guard manuals—steps meant to slip a fighter through dense underbrush without losing their footing.

He flows closer, spinning on the final step to strike, a testing blow aimed just past her shoulder.

Lumira counters with deliberate imperfection, misjudging the third rotation enough to gauge his reaction. "My apologies." She mirrors his stance with careful precision. "Hard to ignore your sudden fluency in territory-specific forms you supposedly know nothing about."

"I never said I didn't." The words glide out, effortless—like the forms themselves.

She snorts. "Of course. Easier to keep your secrets when no one knows what questions to ask."

The ravens wheel in silence, their motion seamless. Their formation tightens, not from instinct, but intention. They circle her as if summoned, light trailing in designs no accident could create.

Hadralis, at her flank, lifts his chin, passing as unconcerned. Almost convincing.

The faintest pull tugs at the corner of her mouth.

"You mistake what I've kept for where I stand." He meets the counter with unsettling ease—each step a memory made flesh.

She doesn't press him further. Not yet.

Only watches. And waits.

"Diversion drill," Hadralis calls out. "Outer ring breaks formation to scatter the guards' reactions. The inner ring locks into a shield, fluid and reactive. The center simulates distraction. That's all."

At his signal, the outer ring fractures: pairs slipping behind stone outcroppings, reappearing to pull invisible threats away from the core. The inner ring flexes with them, catching the gaps, bending instead of breaking. A footman misjudges and clips another's shoulder—a sudden curse, a clipped correction. They flow on.

Lumira steps into place at the center as her network closes around her, movements honed by repetition.

"Your role isn't confrontation. It's confusion," Hadralis continues, weaving through the ranks, a thread tightening the whole. "You pull attention where it doesn't belong. You open doors with noise, not tools. It's not strength that matters—it's misdirection."

He adjusts a shoulder here, a grip there, each correction quick and exact.

A pair in the outer ring fumbles, nearly exposing the decoy. Hadralis doesn't bark—he angles a hand, a subtle correction, and on the next pass, they slip through clean. Imperfect, but the misdirection holds. Each alteration makes the formation look less like drills and more like instinct.

"Speed over strength. Noise over violence. You're not here to win. You're here to ensure the real objective disappears before anyone thinks to notice."

It's not what he says, it's how he says it. Inevitable.

Not theory. And not his first orchestration.

The sun's barely up, but already merciless, a warning for those who choose to train in its glare. At Hadralis's signal, Lumira's network breaks formation, each member moving toward the water stations with the composed urgency of soldiers trained not to show strain.

She retrieves a flask without comment, her limbs thrumming with exertion. Though her body craves deep, greedy gulps, she drinks in slow, measured sips—even thirst obeys the performance.

Hadralis approaches, unhurried, the slight sheen on his brow the only concession to exertion. "Your progress is impressive." If there's meaning behind it, it doesn't show. "But your timing drags—a beat longer than it should be between guarding and advancing."

"How tragic," Lumira replies, capping the flask with sure fingers. "To fall short despite such… specialized instruction."

His smile is narrow and calculated. "Your sister never faltered."

The words land exactly where he intends. The Blood Key pulses—soft but certain, a steady rhythm that refuses to fade.

"How unexpected." She sounds amused, but the way she holds the flask says otherwise. "That you'd hold her up as the model of precision, given her reputation for gentler pursuits. She wasn't some godsdamned weapon."

"She understood more than people realized." Hadralis's gaze stays locked on hers. "Patterns. Movement. The kinds of things most overlook."

Lumira's tone stays light. "You were that invested in my sister?"

He shrugs, unconvincing. "One picks things up in the course of duty. She spent hours in the eastern tower observatory. Always writing."

The eastern tower. Off-limits to most. Nearly empty. And he'd seen her there.

"Studying the habits of a girl sketching birds?" she remarks, dry.

He doesn't flinch. "She wasn't studying them."

A pause. A colder truth.

"They were studying her."

The words land like a knife. Of course he knows more than he should—he always does. She tucks that fracture away. Another piece of him she'll crack when she needs to.

The others have drifted away, leaving them on an island of tension beneath the unforgiving sun.

Lumira examines him with renewed clarity. The Blood Ravens had swept across the training grounds today, their flight methodical and perfectly aligned. And Hadralis had responded like someone who'd trained beside them once, not against them.

"The birds seem especially watchful today." Her tone is light, almost playful. "Makes you wonder what they see in us, doesn't it?"

He snaps his focus to her, whatever flared vanishing just as fast. "Birds recognize more than most realize," he replies evenly. "As do some people."

The moment presses in, but he holds his stance.

"Is that what drew your interest to Emberly's work?" Lumira pushes. "The way she saw through everything?"

"Your sister never faltered in recognizing what others missed," he answers, each word precise. "She saw connections where everyone else saw coincidence."

She doesn't blink as she studies him over the flask's rim. "So when did your specialized training start—before or after you became Crimsun's Master at Arms?"

"Qualification is proven by outcome, not chronology," Hadralis replies, his tone perfectly composed. "Though my preparation began long before my current position was... arranged."

Arranged. Not earned, not appointed. The word settles with quiet weight, suggesting influence far beyond the palace walls.

"That will suffice." His voice drifts over the gathered faces.

The comment earns him a few glances—equal parts irritation and exhaustion—swiftly masked behind disciplined composure.

Lumira doesn't challenge it aloud. She only exhales, letting her shoulders ease enough to release the tension without showing strain. The drills were demanding, but it's not the physical toll that unsettles her.

It's the discipline. The language. The feeling that every beat had been rehearsed before—in places none had seen.

"Dismissed." Her tone is cool, final—offering no room for argument.

As the others begin to disperse, Hadralis turns back to her.

"Blood Descent," he adds, almost as an afterthought. "Remain for individual assessment."

Her network slips away, leaving only the two of them in the full glare of the midmorning sun. Lumira doesn't speak right away, and neither does Hadralis.

Hadralis gestures with a sharp tilt of his chin. "Again. From the beginning."

Lumira rolls her shoulders back, jaw set, and drops into position. She carves through the sequence without a word—each step controlled, each transition clean, until the final pivot drags a fraction too long.

He doesn't bother to mask his disappointment. "Your form's clean enough," he says at last. "But there's hesitation in your transitions. The forest won't forgive that."

She wipes sweat from her brow, unbothered. "I told you—I'm going after it."

"And I haven't forgotten." He takes her in as though committing every feature to memory. "The Thallen Forest doesn't surrender its secrets to strangers. It barely tolerates them."

"Good." She meets him, unflinching. "That's why I'm bringing someone it already knows." A beat. Then colder: "Let them try to stop me."

Approval, maybe. Or calculation. Either way, he angles toward her. "When you reach it… don't assume it wants to be taken. Some things resist—even when they recognize you."

The phrasing isn't casual. It cuts clean, aimed with unnerving accuracy.

She turns to leave.

"Lumira."

Her name—not her title. It stops her mid-step, but she doesn't turn.

"The ravens observe." His words carry soft power. "They mark what matters. But they won't save you."

A muscle ticks in her jaw. "Charming bird wisdom," she mutters. "Though your suspiciously specific knowledge needs a story."

"Official positions are rarely the whole story," he calls back. "But you know that better than most."

He's gone before she can answer, leaving her with the Blood Key warm at her chest.

Alone now, Lumira steps into the clearing's center, her boots rasping across the dry earth. She takes her previous place—where the ravens had been most fixed on her.

"Well," she murmurs to the trees, birds, and unseen, "you've assembled quite the audience. I do hope I live up to expectations."

The ravens hold their ground, adjusting along the branches in unnerving unison—until one drops to a nearby sapling, and the rest follow, filling the grove in symmetry so exact it borders on ritual. Naturally, they're immune to sarcasm.

She begins the final sequence they practiced. Her muscles ache, but she moves with precision, not grace. Will, not surrender.

"Subtle," she mutters, unmoving. "But I'll give you credit for commitment." Surrounded by scrutiny, she keeps her steps steady.

The Blood Key flares.

Heat sears through her ribs—sharp, blinding—and the world whips sideways. The training ground rips away in an instant, smoke on the wind, leaving her in a forest that defies reason. Trees tower past reason, ancient canopies knitting overhead until the sun is gone. Branches twist and reach with intent, gnarled limbs drawn toward her as if aching to remember. At their center rises an oak so vast it swallows the horizon. Its trunk throbs with golden light, the radiance bleeding from deep within, where it waits beneath bark dense with age and power. Not theory. Not myth. *The Living Branch.*

She doesn't hear the words, she understands them. Not sound, but knowledge—immediate and whole, unfurling through her like blood memory.

Blood remembers what flesh forgets. The pattern completes when twelve unite.

It lasts only seconds, but its pressure lingers, heavy enough to disorient. Lumira pulls herself out of the vision's grip through sheer force of will, not magic. Her legs tremble, spine locks. She stays upright on pride alone—no magic, but a refusal to yield.

She won't kneel. Not to this. Not even now.

"How considerate," she murmurs, steadying her breath despite the hammering in her chest. "Though I'd have preferred coordinates. Maybe a map. Hell, even a note."

The ravens say nothing. They hold their perches, black eyes unblinking. No retreat. No advance. Only waiting.

The largest among them regards her with an intelligence that feels almost mortal—then lifts into the air with a single sweep of its wings.

The others follow, formation shifting mid-flight, curving eastward in perfect synchrony—every wingbeat charting a path toward Thallen Forest.

Heat surges from the Blood Key, stirring as if it recognizes what the ravens reveal. She's read signs before, but none this precise.

No translation required. No ritual words, no mysticism—only a truth too clear to deny.

This way. Soon.

Lumira's chambers greet her with the indifference of a space built for function, not comfort. She locks the door, checking visible and hidden mechanisms before activating the privacy wards installed years ago—subtle enchantments designed to discourage casual eavesdropping through methods best left unexamined.

Her mind reels from the vision: the Living Branch, the ancient trees, the presence—powerful, trapped, and waiting with inhuman patience.

It wasn't the birds directing her vision, but the force behind them. Older. And aware of it all.

She turns to the terrace doors, throwing them open to let the late-morning air clear her head. The ravens may be messengers, but she's not ready to be their puppet. Not when she doesn't know who pulls their strings.

Whatever they are, whoever controls them, they killed Emberly, or they let it happen. Either way, their debt to her will be paid.

She starts preparing for the journey, checking her pack. It holds weapons suitable for forest travel, navigation tools, and supplies for two days, enough to reach Thallen's outer ring and return, assuming everything goes according to plan.

Which, of course, it won't.

A shadow falls across the terrace. The largest raven—the same one that led the others in the training ground—is there, waiting on her windowsill.

She doesn't bother to acknowledge it. "I see subtlety's not on today's schedule."

The bird twitches, as if amused.

Of course it is.

She turns away, checking her timing against the guard rotations her runners have tracked for weeks: gaps and intervals scribbled on stolen ledgers, memorized by firelight. There's a three-day window—enough space to slip through the eastern defenses before reinforcements head south.

"Let them know," she said, her voice cold. "I'll retrieve their artifact. But I'm not their puppet. They touch my body or mind without a godsdamned invitation, and I'll set their forest alight from root to crown."

The bird's response is wordless: a slight nod, then flight. Purposeful. Direct. As if delivering her terms to whatever force waits beyond bark and bone.

She finishes her preparations, checking every detail twice—cover stories, diversions, exit plans.

The Brotherhood has dug deeper than she thought. Hadralis knows more than he's been told. And the ravens know it.

And she plans to use it all.

This isn't just politics anymore. It runs through the land, through feathers and ash. Maybe the gods are involved. Maybe they've been watching longer than she imagined.

She lingers only a moment at the window. The stars beyond are fixed, impassive. But the raven's absence hums. Whatever ancient forces speak through these birds, they've gravely misunderstood her.

Let them mistake cooperation for obedience for a little longer.

Tonight, they'll pay the price for underestimating the wrong Kyrvayne.

16

THE RETRIEVAL

Night folds over the palace, thick and deliberate, slipping into corners even lanterns forget. Lumira straps the final blade to her thigh in one smooth, practiced motion—ritual made muscle. Steel hugs her thigh like instinct, anchored in necessity. Beneath her tunic, the Blood Key thrums: a heartbeat not her own, steady and insistent. After the vision in the training yard, she knows what it means. The Living Branch waits, entombed in the root-riddled belly of Thallen Forest in Grovenar territory.

And tonight, Lumira will find it.

Beyond her window, the ravens gather. Not a single sound— only the gleam of copper catching moonlight. Sentinels shaped by prophecy. Their presence says more than noise ever could.

She turns away.

Let them bear witness.

Emberly's journal lies before her, the inked lines like veins pulsing with possibility—notes in her sister's spidery hand bloom across the parchment, coded with grief and genius. A sketch of the Naiad River, a shoreline circled twice in red, stands out amid warnings of "shadow witnesses." But that secret will wait.

A knock. Three sharp, two slow.

She sweeps Emberly's journal into the hidden compartment within her vanity—pressing the carved catch until it clicks shut—and turns as the door creaks open. Quinn enters, serene as snowfall.

Her handmaiden curtsies. "Your evening tea, Blood Descent."

Lumira's brow lifts. "You always make espionage feel so civilized." She accepts the tray with a fluid motion, porcelain clinking softly as she lifts it.

The door clicks shut behind Quinn. Her poise dissolves with it, edge bleeding through calm. "They believe in your illness. Court physicians are arguing over fevers and invented deficiencies."

"Perfect," Lumira murmurs. "And the patrols?"

Quinn unfurls a map from her apron's pocket. "Diverted east. Wrenna's misinformation worked better than expected. The southern tunnels are thin. Almost unguarded."

"Too easy." She doesn't raise her volume, but the edge cuts the same.

Quinn's mouth uplifts. "Exactly as planned."

Lumira turns toward the armoire, donning a cloak. The Blood Key answers with a quiet pulse, ready in its own way. "Quinn." She fastens the final clasp. "Hold the cover story. Keep the physicians circling and the court guessing."

"You'll have your silence." Quinn gives a brisk nod.

"Good." Lumira moves to the velvet-draped alcove in the corner of her chamber. "Send word to the others. It's time. They know what to do—noise at the gates, flickers in the wrong corridors. Keep the guards chasing phantoms."

Quinn nods once and turns to the wardrobe.

Lumira kneels beside the shallow cabinet at the alcove's base, pressing two fingers to the worn edge of the panel—a soft click. Hinges groan as it loosens, this same hidden passage Hadralis emerged from days ago, a secret taking form in the shadow. She hasn't forgotten. Now, it opens for her. The narrow corridor slopes downward, carved in stone and smudged with ash and time. Dust exhales from its throat, the stir of a memory waking.

"Quinn." The name leaves her lips without a glance behind.

"On it," Quinn replies, dragging the wardrobe into place.

By the time Lumira slips inside, the panel has closed again, and her room looks untouched, save for the slightly skewed rug that will cover the scuff.

The palace tunnels swallow sound. Walls press close, their surfaces slick with age and damp secrets—passageways once traversed by servants, soldiers, smugglers, and spies, and now by those loyal to Lumira when shadows are safer than halls.

For now, it's only her.

The lantern casts pale, flickering light across her tense face and the blade she won't sheath.

Secret entrances stitch the city together: garden walls, library floors, hidden columns. All of them feed into these tunnels under Altareth.

This time, they're her way out.

She goes alone, letting the weight of the stone settle over her. History presses in on all sides, but so does purpose.

Soft footsteps join hers a corridor later—Wrenna, emerging from a shadowed side passage, lantern held low, her satchel heavy with parchment and intent. She falls into step without a word.

A hundred paces on, another presence stirs—Ilara steps from the narrowing dark, her hood drawn, boots hushed over worn stone. The air around her hums faintly, like roots creeping on stone, Ilara carries the forest's memory in every step.

No orders are needed. The exchange is brief, decisive. The network topside is ready; they'll cover their exit.

Wrenna adjusts the lantern's glow to keep their path dim but readable.

Lumira's voice is low when it comes. "What are we walking into?"

Ilara's gaze is piercing. "There's a twenty-minute gap in the patrol rotation near the forest boundary. But they've brought in void-steppers. I saw the shadows writhe before they emerged."

"Shadowspire," Wrenna murmurs. "Not palace guards."

For a split second, Lumira thinks of her shadow—the one she can't seem to outrun. She shoves the thought aside. "They're not guarding." Observation settles into certainty. "They're circling. Waiting."

"Then we strike before they realize where the real threat lies." Wrenna unrolls the parchment they'd pulled from Emberly's painting and presses it flat against the tunnel wall. The ink has faded in places, but Emberly's careful marks remain—shadow roads sketched in the same stroke that once hid secrets in oil and pigment.

"The primary approach is through the western shadow roads. Emberly marked them for discreet transport: narrow, unused, but intact. Contingency paths branch south through older channels if patrols tighten sooner than expected."

"And the gear?"

"Distributed," Wrenna confirms. "Packed per Hadralis's specifications. I swapped the outer casings, nothing traceable."

Ilara's brow furrows. "He shouldn't have known what we'd need before we chose the route."

Wrenna exhales through her nose. "He's known a few things he shouldn't."

Lumira doesn't answer. She draws the Blood Key and sweeps it over each of them in turn. Ilara registers as expected—warm, loyal. But when it passes over Wrenna, the heat intensifies, too eager to trust.

"Interesting," Lumira murmurs, sliding the chain back into place.

Wrenna stiffens. "That's new."

"It sees something in you. Or someone keeping tabs on you."

Before Wrenna can speak, something in the air changes. Lumira angles herself toward the dark behind them, struck by how endlessly the tunnels stretch.

"We're not alone." The words slip from Lumira.

Ilara's expression darkens. "They're waiting for us to act."

Lumira lets the thought settle like dust, then directs the key toward the open throat of the tunnel behind them. It pulses cold—warning coiled in iron. Good. Proof enough.

"Stick to the plan. Trust nothing outside this circle. And if either of you dies before breakfast," she adds dryly, "don't expect a eulogy."

Ilara huffs. Wrenna smirks.

And they advance.

The tunnels narrow as they quicken their pace, the air thickening around each footfall—time slips, hard to measure beneath so much stone. Once dry, the space grows warmer with their shared breath—the closeness of three women bound not by orders, but by trust earned in darker places.

No words pass between them now, not because they fear what's left unsaid but because some truths resonate best unspoken.

They descend through low, arched corridors where roots creep like veins through ancient mortar. Somewhere above them, the palace sleeps in candlelit ignorance. Here, the city's underbelly unfurls in resistance.

A final turn brings them to a slant in the earth where stone meets soil—an opening no wider than a servant's burdened shoulders. Moss clings to its mouth, a secret held past its time.

Ilara goes first, slipping into the passage with the fluid ease of someone born between tree and shadow. The roots realign slightly around her steps, not parting, but adjusting, as if they know her tread and welcome it. Wrenna follows, tucking her satchel tight to her chest. Lumira comes last, brushing the frame once carved with the seal of Crimsun Territory. Faded and forgotten. But not erased.

They emerge into the night. Moonlight spills silver over the rise, catching in the soft undulation of moss and root. At the edge of the final bluff, where stone surrenders to soil and thorns, the forest rises like the pause before a storm: vast, bracing, waiting.

Thallen Forest.

Outside, the undergrowth swells—rich with bark and bloom and the unsettling sweetness of magic left untended. No border wall marks the edge, but the land changes all the same. This isn't a place one enters; it notices, measures, and decides if you belong.

Ilara drops to a crouch and scans the horizon. "We're inside the guard's sweep. This bluff shields the entrance. Patrols pass east and south. Fifteen minutes, maybe less."

Lumira adjusts the strap across her chest. "Then we don't waste it."

Wrenna leans in. "Do you feel that?"

The atmosphere constricts, the night holding its breath—no crickets, no owls, not even the wind dares to stir.

"I think the forest already knows we're here," Wrenna murmurs.

Ilara rises, unsheathing her blade—not in alarm, but in respect. "It knows me. Walk like you've earned your place."

Lumira steps forward, eyes fixed on the shadowed path opening between the trees. It wasn't carved by foot or wagon, it parted, as if the forest itself had chosen to make way.

She keeps moving. What matters is where she's going, not what she's left behind.

And they fade into Thallen Forest.

The trees close around them like a cathedral—not with bells and incense, but one older, formed by time and root. Massive trunks rise like columns, their bark scored with age. The canopy above tangles so thickly that moonlight falls only in trembling shards.

They've been traveling for hours—those slow, suspended hours between night and morning, when the cold seeps in and thoughts begin to bend. With every step, the forest draws tighter. The leaves don't rustle, they murmur truths etched into the bones of the world.

Ilara leads, steady and sure, the earth moving with her, stillness her strength.

Wrenna stays just behind, tracing the carved bark, matching each symbol to Emberly's notes by memory and feel.

And Lumira—Lumira carries the key against her heart, its rhythm no longer faltering. It beats in harmony with an ancient force, vibrant through the forest's surface.

She doesn't want to name it.

They come upon a clearing unmarked by any map, a place that seems to rise not from geography but from memory. The trees circle like sentinels, their trunks bowed in solemn council, roots entwined under the forest floor in a braid older than the borders of any territory. Overhead, branches arch and lace together, forming a canopy so precisely woven it feels intentionally designed, not by chance, but by will. Even the air feels suspended, as if the forest itself is waiting to exhale.

And then it comes—faint at first, like the air tightening, a dream brushing the edge of waking.

She doesn't hear him. Doesn't see him. But her body reacts before her mind can name it—every nerve pulled taut, every hair lifted by a recognition older than understanding.

Not fear or a threat. But attention, fixed and intimate, unbearably close.

Slowly, Lumira turns.

He stands at the edge of the clearing—not carved from shadow, but absorbed by it, as if the forest has drawn him in and isn't quite ready to let him go. The Shadowspire guard. Cloaked in black, hood drawn low, shadows swallow half his face—except for his mouth, curved just enough to remind her what it felt like in the dark. What she let brand her when she should have run. She should've screamed, but the fear took her first. And now he regards her with that same calm intensity, like she's already his—a secret he means to keep, body and soul.

Every time he appears, he unspools her from the inside out—never closer, never gone. Only that insufferable inevitability, a promise that he's always there, no matter how deep she tries to bury him. She hates how those stolen kisses endure, etched into her, wounds that refuse to close.

Her body goes rigid, instinct older than reason etched into bone by encounters like this one. Unfinished and inescapable.

His presence is a trespass she can't bar the door against, and worse—some traitorous part of her wants it left ajar.

The Blood Key warms against her chest, not a flare of danger but a conspiratorial hum. As if it, too, feels him in the dark, coiling closer, wrapping himself around her future whether she wants him there or not.

She doesn't call out. Doesn't signal Wrenna or Ilara. The moment stretches taut, refusing to snap.

A single, searing look and a claim he never voiced. Then the Shadowspire guard steps back and the forest swallows him whole: leaves rustle, darkness folds, and he is gone. The clearing stands empty once more, but the air refuses to exhale. She knows better than to believe he's truly gone. He never is.

A soft question from behind—Wrenna. "Did anyone else feel that?"

Ilara answers before Lumira can speak. "Yes."

Lumira doesn't turn around. Instead, she grazes the Blood Key, feeling it steady under her touch, and lets go of the tension she hadn't realized was there.

They aren't alone in this forest. But they aren't hunted, either. Not yet.

She turns from the clearing and the trees close behind her, a curtain falling on a performance not meant for an audience. "This isn't it," Lumira mutters. "The oak in the vision glows from within—light bleeding through the bark. We haven't reached it yet."

And without another word, the three of them slip further into the forest, swallowed by its darkness, guided not by certainty but by whatever has chosen to notice them.

The forest grows tighter around them, not with malice but with intention. Pressure building in between steps. Above, the forest curves into shadowed vaults, catching moonlight in scattered silver shards. No wind stirs. The trees aren't sleeping anymore. They're listening. The Blood Key grows warmer against Lumira's skin, the heat no longer pulsing but pressing, as if it recognizes what lies before them and isn't entirely sure it approves.

Wrenna pauses, moonlight catching on the parchment as it rustles softly in her gloves while she scans Emberly's markings. "There should be a split here." Her fingertip traces a faded line. "A marker. But…"

Ilara steps forward, eyes scanning the twisted trunks. "It's gone. The path reshaped itself again."

It is not empty but rather like the forest is pressing in, waiting to see what they'll do next. Lumira glances between the twisted trunks, trying to trace a way forward, but every path feels like a trap disguised in green. She turns slowly, scanning the dark.

Then, off the path, a quiet voice cuts through.

"You made it." Hadralis leans against the base of a twisted tree, half in shadow, arms crossed like he's been waiting the whole time, and maybe he has. The way the forest hangs around him is unnerving, as if the trees aren't sure whether to welcome or reject him.

Ilara's hand moves toward her blade. Wrenna halts, waiting at her side. Lumira doesn't flinch.

"We didn't need a welcome party."

There's a shift at the clearing's edge—soft, leaving the moss untouched. One moment, he's part of the tree line; the next, he steps forward, the forest almost urging him on. Hadralis stands nearby, posture loose but too disciplined to be mistaken for harmless. "The forest doesn't welcome," he says. "It decides." His focus drops to the chain under Lumira's cloak. "You knew that before you stepped this far."

No answer comes from Lumira.

From within his coat, he produces a small token: carved bone, edges worn smooth by age, its etched lines winding like roots through flesh. "This is the key. Use it right, and the forest lets you through—to the Living Branch, and back out alive."

Wrenna leans closer to study the markings by thin moonlight, but she doesn't reach for it.

Lumira lifts it with care, avoiding the faintest brush of contact. It's warm, as if it remembers every soul that ever held it.

Ilara's expression tightens. "That's old magic."

A faint smile flickers at Hadralis's mouth. "The forest taught it once. Even the oldest trees forget their own songs."

Wrenna arches a brow. "And yet you keep it tucked away."

There's resignation in Ilara's tone. "Shadowspire always did teach its own to hold things close."

"I earned it," he says, softer than the wind threading through the roots. "Shadowspire doesn't offer trust—or training."

The token sits heavy in Lumira's palm as she tests its edge with her thumb. "You weren't sent to guide us."

A ghost of amusement flickers in his eyes. "No."

"Then why stand here at all?" she presses.

What follows isn't sound, but something slower—patient, as if the forest has settled inside him. She waits for him to name Thara, to admit he's here on someone's leash, but he doesn't. There's no leash. Just roots, old and winding, pulling him deeper, the same way they pull her.

He doesn't look at her when he finally speaks. "This place doesn't test the ones who come seeking its secrets." The words seem to belong more to the forest than to him. "It tests whatever dares return—and expects to walk away unchanged."

No further explanation. He steps aside, and the forest yields with him, parting to reveal a cradle of roots—shaped with intent, not accident. It waits, older than any map, older than him. The forest does not speak, but its welcome is clear enough.

Without prompting, Lumira steps forward and places the token into the cradle.

At first, nothing stirs. Then, the forest exhales. Branches twist inward, enclosing the token, a treasure remembered after centuries. Bark creaks. Leaves shiver. A low pulse hums underfoot: deep, ancient, as if the earth itself turned over in its sleep.

Her crescent birthmark ignites—searing through her, a mark carved in fire. It is not a warning, it is a signal. The Living Branch is close.

A strange awareness stirs within her, as if the forest has inhaled her presence and exhaled its own into her bones. She doesn't see the creatures hidden in the canopy or hear the insects buzzing along the moss, but she *feels* them now—soft impressions of essence, brushing against her thoughts. Not apart from her. *With* her.

She gasps, clutching her chest where the birthmark throbs—answering the same magnetic call, two divine relics locked in resonance.

Through the trees, a slender path unfurls, lined with ferns, veiled in mist, scattered with light. Moonbeams bend strangely through the canopy, shimmering as if they, too, have been summoned.

And then, above, the slow grind of scale against bark. Nestled in the vaulted canopy, a Grove Dragon stirs—half-concealed in shadow. Its emerald eyes open, locking on Lumira with unnerving clarity. It isn't inquisitive or hostile, just certain. As if it recognizes what she carries without needing to understand it.

Wrenna lowers her lantern. Ilara bows.

The forest stirs around them, attentive and alive, opening a way forward.

Hadralis doesn't speak. He turns once, as if brushing the clearing with memory, then disappears into the trees.

Lumira doesn't track his retreat. Her mind is already on the path meant only for them.

They move in step, the three of them—past the shimmer, the silence, and the ever-knowing green—until the forest opens.

The grove unfolds, rousing with the patience of a place that remembers being forgotten. Perfectly round, the trees encircle the space like sentinels. Their trunks twist skyward, bark marked by weather and age, limbs arching into a vaulted canopy aglow with silver and gold—dusk held in a glassy shimmer.

And at the center—

The Living Branch.

It rests at the grove's heart—slender, spiraled, no longer than her forearm, slim enough to grasp with ease. Elegant yet wild, its form is shaped by intention, not age. A branch, yes, but no ordinary piece of wood. It holds its own gravity. Its own memory.

The bark is dark as ironwood, smooth where it isn't ridged, and laced with gold filaments that weave through faint, glowing veins—each pulse keeping time with a force just beyond perception. The glow isn't constant; it throbs with a rhythm all its own. It neither towers nor gleams, yet radiates purpose, waiting centuries for her alone. A divine artifact cloaked in simplicity, fashioned to endure rather than dazzle.

Standing before it, she doesn't need the Blood Key's guidance, though it stirs in quiet recognition. She rests her fingers against the branch, warmth meeting her—free of flame or spell, yet undeniably real. Elemental. A pause steeped in unspoken truths, like sunlight remembered in the bark.

The gold threads brighten, not in alarm, but as if completing a circuit, accepting the contact. A current surges from the point of contact, racing up her arm and down her spine.

Behind her, Wrenna steadies. "She never saw this clearly— not even through the ravens." The truth unwinds slow, fragile. "Emberly only reached the edge."

"Then we've already gone farther." The words are quiet, but they land.

Ilara says nothing, fingers settling on the hilt, ready.

The grove holds still—no rustle, no sound. Only a sense of knowing, as if the forest has already decided.

The Blood Key throbs once while the Living Branch remains steady in her grip.

She does not feel chosen.

She feels discovered.

A gentle wind flows through the treetops, a calm reminder. It's time to go.

They turn as one, and leave the past untouched. Some things, once claimed, are meant to be carried forward.

Then the rupture comes—sudden and brutal. The air thickens with pressure, crushing, the pause before a scream.

The forest no longer waits. It braces.

The Blood Key turns cold, ice spidering from the chain like frost across glass. Lumira freezes. She doesn't hear anything, but she knows.

"What was that?" Wrenna asks, voice tight.

Ilara scans the trees. "We're not alone in the grove."

The hush unspools, thread by thread. From the east, the forest lurches, not physically but in intent. The air no longer feels sacred; it feels damned and strangled.

And then—footsteps. Heavy. Plentiful. Loud enough to bruise the air. Intent crashes through the trees, unmasked and unrepentant—nothing restrained about it. Shapes flicker between the trunks, impossible to count in the dark, a single body in motion. And behind them, darkness blacker than shadow clings to their heels, pulsing through the underbrush.

Ilara tenses, one breath from drawing, when a shout cracks through the trees, close and commanding.

"Secure the Blood Descent. Leave the artifact, she's the priority. She's connected to it."

The words hit, as a stone through stained glass. Male—clipped, trained. Out of place. Uninvited. And not alone.

Brotherhood, Lumira mouths to the others, though the word tastes uncertain even now. They shouldn't be this close, but the tone is unmistakably sure, unnervingly organized.

"Shit." Wrenna inhales—a quick, shallow pull of air. "They know."

Lumira's grip on the Living Branch tightens—the Blood Key shudders, its cold intensifying.

"They're sealing the paths behind us." Wrenna's eyes dart around them. "Trying to funnel us toward the cliffs or the river. Force us into a trap."

"No," Ilara replies, stepping toward the trees. "They *think* they can. That's different."

Above, the canopy stirs, not by the wind.

Wings.

A Grove Dragon peels from the mist-thick branches, its massive body the shape of a dance forgotten by time. Its scales shimmer like rain-slicked bark, mottled in shades of deep green, ash black, and glints of copper where the light catches at the perfect angle. Moss clings to its joints, and ferns grow from the crooks of its wings. Then another arrives. And another. Ancient. Terrifying in their grace.

"Wrenna." Ilara speaks with certainty. "Take her. Get to Pigments & Pints."

"What about you?" Lumira demands, already stepping forward.

Ilara smiles—that crooked, wild thing she wields as defense. Wind-tossed. Knowing. "Someone has to show the dark it's not the only thing that bites."

She turns and speaks a word older than language, and the trees bend closer to hear. A golden shimmer blooms beneath the soil, slow and patient as wrath. Leaves tremble. Roots tighten—the forest starts to respond to her call.

"Go," she demands, already facing what comes next. Then Ilara is gone, vanishing into the trees with her Grove Dragons, all flame, fury, and motion, as if the forest has unleashed its wrath in her shape.

The ground trembles, shadows collapsing fast around them.

Wrenna turns, every line of her body suddenly rigid. "We'll only have one shot at this."

"I know." Lumira checks the canopy. "You navigate. I'll cover."

A smaller dragon drops through the branches—sleek and coiled for speed, its scales veined with moss and smoke. Wings snap wide like banners unfurling. Wrenna scrambles up first, pivoting into position behind the ridged neck.

Lumira doesn't hesitate. She vaults up after her, the Living Branch tucked against her side, gripping the thick edge of the dragon's spine as if it were the hilt of a sword waiting to be drawn.

Below them, the forest roars. Above, the dragon takes flight. They tear through the canopy—leaves slicing past in a blur of green and shadow, bark, wind, and sky. The air tightens. The treetops fall away.

And then—they break through, the world exhaling them into the night.

They surge into the open sky, mist trailing behind.

Far below, the forest churns. Shadows move in deliberate lines—formations precise enough to defy accident, ruthless enough to strip away doubt. Whether it's the Brotherhood or a darker force, it doesn't matter. They're being hunted.

But up here, they are untouchable, for a moment that steals the world away from them.

Moonlight kisses the dragon's scales below them. The Blood Ravens are waiting there, etching graceful loops against the sky—a dozen, maybe more—circling, guiding, and unseen. Their flight isn't random; it weaves into a shape and rhythm, a sky-written sigil that pulses with intent.

Lumira's head snaps back. "I see it," she whispers. "They're showing us the way."

The Grove Dragon rumbles, its wings adjusting to Wrenna's grip and Lumira's command. It doesn't follow the pattern itself, but it senses the urgency in their bodies and the hunger in their choices, and obeys.

From behind, Wrenna says, "Then hold on."

And the Grove Dragon dives.

Straight into the dark.

They tear through the night, wings carving open the waiting dark. The sky above Altareth opens like a wound, moonlight bleeds over rooftops and towers tangled in slumber. They circle once, low and wide, before the dragon folds its wings and drops toward the far edge of the city's lower district.

Pigments & Pints rises from the street below—windows shuttered, chimneys cold, and roof sloped steeply with clay tiles faded by sun and rain. The dragon touches down with surprising grace, its moss-mottled body settling against the roof's slope as if it has landed there a hundred times before.

Lumira presses a hand to the dragon's scaled shoulder in thanks as she dismounts. The steep roof pitches beneath her boots, slick in the moonlight, and she braces against the ridge beam to keep from slipping. Beside her, Wrenna drops down, too, boots skidding before she catches her balance with a hissed curse.

The dragon nods in acknowledgment, the moss along its brow catching a faint glint of light. Then, with barely a sound, it turns and vanishes into the streaked sky above.

They flow as one, slipping to the rusted maintenance hatch under the chimney eaves. Wrenna crouches first, working the warped latch free with a twist she's done a dozen times before. The hatch groans open, and they slip through, dropping into the attic. The narrow service ladder creaks under their weight.

They land behind the supply counter, soft as a brushstroke in the artist's café. The walls hold the ghost of cinnamon and ink—warmth lingering where memory can't forget. Moonlight slips through the rafters, catching on drifting dust and splintered glass.

Below, the city dreams on, unaware of the divine slipping through its chimney flues. It is not yet dawn. They have not yet been noticed.

Wrenna nods toward the back door, voice level, untouched by urgency. "The eastern corridors will hold. Keep to the shadows."

Lumira snorts. "Oh, good. Never done that before."

A smile flickers across Wrenna's face as she presses a ribbon-wrapped bundle into Lumira's palm. "Sugar helps."

Lumira arches a brow. "You think I can be bribed with pastries?"

The grin that answers her is pure trouble. "You already have been."

Lumira rolls her eyes and grabs the bundle, its warmth sinking into her palm as she pushes through the door and steps into the alley. Behind her, the door is closed and the soft scrape of the lock slides home.

The way back to the palace cuts through garden walls and servant paths: veiled passages few remember and fewer dare to use. Her network has done its part. She slips past distracted patrols and illusion-slicked walls, a shadow until she reaches the eastern entrance, where two cloaked figures wait. They don't ask or speak. One simply nods and opens the old door carved into the stone, the one closest to Emberly's rooms.

Fitting.

Lumira slips through as the palace closes behind her. When she reaches her chambers, the sky is beginning to pale, thin streaks of silver brushing the highest towers. Inside, Quinn is there, fluid as she sets a fresh tray of tea at the bedside. Their eyes meet—understanding passing between them. She gives a small, knowing smile, then leaves the room, the door closing gently behind her.

The latch clicks shut as Lumira turns the key in the lock, then she crosses the room without a sound. Passing the table, she sets the ribbon-bound bundle down before sinking to her knees at the vanity, her palm finding the hidden catch under the drawer.

A dull snap. The panel opens.

She reaches within her tunic, drawing the Living Branch from where it's nestled against her side—warm, like it holds the echo of her body heat. Carefully, she lays it into the shallow hollow behind the drawer's false bottom. Her fingertips linger on the hidden wood. The stillness in the room isn't peace—it's the weight that settles when all senses tilt toward the same unspoken threat, clinging long after the danger has passed.

She presses the panel closed until it clicks, then crosses to the small table, letting her touch skim the ribboned bundle she'd set down earlier. Its shape is familiar and comforting—the same pastry Emberly used to sneak to her when the nights dragged on, when her bones ached from holding composure, and sleep felt miles out of reach.

The chair takes her weight, the ache of the night catching up all at once—muscle by muscle, thought by thought. For the first time in hours, she lets herself sit.

With a gentle tug, the ribbon loosens. A honeyed pastry: golden, flaky, filled with spiced almonds, and faintly warm. A rare indulgence. A relic of care tucked among chaos.

She bites into it—and for one stolen moment, the sugar soothes everything. Syrup and cinnamon bloom on her tongue, cutting through the weight that has clung to her since dusk. For a moment, she is not a Blood Descent or the keeper of anything sacred. She is a girl, worn down to skin and willpower.

But sweetness is fleeting. The forest returns like a ghost, roots and shadows curling through her mind, reminding her of what waits to be carried.

Memory coils tight—storm-gray eyes pressing from the dark, not just seeing but binding. Something unseen has already claimed her.

And it isn't done.

17

THE SHAPE OF HUNGER

The honey clings to her lips, sticky and sweet, as she leans back against the chair, exhaustion pressing into her bones. The pastry is gone, but it lingers—rich and unshakable, lodged at the back of her throat like a truth she isn't ready to name. The sensation ghosts over her, an old bruise that refuses to fade.

It's not the sugar that unsettles her. It's him.

The Shadowspire guard.

She can still feel the weight of him in the clearing—storm-gray, unreadable. He hadn't seen her as an enemy or ally, but as a force he hadn't yet decided to fight or follow. An unknown with the instincts of a predator.

Without rushing, she unhooks the last of her gear, placing each blade in perfect order. From its hidden compartment across the room, the Living Branch sits at the back of her mind—its power pressing in, sealed away. An artifact of immense power rests within reach, but that's not what's caught beneath her composure.

That heat, that ache—it's his. And it's not gone.

She rolls her shoulders, willing the tension away, but her body refuses to yield. It remembers, in the ache that drags behind her knees, the slow heat that sits low in her belly and refuses to fade.

And the worst part? It wasn't imagined—it had happened. Undeniable. Unshakable. An uninvited flash of his voice from the summit echoes through her mind. *"You're losing your touch, little fox. I counted at least three openings where I could have killed you."* She'd scoffed, played it off like a jest—but the way he said it, a man recalling exactly how close they'd once been, lodged deep in her mind.

Because he had known.

And so had she.

The words slither through her mind, wrap around her spine, tighten around her ribs. Fast. Unforgiving. Her body understands first.

A flicker of memory—intense and vivid—rises and envelops her senses.

Samhain night, two years ago.

While the palace prepared for garlands and gold-laced wine, she officially opted for a different purpose for the night— intelligence gathering. But the truth ran deeper: she wanted no part in the celebration. No masks. No posturing. No endless waltz of pleasantries offered by people who would trade her name like currency.

She wore intentionally distressed leather, tailored for mobility and crafted to conceal her rank while allowing her weapons to remain visible. It was a night intended for risk, but risk on her terms.

The tavern's appeal had always been its rough edges—scarred tables darkened by old burn marks and bloodstains, shadows thick with smoke and intent. The air reeked of Darkroot cider and burnt herbs, sharp enough to sting the back of her throat with every breath. Patrons wrapped themselves in anonymity and intrigue, speaking in dialects long since scrubbed from the palace's education.

It wasn't safe; however, survival was never the point.

Lumira knew exactly how to start the brawl: a spilled drink, a pointed insult about someone's questionable lineage, and the right jostle near a volatile patron to ignite the room. A dozen fists followed, none aimed at her. All of it was noise—used to mask a meeting in the corner, with a contact whose accuracy blurred the line between help and betrayal.

And then—

She spotted him across the room with the particular awareness she reserved for potential threats—smoke among flame, a battered glass of Ashbrand whiskey turning lazy circles in his hand. He hadn't joined the surrounding brawl—only watched it unfold, cool and unreadable in the shadow of a hooded cloak, despite the tavern's heat.

His posture screamed professional training beyond that of a typical guard or mercenary. The way his weight was distributed suggested combat readiness in the guise of a casual stance—limbs angled for optimal weapon access, eyes tracking the room with the precision of assessment, not idle observation.

A head taller than her at least, a wall wrapped in cloak and leather. She couldn't see the muscle, but she could feel it—waiting, compressed, more than enough to shatter the room if he chose to unleash it.

Their eyes met briefly across the chaotic room, storm-gray with gold flecks that caught the lamplight like molten metal. There was nothing idle in his stare. It struck fast, igniting a heat she couldn't blame on the tavern fires or the exertion from the fight she had orchestrated.

His hood shadowed most of his face, but his mouth remained visible, cut clean—a feature that needed no voice to command. There was restraint in it, not smugness. A mouth that never begged, only sinned. And she hated how much she wanted to ruin it.

The intensity he demanded suggested more than attraction: recognition, not of her face, but of the truth masked from the world. He sliced through every layer of her disguise with unnerving precision—through the leather, the false dialect, the carefully modulated posture—until he saw her for what she truly was.

But he hadn't reacted like the others when they caught the scent of her bloodline. There was no deference, no thinly veiled ambition. Only amusement, interest honed to a point, and a calm that settled in her bones and refused to leave.

Being the center of the room was nothing new to her. Men had pursued her title, her rank, and the challenge of unraveling what was cold and kept out of reach. They arrived with flattery as slick as oil, awkward charm, and a hunger that reached without permission.

However, his approach was distinct.

There were no compliments, no feigned seduction. He simply appeared beside her as the brawl reached its crescendo, slipping through the chaos with a lethal poise that spoke of training far beyond tavern fights.

"Interesting technique," he said, as she incapacitated a particularly persistent drunk with a single, well-placed strike. "Unusual education for someone raised to wave from balconies."

The comment struck her like a knife—too accurate to be mere speculation. He hadn't discovered her identity by chance. He had seen through her from the beginning, beyond the faded leathers and gentle accent, beyond the stance and the ground-in dirt beneath her nails.

Not a coincidence. Recognition.

"Perhaps you've only met useless nobility," she replied, cool as cut glass, despite the traitorous heat blooming low in her abdomen at his nearness.

His laugh surprised her—low, genuine, entirely unbothered by the barbs in her tone. "Perhaps I have." He caught an oncoming brute by the wrist and redirected him effortlessly. The man stumbled backward, dazed, collapsing in a heap before realizing he'd been handled. "Though clearly not in present company." His tone remained unfazed.

The way he moved called to a part of her built for war, not romance. It was clean and contained, an economy of motion that spoke not of brute strength but of practiced lethality. Every step, every shift, and every calculated use of momentum revealed training that surpassed tavern scraps and barroom swagger.

Her interest stirred, despite herself. "Careful," she said, tone honed to gleam. "Someone might mistake that for a compliment."

He didn't flinch. "Some company deserves better walls… and fewer witnesses."

She should have bristled and walked away with some clipped remark and a bruised ego trailing in her wake. But she didn't.

Because the truth was that she wanted out.

Not only from the tavern but also from the careful control she wore, a mask she never dropped. Of the lineage, the pressure, and the endless choreography of noble expectations. And this stranger, with his storm-gray eyes and maddening calm, offered a kind of certainty she hadn't realized she was craving.

An opportunity to let go.

The suggestion in his tone didn't provoke—it ignited. Heat curled through her spine, unmistakable, seeping through defenses forged for strategy, not seduction. Her body didn't hesitate. It recognized the moment for what it was: invitation, challenge, and release.

He reached out—scarred knuckles, ink curling along the back like smoke—and she took it, cider burning in her veins, fueling a recklessness she hadn't allowed herself in ages.

Their walk to The Shadow's Rest was laced with verbal sparring, testing boundaries rather than enforcing them. He revealed little.

She revealed less. However, every glance, sideways smile, and evasive answer served as foreplay in its own right.

And though she told herself she was reading him, studying how he asked questions without asking and coaxed truths from her without force or flattery, the truth was more straightforward. She wanted him—not for answers, nor leverage.

Only for the night.

She hadn't intended to go with him. Not truly. She told herself it was about shadows, anonymity, the way his presence offered sanctuary without demand. But her palm met his, their clasp effortless—familiar in a way that defied time. As if it remembered.

The Shadow's Rest welcomed them—dim and discreet, tucked behind an alley scrawled with ancient sigils. It was the kind of place where questions dissolved into smoke and sins never saw sunrise.

He didn't press her, nor did he touch her again until the door shut behind them. And then—

Before she could react, fingers caught her hips—firm enough to freeze her in place.

His gaze met hers in the dark, storm-gray and unreadable. But in the silence between them, the message was clear. He wasn't asking. He was offering. And yet, he waited—infuriating in his restraint, letting her be the one to close the distance.

So she did. She surged forward—a crashing tide, fingers tangled in his cloak, pulling him down to her mouth with a force that signaled no more games.

The kiss was not gentle.

It was a clash of heat, instinct, and carefully hidden truths colliding in the open. Teeth, breath, bodies—all fire and friction. His mouth met hers with restrained hunger, long denied yet never desperate, certain of what he wanted and how to take his time getting it.

He tasted of winter spice and dark heat, smoke swallowed before the burn could settle. His touch slid beneath her jacket, not fumbling, not pleading—claiming. But only where she allowed.

And, gods, she allowed.

Every barrier she'd spent years constructing—stone by polished stone—cracked under the weight of him, of this, of the aching, glorious surrender that curled her toes and set fire to her lungs.

He edged her toward the narrow bed, slow and relentless, breaking only when air became necessary. Even then, he said nothing. He only stayed, present in a way that scraped against her nerves.

She stood at the edge of the bed, chest lifting, lips bruised and tingling, pulse a drumbeat in her throat. Her fingers hovered over the buckle at her waist.

He stayed where he was, waiting. For her. For yes. For consent that resided not in her body but also in her blood.

She unbuckled the strap with precision that felt like defiance. Then she whispered, "Don't go easy."

His smirk was the last thing she saw before her world vanished in flames. He didn't go easy; he went slow—deliberate, maddening, leaving her shaking by the time his mouth found her throat, his tongue tracing the hollow, a map and a promise. He kissed the pulse there, then let his lips wander down the line of her collarbone—pausing where the crescent birthmark burned hot beneath his mouth.

She gasped when he bit down hard enough to sting. His mouth soothed the bite instantly afterward, his tongue trailing in a molten stripe that sent lightning down her spine.

But he did not stop there.

His tongue made slow, patient circles across her chest—warm and steady—before drifting lower. Not simply tasting. Memorizing.

Palms braced along her ribs, thumbs brushing over her nipples until they pebbled under his attention. Then his mouth closed around one—gentle at first, then deeper, until her back arched and a sound broke free before she could swallow it.

A low hum pulsed through her, cataloging her reactions like scripture—trembles noted, stored.

He descended further, no hesitation in the way his mouth continued its descent.

Heat bloomed as lips followed the curve under her breast, down the flat of her abdomen, circling her navel in slow, spiraling fire. His touch followed, broad and possessive, sliding over her hips, settling firm at her sides, thumbs moving slow circles where thigh met torso. He moved with excruciating intent, his touch orchestrated to devastate.

And he was talking now—soft murmurs against her skin, rough with desire. "Look at you." He was rough with awe. "Gods, you're soaked."

His fingers slipped between her thighs, teasing through the slick heat gathered there, and he groaned—deep and guttural, like the wetness on his skin was the most sacred offering he'd ever been given.

"All this for me?" he murmured, brushing his mouth over her inner thigh, biting gently before licking the sting away. "So eager. So perfect."

She tried to respond, but the words dissolved into a whimper as his tongue followed, trailing higher. Closer. Circling the inside of her thigh, then dipping to taste her. And when his mouth finally found the center of her, his tongue sliding through her folds—a secret learned by heart—she shattered.

Because it was not merely hunger, it was not simply lust. It was an act of worship.

And he didn't stop. If anything, he devoured her with greater hunger—desperate for absolution, licking her slowly, religiously, his tongue curling against her clit before retreating, only to return harder, hungrier. His hands gripped her thighs, holding her open like he needed to be there, needed to know every inch of her. He moaned against her, like her taste undid him—like she was his salvation.

Then his tongue dragged lower, circling her entrance—slow and torturous—before plunging inside, stroking deep while his nose pressed firm against her clit. She cried out, body shaking, legs locking around his shoulders, but he didn't ease up. Not for a second.

Doesn't even pause.

He licked her in a steady, devastating rhythm, tongue moving inside her, while his grip on her thighs held firm, grounding her like he feared she'd vanish if he let go. Flicks, curls, and deep presses came with purpose—drawing more slick from her with every pass. Soon she was panting, begging, clinging to the sheets like she might otherwise fall into nothingness.

She reached for his hair, threading through the strands and tugging hard as her climax built—fevered, biting, and overwhelming enough to scare her.

And when she came—gods, when she came—it was with a full-body quake that tore her apart.

Nevertheless, he didn't stop.

He held her through it, tongue softening, drawing out each aftershock and tremble until she sagged against the mattress, boneless and wrecked. Lips pressed to her inner thigh slowly and lingeringly, as if he were grateful for the privilege.

When she blinked back into awareness, he was above her, bracing himself on his forearms, eyes searching hers.

"You said not to go easy," he murmured roughly, brushing his lips against hers. "I obliged."

This time, when he kissed her—really kissed her—she tasted herself on his tongue, and gods help her, she kissed him back as if she wanted to drown in it. His mouth devoured hers like she was the one thing he wasn't supposed to touch. It was as if he had waited for this.

His composure never wavered, all coiled heat—tempered and taut. He touched her with the certainty of someone who had already memorized her, every contour mapped with his tongue and etched into him.

When he rose, smearing his mouth dry with a rough swipe, only half sated, she grabbed his collar and kissed him hard. Her taste lingered on his tongue. Her ruin hadn't left him yet. He growled, the sound vibrating through her bones—and then they were moving. Staggering. Half wrestling. Lips colliding. Cloth shredded in a frenzy, as though it had earned their wrath.

She dragged his cloak down his arms, knuckles whitening as she clutched the fabric, refusing to let go until it crumpled at his feet. He reached for her again, every motion a suggestion over skin: bare lines, soft curves, craving the next gasp, the next surrender.

Boots thudded somewhere behind the bed.

They didn't pause, not even when he spun her and pinned her briefly against the wall, mouth devouring the underside of her jaw as she fumbled with the fastening at his waist. She laughed into his throat, and then he was kissing her again, walking her backward toward the bed with coordination only sinners possessed.

They tumbled onto the mattress in a tangle of limbs, her knees bracketing his hips as the last scraps of clothing vanished with desperate, half-mad efficiency. She barely remembered tugging his shirt off.

But then, there they are.

Naked. Shaking. Enveloped in shadows so thick they could've been in a void, somehow making everything more real.

She burned under him—sparks in the scrape of his palms and the bite of his teeth, heat ready to catch.

"Tell me what you want," he rasped, lips brushing her throat.

"You," she breathed. "All of you." And that's when she slid down his body again.

His outline was all angles, haloed in shadow. His face remained obscured. Not even the faintest glint of an eye or edge of a jaw appeared. Only the memory of that mouth—already etched into her bones—and the way it had rewritten her understanding of pleasure.

She wanted to see him.

The mystery unsettled her more than any revealed face ever could. He could have been anyone. Anything. A god. A beast. A myth woven in sensation. Her body didn't care; it responded as if it knew him anyway.

The anonymity inspired her recklessness.

Her limbs tangled with his as she climbed over him, the weight of her body pressing him into the mattress, but not with force. With intent. With the mastery of someone who knew exactly what she wanted and how to take it.

And she wanted this.

She leaned down, her mouth brushing what she believed to be his jaw—searching in the dark, tasting sweat, chasing his shape without ever seeing. Warmth stuttered against her ear, and her lips curved into a wicked smile.

She slid lower—fingertips gliding down his chest, nails scraping lightly through the soft trail of hair below his navel. A beat passed before he moved again, and she smiled into the dark.

His face remained a mystery. But everything else? She had memorized it by touch.

She took her time as her hand slid to the base, relishing the heat and weight of him.

"Fuck," he muttered, the word dragged from deep within.

Good. She wanted him wrecked before she began. Leaning in, her lips brushed the tip, tongue flicking once over the crown—

light as air, teasing. And then, without warning, she took him into her mouth.

Not gently or shyly—all in.

He swore again, louder this time, his hips jerking instinctively, but she held him down with one arm flung across his stomach, her forearm pinning him in place. Her other hand worked in tandem with her mouth, stroking what her lips couldn't reach, her tongue circling him with maddening precision.

She established a rhythm—slow at first, then faster, then slow again—unpredictable, never rushed. In that moment, she owed him.

He reached for her, fingers threading into her hair, not to steer but to steady. His grip tightened the moment she hollowed her cheeks and sank deeper. She moaned around him, letting the vibration do its work.

And gods—he groaned, deep and raw, as if the sound was trapped in his chest and she had pulled it free.

He tasted of heat and hunger, desire's metallic edge barely held in check. She can't see his face, but she doesn't need to—his thighs tense, voice splintering, and she feels him coming undone.

"You're going to be the death of me," he choked out.

She eased back, tongue slick with mischief, smirk curling through every syllable like a dare. "Not yet." Then she went right back down—deeper this time, jaw relaxing as she took him to the back of her throat. She held him there until his whole body seized, then eased back, lips locked, tongue mapping the long, unyielding heat of him.

His curse broke into a guttural sound, his grip tightened in her hair. "Don't—" he managed, equal parts warning and desperation.

She thrived on it. "Let go," she rasped, lips dragging up and across his tip. "I want to feel you come undone."

He was close, she felt it in the way he trembled and tried to hold himself motionless.

A ragged laugh slipped out—part disbelief, part surrender. "You're insatiable, little fox."

The words slid over her like oil and heat: sudden and unexpected. A name no one had ever called her before, but the moment he said it, it felt as if he always had. And part of her liked it more than she should.

She gave him everything. Her mouth. Her hand stroking the base of him. The other braced at his hip, holding him steady as she worked him—wet and relentless. She sucked harder, quickening her pace, tongue flicking in rhythm until—

He shattered.

With a hoarse groan, he came undone in her mouth, hips stuttering as she swallowed him as if it was holy communion, not stopping until his muscles slackened and his chest rose like he'd survived a war.

Despite everything, she hadn't truly seen him. But in the dark, she smiled against his thigh because she had heard him. Felt him break. And in that aching, weightless moment, he was hers.

She didn't allow him much time to recover.

Flushed and panting, she dragged herself up his body, every inch of her brushing against him, a threat dressed as desire. Her lips found his throat: nipping, licking, tasting the sweat blooming across heated flesh. She felt him hardening against her—already— and it lit a fresh ache between her thighs.

He grunted when her hips settled over him, and she reached down, curling her fingers around his length, slick from her mouth and the last remnants of his release. He twitched in her grip.

"You're not done," she said, voice soft but unyielding—each word brushing his ear like velvet and steel. "Not until I say you are."

He laughed, barely. More tremor than sound. "Is that so?"

She didn't answer. She guided him to her entrance, dragging the tip through her folds, letting him feel how desperate she was. The stretch of him was deep, every inch an ache, and as she sank onto him, her mouth parted in a gasp that neared a sob.

His fingers gripped her thighs.

She grasped his wrists. Not rough—but firm. Commanding. Then she lifted them, pressing them into the mattress above his head.

"Don't move." She frayed at the edges, lips brushing his ear. "No touching. Just feel."

He did not resist, and that made it worse—better.

She rocked her hips once, slow and deep, as his breath broke ragged, muscles tensing as if he wanted to grab, flip, and own her.

But he didn't.

She had him pinned, his wrists trapped under her hands like some dark invocation, and she sank into him again, grinding down until she felt him everywhere.

Each roll of her hips sent fire licking up her spine. Every slide and slick drag of his cock inside her made her whimper, soft, involuntary sounds pulled from someplace deeper than breath.

She clenched around him—searching for friction, for release, for that perfect edge. Her thighs trembled from the strain; sweat bloomed across her chest as she chased it.

She was close, too close. Pleasure knotted hot and tight, pulsing with each grind of her hips and maddening drag of him inside her. All she knew was the tension—tight, blistering, almost overwhelming—and the way her body clenched around him in greedy rhythm, searching for that final, glorious break.

Her rhythm grew ragged—whimpers twisting into hoarse, high-pitched cries, nearly a scream. She didn't let go of his wrists. Didn't stop or slow. Because she was falling and she meant to take him with her.

"Fuck, I'm close," he growled, the strain evident, trembling below her.

"Then hold on," she gasped, picking up her rhythm. "I'm not finished with you." She rode him hard—no finesse, all hunger. Her breasts bounced with every grind, her nails dragging red lines down his forearms as the pleasure mounted.

But then, the contact broke—his touch abrupt and certain—and suddenly, she wasn't in charge anymore.

In one fluid motion, he flipped them, her back hitting the mattress with a sharp exhale, his body caging hers in the dark. His hips snapped forward—deep, possessive.

Her cry split the air.

He thrust again—faster now, unforgiving, driving into her with the kind of power that said *mine*, even if neither of them would ever dare speak it aloud. Her legs wrapped around his waist instinctively. Her nails dug into his back.

"Thought you were in control," he rasped into her throat.

She arched up to meet him. "Let me pretend."

He grinned against her neck. "Not a chance." Then he thrust into her—deep and devastating. His rhythm was relentless, built to ruin. Each stroke hit a place that made her gasp, made her claw at his back, made her forget everything but the sensation of being filled, again and again.

She kissed whatever she could reach, her mouth wild against his shoulder, her nails leaving desperate crescents across his spine. Curses tangled with prayers on her tongue, none coherent, all his.

And when she was about to shatter—

He slowed.

Pressed deeper.

Held her there, pulsing and aching.

Torment, drawn out like a bowstring.

She writhed beneath him, her whole body begging without words. And she broke when he finally gave in and surged forward with a growl that echoed through her bones.

Harder than before, louder. Her cry was raw with reverence, spine arching, body clenching tight around him in a shuddering wave.

He followed her over the edge seconds later, spilling into her with a hoarse, broken sound that ripped straight from his chest.

And then came silence, thick with aftershock and trembling restraint.

But not done.

Not with each other.

The air between them felt heavier than before—a raw charge neither dared to name.

He didn't stir, not at first. He hovered above her, chest heaving, muscles trembling from restraint and release. His chest rose and fell against hers, their sweat mixing, heartbeats syncing. With her legs wrapped around him in the dark, he was reduced to shadow and weight against her.

She could feel the way he watched her. Not with softness. Not with guilt—with appetite.

A need that didn't fade after climax, but grew.

He rolled off her slowly, the mattress shifting, and she turned, drawn to the sound and scent of him. A smirk danced at the edge of her lips. Not sweet. Wicked.

She could taste him on her tongue and feel him between her thighs—a delicious ache. "You're not very good at letting someone else lead," she said, hoarse but smug.

"And you're not very good at giving up," he replied, equally wrecked.

A dry sound escaped her—rough, but not quite a laugh. "Then it's a good thing we've got hours."

A beat.

Then he was on her again. Not gentle. Not urgent—intentional.

Warmth skimmed her ribs, a thumb brushing beneath her breast—as if retracing ground it had once conquered. His mouth followed—slow, slow, slow—dragging over the curve of her hip as she twisted to straddle him again.

They didn't speak after that.

They fought with tongues, searing touch feeding searing touch—a rhythm of heat and hunger, power trading hands with the rise and fall of breath. One moment, she was on top, hissing through her teeth as she rode him until he begged. Then next, he had her on her knees, fist knotted in her hair, the other splayed possessively over her spine as he drove into her with a rhythm that left her clawing the bed for mercy she didn't want.

It wasn't lovemaking, but a war of wills.

Orgasms became victories.

Surrender was a calculated strategy.

And every hour dragged them deeper into a hunger neither of them knew how to express—only how to chase.

When exhaustion finally pulled her under—limbs trembling, lips swollen, thighs aching—he remained a mystery beside her.

He remained faceless. Nameless.

But gods—she already knew she'd remember how he touched her for the rest of her life.

Sleep came not as surrender but collapse—her body giving out long before her mind could catch up, limbs slack against unfamiliar sheets, heart steadying in the wake of ruin.

And when she woke, he was gone.

No name. No note. Only the ache in her hips and the phantom heat of his mouth on her skin. Her cloak had been folded neatly over the chair. Her dagger was untouched—as if he'd never been there.

As if he hadn't touched her at all.

As if he hadn't destroyed her.

Even now, she lies below the hush of her ceiling, barely moving, the memory wound tight and pulsing low in her belly—unspent, unfinished.

The room waits, breathless, but her body hums with it. The ache persists. It lingers, heat between her thighs, in the places he touched, in the tension that snapped the moment she took over.

She rises, slow and bare, and crosses to the bed.

Cool sheets greet her, but the heat clings—curling behind her knees, blooming in the hollow between her thighs. She sinks under the covers, palm gliding down her stomach to where his mouth had lingered. The reverence in his touch. The slow spiral of his tongue. The low, guttural praise when he'd found her soaked for him. The memory alone pulls a sigh from her lips. Her hand drifts lower, circling the ache in tight, deliberate circles—mirroring the maddening rhythm he'd left in her. Her hips rise, chasing it.

She's never seen his face, and maybe that's why he remains so sharp in her mind, faceless yet unforgettable. The rest of him lives vivid behind her eyes: the weight of his body, the sound of his voice, the brutal tenderness in his grip.

She comes quietly, not for release, but for remembrance.

When sleep finally claims her, it pulls her down into the darkness, where shadow takes shape, and memory presses its mouth to hers—hungry as ever.

18

BLOOD TIES

Lumira lifts the porcelain teacup, willing her fingers not to tremble. Even fine china feels heavy today. Her limbs ache with a fatigue that sleep can't fix—born of countless lies, endless decisions, and no space between them to recover.

Two days since Thallen Forest, and the promise of rest has become nothing but a fleeting rumor. Every hour since, she's pressed harder than the last, her mind wound so tight it refuses to uncoil in the dark.

"Darling, you seem particularly... refreshed." Thara savors the pause before the last word, letting it land like a slap dressed as a compliment. Her teacup is lifted with practiced ease, her face unreadable. "A certain glow clings to you. I suppose vanishing for days is the new elixir for beauty." Her gaze dissects with calculation, hunting for the fractures fatigue leaves behind—truths Lumira hasn't voiced but may betray in the set of her shoulders.

The emphasis on absence does not ask; it accuses.

The breakfast table stretches long between them, burdened with silverware and delicacies no one truly wants, yet tradition insists they feign enjoyment.

"Nothing like solitude to stitch yourself back together," Lumira says, her tone light to mask the gravity behind it. In truth, she has spent the last few days after Thallen Forest hunched over Emberly's journals, piecing together artifact clues by candlelight and listening for phantom footsteps outside her door. "Although, tea and veiled insults have their own restorative charm."

The Blood Key cools slightly against her the moment Pyraxus enters—as if the artifact itself acknowledges him, recognizing yet not fearing.

He moves with sparse elegance, each step measured, stripped of flourish or waste. He passes behind her chair without touching— he never does. Pyraxus is the kind of man who speaks only when holding his tongue would do more damage.

He takes his seat without fanfare. A moment passes. Two. Then: "Resistance"—spoken softly, no louder than a thought—"is surfacing in unexpected places." No elaboration follows. In his world, every word carries power by design.

Lumira selects a pastry with all the disinterest she can muster. "I imagine that's proving… inconvenient."

"It will be corrected." He glances at her, then back to his tea. He doesn't stir it; instead, he lets it cool.

Further down the table, Jaggard's unnatural composure is louder than most people's shouting. He sits opposite Lumira, focused on buttering his toast with obsessive exactness—alarming for a man who usually pollutes the air with smug observations and poorly timed jabs at her expense. It's not appreciation—it's avoidance that only appears when he knows better than to insert himself. And the fact that he's actually exercising discretion? That means a threat is in motion or waiting to strike.

"I heard there was light in the forest. They say the ground glowed—like the roots burned from within." Aviah looks at Lumira, filled with wonder and the kind of questions that don't yet know how sharp truth can be.

Rumors, Lumira thinks. A child's version of the chaos Ilara unleashed to buy them time. No one really knows and that's exactly how Ilara wanted it.

The Blood Key remains calm and still, completely unbothered. Of course it does—there's no danger in a child's rumor. Aviah's curious, parroting stories she shouldn't have overheard, let alone cling to like truth.

Lumira manages a smile, careful and noncommittal. "That sounds like quite a story," she murmurs, though a small tremor runs through her.

"Thallen Forest." Thara's tone is smooth, delivered with the crisp elegance she reserves for treacherous threads without seeming to. "It's hardly a suitable breakfast conversation." She lifts her teacup with practiced grace, composure unshaken. "I'm certain these… security murmurs have nothing to do with our family." Her pivot toward Pyraxus is sharp, charged. The kind of signal that makes its meaning clear: *this has everything to do with us*—no words needed.

"Recent council reports noted an anomaly." Pyraxus speaks at last, calm enough to make the words feel worse. "Careful, persistent inquiries about artifacts. No names. No affiliations. And questions asked in the wrong rooms." He sets down his cup with a deliberate click. "It's not the frequency that's concerning. It's that there's no interest at all."

Then his attention fixes on Lumira, a pause wrapped in implication.

Jaggard suddenly chokes on his toast, converting the suspicious noise into an unconvincing cough that implies knowledge beyond a casual reaction to sibling verbal sparring.

"Quite right," Thara agrees smoothly. "Information, properly applied, is worth a legion of soldiers. And far less traceable."

Her phrasing is careful, carving a subtle yet unmistakable divide between family interests and outside allegiances. She rarely acknowledges this boundary, especially not over breakfast.

Lumira catalogs the sequence: Pyraxus's pointed calm, Aviah's childish rumor, Thara's veiled warning. None of it is accidental. This is how her family speaks when naming the truth risks everything.

They know someone stirred up Thallen Forest—they don't know how deep she was in it. They're probing, caution wrapped in civility, searching for fractures she might widen if she answers carelessly.

A small voice pipes up from further down the table—eager, unfiltered, and far too loud for the moment. "I heard that Thallen Forest caught on fire," Marnox announces brightly, proud to offer a crucial insight to the grown-up conversation. "One of the guards said the flames were blue. Like a firestorm! I wish I had seen it." His fork makes an enthusiastic arc in the air, nearly launching a slice of salted venison across the polished table.

Sitting beside him with the grace of a painted portrait, Arabella doesn't blink. "Manners, young man." Her words are clipped and icy. "A nobleman does not wave his utensils like a conductor."

Marnox ducks, his cheeks turning pink as his excitement crumbles under her disapproval.

But Lumira notices it, an exchange between Thara and Pyraxus across the table. Quick. Weighted. It's not the fire that induces fear, but the fact that someone is discussing it.

She neither reacts nor falters, her composure unbroken. Relief flickers—Ilara's note had come before breakfast: *unscathed, in hiding, no pursuit.*

Jaggard rises with theatrical stiffness rather than simply standing up from breakfast. He folds his napkin exaggeratedly before setting it beside his plate, as though preparing an exhibit for inspection. "Some of us have council obligations to attend," he announces to the room at large, pitched loudly enough to imply importance. "Preparations must be made. Briefings, naturally. Intelligence doesn't organize itself." He offers Thara and Pyraxus a slight bow, polished and unreadable. "Mother. Brother."

Thara gives a single curt nod, both validating and brushing off at once.

And then he avoids Lumira, pointedly and purposefully.

She waits until Thara and Pyraxus turn away, then allows the pull of him to take hold again. Jaggard walks like someone trying not to care—his posture rigid, his movements betraying the effort. Under his coat, a faint, angular shape presses against the fabric, documents most likely. Not posturing. Covering a trail.

"I should prepare before my duties resume," Lumira announces, rising from the table. "My... absence left a few things unattended."

The pause is significant. Let them interpret it however they like.

Thara's smile arrives on cue—slow and polished, with all approval and implications. "Of course, darling. Ensure you're properly prepared before engaging in more strenuous endeavors." The words are velvet-coated barbs. She's not oblivious, she's assessing.

Lumira sweeps a hand across her torso, insolence threaded through every graceful line, and glides from the room. Only when the last sconce vanishes behind her does she let the mask drop. Her pace quickens.

The servant corridors are faster, narrower, unadorned, and ignored by courtiers who fear dust more than knives. Her footsteps ghost over stone as she follows Jaggard's route toward the western wing. It is not where the ceremonial council chambers sit, but where the real work occurs.

Where secrets are stored and, at times, relocated.

She maintains a careful distance, using corridor bends and the rhythm of servant traffic for cover. The Blood Key stays cool against her skin, unbothered by the chase, indifferent to sibling surveillance—it has offered only a neutral pulse at best where family is concerned.

The scriptorium hasn't been used for years, officially. But Jaggard operates on muscle memory, slipping through the door with a key he absolutely shouldn't have. Palace security should have flagged the entry. Instead, he walks in as if it's his office.

She gives him four minutes. Time to settle, not enough to finish. The door handle turns easily under her hand—no lock, no ward: carelessness or invitation.

Inside, the room is a forgotten chamber lined with dark shelves, dust-furred ledgers, and a single massive table under a low chandelier. Jaggard stands at the helm, papers spread across the tabletop. From the doorway, she catches the sprawl of maps—Thallen Forest in sharp ink, patrol routes looping in red. A polished stone pins one page; half-buried ledgers disguise the rest.

He doesn't bother to sit. One hip rests against the table's edge, posture loose, though he keeps shifting the documents out of her line of sight.

"You might as well come in," Jaggard calls, not glancing up. "Lurking in the hall is tiresome."

Irritation cuts through, she'd been careful. Too careful for him to have noticed. Yet he handles the detail with begrudging competence.

She smooths her expression into aristocratic disinterest, posture languid, as if being caught were always part of the plan. "Council meetings must have changed since I last attended." Her tone is silk over steel. She drifts past the table, gaze skating over his careful arrangement. "I don't recall quite so many… unofficial documents." Everything about it is too tidy for chance—plausible deniability laid out like décor.

"Perhaps if you attended actual council sessions instead of inventing excuses, you'd already know." As Jaggard speaks, he shuffles the papers: shielding some, revealing others, all too casually.

Lumira closes the distance with certainty, cutting through the act. "Strange place for honest politics. Unless decay's creeping behind those doors."

"One might also wonder," he replies smoothly, "why Crimsun's Master at Arms—your loyal commander—becomes unreachable the same day patrols report… irregular activity near Thallen's edge." His gaze stays fixed, steady. "Particularly when his absence aligns with yours—even if you were, as the official word claims, indisposed in your chambers—and neatly sidesteps any formal report to family members concerned for your safety."

The words settle like smoke across a battlefield, unthreatening yet impossible to ignore. He knows, not from rumor, but from experience.

"An interesting kind of concern." She steps to the side, enough to glimpse the document he tried and failed to hide. A torn letter. Its edges are scorched, the ink faded, but the mark is unmistakable: a jagged crown, split clean down the middle.

She freezes, chest tight.

"Concern takes many forms," Jaggard continues. "Some brew potions and whisper bedside reassurances. Others—like me—scrub away the footprints left by family who trespass where they shouldn't… and draw Brotherhood interest we can't afford."

Lumira halts, stillness seeping into her. Not because he named the Brotherhood, she's spat the word plenty of times, but because under the smooth insult, raw truth bleeds through. Of all people, Jaggard—her brother, that arrogant fixture of court theatrics—has been carrying this weight alone.

"What exactly are you investigating?" she asks, the formality stripped bare. "And how long have you been running your operation out of forgotten palace rooms?"

His smile withers, the fondness thinning into a bone-deep fatigue. "Longer than you've been hunting relics." The words land without inflection. "And with far less noise."

He lifts a sheaf of papers and slides them toward her without ceremony. Courier logs, guard rotations—Emberly's name is written again and again in the margins, circled, underlined, as if by repetition he could hold her here.

Lumira stares at the ink. Her sister's name repeats like a prayer disguised as a ledger. This isn't strategy—it's grief, buried in margins and masked as duty. Damn him for hiding it so well, the closest thing to mourning he'd ever allow.

"So it wasn't all theater, then," she murmurs, eyes locked on his scribbled lines. "You were chasing her trail too."

He doesn't nod, doesn't smile—watches her, letting her piece it together for herself.

"Among other connected matters," he confirms, revealing additional documents. "Including the Brotherhood's interest in specific bloodlines and how they react to artifacts." He taps a page stamped with an official seal, with neat notations questioning conclusions about "inherent capabilities."

It aligns closely with her own work: two paths, same quarry. She took the visceral route—relics, ruin, blood, and memory. Jaggard went cerebral: ledgers, council reports, the brittle language of bureaucracy turned against itself.

"I think," he adds, choosing a parchment with no wasted motion, "you'll find this particularly interesting."

The parchment speaks for itself, her silence carries the rest.

She recognizes it for what it is: not Crimsun's secrets, but moldy fingerprints of a plan buried under forgotten ledgers and half-buried archives. Emberly had found the first pieces; Jaggard picked up where she left off.

The Brotherhood's mark is there—stamped across birth records, sealed correspondences, half-burned inventories that tie specific families to artifact resonance tests.

The bedtime stories she'd once mocked as superstition, shadows stealing children who strayed too far, now feel almost harmless by comparison. The truth is colder, older: a machine disguised as myth, patient enough to engineer its will across generations.

Jaggard's margin notes stitch it together: this wasn't chance or divine blessing—it was designed.

"They haven't been hoarding artifacts," he says, voice cold. "They've spent generations breeding for the one who could bind what they can't control."

The truth lands, cutting clean: not inheritance, not fate—a system.

He slides a salvaged scrap of paper forward, edges charred, ink half lost yet still legible. It references a sealed chamber far below the palace, the place where the Blood Key was hidden generations ago to keep it out of the Brotherhood's reach.

Her pulse spikes.

But they never stopped trying to reclaim what had been kept from them—shaping bloodlines in the dark, pairing families like livestock, each generation more precise than the last. Determined to create what they'd been denied.

"What were they trying to make?" she asks, quiet in a way that drips with menace.

"Not what," he replies, meeting her eyes. "Who."

Tension pools in the air, as if the lack of questions speaks louder than any answer could. She'd been constructing a roadmap, and Jaggard, somehow, followed the path.

His investigation isn't a diversion, it's a continuation—a thread winding through secrecy, shadow, and sharpened instinct—three paths, cut from different cloths. But now, impossibly, they're braiding into the same line.

"How extensive is your information network?" Her tone is marked by professional curiosity rather than sibling rivalry. The documents before her suggest a reach far beyond what one man alone should manage.

"Less extensive than Wrenna's merchant connections but considerably more official in appearance." His calculated modesty fails to disguise pride. "Council membership provides access beyond suspicious questioning, particularly when one maintains appropriate public disinterest in sensitive topics."

The emphasis on disinterest is a blade wrapped in silk— criticism cloaked in courtesy. Her methods are effective, yet visible. Blood and artifacts don't exactly invite plausible deniability.

"I've heard," he replies, lightly veiled, "that Pigments & Pints has become a haven for… unorthodox perspectives. The kind that don't align with council doctrine." The words hover, casual on the surface, but calibrated. Not a warning. A signal.

"You've been monitoring my contacts?" she asks, tighter than intended. The protectiveness flares before she can temper it.

"I monitor sources with operational value." His tone is diplomatic, edging on bored. "Some establishments attract people worth listening to—sometimes for what they know, sometimes for what slips out by accident." A simple fact, not a threat. But the message lands: her shadows aren't as private as she thought.

His network observes the patterns, while hers enters them. For the first time, she starts to question which is the greater threat.

"I should return to my chambers." Her words are clipped, more exit strategy than excuse. There's much to unpack, and she needs space to process it.

Jaggard nods once, approval without praise. "Routine is your best alibi. People believe what they expect." There's no affection in his voice, just tactical advice. Yet, it lands with a steadiness that feels stronger than loyalty.

She leaves the scriptorium with even strides, letting habit guide her through the hum of service corridors. Her body moves, but her mind is a spinning loom—threading revelations into shape. Jaggard's investigation. The sealed letter. The bloodline research. It's not a tangle anymore—it's alignment. His method, her instinct, Emberly's foresight. Three angles folding into one.

She walks faster, needing distance and seeking clarity. What she thought were separate pursuits are converging—again and again—on the same name.

Her chambers appear undisturbed. Locks respond as expected, and hidden markers remain in place. Subtle tests confirm what her instincts already suggest: no one has gotten in. Quinn's touch doesn't count—the girl has always known how to slip past locks when needed.

Lumira eases the false panel open to reassure herself. The Living Branch rests within its containment box, its golden light pulsing softly, like breath, like heartbeat, synchronized with her own. Satisfied, she slides the panel shut. The Blood Key lies dormant where it touches her, its presence constant, steady—neither warm nor cold, simply… aware.

On her correspondence tray, a message lies slightly askew—neither accidental nor routine. Quinn's way of telling her this matters.

No—two messages.

The first bears Wrenna's seal: a merchant guild insignia refined with her signature flair—official, yet unmistakably personal. The second carries only Lumira's name, written in elegant script—educated, restrained. The kind of handwriting shaped far from palace walls: refined, distant, a signature that doesn't quite belong here.

She opens Wrenna's first—her professional instinct taking precedence over mystery.

Multiple parties are asking pressing questions—your name is being linked to the Thallen Forest blaze. Some believe you set it. Tomorrow evening, at my place. We need to talk. —W

The lettering is plain: stripped of embellishment, devoid of comfort, and brutally to the point. It conveys a message meant to inform, not to soothe.

Jaggard's earlier revelations churn under the surface, now echoed in Wrenna's warning. Different voices. Same thread. Not a coincidence—a pattern emerging, undeniable in its alignment.

The second letter crackles as her touch skims the brittle surface. The parchment is thick, and the ink is slightly raised. It's a short message, but every word cuts deep.

You're asking the right questions. Let's see if you're ready for the answers. The Silver Chalice. Seventh bell tomorrow night. Don't be late, little fox. —Your Shadow

She doesn't need a name. The phrasing is his—etched with intent, claimed without question. The Shadowspire guard: precise, familiar, and anything but accidental. *Your Shadow.* Not *a* shadow. Not *their* agent. Hers.

She rereads it. And it infuriates her off more than she'll admit.

The Silver Chalice isn't far from Pigments & Pints—a proximity that feels deliberate. Two meetings. Same night. Different messengers. No one speaks it outright—but each question scrapes the same vein: who she is, where she comes from, what her blood might be worth.

She tucks both letters into the false bottom of her vanity drawer—a place for things that can't be left to chance, but won't stay there forever. She lingers on the second note longer than she should, as if it might say more if held just right. Intelligence and entanglement—tightly woven now to separate cleanly. Both are perilous.

From there, she returns to her planning desk with the cold discipline of strategy—but under it all, a low hum of anticipation builds, shaped by the weight of truths converging at once.

"*Blood ties*," she murmurs into the hush, testing the words. Not family—but older, twisted deeper than she can see. She doesn't know. Not really. But it clings to her now, the possibility that her blood was shaped for a purpose she never chose.

The key hums, a low note of agreement.

She builds the plan in her head—timing, alibis, escape routes—each an answer to the day's tangled truths. She sends Wrenna a brief confirmation: she'll stop at Pigments & Pints first, then The Silver Chalice to meet the Shadowspire guard. No warning for him, though—he'll have eyes on her anyway. He always does.

Tomorrow, she ventures beyond the palace walls, toward Pigments & Pints, The Silver Chalice, and the threads of conspiracy, inheritance, and memory. She does not go to represent but to reclaim.

The pieces are aligning: artifact, bloodline, betrayal, truth.

She smiles—dry, with a touch of defiance.

Let them try.

Blood never lies.

19

WATCHING EYES

The cold bites harder three stories up. The air is cleaner—crisp, as if altitude alone can scrape the chaos from her skin. From this height, danger feels smaller. Manageable. Almost laughable. Maybe that's why she remains steady, curled into a ledge etched into the northern face of Pigments & Pints, counting heartbeats as the Blood Legion guard passes below.

It's been one night since the letters arrived—just one—and the city feels transformed, stretched thin under her boots. The Blood Key rests against her, a heartbeat held in suspension, ready to bite. Since claiming the Living Branch, the artifact has begun to behave differently. It doesn't merely respond anymore; it listens and anticipates—as if it, too, is preparing for what's coming.

She waits for the last echo of boots on stone to fade before slipping through the third-story window. The narrow corridor beyond smells of linseed oil, turpentine, and the slow decay of pigment left to spoil in the open air. Canvases lean in crooked stacks along the walls, their surfaces dust-dulled and warped at the edges, as no one has touched them in months. Everything here feels abandoned—but not forgotten, a space meant to be seen by no one at all.

There's no welcome on this path, only shadows and the feeling that whatever mattered has slipped past her.

"Breaking and entering now?" Wrenna's voice slinks down the corridor, amused and unimpressed, already in command of the space. She steps from the shadows near the far wall, arms folded, her expression a blend of mockery with a knife-edge of concern. "The front door still works for people who haven't become the Brotherhood's latest obsession."

"I prefer 'creative access.'" Lumira sweeps the hallway for movement. Wrenna might sound casual, but the rigid set of her shoulders screams otherwise. Lumira continues carefully, keeping her tone deliberately casual. "And last I heard, my name wasn't on anything official."

"Funny. Four Dusk Agents seem to think otherwise. They've been crawling the market district with your face in mind and orders they're not sharing."

Lumira stops. "Dusk Agents?"

"One level above Watchers." Wrenna's already moving. "Watchers collect information. Dusk Agents act on it with missions, sanctioned retrievals, disappearances with strings attached. If they're here, it means the Brotherhood wants you alive, compliant… and entirely theirs."

Lumira follows, slower now. "And where exactly did *that* bit of knowledge come from?"

Wrenna glances back, voice dry. "Let's say someone who talks more than they should wants me nervous. It worked."

A strange certainty settles over her as they navigate the labyrinth of halls above Pigments & Pints, like stepping into a space that was always waiting for her, hidden until she needed it most.

"You could've mentioned the obstacle course in your invitation," Lumira mutters as they descend another narrow staircase tucked behind what appears to be a solid wall.

"And deprive you of the thrill?" Wrenna's grin flashes in the half-light. "Besides, these passages aren't common knowledge. Emberly designed most of them—had them built during 'renovations' that never quite matched the plans submitted to the guild."

At the sound of her sister's name, the Blood Key pulses, a wave of heat rising fast and unrelenting. She suspected Emberly had hidden layers here, but feeling them stir under her boots rewrites everything.

The room beyond is nothing like what Lumira expected. There are no windows, and there are no exits aside from the one they entered. It is a hexagonal chamber, walls covered in what initially appear to be decorative panels. In the center stands a single table, its surface inlaid with a meticulous map of the café below, complete with moving markers.

"Observation mirrors." Wrenna taps one of the panels. The decorative surface shifts, revealing a pane of one-way glass that provides a flawless view of the café's main seating area. "Emberly had them installed as 'artistic features'—which so happen to offer a line of sight to every corner below."

She circles the room, brushing each panel in turn. One by one, the walls unfold to reveal the entrance, the reading alcoves, the service counter, and the studio space where classes are held—the entire establishment is visible to anyone from above.

"The acoustics are the real masterpiece," Wrenna adds, flicking a small copper switch embedded in the table. Conversation swells from below—separate threads, each one precise. It's not a blur of background noise, but isolated conversations, easy to tune in or out. "Emberly worked with a Naiad Songweaver who usually designs concert halls. Each arch and beam downstairs was placed to channel sound into specific collection points."

"She built a surveillance system disguised as design." Lumira steps closer to one of the glass panes, her gaze sweeping the café beyond. "No one questions it because it's beautiful, clever, and exactly the kind of unconventional gesture they've come to expect."

"And all while running a completely legitimate business that so happens to attract all factions worth eavesdropping on." Wrenna's pride curls in her voice like smoke. "Merchants trade route secrets over breakfast. Artists share gossip during classes. Nobles whisper politics in the reading alcoves. And Brotherhood agents interrogate my staff while pretending to care about herbal tea blends."

She adjusts another switch, isolating a conversation from below. Two men in merchant attire sit at a corner table, their discussion of textile shipments serving as a flimsy veil over border patrol rotations and security breaches.

"Emberly tracked their pattern for years," Wrenna said, the weight of it evident in her delivery. "She didn't know what to call them, but she knew what they were. Men who dress to disappear. Always long sleeves, even in sweltering heat. Said their arms were the giveaways."

Lumira flicks to one of the men below, and he adjusts in his seat, revealing a brief flash of ink winding down to his wrist. His sleeve pulls back.

"What are they hiding?" she asks, although part of her already knows.

"Tattoos," Wrenna answers softly. "Intricate ink winding fully along their arms, spiraling down to fingers and curling toward their necks if they feel bold. But they all share one unmistakable mark: a jagged crown split down the center, etched always upon the left forearm. They hide it under cloth or weave it into dense patterns, but it's always there—the Brotherhood's mark."

Lumira remains unreadable. The point's been made.

That moment is forever etched in her memory—the sudden lunge, the ripped sleeve, the intruder recoiling as her blade brushed against him. A mere scratch, but sufficient. His left forearm lay bare for half a second. The same mark Emberly carved into her desk. The exact shape that has haunted the edges of every unanswered question since.

Her jaw tightens. "She saw it before any of us." Lumira holds the connection. "Didn't she?"

Wrenna nods, her jaw tightening. "She noticed the signs: security tightening between territories without formal justification, noble disappearances drowned in reports no one was allowed to question, ancient sites suddenly restricted under vague preservation orders that felt more like suppression than protection."

Lumira observes the Dusk Agents below, her voice sharper now. "What are they after?"

"You," Wrenna replies. "Specifically. They've been straight-forward, asking about a 'Blood Descent noble' seen near Thallen Forest during the disturbance. The label applies to all of you—but it isn't your brothers or the little ones they care about. They want you—your movements, contacts, forest access points." The words land harder than they should.

She recalls what was shouted during her extraction—half lost in the chaos but burned into her memory: *"Secure the Blood Descent. Leave the relic—she's the priority. She's connected to it."*

"Well. So much for ambiguity." The sarcasm cuts through Lumira's clenched teeth. "I'm their favorite fucking problem now. How flattering."

"Security's tighter." Wrenna adjusts a dial, tuning the acoustics from the Brotherhood's table. "They're monitoring anyone remotely tied to your family, and they keep circling back here like they're waiting for someone to slip and turn you in."

A chill threads along Lumira's collar despite the room's warmth. Their focus on her rather than the artifact is unsettling—what do they know about her bloodline, about how it ties to the relic? She doesn't know the full story—yet the Brotherhood's questions suggest they've pieced together things she's barely begun to unearth.

"According to my palace contacts," Wrenna continues, tension threading through her words, "they've reassigned elite units to interior patrols. Not standard guards—void-steppers. The kind they use for high-value retrievals."

Lumira's jaw tenses. "That would explain the security tightening near my chambers." She pauses, her spine prickling as if the cold itself has found a purpose. "And if they've been observing that closely…" She returns to the scene below. "Then it's more than my habits they're keeping record of."

Below, the Dusk Agents lean in, their voices dropping despite the improved acoustics. Wrenna adjusts a dial, refining the resolution.

"—confirmed sighting near the eastern quarter yesterday," one murmurs, his merchant disguise betrayed by the clipped formality of his posture. "Orders are to observe only. Maintain distance unless the acquisition is clean and discreet."

"Priority remains Blood Descent retrieval," his companion replies, calm and mechanical. "Artifact is secondary."

The Blood Key stiffens against her chest, cold threaded with warning.

"Have they tied anyone to the night I escaped?" Lumira asks, calculating the fallout if the Brotherhood's reach spreads beyond her.

"Not yet," Wrenna replies. "They know you didn't act alone but haven't linked anyone directly. No mention of Ilara. No signs they care what I'm doing either." She nods subtly toward the café's main floor, where casual conversations mingle with the low churn of surveillance and subterfuge, calm only on the surface. "In the meantime, we've been feeding them carefully planted falsehoods: sightings in other districts, ties to irrelevant nobles, false trails about artifact locations."

A group of merchants erupts into laughter—fast and loud, a cue well-rehearsed. One leans back in his chair, owning a victory that didn't cost him anything.

Wrenna stays fixed on her work, but a sliver of satisfaction seeps into her tone. "Everyone plays a part," she says. "They think they're gathering intel. Really, they're bleeding it."

Wrenna's tactics catch Lumira off guard—not the kind she's trained for, but effective. It isn't brute force or intimidation. It's elegance, honed to slip past resistance.

Her fighters extract information through pressure. Wrenna's staff skirts the edges. The room bends around them until secrets fall out on their own. While she's trained nobles to vanish into shadows, Wrenna and Emberly have built a network that thrives in plain sight.

"Watch closely," Wrenna murmurs as the Brotherhood agents signal for their bill.

Across the café, a student fumbles a water jar near the studio tables, causing brushes to clatter and laughter to ripple through the room like a thrown stone. In the same breath, one of the café staff glides past the Brotherhood table—another server clearing a cup—and casually palms a folded slip from the agent's coat pocket.

Lumira nearly misses it. "What did they take?" she asks under her breath, more thought than question.

"Their observation notes," Wrenna replies, smiling. "Descriptions, territory paths, potential witness names—details they think they've kept to themselves. We'll have copies made and returned before they reach the door."

"And they never suspect?"

"They suspect everyone but the staff." Wrenna smiles, clearly pleased. "Self-important men never see the hands that carry their tea."

Below, the performance continues with effortless precision. The Brotherhood agents rise as a discreet bell chimes, signaling a ripple through the room's rhythm. A nearby card game ends with theatrical groans and exaggerated loss. At the studio's far end, one of the painters adds a final stroke to a portrait—a face rendered with startling accuracy. Each person who entered or exited during the past hour was captured in careful detail.

"What you've built is remarkable." The words are soft, meant more as recognition than praise. She sees now why Emberly returned to this place again and again. "An intelligence operation set up where no one thinks to check. Pulling from every side."

"Emberly created it," Wrenna utters. "I'm keeping it alive. She saw what this place could be—how art could hide things in plain sight. How beauty could be used as a weapon." She exhales slowly. "They never took her seriously. Thought she was another palace artist painting to please nobles with more wealth than taste."

A pang rises in Lumira's chest, the weight of Emberly's unfinished work lodging sharp beneath her ribs. Her arm lifts before she thinks to stop it—a reflex burned deep, shaped by an absence that's refused to sit right. The ache lingers, a bruise pressed past comfort. She almost touches her collarbone, but the movement stalls, held back before it can mean anything.

A quiet release escapes her. The ache fades, overtaken by what matters more.

"I've had people keeping tabs on The Silver Chalice since you told me about your next meeting." Wrenna checks a slim copper timepiece. "He arrived early. Took the northeastern private room—multiple exits, strong vantage points."

Lumira nods. "His note said I was asking the right questions… and that it was time for answers."

Wrenna's expression tightens. "Cryptic, arrogant, and dangerous."

"A perfect assessment," Lumira murmurs.

"He's been careful." Wrenna doesn't bother to mask her suspicion. "No affiliations beyond the Shadowspire front, but choosing a private room with multiple exits? Arriving early to secure it himself? That's not casual. He's treating this like a tactical meeting."

Lumira doesn't respond right away. "I can handle him." What that entails—interrogation, seduction, or a choice more ruinous than either—remains hers alone.

Wrenna doesn't argue, but her tone hardens, calm edged in restraint. "Make sure he's giving more than he's taking."

A bell chimes below—three short, two long.

Wrenna straightens, her words edged with resolve. "That's more Dusk Agents than we planned for. Get moving."

She guides Lumira through a narrow stairwell that twists like an architectural oversight. They emerge into a storage room stacked with musical instruments: violins, cracked bows, and cello cases dulled by dust and time.

"Service exit." Wrenna nudges aside a wall of cases to reveal a narrow door. "Opens behind the Hollow Mantle. Close enough to The Silver Chalice, and no direct street exposure." She pauses— taking the time to face Lumira directly. "Come back soon." It's not a plea, but an expectation. "We'll both want answers after this."

And Lumira slips into the alley without a word.

Altareth hums under her boots—the stone streets alive with foot traffic, lantern light, and the low murmur of a city that seldom sleeps. Lumira threads through its outer veins, slipping between alleyways and half-lit corridors that wind behind closed taverns and shuttered storefronts. The Hollow Mantle fades behind her. Ahead, The Silver Chalice awaits.

The Blood Key rests against her skin—chilled and enigmatic. Not vigilant—poised. And that unsettles her more than any flare of heat.

The Silver Chalice occupies a peculiar position in the city's social hierarchy—refined beyond a drunkard's comfort, yet lacking the gloss to satisfy aristocrats. It caters to merchants, information brokers, and those who require multiple exits and no questions.

Surveillance isn't avoided here—it's misdirected. Guards are trained to identify the wrong threats, filtering out anyone who dresses plainly or walks with confidence.

Lumira walks in through the kitchen, unnoticed by anyone. Dressed in worn clothes, with a steady stride and a half-filled satchel on her shoulder, she seamlessly blends in with the staff. The cook remains unfazed, and the servers barely acknowledge her presence. There's no need for her to seek approval; she claims her place. At the corridor's end, she pauses—marking exits, blind spots, and potential weapons. Nothing is truly harmless. Not here.

A serving girl intercepts her before the dining hall threshold. She is young, not far from Lumira's age, with shadowed features and a smile that guards more than it gives. Her bow is shallow and crisp, her apron smudged, and her posture exact. "The gentleman in the private room asked me to let him know if someone matching your description arrived." She is calm and methodical, resembling a recital of instructions instead of assistance. "If you'd like to follow me, my lady."

The title lands with weight—pointed, knowing. Nobility, seen through the disguise. As Lumira passes her, she catches a glimpse of darkness at the girl's wrist—half-concealed by a rolled sleeve. Ink? Markings? She can't quite tell, but it sets her on edge.

Then the girl gestures gently, the flicker of it nearly lost to sight. A presence unfurls across the space behind them, smooth and subtle. A tingling hum ripples across Lumira's senses—reminiscent of when magic alters the boundaries of a room.

She glances back.

The hallway behind them seems the same, but the light has dulled slightly and the angles are muted. Her pulse slows as she recognizes it—not illusion, not concealment. A mirage. Room-altering magic designed to protect rather than deceive. It ensures what happens next goes unseen—and, more importantly, is forgotten.

The magic wasn't active when she entered. He wanted to be seen—up until the moment she arrived.

Now he doesn't.

And the girl? Not a servant after all—probably one of *his*.

The private dining room is situated in the building's northeastern corner, a strategic choice that offers street visibility and a secondary exit through an adjoining storage corridor. A table anchors the center of the room. A figure sits at it, their back to the wall, positioned for clear sightlines without appearing defensive. His cloak lies draped over the opposite chair, the fabric slouched as if it was quickly peeled back.

And Lumira nearly stumbles.

She has never seen him completely, not like this. But the sight strikes her, a dream recalled in perfect clarity, heat rising up her spine before she can stop it.

Storm-gray eyes, laced with those impossible gold flecks, follow her approach with the same unnerving intensity she remembers. But now... now they belong to a face almost unreal. High cheekbones cast sculpted shadows across features refined past the point of chance. His jawline is a study in aristocratic defiance, clean-shaven, each line drawn like it knew the effect. A single strand of dark-brown hair slips artfully across his brow, catching the lamplight like polished brass—an accident, she's sure, carefully staged to seem unplanned.

And then—that mouth.

Exactly as she remembers it from the shadows: honed, measured, cut like it was designed for silence and sin. But in the light, it's worse because it's real. A mouth made for biting words and whispered ruin, frozen with intent, like speech is the only thing keeping it from destruction.

Each feature on its own might be striking. Together, they are ruinous. As if some bored, cruel deity had sculpted a man solely to test her composure.

And gods, is he succeeding.

The Blood Key responds almost instantly as she approaches, matching the sudden quickening of her pulse. It's not the warning she might expect when confronting a potential enemy, but rather a steady, insistent warmth. Heat spreads across her chest in waves that mirror the inconvenient flush she's fighting to keep from her face.

And it's not the artifact reacting.

Because her body remembers—his mouth, unbearably intimate; the press of his tongue... wrong place, wrong time. Yet the memory flares anyway, slow and searing, a match drawn across oil.

The key's warmth deepens—in agreement, as if it remembers what he did to her.

"You're early." His voice settles over her like velvet pulled taut, a softness with edges. Controlled. Even. Designed to resonate. "I appreciate punctuality in someone so deeply entangled with me."

"Is that what we are?" Lumira replies, her annoyance doing the explaining for her. She sinks into the seat across from him, deliberately choosing the one that complements rather than blocks her sightlines to the door. "Entangled?"

He remains fixed on her for a beat too long, then lets a slow smile carve its way across his mouth—angled, never careless. "That depends entirely on what you do with the information I'm about to share," he murmurs. "And whether you can trust someone who's seen you at your most... vulnerable."

The reference strikes with accuracy—not a weapon, but truth, laid bare between them. He places it on the table like a playing card that doesn't need to be turned over to matter.

"Call it what you like." She gives nothing away. "But don't confuse *vulnerability* with an invitation." She lifts her chin. "What do I call you—besides 'the infuriating Shadowspire guard who keeps appearing at the most inconveniently strategic moments'?"

He lets out a soft laugh, a hint of a smile appearing at the corner of his mouth. "That has a certain charm." He stays fixed on her—warm and playful—and for a brief moment, the atmosphere seems relaxed. Almost carefree. But then his expression settles. Not cold, careful. "Names have power," he says gently. "And mine isn't given lightly."

"You're avoiding the point." Her lips twitch with the threat of a smile she refuses to let slip. "What kind of information justifies this much theater and layered security?"

He doesn't answer immediately. Instead, he reaches for a small copper device at the center of the table and activates it with a flick of his thumb. A low hum fills the air—not loud, but dense. Like pressure building in her ears—the way the world waits, taut and expectant, before a storm breaks.

"Sound disruption field," he explains. "The mirage keeps us from being noticed. This keeps our words from being heard." His mouth quirks, but it stops short of a smile. "Anyone listening in will hear a dull conversation about agricultural trade routes."

Her spine snaps straight—not because of the field, but from the sight before her. That brief motion, that careless reveal of skin, has already cost him.

Because she sees it now.

Ink, dark and intricate, winds over his fingers and up the edge of his left forearm before disappearing beneath his sleeve—swirling lines that are familiar in a way she can't dismiss. Hidden within the pattern is the Brotherhood sigil she glimpsed that night in Emberly's bedroom—her only warning before he forced her hand.

It pierces before she can flinch—realization, swift and needled, already sinking deep. He was there. The figure in the dark. The one who cornered her, made her run.

And for the first time, she understands—*he wasn't trying to hurt her*. He could have. He didn't. He pushed her, tested her, forced her to see what no one else did. He didn't underestimate her. Not like the others.

She says nothing, yet the Blood Key warms, recognizing a truth that shifts everything.

"The Brotherhood isn't a security force acting on its own." The Shadowspire guard's tone is precise and steady. "They serve an agenda that threads through all twelve territories—all alliances, bloodlines, and generations of carefully preserved power. Obedience isn't optional. Especially when it comes to mixed bloodlines."

Mixed bloodlines. The phrase hits a nerve. Connections long buried rise fast: Emberly's research, her mother's careful matches, Jaggard's brittle ledgers stitched with secrets. Generations of pairing families like livestock—breeding for power they could never claim on their own.

He examines her closely. "Certain combinations can access the relics in ways no one can predict. It's not power—it's affinity. The Brotherhood believes the artifacts aren't merely enchanted. They're fragments of what came before. Pieces of gods, sealed away. And mixed bloodlines…" His voice barely carries—more vibration than sound beneath the hum of the field. "They don't draw power. They help uncover it."

The Blood Key flares where it rests—sharp, insistent, alive. She gives nothing away, though her thoughts are already fracturing.

This isn't about the artifacts alone.

Every move—the palace surveillance, the Dusk Agents in Pigments & Pints, the Brotherhood's narrowed focus—leads to one unavoidable truth: it isn't what she carries. It's why she can hold it.

"Fragments of gods," she says at last. The words taste like half-truths—stolen from Emberly's journal, murmured during long-forgotten festival nights. "You mean the old claims—the gods were bound, and the artifacts hold what couldn't be destroyed?"

The question feels childish to ask. But it escapes anyway.

His expression holds steady. "They're not stories, Lumira," he replies. "They're history. Rewritten. Buried. But not erased."

"And you think it's *my* blood that unlocks it?" she questions.

A pause, as if time itself were being sifted through steady hands.

"You seem to intimidate them," he concludes. "And I believe their fear is justified."

The Blood Key pulses in answer—now hotter, more insistent. Confirming.

The realization slams into her chest, leaving her breathless. It was never about what she found but what she is.

"Why tell me this?" She keeps it low, attempting to steady the tremor under her ribs before it climbs higher.

"Because you need to understand what they're chasing. The Brotherhood's been forcing bloodlines—splicing legacies, marrying for magic. They're trying to cheat their way in. But you... you may be the result of older plans. Intentional ones." He scans her, eyes sharp enough to hold pity. "Your father's name keeps surfacing where it shouldn't. Disappearing where it should matter. If he's behind this—if it's been generations in the making—then you're not a coincidence. You're a conclusion."

The words hang.

And Lumira—jaw tight, chain clutched between her fingers— lets the truth settle.

She's not the beginning.

She is the end.

The words settle like prophecy. Not offered or earned— just true.

It takes a breath—maybe two—before she finds her voice again. "Then what happens now?"

He doesn't hesitate. "The Aethervoid is thinning, and the Red Night is rising."

She frowns. "The… what?"

"It's not a name that survives in common memory," he responds carefully. "The Brotherhood ensured that—scrubbed the records, removed anyone who might contradict them. But it's real. And it's starting again. The Aethervoid isn't a magical theory," he continues. "It's a veil—a boundary that separates this realm from the divine. It keeps the gods locked out. Keeps us from reaching them."

"And the Red Night?" she asks.

"A rare celestial convergence—one that comes only once every eight hundred years. As it draws near, the Aethervoid begins to fray, weakening until it finally breaks." The words fall softer, heavier. "Magic becomes unstable. Artifacts awaken. And things that should remain hidden start to emerge."

"The Red Night," she echoes, frayed at the edges. "Painted skies, caged gods, the world coming apart." Her mouth twists. "Because everything else hasn't been sufficient."

He doesn't waver. Not even for her. "It is a reckoning. And it's begun."

It scrapes raw—the absence, the weight, the unsaid.

He says it low, but certain. "It's coming—whether you're ready or not."

The sound disruption device hums once before clicking off. The space between them tightens—thick with unspoken weight, electrified by what neither will say.

Rising to his feet, he smooths the fabric—each motion restrained, like tucking unfinished truths out of sight.

"You don't have to believe me. Not yet. But think, Lumira," he says, stepping toward the door with unnerving tranquility. "Certain truths only surface when you cease fleeing from them."

Her question slices through the hush, delicate but barbed. "And when exactly do I get to choose what I'm ready for?"

He halts mid-step. He rotates slightly, the lamplight catching the hard line of his mouth.

For a heartbeat, a flicker of restraint threatens—then buckles under age-old certainty.

Possessive. Knowing.

"You always decide, little fox." It lands somewhere between a caress and a caution, like he's savoring the truth of it.

The nickname strikes deep, a secret spoken aloud, a reminder that he's watched long enough to name her in ways no one else dares.

"And if I know you at all…" His gaze pins her in place, dragging over every inch without mercy. "You'll dig until the earth bites back. You'll take what they buried, even if it unravels you." Amusement cuts through the shadows below his eyes. "Remember—I see more than they do. Always have." He angles toward her, and the faintest curve touches his mouth. Not soft. Dangerous. "They want you secured. But you're mine. And I find what's mine. Always."

And then—he's gone.

Lumira doesn't move. Her pulse stays steady as the truth rearranges itself like blades in a sheath. The Brotherhood isn't rogue, it's sanctioned and hidden in plain sight. Woven through the ruling structures like old blood in new veins.

And the man who delivered that truth? A walking contradiction in flesh—tattooed, measured, and far from ordinary. He spoke of the Red Night but left other things unsaid: the Living Branch, and how much he truly knows of her. Yet, the timing, the intent, and the way his attention held—none of it felt accidental.

She rises only when silence settles, the echo of revelation no longer vibrating through her bones.

Outside The Silver Chalice, the city stretches wide and alert. Stone whispers with each step. Stars carve through the velvet sky, silver and cruel. And the sky ripples—red smudging the dark for one breathless moment.

Gone before she can blink.

She doesn't chase it. The key remains warm, acknowledging. Accepting. A quiet pact. Her cloak snaps in the wind as she slips into Altareth's shadows. Her thoughts keep pace with her: cataloging threats, allies, and truths.

If the Red Night is rising—let it.

She's no longer running. She's the reckoning.

20

HUNTERS AND SHADOWS

"**S**tart from the top." Ilara is steady, arm raised—not to command, but to center the room. "Everything he said. No theatrics. Facts and nothing more."

Lumira braces herself on the worn oak table in the surveillance room above Pigments & Pints, her knuckles turning white. "He termed it the Red Night." She keeps her head down. "He insisted it's more than a theory. It's a cycle. And it has already commenced."

Wrenna exhales through her nose, not quite dismissive or convinced. "Feels like the kind of tale born in the dark—when the bottle's empty and egos are full."

"He wasn't telling stories." Lumira finally meets their eyes. "He spoke like a man running out of time."

But that isn't the worst of it.

Not the Red Night. Not even the gods.

She's still reeling from the other truth—the one wrapped in lineage and calculation.

That she might not be a mistake, or even a miracle.

That her blood was shaped on purpose.

And if that's true...

"You ever heard of it?" she asks, clipped. "The Red Night?"

Wrenna doesn't hesitate. "No." Her voice is firm, unapologetic. "And I've dug through enough half-rotted scrolls penned by fever-struck scribes to recognize a pattern if there was one."

Ilara traces the wood grain, tension drawing her features taut. No flicker of recognition—only unease. She sits back slowly, refusal in each line of her posture.

"I don't remember ever seeing it—not in Emberly's notes, not in the archives, not in the deep court records I wasn't meant to touch," Lumira remarks, her jaw tight. "It's... gone."

Wrenna reaches for the worn ledger, flipping it open in a distracted motion. "I've cataloged everything from solar anomalies to dead-raven omens and that ridiculous river-frog superstition. But not this. Not even close."

"He mentioned the artifacts are affected by it." The words slip out, nearly swallowed by thought. "It thins the barrier between our world and... whatever exists beyond. That's the effect of the Red Night—it unravels the veil. And when it shatters..."

She doesn't finish.

"That's not magic." Ilara's reply is low. "That's cosmology—the kind the academy buries in the back of locked archives and pretends it holds no substance."

Wrenna taps a restless rhythm against the table's surface. "Sounds like a bard with good lighting and a flair for dread."

Lumira lets out a short, bitter laugh. "You think I didn't want to dismiss it too?" She draws the Blood Key from beneath her cloak and lets it swing once before closing her fist around it. "But this doesn't care about performance. It reacts. And lately… it's been listening."

Ilara blinks. "Listening?"

"You mean it talks to you now?" Wrenna adds, half joking, half not.

The interruption is sharp, unapologetic. "No. It doesn't speak. It pulses. Burns. Freezes. I thought it was random." Lumira holds her ground. "It's not. Heat means alignment," she says, voice even but edged. "Cold means threat. Everything else—it's waiting." She slips the key back into place. "Lately, it's been doing a lot of that."

Wrenna whistles. "Lovely. So we're dealing with divine mood swings."

Ilara doesn't smile. "You waited until now to say that?"

Lumira shrugs. "I needed to be sure. Now I am. And if what he said is true—if the Aethervoid is thinning—then this isn't prophecy anymore." She plants both hands on the table. "It's a countdown."

The aftermath settles, bitter and suffocating.

Wrenna offers no words—just crosses the room and opens a hidden drawer. The bottle of Naiad Flame-Brew catches the lamplight, a spark about to bite. She sets it down hard, making the glasses tremble. "If it's a countdown," she mutters, uncorking it, "we're late."

The liquid flares amber-red as she pours it, flickering like fire trapped in glass. There's a slight tremble as she passes the first glass to Lumira, then the next to Ilara.

Ilara takes hers with a faint wince, the smell alone curling her lip. "Gods." She swirls it once. "Even the bottle smells like consequences."

Lumira doesn't answer. She lifts her glass and drinks—cool, crisp, and without hesitation. It hits like heat and revelation.

Ilara speaks next, low but unyielding. "So we believe him now?"

"We have to." Lumira sets her glass down. A beat stretches, allowing heaviness to land—before her voice hardens once more. "The Brotherhood's ties to the Crown... Did Emberly leave behind anything—names or clues regarding who in the royal lines could be involved?"

Wrenna and Ilara hold the moment between them, heavy with meaning.

"That's where things become... complicated." Wrenna crosses the room, kneeling beside a loose floorboard near the corner bookshelf. She settles into the groove as if she's done it a thousand times before. "Emberly suspected the connection went all the way to the top, but she never committed to names outright—not in the journal you have. But she kept a safeguard."

With a soft scrape of wood, Wrenna lifts a hidden panel and retrieves a thinner, weatherworn volume—its leather rubbed smooth at the corners, the spine reinforced with mismatched thread. She brushes away the dust.

"It's not like the others." She frowns. "No riddles, no verse—only patterns. Movements. Names that don't belong together." She gently sets the journal down. "Her surveillance log." Wrenna flips to a page marked with a slender twine ribbon. "She recorded guard rotations," she observes, scanning the ink. "And noted individuals who strayed from standard procedures. Those who behaved as though they had their directives."

She slides the log across to Lumira, the pages rustling as they shift.

The log showcases detailed entries: dates, times, locations, and names. Small sketches of guard insignia adorn the margins. Through meticulous examination, irregularities emerge—specific guards are found where they shouldn't be, some are inexplicably missing, and rotations change without approval.

One name appears increasingly often as Lumira turns the pages.

"Hadralis," she murmurs. The name used to mean strategy, discipline, loyalty. Now it tastes like a lie.

There it is, Emberly's handwriting, every letter etched with intent. A record of Hadralis pressing for answers he shouldn't seek. Inquiries were made of staff low-ranking, the sort who follow orders without asking why. Discrepancies appear where his presence overlapped with locked corridors and sealed wings. Mentions of shadowed meetings—always brief, always off the books—with men no one could correctly name afterward.

"I trusted him," Lumira states, not numb, but honed. "He's trained me since I was twelve."

"Which would make him the perfect choice." Ilara halts momentarily. "No one sees more clearly than someone meant to protect you."

The thought lodges deep within: years of drills, counsel, and wounds bandaged with a mentor's patience. Laughter exchanged in shadowed halls. All of it is seen now through fractured glass.

Lumira lets the glass settle without flourish or fuss.

Wrenna settles beside them, thumbing through the final pages of Emberly's surveillance log. "There's more." She holds the page steady. "This is the last entry she wrote."

The lettering slants differently here—rushed and uneven. A name is circled three times. *Hadralis*. Beside it: *Too close to the source. Must warn L.*

L. Lumira. Her sister had known. She'd tried to sound the alarm.

Lumira stills. Doesn't blink. "When?"

"Two days before she died." Wrenna stares at the floor.

Ilara leans in, her fingers brushing a faint seal in the corner. "Here. This mark." The mood alters, urgency bleeding into every word now. "I've seen it before—at Grovenar ranger stations. It was stamped on documents we had to incinerate without examining." She pulls a folio from her satchel, a collection of accusations fanned across the table. Each one features a seal from a different territory, and tucked in the corner is the same symbol found in Emberly's note. Subtle. Designed to be overlooked. But not by them.

"That's his." No doubt. No pause. "Hadralis uses that mark on training reports. Field requisitions. Even my own clearances."

The moment closes in. Not disbelief, just an answer neither needs to voice.

"He was close enough to intercept Emberly's research." Ilara doesn't blink. "Close enough to know exactly what she found."

Wrenna drops her voice. "And close enough to make sure she never told you."

The implication lands hard, stealing the space in her chest.

Lumira closes her eyes. When she opens them, she speaks with careful control, though bitterness coils just under the surface. "He knew," she says. "I don't know how much. Or how early. But he knew *something*." She swallows hard, disbelief lodging in her throat as heat builds—not certainty, but suspicion. The kind that spreads when answers come only after the damage is done.

"What will you do?" Ilara asks the question without judgment and only with practical consideration.

Lumira drags her fingertip over the damning evidence, memorizing each detail of her mentor's betrayal. "I'll do what I've been trained to do," she replies, carrying the particular calm that precedes violence. "I'll confront him directly."

"That seems," Wrenna observes with delicate care, "potentially suicidal."

"Only if I'm unprepared," Lumira counters. "And thanks to this"—she taps the leather-worn log—"I won't be. I'll make him face me on the training grounds—his arena of supposed expertise. He won't expect me to know, which gives me the advantage. Search for anything else about the Red Night," she instructs, mentally planning the confrontation. "The Shadowspire guard seemed to think it's significant beyond poetic imagery."

Ilara nods, gathering the scattered papers into organized piles. "If it's mentioned in ancient records, the Grovenar archives might have references. I'll send word to my forest contacts tonight."

A sharp knock on the door interrupts her mid-sentence—three rapid taps followed by two slower ones—Pigments & Pints' danger signal.

Wrenna moves to a small peephole disguised as a decorative knot in the wooden paneling. "Brotherhood patrol," she reports, dropping to barely audible levels. "Four agents, main room."

"I need to leave." Lumira gathers Emberly's secret log. "If they suspect anything, they'll push past the front—it's only a matter of time."

Wrenna nods.

"We'll keep digging," Ilara promises, tucking the last folio into a hollowed-out book spine. "And I'll have eyes on Hadralis before dawn."

Lumira hesitates at the threshold, knowledge pressing into her, rigid and unyielding against her skin. "If I don't come back after tomorrow's session…"

Wrenna doesn't flinch. "We'll know who to bury." The line lands soft, almost elegant—like silk hiding steel. "And we'll make damn sure the rest follow."

Lumira nods once before vanishing into the concealed corridor, her boots making no sound against the narrow planks. The rooftops of the merchant district stretch below her, oblivious to the conspiracies and betrayals that loom over its existence. She expertly maneuvers across the slick tiles and tight spaces, relying on her tactical instincts and skill rather than fear.

Three Blood Ravens perch along the wall, their dark forms nearly invisible against the night sky. As she walks beneath them, the air tugs—an unseen thread drawing taut between past and present.

Lumira promises the watching birds, "I'll finish what she started. Whatever it costs."

The ravens circle, intelligent eyes tracking every step, unblinking. If Emberly's research—and what Hadralis told her—proves true, they are not mere birds but conduits for an ancient force, witnesses to events beyond mortal comprehension.

Lumira slips through the palace grounds undetected, the weight of Emberly's surveillance log pressing against her side where she has secured it—evidence of Hadralis's betrayal and a reminder of what's at stake.

Entering her chambers through the servant passages, she carefully secures the journal in a hidden compartment behind the weapons rack. Tomorrow, she will confront the mentor who has shaped her into a weapon while simultaneously betraying her to her enemies. The particular irony would be amusing if it weren't so fucking infuriating.

She passes along the row of training blades, pausing on the one Hadralis gave her after she mastered the defensive forms he carried from Shadowspire. How fitting that it might draw his blood.

Tomorrow, Hadralis will face the consequences of his choices— and maybe then she'll finally see how deep the Brotherhood's reach really runs.

Outside her window, a Blood Raven quietly perches on the sill, its eerie copper eyes observing. It neither warns nor reassures; it simply witnesses, as if her journey was scripted in some ancient manuscript, and she is only following lines etched long before her arrival.

Either way, blood will spill before the next sunset. Betrayal demands nothing less.

21

TRUTH AND TREACHERY

Lumira's blade cuts through the morning air, a verdict delivered. Each arc is precise: third position to seventh, defensive to offensive, form to fury. She trains not to practice but to *prepare*. The rhythm should anchor her, but it doesn't. Not with his name circling like carrion above a battlefield.

Hadralis.

Once, a name that conveyed strategy, safety, and certainty. Now it tastes like iron on her tongue. Familiar. Poisoned.

She meticulously chooses her practice blades—shorter, duller, and always safe. They're designed not to kill with a single strike, but they can be deadly in skilled hands. Her grip remains firm, yet tension spirals unseen—a bow drawn tight. Her breath holds meaning unspoken, and her bones echo memories with unsettling clarity.

The sky fades from black to indigo, light bleeding into the horizon, an old wound reopening. She doesn't stop moving.

Her blade whispers through the cold, carving arcs that echo the violence honed into her.

But her thoughts do not obey.

The past presses close, stitching itself into every step—each a memory bound by intent. She fights ghosts before she's even drawn blood.

Then—

The air tightens—barely a tremor, but enough.

At the edge of the training grounds, space bends: one breath in stillness, the next revealing a figure where none should be.

She remains unshaken, her blade already in hand. If it's him—and it is—he already knows she's prepared.

"You're early." Hadralis emerges from the shadows, moving with purpose and fluidity. She once admired his grace, but now sees it for what it truly is: Brotherhood training, not the Shadowspire loyalty she once trusted, a deception honed in plain view.

"Couldn't sleep," Lumira replies, each syllable smoothed into composure, emotion sealed tight. Her aristocratic training proves helpful beyond court appearances.

He circles her with the careful precision of a hunter. His eyes skim over the details others might miss: the unspoken defiance in the space she refuses to yield. Recognition flashes, brief but clear. Not alarm. Not approval. The look a predator gives when what once was prey begins to alter, sharpening into something with teeth.

"Nightmares again?" he asks, selecting his practice weapons with his usual precision.

"Not quite." Her gaze meets his directly, refusing to look away first—a small act of defiance, but significant in its execution.

No questions arise. No challenge to the change in her posture or the tension radiating from her. He nods once, accepting the game without naming it. "Start the Shadowspire defensive sequence," he directs, falling into their usual training cadence as if nothing is different. As if everything remains the same. "Complete extension. Half speed."

Lumira complies, moving through the forms with mechanical perfection. Each position lands with textbook precision, lacking her usual adaptive flow. This isn't a fight—it's a statement. A calculated exposure to the rhythms he's spent years instilling in her.

Evidence that she is aware.

Hadralis notices immediately. A slight adjustment, barely perceptible—the only visible reaction to her uncharacteristic approach. He adjusts his stance in response, moving to counter with the traditional offensive sequence instead of his customary adaptation.

They circle each other without speaking. The student and mentor converse beyond words, communicating through blade position and foot placement instead of direct accusation.

"The palace assigned extra patrols last night," she says, casual in tone, pointed in intent. "No official documentation."

Hadralis deflects her attack with the same graceful accuracy that once garnered her respect. "Palace security adapts as needed," he states, his tone inscrutable. "Not all threats produce a paper trail."

Lumira lets her next move drift into a technique he forbade, wholly hers. "Save the excuses. The Blood Legion's routes don't align with the Brotherhood's anymore." She pivots, more predator than target. "Almost like you're taking orders from someone else."

The word resonates with purpose.

Brotherhood.

It hangs there, undeniable and unsoftened—poison in a gilded room.

Silence blooms in its wake.

But she's attuned to him—the quiet tell in his posture, the coiled readiness masked as ease. Others would see control. She sees the build before the break.

To Lumira, this is a reckoning. She hears it clearly: he's not surprised.

"The palace maintains multiple security protocols," he replies, steady despite the near-imperceptible change in his stance. He is more defensive now, guarded. "Redundancy prevents systematic vulnerabilities."

"Redundancy," she repeats. "Or competing authority structures?"

He continues without pause, unreadable as ever. No break in expression, no change in rhythm—that smooth, practiced ease. "You've been busy." It isn't a denial. It's a blade, sidestepping cleanly.

"I've been studying a lot." Her tone is light, yet purposeful. Her stance eases, restraint tempered by a softer edge. A hint of vulnerability emerges, presented as if inviting a response.

She observes, not for haste, but for intuition. In the hush that follows, she reads the truth in his stance.

"The Red Night approaches." She intentionally uses this phrase, observing his reaction with unwavering focus.

Hadralis halts completely. Not from the frozen shock of surprise but from the calculating pause of a predator reassessing. Two heartbeats. Three. He holds steady. "Where did you hear that phrase?" He drops to barely audible levels despite the training ground's apparent emptiness.

"Does it matter?" Lumira counters, maintaining her position without advancing.

The space between them transforms—no longer mentor and student, but operatives evaluating a threat. Pretense falls away like unnecessary weight before combat.

"You're Brotherhood." It's not a question; there's no space for denial.

Her eyes catch on his arms as he adjusts his grip on the practice blade, the faint edge of intricate ink peeks out from his cuff. What she once took for simple ornament is now clear for what it is: the Brotherhood's mark, worn without apology.

Hadralis does not attempt to deny it. He's motionless—the pause before everything shifts.

The Blood Key burns against her skin, intensifying with proximity.

"Yes," he acknowledges. A single word that carries years of deception. "But not how you think."

"Enlighten me." Her tone is flat, stripped down to serve the task at hand.

"My role has always been about protection, not elimination." He subtly modifies his stance. "The Brotherhood's external image centers on security and the guardianship of artifacts. However, its internal purpose is much more complicated."

"Complicated," she repeats with increased disdain. "A convenient description for infiltrating noble houses, manipulating bloodlines, and executing those who ask inconvenient questions."

"Bloodlines aren't meant to be erased." It's not said in defense; it's spoken like truth he never doubted. "They're meant to be preserved—protected against forces that would exploit them."

"If you truly cared about preservation," she counters, "why has the Brotherhood pursued me since Thallen Forest? Why did that commander instruct his men to 'secure the Blood Descent'?"

His expression changes subtly—he is surprised by her choice of words. "Because you are important." The declaration slices through the moment. "More than you might even realize." This remark arrives with frustrating vagueness, serving neither as a confirmation nor a denial, creating another barrier to her accurate understanding.

"Important enough to lie to for years? To manipulate? To fucking craft me into a weapon while betraying the enemies I was trained to destroy?" The truth clicks into place—awful, undeniable. "You stood beside me at her funeral." Her control splinters under rising fury. "You let me grieve a sister you helped kill."

His expression reveals nothing that could quell the rage building behind her sternum.

"All this time, you were one of them." She pauses, searching for any hint of emotion—a sign that he understands the gravity of his actions.

The void is excruciating.

The blade strikes before she reacts, an embodiment of sorrow honed into rage. Hadralis moves faster, intercepting her wrist with brutal precision. A tilt of weight and a twist, her blade wrenches free before she registers the loss.

The weapon clatters to stone, the sound louder than it should be.

"Too obvious." He's calm but edged with disappointment. "If you're going to kill me, at least be smart about it."

She dives, scoops up the blade, and lunges—reckless, desperate. The steel slices through the air, narrowly missing his throat as he pivots at the last moment.

Hadralis doesn't retaliate. A sidestep, a redirection, and her own momentum is turned against her.

Spinning with the miss, she drives her knee toward his ribs. He finds her shoulder, pivots, and sends her stumbling. She catches herself at the last second. Air comes in shallow bursts, her rhythm fractured. He hasn't broken a sweat.

The training grounds become a battlefield—her raw emotion against his restraint.

"Fight back, damn you!" She lands a glancing blow. "Stop treating me like a child!"

"Then stop acting like one." His response conveys a frustrating calmness, lacking any heat.

Everything goes into the next strike—faking high, cuts low, and driving an elbow into his ribs. The impact lands and knocks his stance off balance. Just briefly, it feels like the way might clear.

Then he turns—no retreat, no resistance. Space vanishes. He clamps her wrist and wrenches the blade free before she registers the loss. A twist at her center sends her sprawling—stone smashes her back, cold steel touches her throat. Light. Final.

"If I wanted you dead," Hadralis murmurs, infuriatingly even, "you wouldn't have made it past your first mistake."

She has never felt fury like this—white-hot, bone-deep, tangled with helplessness until she can't tell them apart. It burns worse than any wound, a scream caught behind her teeth. "You killed her," she snarls, the words ripping free before she can stop them, locked on the Brotherhood mark inked across his wrist like a brand. "You killed Emberly."

His demeanor falters, revealing the edge shrouded in elegance—untamed, waiting. "No." The denial comes soft, but absolute. "I had no part in it."

"But you knew." Her voice doesn't rise, its restraint is what makes it dangerous. "You were aware and chose not to stop it."

"Do you really believe I had a choice?" The words cut, clean and merciless. "Do you think I don't bear her death with me every damn day?"

The Blood Key stirs—heat blooming like a truth layered in misdirection.

"The Brotherhood serves the Crown," he continues. "The Crown answers to powers more ancient than we can grasp. The Red Night isn't a metaphor, Lumira. It's not prophecy. It's a cycle. And it's coming—whether we're ready or not." He withdraws the blade from her throat but keeps his stance. "Emberly uncovered links that endangered individuals much more influential than us. She was advancing swiftly, attracting unwanted attention she couldn't defend herself against. I attempted to slow her pace and redirect her investigations."

"But you failed."

"I failed," he acknowledges. "And she suffered because of my indecision."

The confession lingers in the air, evoking neither forgiveness nor complete condemnation. Simply truth, at last articulated.

"Who ordered it?" she demands. "Who gave the command?"

"I don't know." His response carries the weight of truth rather than evasion. "Brotherhood chains of command are designed to obscure the source. Orders come through, but no names are attached. That's the point—compartmentalization protects the whole structure when pieces fall."

"Convenient," Lumira growls.

"Strategic," he corrects without emotion. "The system protects itself even when individual components fail."

The blind fury ebbs, giving way to cold strategy as she reassesses him. Not forgiveness—never that—but a recognition of complexity.

"I had an interesting conversation recently." She adjusts her approach. "With a Shadowspire guard remarkably well-informed about Brotherhood operations."

Hadralis's reaction is subtle but unmistakable—a brief pause, then careful recalibration. "And what exactly did he tell you?"

"Enough to confirm what I'd begun to suspect: the Brotherhood's true interest in these artifacts and their obsession with bloodline preservation."

A tell in his posture, a subtle realignment suggesting private calculation. "Be careful where you place your trust," he advises. "None of us are free agents in this war. Each decision answers to a deeper cause."

The caution carries weight when it comes from someone who has admitted to years of deception.

Hadralis almost continues. She catches the hesitation in his shoulders—a tension that hints there's more he could give her. But he wavers, as if weighing the cost, then lets it go. "The Red Night approaches," he offers instead—quiet, grave. "Whatever comes next will change everything we thought we understood about bloodlines, artifacts, and the barriers between worlds." He releases her completely, stepping back to allow her space to rise. "Lumira, it's time to decide: will you expose me, end my life, or utilize me as the resource I was meant to be?" This question highlights their circumstances with stark clarity—devoid of emotion solely on strategy.

She rises without responding to the barbed offer, her composure exact—though the storm's already turning in her gut. "We are not done," Lumira asserts, her decision stemming from a practical need instead of emotional clarity.

Hadralis nods once, accepting without clear relief or satisfaction. "No," he agrees. "We're not."

They hold for three heartbeats—mentor and student evolving into a more perilous ambiguity.

"I'll maintain our training schedule." He speaks at last with a firm tone. "Public perception of normalcy provides a tactical advantage while you determine your next actions."

"Agreed." Her response aligns with his pragmatic approach, years of court conditioning overriding personal feelings despite the lingering burn of betrayal.

She gathers her weapons with the ease of repetition, calm and betraying nothing.

"Lumira." Her name escapes his lips with unusual hesitation.

She pauses mid-step, spine rigid, but doesn't turn.

"Be careful. The Brotherhood isn't united in purpose or methodology. Some seek preservation, while others pursue dominance. The distinction matters more than you realize."

She offers a slight nod, nothing more, and continues on.

The training grounds fade behind her, but his words hang in the air: *You need to make a decision.* Each step through the palace corridors is measured, each breath wrestled into steadiness. The weight of Hadralis's betrayal presses in—cold, suffocating. It isn't shock. It isn't grief. It's worse.

Certainty.

He's always been part of the Brotherhood, and he stood beside her as she mourned.

She exhales sharply, pressing her knuckles into a marble column, grounding herself against the feeling of falling.

As a guard walks by, she straightens her posture and rolls her shoulders. She will handle this later; for now, she needs to keep moving.

The door clicks shut after her. Lumira locks and bolts it. Her chamber rests in heavy calm, the air unnatural, the walls aware with an intelligence older than time.

Three Blood Ravens sit on the window's ledge, their copper eyes glimmering in the candlelight.

"I know what he is now." She's barely above a whisper.

They don't move. She doesn't wait.

A quick bag. A clean exit. She takes Emberly's old path—narrow corridors and secret turns carved for escape.

By the time she arrives in the city, Hadralis's warning thrums through her like an echo she can't shake. Patrols have rotated. Guards linger where none should be, their routes deliberate, unmistakable. They're preparing.

Moving like a shadow, unseen and unfollowed, Lumira lets the market noise swallow her whole. A Blood Raven perches from a crooked sign; her stomach tightens, but she doesn't stop.

It's late afternoon by the time she finds what she needs: a cramped room above a dye shop where no one asks questions and glances never linger. She could have hidden away in her own chambers, but the walls there hold more ghosts than comfort, and a suffocating sense of being seen. Here, the stale dye fumes and thin walls offer a place to clear her mind and decide what must come next.

Hours pass. She paces the narrow boards until they groan under her steps, her thoughts pulling apart and knotting themselves back together in loops she can't quite untangle. Outside, the street noise fades, replaced by the hush that settles when the city finally forgets its own heartbeat. Once, she peeks through the warped shutters—and there it is again: the same Blood Raven, perched now on a low rooftop beam across the alley, feathers catching the lamplight like old copper.

When dusk bleeds into the alleys and the last vendors bar their doors, she slips back into the streets and trades coin for a sturdy horse at a stable near the city's edge. No questions. No names. She rides south through back roads and farmland, the chill pressing close as she skirts the edges of Thallen Forest and pushes deeper into the trees—toward the one person who might understand what comes next.

The journey takes the rest of the night. By the time the forest thickens around her, dawn edges over the horizon, her muscles ache, and her thoughts drag like iron. She reins in. A rustle in the brush. Then nothing.

Ilara steps from the trees, a bow slung across her back, her expression unreadable. She scans Lumira once. "You look like hell."

Swinging down from the saddle, Lumira's boots hit the damp earth. "That makes two of us."

Ilara waits; fixed on her approach. "Trouble?"

Lumira meets her gaze. "Not trouble. Betrayal. Wearing a familiar face." The forest hums around them—alive, indifferent—a stark contrast to the chaos coiled inside her.

Ilara squints, much like a ranger observing a wounded creature that could strike. "You're certain?"

Lumira nods. "He's in the Brotherhood." The words feel conclusive, like closing a wound that continues to bleed.

"And alive?"

A pause. "For now."

No further questions. Just a breath held longer than usual—Ilara's version of agreement.

Lumira tightens her gloves. "What have you found about the Red Night?"

A flicker crosses Ilara's face, vanishing before it takes shape. "I don't think you'll like it."

The clearing is secluded, chosen for conversations that cannot afford interruptions. Faint traces of old campfires form uneven scars—a testament to the secrets exchanged here.

Ilara lowers herself to pick up a leather satchel. "Forest scouts have been observing Brotherhood activities. Same routes, same tactics. It's repeating." She spreads a cloth beside a tangle of roots and lays out her findings—maps inked with notations, messages half-burned, names scrawled in the margins like afterthoughts. Not declarations, but patterns.

Lumira inches closer, bracing her hands on the earth as she scans the pages. Her breathing steadies, her body settling into tighter control. The picture they form isn't complete, but it's enough. Patrols have thickened near noble districts across multiple territories. There's been no public decree, but border crossings and trade roads are restricted—merchants turned back, travelers questioned or detained without reason. Word spreads fast when roads once open to everyone grow narrow overnight.

Specific names have stopped appearing in correspondence: trusted intermediaries and familiar contacts. They have not been exposed or arrested, but have been absent without leave. There have been no explanations. Silence has replaced the life that once existed.

"Who are they really after?" Lumira inquires, her tone soft and measured.

Ilara doesn't answer immediately. She runs her finger down the side of one map, halting at a cluster of inked notches—places spaced far enough apart to defy coincidence. "No one obvious. No highborn, no leaders." The words come slowly, finally. "But the balance is unraveling. People with reach—those who kept things moving behind the scenes—they've vanished. And in their place, there's only absence."

A cold knowing settles low in Lumira's chest. *Restructuring.*

"Whoever's orchestrating this isn't removing threats," Ilara continues. "They're clearing the board. If Hadralis is still standing, they haven't finished with him."

Lumira presses her palms to her temples.

Hadralis stated it: the Brotherhood answers to the Crown. If the Crown's grip is slipping, the Brotherhood won't stay steady for long. A larger move is already in motion.

The Brotherhood and the Crown—one force, one mind, hidden behind different masks.

"Are you suggesting they're gathering strength before the Red Night?" Lumira inquires, fixed on the disorganized papers.

Ilara nods. "It fits. They either sense what's coming or they've arranged it. The timing couldn't be more exact. The Brotherhood is preparing for a reckoning."

Lumira straightens, the fire in her chest crystallizing into determination. "We push harder. Discover who's behind these decisions. If the Brotherhood is altering power dynamics, we must know who they're answering to."

Ilara nods. "We'll start with our spies inside the territories." She tugs her cloak tighter. "We should set out before dawn. Rest while you can."

But Lumira knows sleep won't come.

The fire burns low. Lumira shifts upright. Sleep eludes her, not with her thoughts tangled in Hadralis's revelations.

Ilara lies motionless nearby, but Rangers do not truly sleep when they are hunted.

A breeze stirs the leaves, but the tension hangs—unmoving beneath the rustle, like the forest knows what's coming. Lumira stands at the edge of the clearing, her fingers brushing the hilt of her blade, tracking the tree line. It isn't fear that constricts her chest, but a deeper pressure—dense, unseen. She's not alone.

No creatures twitch. No wind blows. The forest isn't untouched—it's conscious.

The Brotherhood reaches widely, its grip extending beyond city gates and noble halls, infiltrating places that should remain untouched. Yet somehow, she has become the axis of it. However, this presence—this feeling—does not belong to them.

Whatever waits now is older and more patient.

She sends one last thought into the darkness before returning to the fire. The scattered reports raise more questions than they answer. Dawn is approaching.

Whatever the Red Night brings, she will face it on her own terms—with nothing but a blade and the will to use it.

22

SHADOW WITNESSES

The fog curls around Lumira's ankles—a patient predator, unhurried in its hunger. It rises from the Naiad River in pale tendrils, softening the forest's harsh edges and transmuting the shoreline into both mythic and unknowable. The air hangs heavy with expectation, the kind that seeps into bones and makes itself permanent.

But she didn't come to wander; she came to reclaim control. And she didn't come here by chance.

Thallen Forest presses against the Naiad's current here—a narrow stretch Ilara marked after repeated patrols disappeared, no evidence left behind. They'd sketched the stakes by firelight, routes disappearing into smoke.

"The Brotherhood's thickening their presence along the river," Ilara had warned, low and certain. "Grovenar's side. Crimsun's too. Whatever they're guarding—it's not random."

So Lumira walked west, past logic and safety, toward the one place that didn't ask questions.

The Naiad drags past her like a forgotten tale—refusing the dignity of reflection. No sunlight. No trees. Not even the outline of her own fucking sorrow. On the far bank lies what she recognizes: Crimsun's stern watchtowers transitioning into Grovenar's thick wilderness. Each territory clings to this stretch of river, as if unable to relinquish it.

Maybe the gods who shaped these lands once had more than borders, she ponders. They may have constructed their palaces close enough to see one another, as being apart would have been too painful. It's a naïve thought—but a beautiful one. And tonight, beauty is allowed.

It's not the cold that unsettles her, or the damp curling along her skin—it's the hush, stripped of birdsong, of insect drone, of the river's chatter. The forest waits, suspended and listening.

Lumira resets her stance. A light touch grazes the sword's hilt—not from fear, but to steady herself. Her body remains composed, though her thoughts race like wildfire. She is not lost; she is attuned. And with chilling clarity, she realizes it's listening back.

The plan is elegant: Ilara mapping Brotherhood movements deeper in the forest while Lumira probes the river crossing, where three territories graze one another and oversight thins into opportunity. It's ideal for covert work—intelligence gathering that, if discovered, could cost her everything.

She used to believe she could identify Brotherhood agents on sight. That illusion shattered with Hadralis's confession. Now she trusts nothing she sees, and everything she senses.

The real blades at her hip mirror her well—curved for speed, unadorned, built to finish the job up close. Once, that honesty was pride. Now, it feels like judgment.

She had been prepared for this—strategy, subtlety, and the controlled use of violence. Yet, none of it saved Emberly.

The Brotherhood has threaded itself through history like a creeping sickness, pulling strings behind the Aethervoid while nobles play their tired games with crowns and courts. Territories realign, alliances rise and fall, and war declarations are signed and sealed with ceremony. But perhaps it's all theater. A grand performance to distract from the power behind the curtain.

If she wants to destroy them, she must first see them. The realization settles in with grim clarity.

Lumira exhales, warmth vanishing into the dawn—swallowed by the morning chill, gone as if it had not existed at all.

Something flickers among the trees to her left. Not quite shadow or form. She finds one of her curved daggers, but doesn't draw it. The motion isn't hostile. It simply shouldn't exist.

Darkness deepens once more. This time, it lingers.

Figures appear—not walking or gliding, but manifesting—as though the forest exhales them into existence. Ethereal and void of light, they hover at the periphery of perception, shimmering like phantoms woven from fog and fading light. Their shadow-slick hair drifts as if caught by an unseen current. It is delicate and vaguely feminine in shape—elegant, unsettling. Without leaving footprints or disturbing the grass, they embody absence.

The Umbra Wraiths. Tales call them silent watchers—drifting shadows that never meddle, never draw close. Yet the name surfaces now as both myth and memory. Emberly's journals flicker through her mind: meticulous sketches, cryptic notes, a shoreline like this one circled in red ink. Shadow-beings, birdlike in their curiosity, collectors of stolen truths. She's seen enough now to know it's true. One phrase Emberly scrawled in the margin hums in her bones:

They remember what was taken.

A chill slides through her. It's not the cold but the way she knows this. Not fear exactly—more a primordial instinct stirring awake. The Blood Key warms against her chest, its heat syncing with her pulse.

She can't shake the sense they're not seeing her as prey or a trespasser, but as one expected.

Her thoughts slip back to Thallen Forest, weeks ago—when she first glimpsed one, distinct from the darkness. Its presence had thrummed through the roots and bark, as if the forest itself had taken notice. It hadn't spoken. It hadn't approached. But it had observed her—assessed every action.

As they do now. Familiar. Unsettling.

The Wraiths materialize where light cannot reach, gliding out of shadow with unnatural grace. They glide—slow, avian, eyes dissecting as if parsing a secret. They don't see her as lost or wandering. They see a hinge in the story. A threshold. A spark.

Emberly wrote that a bloodline alone cannot activate the artifacts—that a rarer force is required. Now, Lumira feels it in her marrow: they aren't waiting for anyone—they're waiting for her.

She raises her chin and keeps her spine straight, undeterred by the Wraiths gathering before her. "Well," she murmurs, smooth as silk and twice as dangerous, "the legends failed to mention you'd be so... theatrical."

The nearest Wraith pauses, inclines slightly, then bows—a figure stitched from absence, not substance. It extends what might—generously—be called a hand. Less charitably, it resembles reality's fracture, a void offering either invitation or undoing.

Lumira stands her ground. She knows what they want—not from palace fables or whispered bedtime tales, but from the last desperate pages Emberly left behind: cramped script, meticulously sketched warnings. Her sister had called them "shadow witnesses," the ones who remember what others strive to erase. She had written of contact, of revelation. They show you truths that can't be spoken. That line was underlined. Twice. The shoreline appeared only once, but once proved enough.

She steadies herself—not out of fear; she has outgrown that indulgence—but because instinct demands precision. Her arm stays outstretched, held in anticipation. "My sister stood here before me," Lumira states, steady and sharp. "She gave you her truths to keep. Let's see if you'll keep mine."

The Wraith offers no response. Of course, it doesn't. How tediously dramatic. Even the shadows refuse to engage in straightforward conversation.

"I didn't come here expecting you." She doesn't flinch in the dark. "But I won't waste what you're willing to witness." She meets the writhing dark where its eyes should be. "The Brotherhood. The Red Night. The people they've vanished, the truths they've buried to keep their secrets hidden. You remember what was taken—remember this too."

A ripple moves through the Wraith—subtle, like wind-disturbing smoke—a reaction, perhaps, or acknowledgment. The outstretched limb remains steady, waiting.

Emberly wrote about this briefly, almost against her will. Contact is required. Disorienting, yet necessary. The note was scrawled in the margins, as if she hadn't meant to record it but couldn't bear to leave it unsaid. They ask for trust, obedience—or worse. Still, Emberly kept returning. She went willingly, and that means it wasn't coercion.

Lumira takes a step forward, reaching out—unflinching, unapologetic—as if offering a limb to the executioner while daring them to tremble first. Her fingertips brush the Wraith's surface—cool, almost immaterial—and the world shatters.

Sound fades. Voices disappear. Only sensation remains—overwhelming, timeless, unbearable. Not words, but memory.

The vision crashes into her.

Not a battlefield—worse. A gathering that bordered on sacred.

The Brotherhood stood in ceremonial lines, armor polished to a mirror shine, etched with symbols she can't name but feels in her blood. They weren't guards. They weren't soldiers. They were worshippers—guardians bound to a force so ancient it reverberates through her bones.

That reverence had already begun to rot—into possession. Into cruelty.

The twelve gods and goddesses stood in majestic presence, vast beyond mortal comprehension, blazing with a terrifying radiance no eye could bear. Their power flowed freely between them, divine connections maintained without the artifacts that typically anchored them to the mortal realm. Today, they had been summoned directly.

This marked the day of treachery, the moment when the Aethervoid would transform from a veil into a prison.

Lumira feels it stir—an instinctive pull, as if a long-dormant note has finally been struck inside her, vibrating through her veins. The Brotherhood didn't lose the gods to time or myth; they sealed them away.

The vision blurs.

The twelve deities formed a perfect circle. Power arced between them, weaving creation, destruction, and renewal into cosmic harmony—until one figure, initially subtle, a shadow among starlight, broke from stillness.

Not outward. Away.

Its form twisted, stepping beyond the sacred pattern. Balance wavered. The others faltered—not from violence, but from absence—as the bond unraveled and an invisible thread was taken, not severed.

The Aethervoid was never intended to be a prison. It had been crafted as a delicate veil—divine magic woven by all twelve, a sacred boundary between worlds designed to balance cosmic powers, not sever them. It embodied harmony, a testament to what gods could create when they stood as equals.

But one god fractured the circle.

Not through warfare, but through secrets passed hand to hand.

The Deceiver slipped through mortal courts like poison, offering forbidden knowledge—rituals, spells, undoings slipped in the right ears. They spoke of divine instability, of gods grown distant and volatile. Yet, balance wasn't the goal.

From the beginning, each god carried an artifact—vessels of their own essence, forged to focus and temper their power. Divided among the twelve, these relics kept the realms in balance and the Aethervoid contained.

But it was a slow and relentless conquest, unraveling trust and stealing strength meant for many, not one. Separated, the gods faltered. Together, they were mighty but exposed. And when the final spell was cast—woven of mortal ambition and divine betrayal—they did not die.

They were incarcerated.

Trapped beyond the Aethervoid, severed from the mortal realm and scrubbed from memory. A final spell ensured their erasure—woven not to kill but to blur, to hollow out belief until the gods became nothing more than bedtime stories and half-forgotten curses.

Memories unraveled. Truths faded before they could ever be written. Bloodlines were thinned, monitored, and quietly reshaped. From the ashes, the Brotherhood rose—not as rulers, but as stewards of a magnificent lie. They hoarded the traitor's knowledge, twisted the Aethervoid from veil to vault, and consigned the gods to obscurity, their names remembered only by earth and shadow.

But the forest remembers. The Umbra Wraiths remember. A buried power shifts inside her, no longer content to sleep.

It knows.

The vision pulses around her, each beat breaking as a different memory cuts through—a sudden sliver from her past.

The Shadowspire guard's voice, so casual at the time, now strikes as a warning:

"The Aethervoid isn't just a magical theory. It's a veil—a boundary that separates this realm from the divine. It keeps the gods locked out. Keeps us from reaching them."

Locked out.

She hadn't questioned it then, lost in the rush of action. But now, each word settles with uncanny clarity—crafted with purpose, and unnervingly close to the truth.

It wasn't the language of someone reciting lessons. It was the language of someone who understood the truth—that the lock isn't distance but imprisonment.

The Shadowspire guard understands. Perhaps not everything, but sufficiently enough to choose his words with painful precision, and to challenge her understanding without speaking plainly.

Her jaw tightens. One time—*one*—she'd like a straight fucking answer without the smoke and riddles. She realizes this hasn't been about reaching the gods but about freeing them.

The vision fragments, then reforms around a familiar figure that leaves Lumira stunned.

Emberly stands on this very shoreline, her face illuminated by the same unearthly knowledge coursing through Lumira's veins. She sees the Aethervoid, understanding what was never meant to be comprehended.

Lumira watches her sister trace symbols in her journal with frantic clarity, mapping connections between artifact sites and documenting which Brotherhood territories held which relics. Most importantly, she witnesses Emberly receiving the same revelation she now experiences—the truth about the Deceiver who betrayed the other gods and continues manipulating events from behind the veil. But there is a more profound betrayal: the spell that imprisoned the gods simultaneously severed mortals from their innate magic. It placed an arcane block in their minds that prevents them from accessing or remembering their true capabilities. It appears a world of rare magic, but beneath the surface lies a realm of stifled potential. Entire populations unknowingly hobbled, their power suppressed by the same spell that clouds their memories.

That's why they killed her.

The truth surges within her—not as a weapon, but a fault line cracking at her feet. It alters everything she believed she knew. Emberly wasn't in pursuit of artifacts or Brotherhood secrets. She had revealed what held everything together, and what could break it apart with a single breath.

Not only had the gods been imprisoned—they had been erased.

And mortals had suffered alongside them, not stripped of their magic, but stifled—severed from the power embedded in their blood, hindered by a lie so thorough it extinguished memory, muted potential, and transformed birthright into mere myth.

Lumira gasps as the connection severs, stumbling backward. Her heart races, the rhythm frantic and disorienting after the strange communion.

"She knew," Lumira utters, the words splintered with disbelief. "Knew what they did to the gods. Knew what they stole from us—the magic buried in our blood."

The lead Wraith inclines what passes for its head; the gesture is unmistakably one of confirmation. It raises its not-quite hand again, but this time, the meaning is inarguable.

An offer. A choice.

It can restore what was taken—not knowledge but power itself—the birthright stolen from her, the magic flowing in her blood yet remaining beyond reach.

Lumira doesn't hesitate. "Yes."

In an instant, the world doesn't transform but rather sheds layers. Colors become more vivid, edges become clearer, and what is concealed between heartbeats snaps into view. The river transforms from mere water into a pulsating barrier—a membrane between realms, vibrating with primeval purpose. The trees don't exist; they listen, their roots creating an extensive network of communication that connects territories and shared memories.

The Wraiths themselves transform in her perception. They are not shadows but beings who chose that form long ago—forsaking physical substance to better preserve what mortals wished to forget.

Magic she never noticed before exists everywhere—coursing through the ground, spiraling in the air around her, connecting everything in patterns too vast to comprehend fully.

"This is…" Her carefully maintained composure falters, revealing raw wonder. The magic courses through her veins like liquid fire, familiar and awakening all at once. Energy that has always been there, dormant, now stirs to life with terrifying potential. Power crackles at the edge of her touch, barely contained, as her senses heighten past mortal thresholds. It's overwhelming, intoxicating, and for a heartbeat, she understands why the Brotherhood dreads this power unleashed among the masses. Such capacity was never meant to be caged.

Lumira staggers, pressing her palm against the nearest tree to steady herself. The world spins—not from weakness, but from abundance. With each breath, she draws in currents of energy she can now perceive; with each heartbeat, waves ripple outward from her core. She closes her eyes, grounding herself against the intensity.

"Fuck," Lumira half-laughs at the inadequacy of words. "This is what they stole from us."

When her lashes lift once more, her vision has stabilized— yet everything stings with vivid detail. She can see the magical networks threading through the forest like veins of light. She can feel the Wraiths' ageless patience, their relief that finally— *finally*—someone can perceive them as they truly are.

The Wraiths glide around her in synchronous movement, their shapes now more defined as she can truly see them. Not exactly man-shaped, but suggestive of bodies that might have once been, before choosing this manner of existence. Their edges blur and reform with each distortion, as if reality itself cannot quite decide how to interpret their presence.

But one Wraith steps closer—taller than the others, its shape radiating a sense of timeless dignity despite its insubstantial nature. This time, it extends both appendages—an invitation, not a test. The first touch awakened what was already hers by right: magic.

This is something else.

Lumira doesn't hesitate. She allows the Wraith to cradle her face. The sensation is neither warm nor cold—only grounding. The world narrows. Even time seems to hesitate.

Then—

Not memory.

History.

It unfurls in her mind with razor clarity, as though it has always been waiting:

Long ago, the gods and goddesses ruled not as tyrants, but as stewards. Each shaped one of Cyrathea's twelve territories in their image—storm-lashed peaks, tangled forests, endless dunes. To their people, they each gifted a sacred artifact, crafted from their own essence.

These artifacts were not forged in war, but in trust. Each was a divine conduit—bridging mortal and immortal, land and legacy. Traditionally, the artifact was passed down through the god's own bloodline, its power awakening most fully in their descendants. Yet even dormant, the artifact amplified life across its region— fostering abundance, protecting the balance.

Then came the betrayal.

One of their own—the Deceiver—turned. Twisting truths into warnings that the gods had become unstable. Unfit to rule.

Mortals believed him. And from their fear, he built a doctrine. A secret order.

The Brotherhood of Eternal Shadow.

They claimed to regulate the artifacts, to restore order. But order gave way to control. Control became conquest. They began isolating bloodlines, rewriting lineage, and hunting anyone with dangerous levels of divine potential.

After the Aethervoid was cast, their strategy adapted—not abandoning the artifacts, but changing how they approached them. In some centuries, they regulated. In some, they hoarded. In others, they erased any who might awaken what lay dormant. The Deceiver's doctrine endured, reshaping itself with each generation—always toward the same end.

The gods saw the fractures forming—temples emptied, trust fraying, their gifts twisted into tools of power. In secret, they hid their artifacts deep within sacred places, each shaped by their essence and fiercely guarded.

But the Brotherhood wasn't finished.

In the name of stability, they cast the Aethervoid—magic beyond comprehension, laced with sacrifice and sealed by betrayal. The gods were not destroyed. They were imprisoned, cut off beyond the veil, and systematically erased from memory.

Their names were buried. Their presence, denied.

But the artifacts endured: hidden in shadow, alive with intent, patient as ever.

In their final act of foresight, the gods embedded a restriction into the relics: only one born of all twelve divine bloodlines could safely wield their combined power without succumbing to madness or death. It was a failsafe—one the Brotherhood has spent centuries suppressing.

And they learned more. Every eight hundred years, the veil thins. The Aethervoid strains. The artifacts stir. It's not prophecy. Not accident. It's rhythm—older than records, older than gods.

The Brotherhood learned to read it. To anticipate it. To tighten their grip before the first tremor breaks the surface.

They call it the Red Night.

Twice before, they've held the line—patching cracks, sealing breaches, ensuring that whatever slips through is buried or bound. Not the Red Night itself—yet—but its echoes. Creatures growing restless. Magic fraying at the edges. Patrols stirring in places that should remain still. The tremors before the quake.

Now, the Red Night looms again—a rare thinning of the veil between realms. The artifacts stir. Bloodlines long thought extinguished have begun to manifest. And so the Brotherhood accelerates its pursuit—not merely to suppress the relics, but to gather them all before anyone else can.

They are no longer content to destroy what threatens their order. Now, they seek to shape it—to create or mold the one who can survive the artifacts' power, and bend the gods' legacy to their own design.

The truth lands in her like a heartbeat:

She is not their chosen.

She is their last chance—until the next.

The Wraith releases her. The vision fractures.

Lumira collapses to her knees at the river's edge, heart pounding like she's sprinted through centuries. She presses a palm to the earth, grounding herself against the spin of a world that suddenly feels thinner, more breakable.

The Red Night is coming.

She can feel it now.

A curse shudders out of her.

The Wraiths remain—motionless and inscrutable. Not retreating. Not finished. Holding their ground. Waiting. As if the choice is hers to make.

The Brotherhood never *caused* the Red Night.

They've only ever sought to own it. And this time, if they succeed, the world will not survive the cost. *Like hell they'll hold the world together with lies*, Lumira thinks, her jaw tightening.

The Wraiths close in without a sound. The tallest nods—slow, exact.

"And Emberly—did she discover how to undermine their hold on her? To forge connections they couldn't oversee?" The idea evokes fierce pride mixed with fresh grief. Forever underestimated, her sister. Always five moves in front, all while feigning compliance.

The Wraiths create ripples that could signify an affirmation.

"She sacrificed her life for what she uncovered about them." Lumira rises, her newfound understanding solidifying into determination. "I refuse to let that be in vain."

The assembled Wraiths dip, a faint bow of shadowed forms that reads as approval. The tallest raises both appendages and gestures with unsettling purpose—not toward the clearing's edge, but beyond it. The motion carries weight, intention, as if drawing back an invisible veil.

Lumira follows the gesture and gasps.

Where moments before she had seen only forest and shadow, a massive oak now stands revealed. Its trunk is broader than three men standing shoulder to shoulder, and its branches create a canopy that devours even the morning light. Ageless beyond measure, it pulses with the same deep magic she can now perceive—as if it had been waiting, hidden in plain sight, for her awakening.

"The paths reveal themselves when needed," she whispers, largely to herself rather than the Wraiths. "Similar to how they appeared for her."

She approaches, examining the tree with fresh insight. Magic courses through its trunk like lifeblood, linking to hidden networks threaded through the forest floor. At the base, twisted roots form natural archways and hollows.

The Wraith points to a hollow between two massive roots.

Lumira brushes the gnarled bark, feeling the quiet hum against her skin. The intricate designs she noticed at Pigments & Pints and the strange patterns throughout the deeper forest suddenly coalesce, like words in a language she is beginning to understand.

They have always been there, waiting.

"The Terran Gnomes," she murmurs. "This leads to their tunnels."

The Wraith stares, agreement thrumming in the silence, then drifts forward with purpose that feels older than language.

Lumira weighs her options. She needs a place beyond noble halls, Brotherhood influence, and Shadowspire schemes—a place to build strength in secret. She recalls Ilara mentioning them: beings who roam freely beneath all territories.

The gnomes do not trust easily. However, necessity carries weight, and few necessities are more urgent than preventing the Brotherhood from seizing the Red Night.

"They've been expecting me, haven't they?" she asks, confident in her assumption.

The Wraith extends both arms in a formal gesture reminiscent of an ancient pledge. The others follow suit, forming a circle around her.

A promise. An alliance.

"I accept." The words come low and firm. "And I swear it back. Whatever the Red Night brings—we face it together. No running. No fucking mercy."

The commanding presence raises one not-quite arm—and the world shifts for the last time.

Light spills across the sky, vivid tones reverberating through her—syncing with a rhythm not entirely her own. Ribbons of brilliance—amber, amethyst, viridian, cobalt—swirl through the void with impossible grace, flowing not as beasts but as motion born of memory. One arcs low, gliding close in a spiral of liquid light. It does not speak. It does not touch. Yet Lumira feels its intent as clearly as if it had slipped past her defenses.

This is a summons, not merely a path. It's a pull, not an endpoint—a calling to what isn't here, isn't now, but waits. She's unaware of their true nature, only that they are archaic, concealed, and patient. This—this stunning convergence of color and motion—represents the Wraiths' final offering.

The vision fades.

The Wraiths begin to dissolve, their forms unraveling into the folds of ordinary shadow. All but their leader vanish. It lingers—long enough to gesture once more toward the hollow threaded between the roots, then fades.

Morning creeps in soft and unassuming. The hollow sits undisturbed, camouflaged by moss and bark, but Lumira feels the faint thrum underfoot. It takes her a moment to register the light—too angled for dawn, too warm for night's edge. She's lost hours. Again.

Not just a place, but a threshold. A seam in the world, stitched shut by something older than stone. And if she means to cross it, she'll have to decide how much of herself she's willing to spend today.

Hadralis betrayed her, yes. But perhaps his motives were more complex than mere loyalty. His mention of the Brotherhood factions—preservation versus manipulation—may be more significant than she initially realized.

She inspects her weapons and fastens her gear. Then, without hesitation, she slips into the hollow.

The Umbra Wraiths have shown her what lies beyond the Aethervoid. The Terran Gnomes will show her how to move outside the Brotherhood's surveillance unnoticed. And somewhere, in the spaces between, she'll find a way to finish what Emberly started.

The Red Night approaches. Soon.

But this time, she wields the Blood Key—beyond their reach, beyond their rule.

The darkness recedes, giving way to soft golden light as Lumira touches solid ground. A tunnel unfurls before her, carved with ancient precision. Its walls gleam with a flawless finish, and intricate patterns flow like rivers through the stone.

She draws in once, steady and certain, and lets a small, knowing smile slip through. The kind born not from joy, but from promise. The Brotherhood stole her sister's life to bury their secrets, believing they could smother her legacy, erase her name, and seal away everything she dared to uncover. They wanted obedience and demanded submission, but they were wrong.

Lumira isn't here to stop the Red Night.

She is here to finish what her sister began—and this time, the world will hear them both.

23

THE PACT BELOW

After the ethereal void of the Wraiths' domain, the gnome tunnels assault Lumira's senses with violent pragmatism. There is no gradual transition, no merciful adjustment period—just the abrupt slap of reality. Minerals thicken the air like unspoken threats. Iron and damp stone fill her lungs, replacing the emptiness of darkness with an existence both primordial and uncompromising.

Her body remembers its purpose—honed in shadowed battles, masked by velvet and diplomacy. Above, the palace flaunts its opulence for anyone foolish enough to admire it. Down here, the stone keeps its history bare and unsparing—a place built to endure, not impress.

The walls tell stories in ancient sigils and glyphs, a language that predates the carefully sanitized histories taught above. Lumira traces them with her gaze, not her fingers—she knows better than to leave aristocratic prints on texts that powerful forces would happily burn. The carvings possess a mathematical chaos that speaks to the part of her that's spent a lifetime decoding the performative order of noble society, finding its weak points and pressure fractures.

Light spills forward—not the palace's cold, industrial glare, but vibrant defiance cast in gold. Citrine flames flicker against stone walls polished to a mirror-like finish, showcasing a level of craftsmanship that might bring the palace architects to tears. The gnomes have shaped more than tunnels—they've built testaments to perseverance, while the powerful bicker over scraps of authority.

The passage unexpectedly expands into a cathedral of stone. Crystal formations capture and multiply the torchlight with suspicious precision. Underground springs create pools of water so pristine that they appear less like liquid and more like windows into some alternative, undistorted reality.

Gnomes materialize from strategic shadows, torchlight glinting off keen expressions that radiate unnerving intelligence. Small but composed, they command attention with subdued power. They aren't startled by her arrival—they anticipated it. Of course they did. The pathetic surveillance network aboveground is a child's charcoal scrawl compared to the gnomes' subterranean awareness.

A figure advances.

His beard—interwoven with metallic beads that shimmer with unnerving precision—frames a face etched by centuries. The metalwork isn't mere ornamentation. It pulses with intention. Sigils, perhaps. Markers. Warnings.

Ilara had spoken only once of the gnomes—half in jest, half in warning. Of an Elder so old the stones answer to him, and the trees lean in, hearing him before all else. A myth dressed in mineral and memory.

This must be him.

The Gnome Elder.

His eyes meet hers with the weight of old judgment, the kind that has witnessed empires rise and fall and found each one predictably unimpressive.

Lumira doesn't waste words. Diplomacy died with Emberly. She cuts through the chamber's stale reverence—controlled, deliberate, and impossible to ignore.

"I need a place to operate," she states, maintaining the crisp enunciation of her class even while standing as a supplicant. "A safe haven hidden from their scrutiny."

The Elder offers nothing but stillness, the survivalist calm of one who has watched more than acted.

"The Brotherhood threatens all who exist beyond their reach." She's anchored by the one thing she trusts: her own resolve. "I don't require your allegiance—merely space. A fortress beneath their world while I dismantle it."

The Gnome Elder gestures toward a circular pool where water trickles down the stone generously. As Lumira approaches, the water's surface distorts—not a reflection but a window forcing itself open. Images form with brutal clarity: Brotherhood guards colonizing sacred tunnels, artifact chambers being retrofitted with technologies that reek of desperation.

"They prepare," the Elder remarks, his succinct words contrasting with the verbose justifications that nobles exchange as if they were money. "They've always known when the Red Night is near."

Though unease stirs deep inside, Lumira answers with composure—every inch the figure they expect her to be. "Then you understand why I need space beyond their reach."

"You step through shadows as if they belong to you now." His words are heavy with soil, dredged from what should have remained buried. "But knowing where to walk is not the same as knowing who walks beside you. Some pursue with purpose beyond capture," he observes. "Some hunters do not seek to cage—but to unleash."

The statement hangs between them, pregnant with implications that Lumira can't afford to ignore. It is not a warning but contextualization—a reminder that motivations rarely conform to convenient categories and that opposition isn't always what it appears.

"We will watch," the Elder offers, as if time itself answers to patience.

Lumira straightens, not out of deference but certainty. "Watching won't save you. The Brotherhood's grip is fracturing. Desperation makes monsters of men—and they're running out of time."

The Elder's expression remains unchanged, but the atmosphere recalibrates—whether judgment tightening or simply the air itself hardening as decisions crystallize from possibility into inevitability. He studies her with uncomfortable perception, peeling back layers she's spent years cultivating. After several moments, he nods—controlled, the kind of motion that comes from someone who weighs every outcome.

"We have observed the patterns." The voice scrapes the air like prophecy etched in bone. "The Brotherhood has grown… ambitious in their reach. Their corruption extends even into our domains."

Lumira waits, recognizing the careful consideration behind his composure. This isn't a refusal—it's negotiation.

"Behind the Western Ridge," he begins, every word placed with care, "lies land the surface-dwellers forgot. Old bones of stone run through it—enough to shape, if the right hands move quickly."

A suggestion, but also a challenge.

"I don't need ruins." Lumira's voice is all edge. "I need walls. I need defenses built to hold when the Brotherhood stops lurking and starts burning."

The Elder smiles faintly—a craggy, knowing thing. "The gnomes were building fortresses while your ancestors fumbled with fire from stone." His tone isn't unkind, but time clings to it all the same. "The structure stands. Whether it belongs to you... remains to be seen."

Lumira inclines her head, the motion crisp, acknowledging the offer for what it is. Gnomes don't make promises lightly, but their word is harder than bedrock to break once given.

"I'll also need access to communication channels," she adds, leveling into command. "And methods of crossing territories without alerting the Brotherhood."

"The deep passages connect all twelve territories," the Elder replies with the particular patience of someone explaining basic geography to a child. "The Brotherhood knows of some. Not all." He gestures to a rough stone alcove, where intricate maps sprawl across ancient parchment. "Paths exist beyond even their reach. For those deemed worthy of access."

The implication lies between them, unspoken yet unmistakable. She isn't trusted yet—but she might be, given time and proof of purpose.

Good.

Freedom to maneuver will provide her advantages that the Brotherhood, with its territorial squabbles and bureaucratic inefficiencies, can never match. Their power relies on the isolation of the gods, the territories, and knowledge itself. Connection is their enemy, and these tunnels offer precisely that.

"And in return?" she asks, knowing all gifts carry cost.

The Blood Key radiates warmth—calm and attuned, as if it senses the weight of what hangs in the balance.

"Information," the Elder states. "About Brotherhood operations above ground. About plans within noble circles. About the artifacts they seek." He stares at the key draped at her throat, expression unreadable. "And perhaps… insights about certain objects of power."

A fair exchange. Knowledge for knowledge. Sanctuary for surveillance.

But fairness doesn't mean safety.

Lumira lets the silence stretch, gauging the balance behind the offer—their need for her information and her need for their shelter. Allies, perhaps. But not without agendas of their own.

"The decision will be made soon." The Elder is quiet but edged with intent. "If it is yours, you'll know."

The timeline's vague. Reassurance is nonexistent. But that gnome certainty remains—when a choice is made, it holds.

Lumira allows herself a small, sharp smile—the kind that promises retribution rather than joy. "Then we understand each other perfectly."

24

THE HUNTER AND HUNTED

As Lumira emerges from the gnome tunnels, the forest does not welcome her—it confronts her—not changed but revealed. As if her journey through their ancient domain peeled back the lies she'd once accepted without a second glance.

Colors slash the air with stark accuracy—unnaturally bright, as if placed with intent. Shadows collect where sunlight should dominate, pooling in folds that feel older than dusk. The trees seem wrong—spaced with unnerving precision, their mirrored forms echoing a design not born of nature.

The absence devours sound. No birds punctuate the air with trivial melodies, no leaves dare rustle against one another, and the wind itself holds its breath. Only the expectant hush of the unseen fills the void—the deceptive calm that comes before devastation rather than peace.

The heightened awareness gifted by the Umbra Wraiths persists, pushing her senses beyond mortal limitation. Realities no longer stack neatly atop one another but bleed through—overlap—like pages of a book soaked through, text from one seeping into another until meanings tangle and transform. Worlds overlap—sharing air, sharing space—yet blind to each other's influence.

The sense of unseen eyes presses against her, invisible but undeniable.

Not the gnomes with their careful neutrality and ancient patience. Not the Wraiths, who observe but do not stalk.

What trails her isn't passive. It circles with purpose, drawing closer with each breath.

It hunts.

Heat pulses from the Blood Key—brief but fierce, sensing not threat but inevitability—and dares her to meet it. The sensation snakes across her skin, a ghost of touch without the mercy of substance. This is no vague awareness of being watched. This is intent sharpened to a single point—predatory, precise.

A thin smile cuts across her face—the one she reserves for those certain they've cornered her. Let them prowl these woods, convinced she's theirs. After all, the best hunters know when to play prey.

She recognized him the instant the air crystallized, the atmosphere rearranging itself to make space for his presence. Not intuition—recognition. A force that ghosts through her senses, shadow given shape, memory given teeth.

Because this time, the ground is hers.

She carries herself with purpose—steady, daring—casual as death to anyone blind to the danger. To the unknowing, it seems incidental, the way wolves circle before the kill.

The trees part around the riverbank, where light slices through in unforgiving shafts. The ground speaks ancient languages through twisted roots, and the water is slow-moving but restless, carrying secrets that haven't been spoken aloud since empires crumbled to dust.

Lumira folds into the margin where trees lean over the bank—half shrouded, half seen—no more than twenty paces from the open water. She becomes the pause between heartbeats, a predator frozen in flawless restraint. Waiting.

He arrives—intent as twilight, inevitable as the tide, a blade wrapped in velvet darkness, radiating devastating power that makes the trees lean away.

The Shadowspire guard steps into view, close enough for her to strike before he reacts. He glides through the clearing, measured and unhurried—a strategy disguised as leisure. His movements are precise, measured—a man who doesn't walk these woods, but claims them.

He is no longer merely a guard of Shadowspire, but a weapon far more lethal—one that answers to shadows older than any single territory.

"You know," he murmurs, like silk pulled through teeth, "if you wanted me close again, you could've asked."

She steps out from between the trees, letting the river and clearing frame them both—nothing between them but air laced with peril. "I didn't ask." Her gaze flays to the bone. "I led. You chose to follow."

His smile deepens—unhurried, maddening. "Always. You do have a way of setting the most compelling traps."

"It's not a trap if you walk into it smiling."

"Ah," he murmurs, soft and venomous. "Then maybe I'm hoping to be caught."

She advances confidently, unyieldingly, and the air thickens— heavy with pressure—by the time he towers above her like a god carved from shadow and bad decisions. Broad-shouldered and nearly a foot taller, he carries the weight of coiled muscle under polished control—strength restrained enough to kill.

And yet... she doesn't yield.

"Careful." Her voice left no room for argument. "That sounds far too close to surrender."

"And you'd know what that feels like?" he asks, never once looking away. "You seem more the type to take rather than yield."

"Only when what's offered is worth the cost."

There's a weight to the way he regards her—dissecting, not desiring. Curious who will draw first blood, and who will walk away standing.

"And?" He's softer now. "Do I meet the price?" Steel gleams at his hip, but he doesn't reach for it. Not yet. Not when the real weapon between them is unspoken.

They stand there—war and wildfire, cloaked in dusk and defiance—nearly touching. His hood casts half his face in darkness, the glint of his sword resting inches from her leg, a promise. Or a threat.

Neither blinks. Neither yields.

The space between them trembles with withheld violence and ravenous intent.

She should step back. Should remember the weight of every secret, every betrayal that carved lines into her ribs like scripture. But she doesn't retreat.

Instead, Lumira lifts her chin—slow, unwavering—to meet the only part of him visible: storm-gray eyes fixed on her like prophecy made flesh.

Predator to predator.

And she knows—without words—that if she were to reach out, he'd let her touch him. Let her end him, if that was what she wanted.

But that's not what she wants.

Not yet.

Her lips curl—something between a smirk and a promise of violence. "You haven't even made an offer."

Soft and steady, the river murmurs beside them, a witness to their ritual. The trees remain, stoic and knowing—keepers of a pattern woven through ages.

Time halts between them—hunter and hunted. Neither is willing to name which is which. It should be meaningless by now. A forgotten indulgence. But it lingers, persistent as poison in her veins.

Her jaw tightens. She locks the memory down where it belongs—with the grief, the vengeance, the things she can't afford to feel if she wants to survive what comes next. Even now, her body remembers his touch, each whispered threat and promise left in tatters.

He stands like stone—unmoving, unreadable. Then, with unhurried intent: "I didn't come to bargain."

Her mouth tightens, skepticism simmering. "No?"

"I came to warn you."

She remains unmoving, unreadable. But behind her eyes, the shift is unmistakable—a predator stirred from repose.

"You're watching the wrong people." He speaks without hesitation, voice steady. "The Brotherhood is the distraction you're meant to see."

That lands. Not visibly. But she feels the knife go through her spine.

"Then who," she asks coolly, "should I be concerned about?"

He advances, and the space between them warps. The tension doesn't ease—it changes shape, crackling, unstable, thrumming with unspoken weight. "You already know," he murmurs. "You just haven't said it aloud."

The way he delivers it—a shared secret instead of a threat—sets her even further on edge, nerves singing behind the mask honed for palace halls.

She folds her arms, a clipped, joyless smile playing at her mouth. "How generous of you. Riddles and stalking, all in one package."

Amusement stirs at the corner of his mouth—brief, dark, and tightly leashed. "I followed your trail." The words hum with intent. "You walked it like a dare." Another step. Closer. "Don't confuse that with pursuit." He doesn't waver. "You're many things,

Lumira Kyrvayne." Her name unfolds dangerously on his tongue, a weapon he intends to wield against her—and her alone.

The sound of it—her name in his mouth—cuts deeper than it should, carving through armor she's spent years reinforcing. He's so close she can see the faint scar bisecting his brow, the subtle fracture that makes him more real than beautiful, and she catches the strange alchemy of him—forest after rainfall, sun-warmed metal, menace wrapped in patience.

Her pulse doesn't quicken. She won't allow it. Yet, the heat blooming low in her stomach tells a different story, one her body writes without permission.

"If this is your version of a warning," she says, voice level, the steel carefully hidden under velvet, "you're going to need to be clearer."

He reaches for her face, unhurried, granting her all the opportunity to retreat. Or strike.

She does neither.

His fingers lightly glide over her cheekbone, his touch focusing on detail rather than emotion. Methodical. Exact. It is not affection, but examination—a cartographer charting land previously explored. "I've known your patterns longer than you think, little fox," he murmurs. The nickname curls in the air between them—soft-spoken, claimed, and wholly his. "Before Emberly's death. Before you even understood what you carry in your blood."

Her name detonates in the space between them. It leaves his mouth with the ease of ownership—spoken as if it belongs to him.

And that's all it takes—the wire holding Lumira together snaps with pristine violence. Her blade sings through the air, aimed straight for his throat. But he's already gone—one step back, his expression unflinching.

"Leading with your right again," he says, mild as ever, as if remarking on the weather. "Hadralis would be disappointed."

Her second blade materializes with lethal grace. "Try me again, and I'll show you how disappointed you'll be."

She strikes—quicker now, and far less forgiving. Her body moves with vicious elegance, every blow carrying the weight of betrayal, grief, and something far more ruinous: desire she can't eradicate.

He doesn't raise a weapon—he recedes. He is always beyond her reach, always a heartbeat away, allowing her to believe connection is imminent before it evaporates.

A dance without tempo. A fight disguised as foreplay.

Her frustration only fuels the fire raging inside, and she drives him toward the river, blades flashing in precise arcs. He sidesteps each one with infuriating control, redirecting her momentum with a calm she can't read.

He speaks—unhurried, in full control. "Your form is impressive. But your emotion clouds your decisions." The words aren't mocking. They're observant. And that makes it worse—infinitely worse—than mockery ever could.

She feints left—baiting him—and pivots hard, her body moving faster than thought. A twist, a shove of momentum, and suddenly he's off balance, caught by nothing but instinct and the raw need to win.

The splash is glorious.

He resurfaces sputtering, wet hair clinging to his face as his hood slips back—exposing the sharp lines usually hidden in shadow, all that insufferable grace undone by river water and surprise.

"I suppose I had that coming," he mutters, wiping water from his face, dignity dripping away to reveal wicked amusement.

She stands on the bank, arms crossed, satisfaction curling at the edges of her carefully guarded expression. "You suppose?"

He shakes like a drenched hound, flinging water in wild sprays. The hood sags behind his neck, forgotten. "Though I must say," he adds, that infuriating grin sliding fully into place, "your technique's even more impressive when you're not distracted by my—"

Another splash. A rock breaks the surface beside him, perfectly aimed to miss by inches.

"Careful, little fox." He lets the warning curl slow and warm between them. "The water's lovely. It would be a shame if you were pulled in."

"You wouldn't dare."

He meets her with a spark—lightning suspended in storm light. "Wouldn't I?"

She steps back, but not in time.

He's already moving.

One fluid motion, a surge from the water—he grabs her wrist, and she twists—both breathless, adrenaline-charged bodies locked in primal struggle. They crash into the shallows with a splash that sends birds scattering from the trees in a panicked exodus.

Somehow, she ends up on top. Straddling him.

Reeling. Soaked. Her thighs lock around his hips, braced against the hard line of his chest. His fingers settle—uninvited—at her waist, not holding, but *branding* her, as if the shape of her body has been memorized, carved into the blood and bone of him.

Against the cling of soaked fabric, the Blood Key pulses once, furious, possessive, as if it knows precisely what kind of collision is about to break her open.

Her hair drips onto his collarbone, each droplet a tiny betrayal. His nearness scorches the air between them, brushing fire into the hollow of her throat.

He slides below her, and the drag of wet leather against leather sends a jolt through her spine. But it's the pressure against her that truly unravels her. Her hips tense at the contact, unintentional, aware. Heat blooms—immediate and consuming—pooling where her body meets his.

She doesn't veer—composure intact, offering no acknowledgment. Her body already knows. Knows *him*, in a way language never dared to touch.

And gods, he's hard.

She presses deliberately—not quite bold—a slow grind of her hips against his, testing, confirming.

Contact lands hard—bruising, claiming. "Lumira..." he warns, but it's no real warning. Whatever grip he had—it's slipping, written in every clenched muscle and lingering touch.

She lowers herself, water dripping between them in lines that feel like fate—her mouth brushing his ear. "Still think I'm distracted?"

He chuckles—low and wickedly amused. Not born of humor, but of understanding.

Of recognition.

As if he sees the game she's starting and is plotting how to unmake her with it.

Then—gods help her—he angles his head, and it begins not with a kiss, but faint contact.

His lower lip skims her jaw, a secret held too long—gentle, weighted, aching for release. Then his tongue follows, warm and sure, tracing the path his mouth just marked. His teeth catch next—enough to hint, not devour—

And then, as if sealing the vow he will not speak aloud, both lips close over the spot in a kiss so feather-light it feels imagined.

But she *feels* it—every phantom echo threading through her like wildfire seeking for kindling.

A hiss of air. She seizes his soaked shirt, fists clenched so tight her knuckles blanch.

This is not a moment meant for reason.

And yet neither of them dares to finish it. They hold, suspended between brilliance and idiocy, each waiting for the other to act.

He doesn't let go. Not immediately. He lifts them both in one fluid motion, her hips locked to his, water cascading over them in ribbons that stick like heat. His touch stays low on her thighs, steady and unhurried, like he's memorizing the weight of her there.

The closeness is unbearable. Unspoken things coil between them—tension, history, heat. She braces herself on his shoulders, and fuck, she feels him. The firm strength under wet leather, the barely restrained power in how he holds her—waiting.

A single roll of her hips and—

No. No, no, no.

The heat blooming between her thighs pulses traitorously, unmistakable in its timing. A fierce throb, a flutter low in her belly. The kind of reaction she cannot will away, no matter how tightly she reins herself in.

This is reckless in all the wrong ways.

She slowly lowers one leg, then the other, feet finding the riverbed like she's reclaiming lost territory. He lets her go without resistance, without a word, but his eyes stay locked on hers the whole time—storm-gray and knowing, reading secrets she hasn't admitted to herself.

For a heartbeat, everything pulls taut—the current curling around their legs, the forest hushing as if sensing the tremor, the air close to breaking.

Then his lips tilt into a maddening curve—assured, earned. "Next time," he murmurs, low and rich as aged wine, "try leading with your left. You were always stronger that way."

She glares up at him, composed but seething. "You're enjoying this far too much."

He starts backing away—slow, fluid—water swirling around his legs like it obeys him. "I know," he says, voice silk over steel. "I can wait, Lumira. I always do. I'll listen. I'll learn. And when you finally break—" He meets her, dark eyes gleaming. "I'll be the one you crawl to."

Lumira's pulse kicks hard. Heat blooms low, unwelcome; her nerves singe with a tension she refuses to name.

She frowns, fists clenched, fury simmering under flushed skin. "You are arrogant. Insufferable. Impossible—"

One blink—and he slips into the space heartbeats forget, the forest yielding like it knows him. Gone, but the space he leaves behind hums with his absence—hungry, electric, and impossible to ignore.

She stands there—soaked, furious, and far warmer than she should be—glaring into empty space. As she turns to slog toward shore, she mutters, "Cocky bastard."

From somewhere in the darkness, barely audible—his laugh is low and smug.

25

THE COURT MUSICIAN

Returning to Altareth feels less a homecoming than a trial by memory—a slow passage through once-honored streets that nip at her heels. Lumira moves as a shadow unwilling to vanish, weaving through roads that no longer claim her as their own. Not truly. Not since Emberly's body burned. Not since truths began bleeding through lies like ink through parchment.

The air is thin, tightly laced with unease. Crimsun has always reeked of secrets—cloying and impossible to ignore. But tonight, as dusk stains the sky in deep golds and bruised violets, it hums with anticipation.

The streets gleam as if scrubbed of history. The guards stand with a readiness that borders on aggression. Even the cobblestones resent her steps like they know she's returned a different creature—bloodstained, power-branded, artifact-heavy.

A month prior, she would have been paraded through the courtyards atop a gilded carriage adorned with floral displays and political praise. Now, she stealthily navigates the alleyways, a smuggler transporting illicit goods—and in a sense, she is. Deep within her—tucked behind her ribs and threaded through her core—resides a truth that once led to gods being imprisoned.

The Aethervoid. The buried artifacts. The betrayals draped in the language of loyalty. Lumira carries them all now—not truths meant to change the game, but to shatter its illusion entirely and reveal the board for what it is: a prison disguised as order.

She slips behind a fruit merchant's cart as two Blood Legion guards round the corner. Their boots strike stone in echoing unison—crisp for the hour, synchronized beyond routine patrol.

"Command's doubling routes," one mutters, scanning the street like he expects it to betray him.

"Something near the Naiad stirred." The other speaks softly, but the intent lands hard. "No details. The only response—tighten the noose."

Lumira's lips twitch, not in amusement, but with the promise of retaliation.

They don't even realize what they're hunting.

Her.

She waits until their steps fade, then continues—lower now, deeper, threading herself through the city's forgotten arteries. Not the gold-laced avenues of governance, but the cramped veins of resistance.

And there it is.

Pigments & Pints.

The once-rowdy artist café crouches in the shadows, a beast holding its breath, ready to strike. The paint-peeling sign swings lazily in the evening breeze, and the windows stare back—blank canvases, uncertain whether their story is worth telling.

A single flicker of light glows upstairs, faint and unyielding, barely visible behind the curtain. The Blood Key pulses, calm and aware, as if sensing the fragile thread of trust waiting on the floor above. Ilara will be there. Wrenna too. They wait—not for her return, but for answers she hasn't yet found the courage—or clarity—to provide.

"Was the swamp look intentional, or…?" Wrenna cuts through the air—dry, and twice as biting—as Lumira slips through the back entrance. Her tone walks that familiar line between concern and critique—affection delivered at knifepoint.

"Charming as ever," Lumira replies, brushing a damp strand from her face, her diction pristine despite the mud on her boots and the ruin in her bones. "It's a rare gift, how you manage to flay someone with compliments."

Wrenna snorts and turns toward the stairwell. "Ilara's upstairs. Been pacing holes into my floorboards for over an hour."

"An hour? Gods, she's letting me off easy."

The climb up the narrow stairs feels steeper tonight, like the weight she carries has grown sentient. At the top, the once-chaotic studio space has been gutted of its color. Canvases and paints have given way to rough maps and ink-stained parchment, crimson-threaded with strategy—a rebellion disguised as an art project—or maybe the other way around.

Ilara stands by the window, one palm resting against the glass as if listening to the city's heartbeat through the pane. She doesn't turn at the sound of footsteps behind her, but the tension in her shoulders eases by a fraction. That quiet release from a woman who'd forgotten how tightly she held herself. "You took longer than I thought." Not cutting, but hollowed-out around the edges.

Lumira shrugs off her cloak, arranging it with a precision that masks itself as nonchalance. "Had to take a detour. The gnomes aren't known for haste. Or hospitality."

That earns a glance from Ilara—quick, faintly surprised, like she's revising a mental map.

Wrenna, perched on the edge of the desk like she's been waiting for an excuse to pounce, lifts a brow. "And they didn't try to throw you into a pit of enchanted crystals for breathing too enthusiastically?"

"Tempting, I'm sure." A dry flick of words from Lumira. "But no."

She crosses the room, every step composed and unhurried, lowering herself into the nearest chair like she's preparing for a negotiation, not a conversation.

Ilara turns, at last, focus flickering to life behind her eyes. "You saw it."

"I saw a lot of things."

A beat of silence.

Ilara answers with the calm precision of someone who never misses. "You're dodging. Start with what actually matters."

Lumira's jaw tenses, then releases. "The Wraiths spoke to me."

Her words don't draw surprise, but an instinct older than fear. Familiar. Heavy with knowing.

"They didn't speak. But they showed me more than words ever could."

Ilara straightens. Wrenna leans in slightly, her expression unreadable.

Lumira doesn't stall. She lays it all out—what the Wraiths revealed in the forest clearing—the truths buried in bloodlines, the artifacts' true nature, and the boundary between realms thinning with each passing night. Every word of it, spoken as a report, sharpened into prophecy.

She stops, and the room hangs—caught between reaction and restraint.

"They know who you are?" Ilara finally asks.

Lumira nods. "They know what I carry. Who I am. And what I'm becoming."

What follows isn't peace—it's awareness. A subtle recalibration: shoulders square, air tightening. Something ancient draws taut between them.

"I followed the Naiad border, like we discussed," she says, gaze steady. "The Brotherhood's pulled back."

That earns a shift in Ilara's stance—subtle, but impossible to miss.

Wrenna's brow lifts. "Pulling back... or repositioning?"

"It's not fear," Lumira replies. "Or a retreat—it's a handoff. The real threat hasn't arrived yet. And the Wraiths are watching."

Wrenna exhales through her nose. "Then so should we."

"I went to the gnomes next. Negotiated sanctuary beneath the Western Ridge. Temporary for now, but it'll hold."

Ilara folds her arms. "And?"

Lumira pauses. "There was someone else."

"Brotherhood?" Wrenna asks instinctively.

Lumira's answer is slower. Thicker. "Yes. And no."

Wrenna frowns. "That's not exactly reassuring."

Ilara's jaw tightens. One word—cool and unforgiving. "Who?"

Lumira refuses to engage—visually or otherwise. "The guard. From Shadowspire."

Wrenna's tone goes razor-thin. "You're certain?"

"I saw the tattoos," Lumira admits, low. "At The Silver Chalice—the night he summoned me."

Ilara rounds on her, disbelief flaring. "And you *waited* until now to share that?"

Lumira lifts her chin. "I wasn't sure—"

"Since when do you need certainty to act?" Ilara shoots back. "You saw Brotherhood ink on someone you let *summon* you, and you just... said nothing?"

"I needed to understand what I was dealing with—what he was," Lumira replies, clipped. Composed—unnervingly so.

Ilara's mouth twists. "Right. And how close did you have to get before you started understanding?" The accusation is casual in tone, but the meaning slices clean.

Lumira doesn't rise to it. Doesn't snap, doesn't scoff. She doesn't move, but the calm is a lie—her body remembers, traitorous and uninvited. The press of his hands at her waist. The whisper of lips and heat at the place under her jaw where memory now pulses like a wound. She feels it again—low and molten, blooming where it shouldn't. And gods help her, it shows. Her fingers give a single twitch at her side.

She clamps it all down, chains it inside armor forged from years of self-control. But the pause? It is its own confession.

Wrenna, from the side, breaks the tension with a sigh edged in exasperation. "And now?"

Lumira exhales slowly. "He warned me. Said the Brotherhood's just noise—there's a deeper hand behind it all."

Ilara folds her arms, expression hard. "And you think that makes him trustworthy?"

Lumira doesn't answer. But it has a way of sounding a lot like yes.

Wrenna rises without a word, moving toward a canvas draped in tired linen. Quick, practiced, she finds the edge—betraying how many times she's played this moment in her mind. "I've been combing through Emberly's paintings." Her voice is stripped of its usual edge. "Ever since the tea party one cracked open more truth than we were ready for. Most of them are a mess—unfinished, scattered. Like she knew it was coming but couldn't piece the whole picture together in time." Her fingers pause above the fabric, motion stalled mid-thought. "But this one... this one kept pulling at me." She leans back, the raw edge of her expression barely held in check. "You'll want to see it. Before the next complication catches up." With a flick of her wrist, the sheet slips away like a curtain on truth.

The painting beneath is unmistakably Emberly's—each brushstroke taut with intention, each layer humming with withheld meaning. On the surface, it's a familiar courtly scene: nobles preening like caged birds, servants dissolving into the margins, and at the center, a musician seated before a crystal harp.

Lumira steps closer. Her heart knocks once, hard, out of rhythm.

The central figure is partially turned, his face nearly in profile, yet the posture is unmistakable—that poised curve of the shoulders, the precise tension in the wrists.

"Is that—"

"Zylven." Wrenna doesn't budge. "*The Court Musician*. One of her last. She finished it three weeks before she died."

The name drops into Lumira's gut like iron.

Zylven Meridian—High Sovereign of Vesper. The man who wept at her sister's funeral, who spoke of legacy and love like they hadn't cost him a thing. A man of beautiful performances—always too careful, too perfect to be trusted completely.

The Blood Key responds—cold and intense—repelled by the rot woven through the foundation.

And then she sees her.

Half-shadowed behind a carved column, hair pinned in the style she wore when she didn't want to be noticed—but always was.

"Emberly painted herself in," Ilara observes, stepping closer. She delivers the words with calm certainty, soft but unwavering.

"Always," Wrenna responds, carrying a softness that transcends sorrow. "Not out of vanity, but as proof. And she left her name off—she simply interwove herself into the world."

"She wasn't hiding," Lumira murmurs. "She wanted us to know she saw it, that she knew."

Wrenna's expression tightens, her eyes keen. "And left the truth exactly where we'd be forced to find it."

Lumira's attention fixes on the harp. At first, it appears as delicately painted as the rest—glass strings glinting under morning light. But then she sees them—fine threads of copper leaf worked so subtly into the paint that they seem to flicker when the light hits them right.

The strings don't end at the instrument.

They stretch outward, tracing invisible paths through the crowd. Some coil around throats like leashes. Others loop gently at wrists, binding with the intimacy of familiarity. They branch, diverge, converge again—calculated.

"Not strings," Lumira hesitates. "Lines of control." She follows them—how they tangle around certain nobles, skim past others, how some figures burn with soft illumination while others fade into shadow. "The court musician doesn't play for applause," she murmurs. "He keeps the rhythm of power."

The meaning lands with the weight of prophecy. Zylven's role isn't ornamental. It's structural. Coordinating court influence mirrors a composer conducting an army.

Ilara steps beside her. "These connections—this isn't random."

"She was tracking him." Lumira holds a colder edge now—refined and ruthless. "Mapping the reach of his influence. Every thread a name. Every knot a decision."

Wrenna's jaw tightens. "And hiding it where only someone who knew what to search for would ever find it."

Lumira exhales, the sound edged with a feeling she doesn't name. "It's a confession."

Wrenna nods once. "And a warning."

The copper threads shimmer softly, like silk spun from breath, the design emerging not through boldness but through patience—delicate and graceful by nature, not force. Hidden within Emberly's meticulous work—intended to elude those who do not seek what lies beyond the surface of beauty. Yet now, they observe it—the notes, the symbols, the strength that Zylven commands.

They trace the design together, revealing symbols long concealed under intricate ornamentation. The meaning stirs just below the surface—gradual, inevitable—a secret waking in the dark.

A single sentence emerges, carved not in sound but in copper thread:

The court musician keeps the rhythm of power.

The weight settles between them, not spoken aloud, but felt. A truth that does not blink.

"This isn't about the performance." Her tone, when she finally speaks, is sculpted with noble clarity. "It's about who commands the stage. Who bends the room to match their tempo."

"She was trailing him," Wrenna adds, the softness gone. "Following the thread."

Lumira returns to the painting, drawn back into its depths as if the canvas is still unfolding. Past the central figure, past the sweep of the harp and its copper-threaded lines, something smaller catches her eye.

An ornate side table. A glass of wine, untouched. And beside it—

A crystal: small, polished, clear threaded with topaz. Light clings to it in the painted scene, holding the illusion of depth and life.

A hitch catches in her throat. "What is that?" Lumira asks, the words escaping before she can restrain their edge. She lifts a finger, pointing but not touching.

Ilara leans closer, her brow furrowing. "That's a Deepvane Crystal. Mined from fault lines in Terravox—places where the stone remembers. Rare. And not usually left lying around." She hesitates, then adds, "They're used to store memory—sound, vision, whatever lingers."

But Lumira's no longer listening.

She knows that crystal she took from Emberly's desk—the same hue and glow. And then, another flash of memory strikes her. The silk-wrapped crystal Lysander gifted her—unopened, untouched, waiting like it knew its moment would come.

Realization doesn't strike—it sinks. Heavy. Inevitable.

"Gods." She whirls toward Wrenna. "Where's the crystal I left with you?"

Wrenna stiffens—understanding dawning fast. "Wait here." She disappears into an adjacent room, returning moments later with a small wooden box. Inside, nestled on faded velvet, sits a deep-blue crystal, its surface gleaming with unnatural luminosity despite the dim light. It isn't the one from the painting, but it could be its twin in power.

"If it works the same…" Lumira begins.

"…then what's inside it?" Wrenna finishes, already reaching for the crystal without hesitation.

The crystal rests in Wrenna's palm, its faint glow tracing soft light along her knuckles and palms. She speaks then—low, almost tender.

"I didn't say anything when you first gave it to me," she admits. "Not because I didn't wonder. I did. The weight, the cut—it carried meaning. But without activation, it could've been nothing more than a decorative shard. And you..." she addresses Lumira, tone dipping, "you weren't ready. Not to carry more than you already were."

She lifts the crystal slightly. It flickers once, then falls inert in her grasp.

"Emberly told me once that the most powerful crystals—the ones crafted with purpose—can't be opened by just anyone. The creator decides who gets to see what's inside. Not through magic exactly, but through meaning. A name. A blood tie. Someone they trust." Her voice takes on an edge as she turns the crystal between her fingers. "This one from Lysander... if he meant for you to see it, Lumira, it will open. But only when you're ready. He could've locked it behind anything—touch, timing, or even a state of mind."

Lumira brushes the edge of the crystal, nearly taking it. "Emberly's didn't react when I found it." The words are more to herself than to them. "It just... sat there."

Wrenna hesitates, lips parting—then sealing shut.

Ilara's breath catches, audible in the pause that follows.

"On her desk. I took it the day they made me clear out her chambers—the day they pretended she was *gone* instead of *taken*."

The word "taken" grates out between her teeth, raw enough to leave a sting.

"Then you weren't meant to see that one yet." Wrenna speaks slowly, thoughtful. "Or maybe she keyed it to respond only after another truth came to light."

A pause.

Lumira closes her fingers around the crystal, warmth igniting instantly—thrumming against her palm like a second heartbeat, one not her own. The light grows, pulsing steadily. Welcoming.

Wrenna steps back. "That's your answer," she murmurs. "It was always for you."

Lumira exhales in a slow, precise breath, regal as ever. "Then let's see what he left me." She tightens her grip, intention sharp. Not for her. *For all of them.*

The crystal flares, and memory pulls the world apart.

The Vesper palace unfolds around them in shadows and candlelight, summoned from memory as if the walls themselves have begun to confess. Not the grand halls or formal reception rooms where nobility paraded their importance for all to witness, but a smaller, more intimate space—a study, perhaps, or a private sitting room. Candles burned low, casting more shadows than light, as if the very illumination hesitated to fully reveal what transpired here.

Zylven sat at an ornate desk, his usual performance attire replaced by simpler, darker clothing that appeared designed for discretion rather than display. The man who delivered mourning eulogies in a reverent hush was gone.

What remains wasn't softer—it was colder, more cutting, and real. His expression lacked the deferential warmth he gave his noble patrons. Every inch of him radiated cold calculation, a predator dissecting its prey before the kill.

"She's seen more than she should," he stated, smooth and modulated despite the content of his words. No emotion colored his tone—not anger, concern, or even the particular satisfaction some might feel when eliminating a troublesome opponent. It was the matter-of-fact delivery of someone discussing the weather. "She'll drink tonight," he continued, lifting the glass to examine its contents against the candlelight. "By morning, it will be done."

He did not delegate—this wasn't a random command passed from shadows to silence. He poured the wine himself—steady and meticulous—then lifted the glass with the care of a ritualist, not a reveler. Taking a sip—not to savor, but to test the death he'd prepared. There was no hesitation, no flicker of remorse. Only the cool precision of a man who delivered poison the way others offered prayer.

"The sister will suspect, of course," he continued, addressing someone beyond the memory's viewpoint—an essence felt rather than seen, a shadowed figure hidden by design. "But suspicion without proof is merely paranoia. By the time she puts the pieces together, events will have advanced beyond stopping."

He smiled then—not the charming, humble expression he wore at court, but a smile honed in triumph—one that belonged to someone who had won a game his opponent didn't know they were playing.

"Everything will proceed," he said, drumming an erratic beat against the desk. "As planned."

The memory fractures, reality snapping back with a jolt. The crystal's glow fades, leaving them once more in Wrenna's studio, where early moonlight spills in slivers across the floor—and *The Court Musician* peers from the wall, its painted eyes now gleaming with menace.

For several long moments, none of them speak. Lumira can hear her pulse pounding in her ears, a furious rhythm that drowns out rational thought, leaving only rage in its wake.

Wrenna stands rigid, fists white-knuckled at her sides, her face a mask of restrained fury that makes her earlier anger look like mere annoyance. Ilara's Ranger training shows in her immediate shift to tactical assessment—measuring distances, checking weapons, already mapping the next step.

"He did it himself." Lumira is lethal—each word drawn tight as steel. "Didn't whisper it to a lackey. Didn't pass it off to someone disposable. He poured the glass. Let her drink. Knew exactly what he was doing." She stays locked on the empty air where the memory had been, as if she could reach through it and rip him apart.

Ilara exhales slowly. "And he planned every moment that followed."

Wrenna is across the room before thought can catch her, a blur of speed. The floor groans beneath her steps as she grips the window frame like it might hold her together. Her shoulders tremble—not with weakness, but with the unbearable tension of a scream caged behind clenched teeth. She stares out into the night as if she might find Zylven there, vulnerable enough to kill. Her voice is raspy when she speaks, trembling with vengeance heavier than words can hold.

"Don't call this fucking justice." The words are low and lethal. "He didn't make a mistake. He chose it. He poured the poison and stayed to see it through." She turns then—slow and seething—cutting to Lumira like twin blades. "You don't get justice for that. You get blood."

No one moves.

Then Ilara speaks—measured, but pointed. "But why would Lysander give you that crystal?"

Lumira doesn't answer immediately. The question cuts deeper than it should—because she's already asked herself the same thing. *To help me? To manipulate me? Or to ease a guilty conscience before the next betrayal?* If the marriage treaty was supposed to unite their territories, this gift feels like a warning: unity won't come without casualties.

Her jaw tightens. "I don't know." The words come at last, clipped and certain. "But I'm going to find out."

The air vibrates between them—taut, electric. The Deepvane Crystal throbs faintly in Lumira's palm, a heartbeat not her own.

"It's time to revisit Emberly's crystal," Lumira bites out, every word dipped in venom. Her fingers tighten until her knuckles go white against Lysander's crystal. "I didn't know what it was then," she continues, the rage now a controlled inferno as she slips it into her pocket. She burns with a fury so cold it scorches. "But I do now."

The crystal settles against her skin with the weight of inevitability—a promise of retribution. One truth was revealed. Another is waiting for its turn. The crystal falls away, her next instinct guiding her straight to the dagger's hilt. The gesture of someone who knows how this ends. What curves her lips isn't a smile. It's a promise—unyielding, edged in blood.

"That bastard dies," Lumira proclaims—each syllable a blade unsheathed. No speeches. No ceremony.

A verdict rendered in blood and bone.

She clenches her fists until her nails bite deep, carving blood-bright crescents into her palms. "And not as a traitor in the shadows," she adds, finally turning to face them, her eyes glittering with murderous intent. "He dies as he lived—drenched in power, draped in lies. And when he falls, the echo will tear through everything they tried to bury."

Against her breastbone, the Blood Key ignites—not warmth, but blistering heat, searing, a fury that floods her veins with ancient purpose. The key doesn't simply agree—it brands its will into her flesh, a soundless scream of *yes, now, let him burn.*

Wrenna doesn't argue. Ilara doesn't flinch.

And in the quiet that follows, not one of them disagrees.

26

WITNESS AND WEAPON

The door to Lumira's chambers doesn't so much open—it surrenders, flung wide with velvet-lined violence that makes the hinges whimper. It slams behind her with cathedral finality, the sound reverberating through the empty space like the closing of a vault.

There's no tremor as she secures the lock—only calm, practiced motion. They quake, conducting the symphony of rage that courses through her with such violent intensity that untempered veins would have ruptured hours ago. The bolts slide home with a click that feels insulting in its inadequacy, as if mere metal could contain what now burns inside her.

Lumira stalks through her chambers with the refined violence of a predator, finally uncaged. These rooms—once a shelter, then prison, now war room—watch her with the wariness of witnesses who know better than to interfere.

"You wove your lies well, Zylven," she intones, every word etched in frost. "But they won't save you now."

She approaches her vanity not with steps, but with intent. Each action is practiced, despite the turmoil simmering under her calm exterior. Her reflection welcomes her—serene, flawless, and completely indifferent. The carefully crafted façade remains intact, while underneath, a primal dread stirs awake.

The Blood Key is maddening in its demand—hot and insistent, as if it has been waiting for this moment to awaken fully. It approves; it *hungers*.

The false drawer opens with a soft slide. Inside, Emberly's crystal rests beside the journal—hidden the day they demanded she strip the chambers clean, her mourning repackaged as duty. While they cloaked their purge in velvet and condolences, Lumira stole what mattered—before they could erase it all.

The crystal gleams with an unnatural patience, its blue surface capturing candlelight and refracting it into an age-old awareness. Watching still.

"Let's see what you witnessed, sister," Lumira murmurs, lifting the crystal with a steady grip through sheer noble spite.

The warmth is immediate—not the comforting kind, but the raw heat of truth contained longer than it ever should've been. She cradles it between her palms, not with reverence but with demand. "Show me," she commands, rich with the particular authority that makes lesser nobility flinch. "Show me what he didn't want found."

Unlike Lysander's crystal, this one hesitates, testing her resolve, identity, and right. The blue glow pulses once or twice, questioning.

"I am Lumira Kyrvayne," she hisses through clenched teeth, "and I will burn this entire kingdom to cinders if that's what it takes to make them choke on the truth. So stop playing coy and show me what she saw."

The crystal flares violently, suddenly—approval and surrender in one blinding moment. Memory floods outward, drowning the room in its cold blue light.

Reality fractures and reforms around her. Not with the gentle unfolding of Lysander's crystal but with the violent clarity of final moments desperately preserved.

Emberly's chambers materialize—not as they were in life, vibrant and chaotic with creation, but as they became in death—a pristine crime scene disguised as respect for the departed. She was lying on her bed, unmoving as a corpse—but her eyes remained full of fire. They darted frantically around the room, the only part of her body under her command—everything else pinned by a slow, invasive dread.

The Deepvane Crystal sat dormant to all appearances on her desk, nestled among half-finished notes and letters. Its surface caught only ordinary candlelight, its true purpose hidden under the guise of a simple decorative trinket—bearing witness, recording while remaining invisible to those who didn't know its secrets.

Zylven Meridian carefully moved through the room, examining Emberly's belongings. He lifted papers, studied sketches, and checked drawers—methodical in his invasion. The mask of benevolent leadership had been discarded, replaced by the cold efficiency of a predator ensuring its kill.

"There's a reason they call it Soulthief," he murmurs, rifling through the debris. "Not for how it kills you, but for what it takes on the way down." He paused by her desk, lifting an empty wineglass and turning it to catch the light. "Earlier, in the Conservatory Hall—you were resplendent, as always." He carried a hint of genuine admiration. "Even you wouldn't refuse a glass poured from the same decanter as a High Sovereign's." There's a faint glint in his eyes. "You should have known better."

Emberly's pupils contracted—the only part of her body able to react.

"Ah." His lips quirked upward. "Now you understand."

For all her care—every guarded cup, every sidestepped trap—Emberly had been snared.

The poison had already been in the wine, long before this evening's gathering. Zylven had ensured he drank from the same source, making it appear harmless. Because, for him, it was. The antidote had been in his system long before the first toast was raised.

He had played the long game.

And he had won.

He returned to his systematic search, finding a half-written letter. He skimmed the contents, lips pressed thin, and dropped it into the waiting hearth. The fire leapt higher, hungrier, casting his face in a cruel shadow. "I did wonder how much you'd pieced together," he continued, as the paper curled inward, darkening to ember. "Your notes about the 'Court Musician' and the influence he wields. Such an interesting metaphor." His tone grew almost appreciative. "You were closer than anyone has ever come."

He turned, examining her paralyzed form with the detached interest of a naturalist observing a specimen. "That's the trouble with brilliance, Emberly. It demands expression. You could have played the game and taken your place on the board. Instead, you insisted on seeing the board itself."

He approached the bed, sitting beside her with perverse intimacy. A finger traced the line of her cheek, following the path of a tear she could no longer shed.

"Your sister lacks your subtlety," he mused. "Lumira burns brighter than is safe, her loyalties exposed like open flame. She'll come crashing forward with the fury of a summer storm." His smile was a bloodless thing. "It's only a matter of time."

Emberly's eyes widened fractionally—the only protest her dying body allowed.

"Yes," he said, noticing. "She has a part to play too. The grieving sister—the avenging blade. A vessel." He stood, smoothing nonexistent wrinkles from his immaculate attire. "The Court Musician builds his symphony from many instruments, my dear. Even those who believe they play their own tune."

Her breathing slowed, each intake shallower than the last. The poison reached for her heart with a chill that clawed from the inside out.

At the door, Zylven paused with his fingers on the latch, a flicker of respect breaking through his expression as he glanced back. "Rest well, knowing you left me no choice," he said. "Few ever manage that much."

The door closed behind him with finality.

Emberly's vision dimmed, the world constricting to a tunnel of fading light. Her gaze found the crystal—an unblinking witness. Not death, but the reckoning ahead claimed her final thought.

Then darkness.

The memory releases Lumira with the violence of a severed tether. She staggers back, the crystal slipping from her grasp, suddenly numb with rage. It hits the carpet with a muted thud, its blue glow receding to dormancy.

She stays frozen for three heartbeats, fury trembling beneath iron will. Then she bursts forward—not the wild thrashing of common grief but a strike honed by pain and purpose. Her hand sweeps across the vanity, sending perfume bottles and jewelry crashing to the floor in vicious destruction.

"Vessel," she hisses, the word torn between clenched teeth. "Your *fucking* instrument."

The Blood Key matches the thundering rhythm of her heart— an urgency that will not be denied.

She drags in a breath, air slicing down her throat like glass. Clarity returns, not gentle but sharp with purpose.

"He's going to die." The words taste final, absolute. "And he'll know exactly why."

Night presses against the windows as Lumira paces her chambers, fury flowing through her in steady currents. The crystals rest side by side on her vanity, their surfaces catching what little light remains—silent and inert now, but no less potent. A shadow stretches at her back, warped into the shape of vengeance, patient and still.

Her mind churns over timing, access, and opportunity, every calculation a step toward the inevitable. Rage has cooled into precision, colder and more focused.

"Soulthief," she murmurs, the word itself a toxin lingering on her tongue. It's a memory—not solely from the crystal's unveiling, but from another place entirely.

She steps to her bookshelf, trailing a familiar path across the leather-bound volumes. Unlike her sister's meticulously curated collection of political treatises, Lumira's tastes run wider, deeper, and more eclectic: history and tactics, botanicals and poisons.

Knowledge is survival.

She pulls down a weathered tome—*Veiled Flora of Cyrathea: Botanical Secrets of the Eastern Territories*—one of many texts she has collected over years of strategic acquisition. Not for political advantage, but for her insatiable curiosity about things others overlooked—a habit formed during countless nights when sleep abandoned her and the boundaries of her world dissolved into a vast, unknowable beyond.

The book falls open to a section marked with a pressed leaf—a habit she picked up years ago, tracking her progress through particularly dense texts. Pages blur as she skims past familiar entries—until she finds it.

Soulthief (Anima Furari): Uncommon flowering vine native to the coastal marshlands of eastern Bravara Territory, particularly the wetlands surrounding the northern shores of the Eirros Ocean. Distinct purple-black blooms with silver centers.

She reads on, pulse quickening.

Properties: Highly toxic when distilled from the vine's flowers. Initial symptoms include sweetness on the tongue, followed by progressive paralysis beginning with the extremities. The victim remains fully conscious as bodily functions cease. Death typically occurs within 8–12 hours of ingestion.

Historical Usage: Favored by ancient courts for political executions. Valued for its stealth, it can be masked in strong wines or spirits. There is no known cure once symptoms progress beyond the initial stages.

Notable Characteristic: Unique among poisons for its selective targeting of motor control while preserving consciousness. Victims experience full awareness until the final moments.

The page crinkles in her grasp, tension blooming white across her knuckles.

Countermeasure: A single antidote exists, derived from the silver heart of the plant's own stem. Must be ingested prior to exposure. Effective window: approximately six hours. Beyond that timeframe, no known remedy exists.

Lumira slams the book shut, her mind piecing together the full horror. Zylven hadn't simply poisoned Emberly. He had *prepared* for it, ensuring the antidote was in his system before they drank from the same decanter at the gathering—the perfect alibi. The calculated cruelty of it twists in her gut, refusing to loosen. Damn him.

Emberly hadn't simply died.

She had suffered—every second, every inhale. She knew who was responsible and was forced to endure his company until the end.

The eulogy. The speeches. The mourning mask he wore in public. It had been rehearsed.

A performance.

He had stood over her grave, speaking of loss, speaking of grief, when only hours before, he had been beside her bed, savoring every moment of her dying agony.

The horror of it sinks into Lumira's bones, carving itself into her marrow, solidifying into a cold, irreversible resolve.

She knew Zylven was guilty.

Now, she knows his death is the only answer left.

She forces herself to move, to think past the rage clawing its way up her throat. Timing is crucial. Politics are important. The game must be played before the blade is unsheathed.

A knock at the door. Three sharp raps, impatient and authoritative.

When she opens the door, one of her mother's guards stands at attention, his posture radiating the particular blend of deference and demand that marks the High Sovereigness's messengers.

"The High Sovereigness requests your presence immediately, Blood Descent," he states, fixed past her shoulder—a courtesy that allows her to compose whatever expression she requires without witness.

He's dressed in ceremonial trim, not the standard palace patrol. Subtle, but deliberate. Which means one thing: this isn't a private summons. It's political. Public.

The sunlight behind him confirms what her body ignored—morning. She hasn't slept. Didn't even notice the hours bleeding out under ink, crystals, and all the things she can't unlearn.

And if her mother's staging is theatrical, there's only one event poetic enough to justify it—the marriage treaty, pushed sooner than expected.

Of course she'd force it sooner. Nothing secures an alliance like pretending your family isn't rotting from the inside.

Lumira straightens, slipping back into the mask of court perfection. The fury doesn't vanish—it simply relocates, settling beneath her.

"Just a moment." The words are cool, deceiving. "I'll be right behind you."

The guard hesitates, searching her face for what she won't give away. But he gives a tight nod and turns, boots retreating down the corridor with obedient indifference.

The Blood Key pulses once against her sternum—a reminder, a promise. Zylven's death sentence has been written.

Lumira exhales softly, slipping into the role of dutiful daughter with the ease of muscle memory. Each fiber of her being screams for blood—for the satisfaction of driving a blade through Zylven's throat, twisting slow until recognition blooms across his face. Until he feels each excruciating second, just as Emberly did. However, nobles who survive don't act on impulse. They plan. They wait. They strike when the moment is perfect, not merely convenient.

She tucks the journals and crystals away, straightens her clothing, and ignores the summons for precisely forty-five seconds—long enough to establish that she's complying of her own volition rather than jumping at her mother's command.

Small rebellions—the lifeblood of children born to power they didn't choose.

The palace hums with tension, every hallway scrubbed, every servant wound tight. And her mother, ever the strategist, has chosen this moment to make her next gambit.

Nothing says *diplomatic unity* quite like parading one's daughter in front of the man who murdered the other, all while offering her up as a symbol of alliance.

Tradition, of course. Her favorite shield.

Light spills across the corridor—staged intentionally, like everything Thara touches.

Thara stands framed in the circular window of her study, fingertips on the glass as if testing for cracks.

"You're late," she observes without turning, carrying the specific note of disappointment she reserves for Lumira's most minor infractions.

"Apologies, Mother," Lumira replies with practiced deference that contains enough sincerity to avoid outright sarcasm. "I had matters to attend to."

A small lie, insignificant in the grand scheme of deceptions between them. A warm-up exercise for the performance to come.

Thara turns, her expression dissecting Lumira with the cool detachment of someone weighing value, not kinship. Whatever she registers prompts the slightest shift—a warning shot in miniature. "You're... different," she states, the pause heavier than the words. Her stare remains on Lumira, unnervingly steady. "Whatever it is... it wasn't there before."

With unwavering neutrality, neither confrontational nor submissive, Lumira measures the distance she'll need to cover if it comes to that. "New cosmetics," she casually suggests. "I've been experimenting with imported pigments."

Another lie. Small, plausible, and utterly beside the point. Thara doesn't care about cosmetics—she cares about the current she senses in Lumira, the dangerous undercurrent of purpose that no amount of aristocratic composure can fully conceal.

"You've been absent from court gatherings," Thara remarks with composed confidence. "Your chambers lie vacant at unusual times. Servants whisper. Guards take note." She pauses briefly. "I have noticed as well." She stops directly in front of Lumira, proximity thick with perfume and power, both applied to choke, not charm. "Enlighten me..." Thara's voice drops to silk and honey, each word precisely spaced and weighed. She takes a step closer, fingers extending toward Lumira with the particular predatory grace of a woman who considers conversation a contact sport. "...daughter." Another pause, loaded with maternal affection the way a crossbow is loaded with bolts. "What. Are. You. Planning?"

How delightfully predictable. When subtlety fails, her mother always resorts to the magical equivalent of a sledgehammer to the skull.

The words brush against Lumira's mind, soft and insidious, unlike any ordinary persuasion. Thara's Compulsion slides toward her thoughts with its usual elegant cruelty. A faint deep-scarlet shimmer gathers in the air around Thara's outstretched arm, coiling and darting like living threads. The glow flickers through the lamplight, unmistakable to anyone present—power made visible, leveled at Lumira.

Because nothing screams "loving maternal concern" quite like magical mind rape in the privacy of one's own study.

A strange pressure blooms at the back of Lumira's skull, delicate yet insistent, coaxing obedience, insisting that compliance would be so much easier than defiance. Her breath hitches sharply, pulse quickening as she sees the scarlet threads slither closer, weaving toward her thoughts like barbed silk.

But the air carries a new weight since the last time her mother tried this particular brand of maternal guidance. The magical veil that once shrouded her abilities has lifted, and with it, her vulnerability to Thara's influence. The Compulsion slides against her mental barriers, a steady pressure that cannot break through.

There's no need to advertise this delightful development. Lumira allows her shoulders to tense, her chest to tighten, playing the part of a daughter struggling against superior magical force. Let Thara believe her decades of practice continue to hold sway.

The Blood Key flares against her sternum, warm and approving— not in response to magical resistance, but in recognition of a truth perfectly delivered. Its heat spreads through her chest, a pleasant counterpoint to the theater she's performing for her mother's benefit.

The Compulsion presses at her defenses with all the effectiveness of rain against a cathedral roof, but Lumira maintains her performance of struggle, allowing the perfect amount of tension as she meets Thara's.

Lumira threads the right tremor into her delivery, the practiced edge of a daughter feigning resistance to a spell that no longer binds her. "I'm planning…" The falter is no accident, expertly placed—but it lands. "To find a way out of this marriage. To delay it, maybe claim illness. I can't—I won't be your political pawn forever."

The confession carries the bitter taste of rebellion that Thara would expect to pry from her defiant daughter under magical influence. And under the lies, there's sufficient truth to satisfy the probing threads—she does want out of being a political pawn, and she absolutely refuses to be suppressed.

Thara accepts the partial truth with all the discernment of a drunk accepting free drinks, the Compulsion easing as her mother's expression slides from suspicion to the particular satisfaction of a predator who believes she's successfully cowed her prey.

"There it is," Thara murmurs, the magical shimmer fading as she withdraws her magic. "I knew you were plotting something foolish." She carries unmistakable satisfaction in her tone. "Did you really think you could hide your little schemes from me?"

Such a charming euphemism for "inconvenient habit of thinking for oneself." Thara had always possessed the remarkable talent for making free will sound like a character defect.

Let her believe the Compulsion worked. Let her gloat.

The truth Lumira offered had been carefully trimmed, polished, and weaponized—sufficient to pass, insufficient to matter.

A chill slithers down Lumira's spine at her mother's words— not fear, but the cold recognition of exactly what kind of woman has raised her. Not for the first time, she wonders if her mother knew about Emberly's murder, if Thara had given her tacit approval for the sacrifice, or if she simply hadn't cared to ask uncomfortable questions when a convenient death furthered her political agenda.

Thara's expression tightens, cold certainty bleeding through the cracks. "You are still a Blood Descent." Each word is chosen with care. "Whatever game you're playing, remember who owns the board."

No elaboration. They both know exactly what Thara does to daughters who forget their place. Years of punishments refined to an art form—scars neither need to name.

"Of course, Mother," Lumira responds with the particular diction of nobility acknowledging an unpleasant but inescapable truth. "Your guidance remains invaluable, as always."

The platitude—empty as a ceremonial chalice—satisfies Thara's immediate need for deference without conceding any actual ground. A diplomatic solution to an impasse neither of them intends to resolve through honest communication.

"The engagement to Lysander moves forward tomorrow," Thara states, returning to safer territory with obvious relief. "Zylven himself will officiate the betrothal ceremony."

There it is.

Not the accelerated timeline—Lumira had half-expected that. This is not strategy—it's panic. And panic, from Thara, is almost as revealing as confession.

But Zylven.

The casual mention of Emberly's murderer sends a jolt of rage through Lumira's veins, molten and vicious. The Blood Key flares against her sternum—so hot she nearly gasps—as if it shares her fury at hearing his name spoken so casually by her mother. Her nails dig into her palms, pressing crescent moons of pain to ground herself. She can almost taste the metallic tang of blood—his blood—on her tongue.

"How appropriate," Lumira murmurs, the words emerging with enough enthusiasm to avoid suspicion while her mind conjures the image of Zylven's throat opening beneath her blade during the very ceremony her mother describes.

Thara studies her for a moment longer, clearly sensing a disturbance but unable to pinpoint its exact nature. She reaches out—rare from a woman who hoards touch as if it were coin—and brushes a strand of hair from Lumira's face, the motion more assessment than affection. "Get some rest." The instruction lands with the weight of command, not concern. "You're starting to appear... unraveled."

Not tired; focused, determined, deadly.

But Thara doesn't need to know that. Not yet.

Lumira offers a shallow nod—polite to pass, hollow to sting—and turns to leave, recalculating, imagining the satisfaction of watching Zylven's face as he realizes exactly who is ending his life and why.

A thrill sparks along her nerves—she can almost feel the blade in her palm, the give of flesh, the guttural sound of a man dying when it no longer makes a difference. She pictures the moment he understands, bending close to let Emberly's name fall into his ear, the last tether before he's gone.

Some secrets are best kept until the blade is already falling.

27

THE SHAPE OF VENGEANCE

J aggard discovers her in the east corridor, approaching with the stealth of someone who deems regular entrances unworthy of his skills. His usual smirk is noticeably missing, substituted by sincere concern that seems strangely out of place on his typically amused face.

"You look like a woman about to make a terrible decision." He falls into step beside her with the practiced ease of someone who's cornered her in empty hallways before.

"And you sound like a man I'm debating whether to stab or tolerate if he doesn't explain himself quickly," Lumira returns, her patience for court games dissolving like morning mist in the presence of her determination.

But instead of the usual sardonic comeback, Jaggard glances over his shoulder, checking for observers with uncharacteristic caution that immediately puts her on alert. Whatever he's about to say, he doesn't want witnesses.

How perfectly theatrical.

"You're being followed," he murmurs, low despite the corridor's emptiness. "Zylven got in yesterday. Didn't make a scene, but he's been hovering. Intent. Comfortable. Like the place belongs to him."

The implication cuts clean and deep: her enemy walks these halls without fear, shielded by alliances she hasn't yet named. The palace isn't neutral. It's his—in function, in loyalty, in every way that counts.

Lumira slows her pace, recalibrating with the quiet precision of nobility, adjusting a freshly redrawn battlefield. "Are you warning me?" she asks, the question layered with equal parts suspicion and curiosity.

Jaggard's expression settles—not into mockery, but into what almost resembles respect. "I'm telling you not to get caught." He leans in, tone low but weighted. "If you're going to do it, do it right."

She freezes.

"Do what, exactly?" she asks evenly, her words as stifled—and dangerous—as the knife beneath her sleeve.

The words hover between them, dense with unspoken meaning. Knowledge, not mercy. Permission, not warning.

He doesn't flinch. "I know what revenge does to a person." The words are subdued. "I'm aware of its effects."

Lumira's expression hardens. "Then you know who it's for."

Not a question—a probe. A trap.

She surveys him carefully. "How long have you known?"

A brief flicker crosses his face—present, then gone. A crack in his armor. "Long enough to know you're not wrong," he answers.

The revelation knocks a thread loose inside her, barely perceptible—but irreversible.

He's not merely a preening opportunist with a taste for velvet and venom—he carries his own ghost, his own reason to let the world unravel.

Shame. He was easier to dismiss when he was just decoration.

"I'll take that under advisement." Her tone is cool, offering nothing more.

Jaggard nods once, the mask slipping back into place—smirk-adjacent, insufferably casual, a man who trades in half-truths and implication. "Do." He's already turning to go. "Oh, and Lumira?"

She pauses, spine taut.

"The Brotherhood's doubling patrols tonight," he adds, but the tension in his jaw tells another story. "They're calling it heightened security. Might want to avoid the main gates."

With that, he saunters away, posture loosening into his usual swagger, like he didn't just commit treason in a hallway soaked in secrets.

Lumira remains motionless as he leaves, the new fragment falling into place within the puzzle of power and betrayal.

Not an ally. Not an enemy. A wild card.

Unscheduled chaos. Noted.

A few hours later, Lumira sits alone in the shadow of the library's western alcove, surrounded by tomes she's not reading and maps she's memorized. She's not here for answers—only confirmation.

One more pass at the terrain, the patrol rotations, the possible escape points. All the variables that might shape a clean kill.

She registers the change in the air but doesn't lift her head. Recognition lives in her spine.

"I know where he'll be."

Hadralis steps from the shelves, a man carved from dusk and certainty, voice cool, presence calculated. Their last conversation ended in a fight—unfinished and charged with tension that doesn't fade, only coils tighter with time.

"Congratulations," Lumira mutters, concentrating on the map. "Should I nominate you for a medal, or have a statue commissioned in your honor?"

He doesn't answer. Instead, he takes the chair opposite her—posture taut, analyzing. A strategist, not a showman.

"Zylven. Crimsun-Vesper river border. Tonight." Each word lands, cold as judgment, impossible to deny. "He's making a discreet visit to the bridge and doesn't want it public. No full escort."

He offers no elaboration, no mention of names, but Lumira doesn't need either. The knowledge settles in her mind with perfect clarity: the Aelric Bridge.

She lifts her head at last, fixing him with the kind of glare that shatters any guise. "And how do you know that?" Her voice carries an even, razor edge—a test threaded with charm and cruelty.

Hadralis doesn't so much as blink under her scrutiny. "I continue to receive Brotherhood movement reports." He pauses, letting the words hang between them before adding, almost as an afterthought, "Thara mentioned how you reacted to your last conversation."

Lumira zeroes in—cold, exact—as if sight alone could strike.

"She said you were suspiciously agreeable. Polite, considering you were supposedly caught off guard." Another beat passes, the weight of deduction threading through. "She didn't trust it. Neither did I."

Damn her. The curse rises in Lumira's mind, swift and fierce.

She'd thought the performance flawless—tone warm, smile practiced, demeanor empty of intent. But Thara, in her ruthless way, had seen enough to send up a flag. And worse—she'd passed it along. Weaponized it.

Of course she had.

And now Zylven crept in silence, thinking himself safe.

Good.

Let him step lightly.

She'd make sure every footfall mattered—especially on the bridge ahead, a narrow arch of black stone spanning the Naiad River. Unadorned, unguarded, it was a thread of diplomacy stretched thin, maintained not for protection but for appearances. It's where emissaries meet. Where pacts are signed.

Where men like Zylven could walk without spectacle and be seen all the same.

Perfect.

Information, location, timing—all falling into place with the groan of a door swinging open.

Lumira keeps her expression neutral, though her pulse spikes. "Why tell me?" she asks, the question carrying more genuine curiosity than her usual defensive edge.

Hadralis meets her gaze. Steady. Unflinching. "Because I want him dead too."

What stands between them isn't alliance or trust. It's strategy, stripped bare. Cold and clean. His unshaken certainty matches her rage—two blades, same target.

The contempt in her gaze isn't suspicion but the loathing reserved for those who break what matters, then pretend to map its ruins.

"You think one good deed scrubs your blood clean?" Low and lethal. "You're not here to help me, Hadralis. You're here because you hate him more than yourself."

For a fleeting moment, a muscle tightens behind his stare—a hit he can't parry before it lands.

Good.

She stands, stepping close, the following words impossible to mistake for anything but a knife to the gut. "I don't need your warnings. I don't need your guilt." Her smile is slow, poisonous. "If you get in my fucking way again... you'll regret surviving it."

Hadralis doesn't argue or explain. He gives a shallow nod and vanishes into the dark—fitting, really.

Evasion suits him better than truth.

Lumira turns, uninterested in his exit.

She has better things to kill.

By early afternoon, the palace gardens are nearly empty—sunlit and brimming with tension no one will name. Lumira sits on a stone bench under one of the myrrh trees, its blossoms barely open and its scent both subtle and piercing. She cannot recall the exact way she arrived here, but she is certain of her reason for staying.

She needs space to think.

It all happened faster than she could keep up with.

She's been reacting, maneuvering, surviving—without a moment to catch her breath.

So she lets herself sit.

Not as the Blood Descent. Not as a pawn or predator, but as a girl wondering if what's left can still be called whole.

The breeze shifts.

A shadow glides across the flagstones, followed by the hush of wings. A silver-winged kestrel lands cleanly on the bench beside her—no jeweled bands, no ornamental ribbons. A creature built for purpose, not display.

Lumira unfastens the scroll from its leg with practiced care. No seal, no signature—only a sliver of parchment designed to vanish if mishandled. One line, inked in tight, meticulous script:

Refuge approved. It is yours.

She falters. The gnomes have chosen—not the fallback, not performance, but loyalty made tangible. The stronghold behind the ridge belongs to her now, shaped by solitude and hidden in stone.

Freed from bloodlines and burdens, with space to exist— and no one reaching to own that freedom. Relief should come. Triumph, even. But the weight only digs in.

The refuge waits, and the future spreads before her, but neither can begin until she finishes this. Zylven Meridian cannot live to see another dawn. Everything else can burn.

Lumira finds Wrenna and Ilara at the upstairs back table of Pigments & Pints, bent over a worn map inked with faded lines and fresh marks—notes, patrol paths, and network routes.

She came straight here after the kestrel's arrival. The sun has begun its slow descent, casting the city in angles and gold. If she wants to reach the Aelric Bridge before nightfall, she'll need to leave soon. It's hours away on foot—and she won't risk a marked trail.

They rise slightly as she approaches. No greetings. No questions. They can see it in her face.

"It happens tonight." The words hang there, undeniable.

Ilara nods once, calm and immediate. "What do you need?"

"A distraction at the palace. Big enough to draw attention. I need to get to the Aelric Bridge without a trail."

Ilara doesn't hesitate. "Consider it done." Her fingers are moving across the map, rerouting runners, rearranging signals.

"I spoke with Jaggard," Lumira adds. "And Hadralis. Separately." She doesn't need to elaborate—they'll understand what that means. "Zylven will be there tonight. Minimal guards."

Wrenna leans back, her composure hardening. "Of course he will. He doesn't need guards when he thinks no one would dare touch him."

Lumira hesitates. "And the gnomes sent word this afternoon."

That captures them completely. Both women still. Listening.

"The refuge is real," she says. "They held up their end."

Ilara straightens slightly, voice cool. "That didn't take long."

Lumira nods. "It was already built. They needed to decide I was worth the risk."

Everything they've built is tilting—accelerating into motion.

"Does this mean I get to paint its walls?" Wrenna's smile is dry, knowing.

Ilara offers a small, steady smile. "You're thinking beyond this. That's good."

The weight coils in Lumira's chest—but for the first time in days, it doesn't crush her. It feels like momentum.

A smirk tugs at Wrenna's mouth. "Might as well make history a little prettier."

Ilara cuts her a sidelong smirk. "Always thinking about décor in the middle of war."

Wrenna shrugs, unapologetic.

Lumira snorts, brittle and dry. "Paint the damn thing however you want—after tonight."

The Blood Key stirs faintly against her, a vow thrumming through her veins.

She takes them in: Ilara, unmoving as stone; Wrenna, all hard lines and loyalty. A thread inside her loosens—barely.

Not relief. Not quite.

But near it—close, and more than ample.

Everything is in motion now: the plans, the players, the price.

And this time, she's not following someone else's path.

She's carving her own.

28

THE CONFRONTATION

Dusk presses low over the Naiad River, bleeding purple into the fog as the last light dies. Lumira crouches near the water's edge, hidden behind a tangle of roots and reeds, out of sight. The Aelric Bridge rises ahead, flanked by pacing Brotherhood guards and shadowed by the man she came to kill.

The mist doesn't simply curl around Lumira's ankles—it *worships* them, coiling like spectral servants bowing before royalty. Each tendril caresses her skin with reverent devotion, as if nature itself recognizes what she's come to do and wishes to participate in the bloodletting. The Naiad River's constant murmur drowns her footsteps, its ancient waters conspiring to mask her approach with the enthusiastic complicity of a fellow assassin.

The elements, ever obliging, seem more than happy to assist in her murderous intentions.

Her pulse hammered her rib cage, each strike a call to slaughter echoing in bone and blood. Yet her hands remain perfectly steady—

elegance, weaponized. This isn't the composure she trained into habit. This is something older—mythic, savage—clawed from the marrow and coiled behind her thoughts, watchful, ravenous.

Certainty doesn't settle in her chest. It consumes her, burning through hesitation like wildfire through dry grass.

Death isn't a choice anymore. It's a vow etched into the dark, tightening with time. As her touch grazes the dagger at her hip, the Blood Key flares beneath her sternum—singing for the blood of the unworthy.

Two Dusk Agents pass fifty paces to her left, their movements mechanical and predictable. They don't see her. They don't sense her or have any idea that they're about to witness the violent collapse of carefully maintained power structures, the death of a man who believes himself untouchable, and the beginning of a reckoning that will tear territories apart at their rotten seams.

History waits for no one—and they arrive woefully unready.

Zylven Meridian stands at the riverbank beside the Aelric Bridge, strolling with the composed assurance of one who views the universe as his own. Not that anyone would question the High Sovereign's riverside walk. It's practically tradition. But Lumira knows better—this is only cover, while the real work unfolds in shadows, not chambers.

Until. This. Moment.

He hums. The bastard actually *hums* to himself, the melody soft but distinct—undoubtedly one of his own compositions, meticulously designed to influence anyone foolish enough to listen. The sound pierces Lumira's ears like needles, each note a fresh confession of his arrogance. Everything he does has a purpose. Even his fucking cursed music.

Her vision narrows, the world bleeding away at the edges until all that remains is the man before her—the murderer who poisoned her sister's wine and stayed to see her die. The architect who built a kingdom on buried gods and stolen power. The performer who wept at her sister's funeral with eyes as dry as bone.

Rage doesn't merely simmer beneath her—it detonates, coursing through her veins with such violent heat that she half expects her blood to evaporate. The Blood Key responds, pulsing with ancient fury that matches her own, each beat a wordless demand:

Now.

Now.

NOW.

She rises from the reeds, slow and deliberate, mist drawing back in a hush that feels staged for a final act. Step by step, she closes the distance, unseen but not hiding.

Claws form where calm once lived, violence trembling at the cusp of release—then Zylven turns.

"Lumira," he murmurs, followed by a chuckle—so precise it might as well have been rehearsed. "What a pleasant surprise." His awareness settles over her in practiced beats—cool, unreadable, every threat cataloged on instinct. "What brings you to this part of Crimsun?"

There's no wit today—no retort, no court-polished mask to shield her. The words come raw, stripped bare, like it was dragged from the pit of her chest.

"Did you murder my sister?"

She closes the distance, positioning herself directly in his path, blocking his easy escape route back toward the Dusk Agents. The guards who once flanked him now trail further up the path—close enough to call, too far to intervene.

The question hangs between them, not a genuine inquiry but a blade unsheathed.

His smile doesn't falter. No, it sharpens, courtesy falling away to uncover the cold calculation she'd seen in the crystal's memory. The truth doesn't slip out; he releases it, confident in its power to wound.

"Lumira," he sighs, like a teacher forced to repeat a lesson to a hopeless student, "your sister was an inconvenience. Inconveniences must be eliminated. It's as simple—as mundane—as that."

The words land like physical blows, each syllable a fresh laceration across her heart. Her soul doesn't merely crack—it shatters, razor-edged fragments slicing through her composure as he continues with practiced indifference.

"Your sister thought she was invulnerable," he muses, tracking her reaction with the detached fascination of a scientist observing an experiment. "I wonder—does that arrogance run in the family?" He doesn't bother denying it. Instead, he holds her in his sights—unblinking, removed—the way one might examine a fragile, irreplaceable relic before shattering it. "Her presence had to be… corrected," he acknowledges, no shame, no remorse, merely confirmation of fact. "Though 'murder' is such an unpleasant term. I prefer to think of it as… a necessary adjustment."

"Soulthief." The word burns Lumira's tongue like acid. "Hours of unending agony. Fully conscious, fully aware, her magic turned traitor inside her own veins. And you sat calmly by her bedside, *savoring* her helplessness as her screams drowned in her throat."

His eyebrows lift slightly—perhaps impressed that she's learned the specifics. "Well researched," he acknowledges, dipped in a kind of lazy, backhanded praise. "Though to be exact—it was closer to seven hours. Your sister had remarkable resistance."

Seven damn hours.

The number sears into her bones, a curse she cannot shake. Seven hours of Emberly trapped inside her own body. Seven hours of soundless screaming. Seven hours of this man hovering and *enjoying*.

A savage heat twists in Lumira's chest, alive and prowling as it spreads through her.

She holds herself in place, to maintain the conversation while her body vibrates with barely contained violence. The Blood Key pulses against her sternum—not warmth now but fire, searing her from the inside out, demanding satiation.

"Why?" she demands, the word scraping her throat raw. "What could possibly justify that kind of death?"

Zylven sighs, as if disappointed by such a fundamental question. "Surely you've figured that out by now, Lumira. She discovered things she shouldn't have. Connections. Patterns. The truth about the territories, the bloodlines, the gods and goddesses trapped within the Aethervoid." He begins to pace, fingers moving in elegant gestures as if conducting music only he can hear. "Your sister was brilliant— brilliant in a way that invited danger. She traced the lines of power back to their source, uncovered the design woven into the divine imprisonment, and realized what we've been doing for generations."

"The Brotherhood," Lumira breathes, disgust thickening each word. "You're not just controlling Vesper—you're puppeteering every territory, every bloodline."

He lets her words settle, then answers in a voice so smooth it borders on rehearsed. "Not both sides—all sides. Each bloodline carefully isolated, each territory held in perfect tension. A system that has served for generations."

"And Emberly threatened that balance." Her fingers twitch toward her blade, muscles coiled for violence.

"She wasn't merely a threat—she was dismantling it piece by piece," he responds, remaining infuriatingly composed. "Mapping bloodlines. Uncovering patterns we've concealed for generations." His voice drops, almost reverent. "She uncovered *you*, Lumira. She knew exactly what your blood could do."

"So you killed her." Each word falls hard, leaving no escape in its wake.

He releases a sigh and opens his stance, the motion elegant and final. "She became a liability. So I dealt with her." A lecturing tone creeps into his words, making Lumira's skin crawl. "One day, you'll understand—when you grow up and become much more accommodating, as your mother has requested. The balance we maintain keeps the world turning. Without containment, the gods would break free, reclaim their territories, and humanity would—"

The rest of Zylven's words blur into noise, drowned by the gleam of her dagger.

Around her, the forest pauses—not with silence, but with anticipation, as if every leaf and beast knows what's coming.

The rage she's been containing—the white-hot fury she's kept chained beneath layers of noble restraint—doesn't simply break free. It detonates within her, atom by atom, cell by cell—not in chaotic fury, but in a far more terrifying form: perfect, crystalline clarity.

Each chain she's clung to breaks in sequence—like bones snapping, vows unraveling, and the scream her sister never got to release.

The transformation doesn't surge through her veins like fire—that would be clean. Simple. And this is neither. This is molten metal, primordial and ancient, searing through her body, burning away everything she was and remolding her into a savage thing, honed and lethal—a reckoning the world wasn't meant to face.

It doesn't burst forth. It flows—cool, sinuous power trailing down her arms, nestling in her palms, a creature preparing to strike. The sensation is unlike anything she's ever experienced—not strength but violation, as if parts of herself previously locked away are tearing free of ancient prisons, awakening beneath the pressure of her hatred, stretching muscles and flexing claws long denied.

She embraces the buzz, the hum, the electric spark that doesn't drift but floods from her chest to her limbs, drowning her in sensation. A delirious giggle escapes her throat—not amusement but the sound of sanity splintering beneath the weight of power, rage, and grief no soul was meant to bear. Lumira tips her head back, rocking slowly, soaking in this newfound raw energy that doesn't fill her—it overflows, spilling from her fingertips in violet sparks that hiss through the air.

It's intoxicating. *Delicious.* Utterly terrifying.

Power thrums through her with each heartbeat, each pulse unleashing fresh waves of destructive potential that snap through her veins and beg for release. She isn't choosing this awakening—it's choosing her, claiming her as its vessel and avatar of vengeance. What was once locked away now crashes through the break—magic unleashed, wild and unrelenting.

Zylven breaks off mid-sentence, tensing as he senses the change in her. His eyes narrow, reaching subtly for hidden weapons. "You have no idea what you're getting yourself into," he warns, dropping to a growl.

"No," she agrees, gaze locked with his, unyielding. The world looks different now, its edges honed to ruthless clarity. Even her voice doesn't sound like her own—it's a stranger's, rich with power and promise. "But neither do you."

Knowledge floods her—unearned, unspoken. Not learned, but remembered. The energy pulsing through her isn't power but potential waiting to be shaped and weaponized. She intuitively understands how to direct it, form it, and manifest it into physical form—not through study or practice but through pure, undiluted intention.

A weapon blooms from her palm in a surge of violet lightning, solidifying instantly into a whip—not a tool but a manifestation of her wrath, pure and lethal. It thrums with searing light, sparks dancing along its length, each burning with the intensity of her hatred. Bronze tips glint at the end, eager for flesh, hungry for blood.

The whip hangs gently from her with deadly elegance, an extension of her will—a weapon that will inflict the most exquisite agony, the loveliest pain.

A smile curves her lips—not the careful, measured expression of court politics, but feral, *hungry*. The smile of a predator that has finally stopped pretending to be prey.

"This will not end well for you, Zylven," Lumira states with a calm more frightening than any rage. She thrusts the whip out and it cracks through the air with a vibrating snap that echoes like thunder, demonstrating its deadly beauty.

His composure fractures, true surprise breaking through the carefully constructed mask. For the first time, genuine fear flickers across Zylven's face. Whatever threat he imagined she posed was never as potent or terrifying as this. Nevertheless, he recovers quickly. A faint glow emanates from his fingers, conjuring a silver haze laced with latent thought—the disciplined unraveling of a Somnifex at work, threading his will through the fractured edges of memory.

"You're full of surprises," he acknowledges, tight with new respect. "But I've been doing this for decades, child. You can't possibly—"

She doesn't let him finish. The moment he begins to speak—pulsing with silver haze—she spins away from where she stood, anticipating the real attack. The magic was a distraction. His sword slices through the space she just vacated, missing her by inches.

The killing calm settles over her now—not the absence of rage, but its refinement. Her fury no longer burns—it carves. She is no longer Blood Descent Lumira Kyrvayne, court-trained daughter of a poisoned throne. She is every secret the palace failed to contain, every scar they taught her to hide—vengeance incarnate, judgment with teeth, retribution finally given a name.

Lumira flicks the whip toward him, streaks of molten light carving through the air before the bronze tips tear into his wrist. The scent of scorched flesh rises an instant before a hiss escapes his clenched teeth—quick, instinctive, pained. Not a scream. Not yet.

She doesn't stop. The next lash carves across his chest, then another—lower, crueler—slashing his abdomen where magic tunnels inward, searching for soft organs to ruin. His body convulses, muscles locking, blood rising in his throat as energy surges through veins not meant to carry it. He chokes, gasps—and then the scream tears free, raw and broken, a sound dragged from somewhere deeper than pain.

It hits like a lightning strike cleaving the world's spine—a sound no man like Zylven was ever meant to make.

And the air carries it.

The Dusk Agents respond instantly, shadows tearing from the tree line with the precision of predators answering a wounded packmate's call. Their footfalls barely disturb the underbrush as they race toward the riverbank, weapons already drawn. They are not simple guards but trained killers, moving with the confident efficiency of men who have eliminated problems without ever leaving evidence behind.

Lumira senses them before she sees them—a prickling awareness at the edge of her consciousness, an intrusion into the perfect bubble of vengeance she's created around herself and Zylven. Her lips curl into a snarl, not of fear but irritation. Of course her retribution would be interrupted by lesser prey.

She doesn't pause her assault on him. The whip continues its dance, opening another laceration across his chest as she inclines slightly toward the approaching threat. The violet energy coursing through her veins splits its attention, a portion diverting toward her left hand while her right maintains its grip on the whip.

"You have guests," she informs Zylven, boredom dripping from each syllable like lukewarm wine. "How rude of them to arrive unannounced."

Desperation gleams through the cracks in his mask, and a vicious satisfaction tightens in Lumira's chest.

"They'll kill you," he gasps, blood bubbling at the corner of his mouth. "The Brotherhood doesn't travel alone."

"Dusk Agents," she corrects him, the term dripping with contempt. "And no. They won't."

The energy in her left palm condenses and shifts—two spectral daggers blossom into existence at once, spinning like conjured spite. They hover above her palm, edges shimmering with barely contained fury, humming with the same wrath that feeds her whip.

She doesn't turn to face the agents. Doesn't offer them the dignity of recognition. They don't deserve it.

With a flick of her wrist—casual and almost bored—she sends the daggers flying toward the approaching men. The weapons streak through the night like comets, trailing violet fire, moving faster than any physical blade could travel. They don't simply fly—they hunt, adjusting their trajectories mid-air with predatory intelligence.

The first Dusk Agent falls without a sound, the energy dagger piercing his throat with such precision that his death rattle never surpasses his vocal cords. He crumples to the ground, fingers twitching around the hilt of a sword left unused.

The second has time to realize what's happening. He watches his partner fall, arm rising to defend himself—a futile, pathetic gesture, but the dagger doesn't slow or hesitate. It slides between his ribs with the particular elegance of a weapon that knows exactly where to strike for maximum efficiency.

He manages a single, strangled gasp before joining his colleague on the forest floor, blood pooling beneath him.

From attack to death, the entire sequence takes less than three seconds. Two trained killers eliminated with the same indifference of swatting flies.

She turns back to Zylven, who stares at her with a new understanding—new terror. The hope that flickered there moments before has been extinguished.

"Now." Lumira turns glacial. "Where were we? Ah, yes." Her whip rises again, casting ghastly shadows across his bloodied face. "I believe we were discussing how long it took my sister to die. Seven hours, you said?" She regards him like a question posed to the room. "I wonder how long you'll last."

Without waiting for his response, she brings the whip down again, echoing through the night. Behind her, the bodies of the Dusk Agents cool on the forest floor, already forgotten.

Some interruptions aren't worth remembering.

When Zylven attempts to regain his footing—literally and in their deadly dance of power—he trembles slightly, the first crack in his decades-old composure. How satisfying to behold fear unravel the mask he's worn so tightly for so long.

Lumira savors the moment and lets it settle on her tongue like fine wine—bitter, intoxicating, and worth every second of anticipation. The whip pulses with renewed hunger, the arcane energy practically purring through her grip as if to say: *more, please, more.* And who is she to deny it, when there's so much debt to collect?

Seven hours of Emberly's muted screaming. Seven hours of Zylven's cold-blooded cruelty. Every second will be repaid—in blood and agony, with interest compounded by betrayal.

Before he can recover, she manifests a knife from her left palm—not summoned, but born, wrenched from raw energy and murderous intent. It doesn't fly, it carves through the air with the trajectory of vengeance long delayed, burying itself in his shoulder with a satisfying, wet thunk.

He falls to his knees, the impact of combined wounds overwhelming even his considerable tolerance for pain. The sight should satisfy her. It doesn't. A man who sat beside her sister's deathbed deserves far more than a momentary collapse.

She knows better than to assume victory. A man like Zylven doesn't break so easily. Doesn't die so easily.

The light skims across him, then bends—coating him in a liquid-silver sheen. Reality blurs, soft at the edges like a painting left in the rain. He's trying to enter her mind. To trap her in dreams, where he holds all the power. The coward's battlefield—when physical confrontation fails.

"You think weapons are the only battlefield?" he snarls, blood trickling from the corner of his mouth in delicate crimson rivulets. "Let's see how you fare in my domain."

The world warps—fragments reform into nightmare shapes. Images from Lumira's deepest fears take form, Emberly's dying face frozen in a scream. Her mother's coldest rejection, perfectly poised and aristocratically cruel. The fortress she won't reach, burning to ash while Ilara and Wrenna scream inside. Blood drips from her fingers, writhing with a life of its own, curling beneath her nails.

But the visions waver, refusing to solidify—like smoke that won't hold shape.

Zylven's expression contorts with effort, then confusion. His power as a Somnifex slams into a barrier he can't penetrate. "Impossible," he hisses, redoubling his assault until sweat mixes with blood on his face. "No bloodline resists dream manipulation—not like this."

Lumira laughs, not the polished performance she's worn for nobles, but a ragged sound that scrapes her throat raw on the way out. "Apparently, I'm full of surprises."

She doesn't fully understand why his powers can't penetrate her mind, but she doesn't waste time questioning the advantage. Instead, she presses forward, her left palm tingling as another dagger materializes—larger, hungrier than the first. It spins toward his other shoulder, sparkling energy trailing behind it.

He deflects it this time, dragging up a shield of shimmering moonlit force—silvery and strange, a weapon pulled from memory or dream. She doesn't know what it is, only that it stops her cold. The collision sends a spray of sparks cascading over the riverbank, the burst of clashing magic illuminating their battle in ghostly, otherworldly light. The water seems to flinch away from the unnatural energies unleashed above it.

"You've been practicing," he acknowledges, rising with cold, unyielding grace despite his injuries. Blood soaks his left side, but he carries himself as if it's a mere inconvenience. "But did your sister tell you everything before she died? Did she explain what happens when bloodlines mix?" He begins to circle her, not rushed, not hesitant—just certain. "The gods never wanted this,"

Zylven snarls. "Power scattered. Divided. You're not a miracle, Lumira. You're the fuse." His sword curves like a sliver of frozen mist, ancient runes etched so finely they seem to ripple across the steel as he moves. "But mortals saw the truth. We saw what they were becoming. The Brotherhood rose to preserve balance. To purify the bloodlines. To make sure no one—*no one*—could ever bring the pieces back together."

He lunges. The blade slices her sleeve, leaving a thin line of blood along her forearm.

"But you," he snarls, thick with disdain, "you're the undoing of that order. Mixed bloodlines. Combined power. You're not a miracle—you're just a weapon the gods left behind to break the seals. And we've spent centuries preparing to destroy you."

Lumira glares. "So you hunted the truth and called it heresy. You built your empire on fear, and now you're afraid of the one thing you can't control."

His smile is thin and cold as winter moonlight. "Of course. What else is there?"

The battle intensifies, physical and metaphysical attacks colliding as they tear through the riverside clearing. Trees splinter and fall as Zylven sends waves of mental force crashing toward her. The ground scorches beneath Lumira's feet as her whip burns patterns into reality, leaving streaks of light suspended in the air.

Blood flows freely now—his from the deep shoulder wound and the lash marks where her whip flayed skin from muscle; hers from a dozen shallow cuts where his blade slipped past her defenses. The pain should be blinding, should scream through her nerves like fire, but Lumira barely feels it. The energy coursing through her veins serves as both weapon and anesthetic, keeping her focused on a single purpose: destruction.

"You can't win," Zylven pants, his perfect composure finally cracking. Sweat mixes with blood, his breathing ragged where once it was held in check. "Even if you kill me, the Dusk Agents remain. The system remains. There are others like me in all the territories—maintaining the divine prisons, keeping the bloodlines separate."

"Then I'll kill them too," Lumira replies, eerily calm. Not bravado—fact. "One by one, until the whole rotten structure collapses."

His face flickers—not with fear, but with the snap of sudden recognition. The understanding that she means every word. That the composure she's worn her entire life was a disguise—for power that wasn't meant to stay contained.

"You'd destroy the world to avenge your sister?" Real curiosity threads his voice as their magic rips the world apart.

"I'd rebuild it—over the corpses of all you bloody bastards." Violet light crackles between her teeth. "Starting with yours as the foundation."

He laughs—a sound of genuine amusement that catches her off guard. "Oh, Lumira. You really are exceptional. It's almost a shame—"

His words die as he releases a final, desperate assault. A shockwave bursts outward, tearing through the air with a howl. The river rises in spiraling columns, frozen mid-climb as reality buckles under the force.

For a heartbeat, Lumira falters. She barely manages to brace before his final blow crashes into her, the impact slamming against her ribs and sending her staggering backward.

Then a rupture—sudden and absolute—tears through her. Not a wall breaking, but a dam. Not magic—*grief*. Not vengeance—*anguish*. The energy building since Emberly's death finds direction—pure and violent.

Her whip splits, grows, multiplies—dozens of radiant tendrils lash through the last shreds of Zylven's defenses like lightning through storm clouds. Each strike leaves glowing scars in the air. Each impact drives deeper. Faster. Unrelenting.

His screams would have once horrified her. Now they satisfy a need she didn't know she carried. She doesn't want to stop. She fucking can't.

He stumbles back, turning to shield himself, retreating into instinct. The bronze tips graze the parts of him he most wants to protect. But Lumira doesn't notice. She doesn't care. She is nothing but the fury he created.

The onslaught slams into him like a final storm. He buckles beneath it and collapses to the scorched earth.

And still, she doesn't fall.

The whip fades to smoke, and whatever held her together splits. She lunges—not with a spell or a blade, but with her fists.

The first punch cracks across his jaw. The second splits her knuckles. The third draws blood—his. He tries to call up magic, but her rage moves faster than his fear. She straddles him before he can crawl away, fists slamming into bone, into lies, into every hour Emberly spent paralyzed.

"She was conscious," Lumira chokes out, driving her fist into his face. "Seven hours. Screaming inside."

Another blow. His lip splits. A tooth hits the dirt.

"You held her hand."

Another.

"You gave the eulogy."

Another.

He doesn't fight back. Only the sound remains—fragile and wet, unraveling.

She doesn't stop until her arms shake, until the fury hollows out and cold seeps in.

The dagger is in her grip—somehow. She doesn't remember reaching for it. Her body trembles, breath uneven. And as she straddles his chest, blade raised, the tears come. Hot. Unwelcome.

He looks up at her, bloodied and fading fast. "They knew," he whispers, vision slipping elsewhere. "We thought… it was always one of you… Chose wrong."

Lumira doesn't hesitate. She drives the dagger into his heart, silencing his words, his life, and the decades he spent pulling strings from the shadows. The blade slides between his ribs with ruthless certainty, sinking deep into flesh and bone.

His body arches once, then falls slack. Whatever light he held fades, leaving his face blank as glass.

The High Sovereign of Vesper, the Brotherhood's puppet master, murderer of her sister, reduced to cooling meat on riverbank stones.

Lumira stands over his corpse, blood—his and hers—dripping from her fingertips. The weapons she manifested have disappeared, the violet energy retreating inward—but she can feel it there, waiting, hungry, forever changed by its first emergence.

In the distance, shouting begins. Others nearby have realized their master has fallen. It's too late to save him—but not too late to hunt down his killer, if she lingers.

She should feel *something*—triumph, perhaps. Satisfaction. Justice for Emberly. Vengeance fulfilled. Instead, she feels hollow, as if parts of herself burned away in the conflagration that consumed Zylven.

Lumira turns to the forest, seeking escape—seeking whatever comes after wrath.

She carries herself with the particular certainty of someone who's crossed a line that cannot be uncrossed, who has become unrecognizable as the girl she once was.

Zylven's blood soaks into the riverbank, staining the soil with the end of his rule. The path is dark and uncertain, crowded with Dusk Agents, political fallout, and the dangerous knowledge she now carries.

Lumira keeps walking. Behind her lies a corpse and a shattered innocence she can never reclaim. Before her, a road carved by blood and violence—a future she both fears and craves.

The mask is gone. The rage remains. And somewhere deep inside, a terrible awareness unfurls, hunger coiled in patience.

Lumira disappears into the forest, no longer the girl who played by anyone's rules.

From this night forward, she carries blood etched into her skin and grief carved deep into her bones.

She is not whole. She is not forgiven.

She is only what vengeance left behind.

29

FOREST'S EMBRACE

Shouts tear through the night like cheap wineglasses at a commoner's wedding—loud, predictable, and dripping with more drama than the moment deserves. Lumira races along the river's edge, every footfall vanishing into the water behind her as if the elements have chosen to become accomplices to regicide. Or whatever term is used for killing a High Sovereign who truly had it coming. Political pruning, perhaps.

Blood—both Zylven's and her own—stains her leathers, the copper scent mingling with river mud as she ventures deeper into the forest's embrace. Her heart hammers against her rib cage with sickening intensity, not from exertion but from the lingering euphoria of vengeance fulfilled. The violet energy that had erupted from her palms like destructive poetry now simmers beneath the surface, waiting for another taste of violence.

How delightfully disturbing to discover one has a talent for brutality. All those years of aristocratic etiquette lessons, and her true calling involves manifesting weapons from pure rage and flaying men alive. Her tutors would be so disappointed.

She allows herself three seconds of vulnerability: the hitch in her chest, the faint tremble of blood-crusted hands, and a flicker of Emberly's face behind closed eyes. Then it's buried—shoved down where weakness has no place. Emotion is a luxury afforded to those who aren't actively being hunted by every guard in Vesper.

She has no time for grief. No space for horror at what she's done—no patience for the strange, hollow satisfaction lodged as a cold stone in her stomach.

The forest conspires around her—branches bending aside, shadows thickening to swallow her form, roots flattening to smooth her path. Lumira does not question this eerie aid—she relishes it with the unique entitlement of aristocrats used to having their desires foreseen and fulfilled without debate.

"Well. Aren't you eager," she mutters to the shadow that slinks forward, swallowing her form as a patrol's torchlight sweeps past. The darkness coils tighter around her ankles, no pet but a weapon awaiting orders.

Of course it is. Apparently, killing a member of the Brotherhood earns you more than stain. It earns attention.

Behind her, patrols churn through the underbrush—torchlight flickering between trees, boots snapping twigs, shouts echoing through the mist. They're hunting a ghost.

As she races through the forest, Lumira envisions the chaos blooming in Altareth—Wrenna's staged blaze dancing across rooftops in mischievous flourishes, an "accident" impossible to ignore and unsettling in its beauty. A distraction painted in flame and spectacle, meant to divert eyes from the bridge.

The docks would be in disarray by now, as Ilara promised: mismatched ledgers, missing cargo, panicked merchants. Enough noise to muddy any response.

And in the city's darker alleys, Ilara's creatures would be moving like myths—Dusk Deer flitting through shadows, Grove Dragons trailing phosphorescent confusion in their wake.

Nature doesn't shout. It confuses. It misleads. It makes you vanish.

The details escape her, and she lets them. Trust is the only thing that matters.

Earlier that night, before reaching the Aelric Bridge, she'd wordlessly pressed a wrapped satchel into Wrenna's grasp. The Living Branch. Too risky to wield in bloodshed. Unthinkable to abandon. Wrenna had nodded—unsurprised.

Nothing like friendship weaponized for mutual spite.

Dusk Agents fan out through the woods with predictable inefficiency, their torches burning little holes in the darkness that illuminate nothing of consequence. They shout to one another with the particular blend of panic and bravado that suggests they understand the political implications of failing to capture their High Sovereign's killer, yet have absolutely no interest in actually confronting someone capable of murdering Zylven Meridian.

Sensible of them, really. Self-preservation instincts are so refreshing in authority figures.

Lumira presses deeper into the forest, following paths that seem to materialize beneath her feet moments before she needs them. The water from the river clings to her boots until no tracks remain visible, then mysteriously evaporates once its usefulness concludes.

A deafening crash of underbrush to her left sends her diving into the shadows beneath a massive oak. Three Dusk Agents hurry past, so close she can smell the sweat of their fear—the stench of men who know they're chasing prey beyond their reach.

"Whoever did it couldn't have gone far," one insists, tight with urgency. "No one kills a High Sovereign and disappears."

"Did you see what they did to him?" another chokes out, cracking with barely contained horror. "I almost didn't recognize him."

The third tightens his grip on his sword, scanning the shadows with the twitchy alertness of hunted prey.

They're right to be afraid.

Power rouses from its slumber within her, a storm answering the call of open sky. Her whole body hums with the terrible anticipation of violence—raw, untrained magic that offers no instructions, no warnings, no mercy. Perfect timing, really. Nothing like unstable magic to make a murder charge more exciting.

The agents approach, their torchlight creeping toward the shadows where she hides. Lumira tenses, ready to fight, escape, or become whatever weapon her rage can forge.

But the confrontation never comes. The forest shifts instead— shadows thickening, the air turning dense and heavy, a barrier between her and the approaching blades. The agents pass within arm's reach, oblivious. Not quite invisible. More like selective blindness, as if reality itself has decided they aren't allowed to see her. How thoughtful of the universe to finally pick a side.

Chose wrong.

The words hit hard, sharp and staggering, echoing in Lumira's ears.

He hadn't meant the gods. He'd meant the Brotherhood.

They watched Emberly. Feared her.

All while Lumira listened. Waited.

And now Emberly was ash—and Lumira was the one walking away.

The wrong sister.

She'll make sure they regret it.

When they're gone, Lumira moves again—deeper into the forest, guided by symbols only she can read: tiny carvings on tree bark, carefully placed stones, paths disguised as accidents. The gnomes' handiwork. Clever. Almost smug.

Creatures slip from the underbrush, keeping pace beside her—not with obedience, but with the easy recognition of kin. A Dusk Deer flickers into view, its antlers faintly glowing as it glides across her path—mesmerizing in its passage, drawing patrols away.

Somewhere deeper in the trees, the low growl of a Grove Dragon echoes, its presence sufficient to reroute the bravest Brotherhood agents.

The forest isn't helping her.

It's *claiming* her.

No longer a visitor, she belongs to it now. It bends with her, not around her—parting without sound, roots sliding beneath her steps, shadows stretching to hide her passage.

She is no longer merely tolerated.

She is sheltered.

By the time she nears the edge of the refuge's reach—where the trees thin and moss-covered markers rise from stone like half-forgotten memories—dawn begins to bloom. Pale grays and muted reds stretch across the horizon, the colors of the aftermath.

There is no triumph. No mercy. Only an unsettling hush, steeped in the aftermath of what cannot be undone.

Ilara waits ahead, steady and familiar. She doesn't speak as Lumira approaches. Her gaze does all the questioning, lingering on the blood, the torn leathers, the faint glow pulsing through Lumira like fire trying to remember how to burn.

"You did it." Soft—like saying it aloud might anchor it in the ruins left behind.

Lumira nods. "He's dead."

Ilara studies her for a beat longer. "And you?"

The question doesn't wound—it lands.

Lumira exhales. "I don't know what… or who I am anymore."

Ilara nods and turns toward the path. "Come. The others are waiting."

They walk together, unspeaking, as their refuge—Sanctuary—emerges: low stone walls curved into hillsides, timber half swallowed by moss, hidden doors that don't look like doors at all.

She never asked for specifics—only a place. A beginning.

And somehow, this is exactly that.

Not a towering fortress carved from ambition, but a place built to contain them—their plans, their ghosts. Nearly all of it lies buried underground, hidden from prying eyes. From their grief. Their defiance.

It hadn't been used in years, but the gnomes had restored it—with care and purpose. They extended its roots, strengthened its reach, opened doors that yield only to those who understand the stillness between stones.

It isn't hers. It's theirs.

A resistance, made tangible.

And for now, it's enough.

As they step through the hidden entrance—where the Sanctuary's wards hum beneath bark and moss—the forest changes. Birds abandon their morning songs, insects still midair, and even the wind seems to hesitate.

The tension isn't natural. It cloaks them, dense as fog and heavy with expectation.

Lumira's heartbeat stutters, recognizing the unnatural hush. Her mouth curves into a knowing smile as Ilara glances her way, question forming.

"Someone's here," Ilara murmurs, brushing the hilt of her blade.

"Yes." Bone-dry and unsweetened. "An irritatingly persistent shadow who can't seem to resist a dramatic entrance."

Understanding slowly breaks across Ilara's features. "I'll go first. Prepare the others." A brief, knowing glint crosses her face before she vanishes through the barrier, leaving Lumira between safety and pursuit.

She reaches the edge of the Sanctuary's wards, the magic brushing against her skin like cool static. One step through—just one—and she sees him.

"You know," Lumira calls out, stepping forward with a deliberate casualness that masks the violent hammering of her heart, "for someone who glides with the shadows, you're remarkably fond of making dramatic entrances. One might almost think you orchestrate these moments purely for effect."

He emerges among the trees like ink seeping through parchment—first absent, then unmistakably there. This time, there's no hood to shield him, no shadow to soften him. His face is bare—bloodied, battered, and unmistakably his. The Shadowspire guard leans against a weathered oak, holding his side where crimson seeps through with disturbing intensity. His smile doesn't falter, that infuriating air of someone entertained by the world, even as it guts him.

"What can I say?" His voice slides through the air like silk over steel, unhurried despite the blood staining his clothing. "Some entrances deserve a proper audience. And yours has been… particularly compelling today."

Pain lances through Lumira's chest as she sees the blood spreading beneath his fingers—undeniable and expanding. Blood. Too much blood. His blood—and she has no idea who caused it, only that he's bleeding and it feels like her fault.

"You're hurt." The words scrape past the sudden tightness in her throat. Not a question. An accusation. "Fuck."

"A minor inconvenience." He adjusts, wincing slightly despite his careful control. "Hardly worth mentioning when compared to your own… accomplishments."

Shouts echo through the trees—angry—but they're distant now, as if the forest itself refuses to let the sound pass.

The magic holds behind her. The Sanctuary remains intact.

But she isn't inside it anymore.

And neither is he.

Lumira steps forward, slow but sure. "You shouldn't be here. Not bleeding in my forest. Not risking yourself for my mistakes."

His mouth curves, dry with pain and amusement. "Mistakes?" he murmurs. "You're not that easy to find, Lumira. Took a few misdirections to keep the Brotherhood guessing."

Her heart stumbles. "You stood between me and them."

His smile is a shadow, worn thin by blood and loyalty. "Wouldn't be the first time."

Curses ring out, closer now—their hunters crashing through the trees.

"Though," he adds, grim and almost amused, "some people seem unreasonably upset about their High Sovereign's… early retirement."

Without thinking, she grabs his arm—bruising his blood-slick skin—and yanks him through the Sanctuary's wards. "Retirement? Is that what we call it when someone is permanently relieved of duty? When that bastard is left in pieces by my hand?"

He doesn't resist her grip, allowing himself to be guided through the veil of protective magic that shimmers around them like heat above flame. Up close, she sees everything: the stubborn cut of his jaw, the raw exhaustion, and the grim determination he wears like armor.

Once through, he leans into her—not by choice, she realizes with dawning horror, but from necessity. His body radiates alarming heat, his weight suddenly heavy against her side.

"Diplomatic language helps in these situations," he murmurs, the usual ease gone, pain threading through each carefully measured word. "I'd say Zylven has certainly… retired from Brotherhood activities. Permanently. Spectacularly, even. Your technique was… impressive."

The casual praise for her brutality should repulse her. Instead, it settles in her chest like recognition—not of what she's done, but of what she is, what she's becoming.

"Sit," she commands, guiding him to a moss-covered stone before he can collapse. "Before you bleed all over my Sanctuary and ruin its aesthetic appeal."

His stare finds hers, amused despite the sudden drain of color. "Heaven forbid I interfere with your vision for the place."

He slumps against the forest floor, half-conscious and bleeding. Lumira drops beside him, knees slamming into moss and stone, her body reeling from what hasn't yet passed.

She peels back the blood-soaked fabric at his side, revealing a deep slash curving from his ribs toward his abdomen. Not immediately fatal—but close enough to terrify her.

She searches wildly, desperate for anything—and finds it: a satchel tucked beside a moss-covered stone. Clearly left by the gnomes. Or Ilara. Or maybe both.

She grabs it, trembling as she rips it open in one jagged motion: bandages, salve, thread, a curved needle already strung.

It will hold. It has to.

Moving on instinct, she presses salve into the torn flesh, her other hand threading the needle through the jagged wound. The skin resists—his blood is slick and hot—but she works quickly, stitching him closed with unsteady care. Her fingers slip once, twice, but she doesn't stop.

Only once the last stitch is in place does she wrap the bandages tight, knotting them off to slow the bleeding.

It's not perfect, but it'll keep him upright.

Only once the bleeding's slowed, once the trembling eases from his jaw, does she realize how close they've become. How little space there is between his pain and her pulse.

"You did this for me." She presses a clean cloth against the wound. Not a question this time. An understanding snapping into place, bringing with it unwelcome weight. "You drew them away. Created a diversion."

"The Brotherhood's hunters are remarkably single-minded," he replies, drawn not to her work, but to the truth written on her face. "They required… convincing."

Lumira adjusts the bandage, her fingers pressing harder than necessary. "Risking yourself to protect me seems reckless—even for you. A death wish poorly disguised as heroics."

A hiss escapes between his teeth. He catches her wrist, expression sharpening—no longer amused, but assessing.

"Someone had to start questioning our dearly departed High Sovereign's methods. The Brotherhood's loyalties… are not what they once were."

"Speaking of complications." Lumira braces a hand against his ribs, not on the wound itself but close enough to make him feel it—partly steadying him, partly punishment. "Why help me? Why risk yourself? Why share Brotherhood secrets? Besides your obvious thrill at playing both sides."

The grin falters as he meets her eyes, amusement evaporating, replaced by emotion stripped bare. "Would you believe I missed our stimulating conversations?"

"Absolutely not," she retorts, though her voice lacks its usual bite.

"Your charming personality?" he offers, the corner of his mouth lifting slightly.

"Try again." Her tone softens, traitorous despite her best efforts.

His stare doesn't waver. "Because you matter, Lumira. More than you let yourself believe."

The simple declaration lands with the weight of prophecy, heavy with implications she cannot yet decipher.

"That's not an answer."

"No," he agrees, his thumb tracing delicate patterns against her pulse point with maddening intimacy, "but it's all I can give you. For now."

She should pull away. Distance herself from this connection that threatens her carefully constructed walls of purpose and rage. Instead, she finds herself leaning closer, drawn by the gravity of unspoken truths between them.

"At least tell me your name," she whispers, the question emerging as vulnerable as an exposed throat. "Your real one."

A flicker of grief slips behind the mask—the careful layers of misdirection peeling back long enough to reveal it. "Kalum." The name breaks free—sharp with meaning, like a promise he hadn't planned to offer but can't withdraw.

The syllables settle into the space between them, reshaping the air and transforming their dynamic with invisible yet palpable force. A name. *His* name. Freely given after so many exchanges of words and blades and secrets.

"How disappointing," she manages, though her voice betrays her with unwelcome softness. "I hoped for something more dramatic."

"Would you prefer 'Shadowlord Dreadweaver of the Eternal Night'?" The familiar teasing returns, though it lacks its usual bite.

"Now you're showing off." But despite her best intentions, despite every instinct honed through years of aristocratic self-preservation, his fingers remain interlaced with hers, and more disturbingly, she hasn't forced him to release her. "Why tell me now?"

His thumb moves lightly across her wrist, a softness at odds with hands that seem forged for destruction. "Because names have power, little fox. And maybe I'm tired of being nameless with you."

The simple admission tears through her defenses with the ease of fire catching dry paper.

"That's…" She swallows, caught off guard by the raw honesty between them, by the sudden absence of their usual protective layers of sarcasm and deflection. "Unexpectedly sentimental."

"You shattered him," he says, steady and sure. "And gods help me, you remain the most beautiful sight I've ever seen." He leans in. "I should fear you, but all I want is to kneel."

The words land like physical blows—not for their content, but for the unvarnished truth behind them. He has seen her at her most monstrous, yet he chose to follow. To help. To bleed for her cause.

Kalum rises slowly, moving with an unbearable steadiness that suggests he chooses each breath he takes. He brushes her cheek with devastating gentleness, claiming nothing but promising everything.

She expects him to pull away.

Instead, he closes the space between them and presses his lips softly to hers. It's not a claim, nor a promise—it's a collision of everything they've done and left unspoken. And when he pulls back, she memorizes every inch of him—the blood, the bruises, the impossible beauty that no longer feels like a secret she's only glimpsed in dreams.

"I'll find you again," he murmurs. "Try not to miss me too much."

"I won't miss you at all." The lie scrapes out of her throat.

His laugh trails behind him, swallowed by the forest. "Liar."

Then, he void-steps.

One blink—and he's gone, lost in the space between heartbeats, the forest folding around him, a secret swallowed whole.

The accusation hangs between them long after he disappears, piercing in its accuracy. Lumira stands frozen, watching the spot where he vanished, a chaotic storm of emotions rising within her chest—concern for his wounds, fury at his recklessness, and beneath it all, that ridiculous flutter of anticipation his promise of return ignites within her.

How inconveniently devastating to learn her heart could still feel beyond rage and vengeance—precisely when such a complication threatened all she'd built, and amid blood, revolution, and the burning wreckage of her former life, it had to be now. When she's begun to care for a man whose real name she's only just learned.

Her fingers brush her lips, where his kiss burns—uninvited, and all the more unforgettable.

The Sanctuary hums with urgency—Ilara barking orders, Wrenna and Quinn hauling crates of stolen supplies, Lumira's network slipping through the trees with blades and secrets.

Neither panic nor praise. Only purpose.

No one speaks Zylven's name, but his death hums in the air—final, and painfully present. And at the center of it all stands Lumira. Not the spare heir. Not the rebel. A different force altogether.

She crouches at the stream that borders the Sanctuary, washing blood off of her. The water turns pink, then clear. It isn't absolution. Just necessary.

The Blood Key hums against her chest—not urgent now, but sated, as if acknowledging the blood price paid.

Her reflection remains unchanged. But she knows better. The power hasn't left. It coils in her depths, quiet and enduring, waiting to be unshackled.

Zylven is dead. And the ripples haven't reached them yet— Aviah and Marnox, suspended in the before. She wonders, briefly, what losing a father might do to them. But she doesn't follow the thought. Not now. Reckoning travels fast.

She shifts her attention to the path where Kalum disappeared into the trees. He called her a liar. He wasn't wrong.

She will miss him. But she won't stop.

The mask is gone. The rage remains.

And from the wreckage of everything she was, rises a threat the world isn't ready for.

30

THE AWAKENING

The meadow beyond the Sanctuary looks serene but is never at rest. The morning wind stirs through the tall grasses in sweeping waves. Wildflowers bow in its passing, their petals catching the first blush of light. Dew clings to every blade, refracting color like glass—bluebells brushing soft against her knees, ferns curling open as if waking. It feels like the earth is listening.

Lumira sinks to her knees, her touch weaving gently through the green—soft stems and petals folding beneath her. Her body aches from wounds she didn't have time to feel. The weight of last night clings to her, stitched into her ribs, the ghost of a scream she did not let free. Grief gnaws at the edges of her resolve, hollow and biting, but she presses her palms deeper into the living earth—as if it might steady her. Creased, weathered, and worn by truths the world wasn't meant to hear, Emberly's journal rests in her grip. She brought it without thinking, pulling it from her satchel like instinct.

The pages fall open to one she hasn't read. A sketch sprawls across the parchment in Emberly's careful script: spirals, arcs, waves of motion that shimmer as if the page itself breathes. The shapes feel familiar, though she cannot say why, the echo of a song unlearned but remembered.

Beneath the sketch, Emberly's script winds across the page—not a note, but a passage that feels like it wasn't meant to be read aloud.

The Rainbow Serpents move where memory gathers—ribbons of light woven through the world's first breath. I have seen their shapes in dreams I cannot name, and their colors are in places the Brotherhood keeps hidden.

They do not answer to those who seek control, but those who remember.

Speak to the earth. Let your power reach downward—the words will come. The names will come.

They are waiting.

Lumira lets go, slipping into the darkness as it folds in around her.

She embraces the scent of morning and moss. Her breath steadies as the earth stirs beneath her touch, and a force deeper than spellwork answers—an old, patient power that flows not by command but by recognition. It doesn't banish her sorrow. It threads through it, weaving grief and wonder into strength.

The earth answers.

Not with violence or fanfare—but with a deeper transformation. Slow and seismic, beneath flesh and soil.

She exhales and lets the words come. Not recited. Remembered.

"Venabs mor feniri."

The ancient language leaves her lips, smoke and song entwined, sinking into the ground as a blessing. Gold light flares beneath her, curling into the grasses in delicate, geometric spirals. The meadow responds—symbols unfurl, etched in glowing lines braided through the living world.

Magic hums. Air thickens. Light bends.

The ground shivers—not in fear, but anticipation.

And from it, they rise.

First, a ripple of golden flame. A colossal form uncoils from the earth: slow, dignified, and divine. Its scales gleam like hammered sun metal, each edged in molten red and deep ember-orange, catching firelight even in the morning's cool haze. Heat rolls off its body in untouched waves, not burning, but commanding. The air bends around it, reverent. It is less a creature than a force made flesh. When its eyes open—twin suns forged in amber and flame—Lumira doesn't flinch. She knows.

"Samir." The name slips out—sacred and uninvited.

Next, a surge of color ripples upward, fluid and alive. Deep green and ocean blue swirl together, formless at first, then coalescing into serpentine grace. Its body flows like tidewater made flesh, sapphire and turquoise coursing across each scale in waves that shimmer with motion. Veins of glowing emerald twist along its spine, flickering with every turn, bioluminescence glimpsed beneath deep waters. It coils midair with impossible precision, as though gravity were a suggestion it long since declined. Silver gleams where a gaze might be—not cold, but sharp with knowing. Amused, almost. Ancient, but never bored.

"Zedriel."

Then the third emerges—not with sound, but with shimmer.

Light bends as it rises—lavender and rose gold, magenta deepening to plum. Its body unfurls, a ribbon caught in a storm, leaving a trail of iridescence suspended in the air, the afterimages of a dream too vivid to forget. Each scale glows with mutable shades of violet and soft blush, refracting light in a thousand subtle hues—evidence of power held, not flaunted. She embodies a cadence that belongs more to music than motion, intoxicating, unknowable. When their stare meets—amethyst and endless— Lumira feels a surge in her chest that no language could contain. A part of her, one she thought was buried with her grief, breaks open—wild, fearless, and fiercely alive.

"Florietta." Not a command, but a greeting—soft, like they've met before, somewhere between starlight and memory.

The three serpents ripple downward in eerie harmony, not to yield but to recognize.

She rises. And with her, the weight she carries does not vanish; it settles, no longer a burden, but a bond.

The golden lines in the earth dim behind her. The grass parts gently beneath her feet. She steps forward and lifts a hand to Florietta's massive head—easily the size of her own—running her palm along the warm, glowing scales with reverence. Not as a conqueror. As if reborn.

The Rainbow Serpent leans into her touch.

Lumira, who once sought vengeance and found truth instead, lifts her chin. "Come." The word lands gently but firm. "We have work to do."

She strides away from the clearing without glancing back, the meadow vibrant in her wake. Magic gathers in her core, dangerous and rising, but purpose holds her steady.

The Rainbow Serpents follow her, silent storms bound to grace.

And Lumira Kyrvayne, who once chased vengeance through broken streets and bloodstained dreams, does not run.

She leads.

ACKNOWLEDGMENTS

This book exists because of many hands and hearts, but first, thank you to every author who created worlds that became sanctuaries when reality felt too overwhelming. And to Rebecca Yarros, whose encouragement during the best damn book tour made me believe my chaos was worth shaping into a story.

To my husband: if you're a bird, I'm a bird. Also, you're the glue. The quiet strength holding everything steady when I'm spiraling through drafts, deadlines, and existential dread. I could not have done this without you—nor would I want to.

My daughter, fourteen going on Oracle, thinks I'm cringey for writing a book she can't read yet, but offers wisdom beyond her years. I'm infinitely grateful you're mine.

My mother deserves credit for the countless trips to the library we took—though I suspect that dark magic and poor decisions weren't part of her master plan.

To my dad, who taught me the value of moderation in all things—except maybe storytelling (and wine, depending on the day).

Michelle survived every rant, spiral, plot twist, and random lore drop. You know how I can tell we're still friends? 'Cause we're connected. (Full Tony Stark sarcasm intended... with a touch of genuine awe.) B.W.A.C. for-ev-er.

Murchison, you've been my hype man since long before this book had a plot—or even a point. Your unwavering encouragement and elite-level hype energy made it impossible to quit (even when I really wanted to). I wouldn't have made it here without you.

Mel, my walking encyclopedia of insight, always ready for deep dives into everything from character arcs to cosmic chaos—your kindness made the difficult parts bearable.

Lora, you brought my characters into the light so the world could feel their greatness—transforming shadows into souls the reader could truly know. You have a gift.

Jessica McKelden, thank you for reining in the chaos without dulling its edge.

To my Delulu HQ girls—my forest sprites, the real MVPs of moral support, caffeine-fueled nonsense, and unsolicited but always correct opinions. You're the best damn street team I could've summoned.

To my ARC readers who trusted a story finding its wings: your early support ignited the flame.

My entire extended family deserves thanks for being my original cheerleaders—every time I'd announce some wild new project, they'd rally around Auntie Lin Lin with unwavering "yes you can!" energy. Their excitement made me realize I've had fans for years before I ever had readers.

Credit also to caffeine, insomnia, and the playlists that made this book feral.

To every reader who cracked the spine, clicked the file, or highlighted a line—you made this real.

And finally, to past me who thought writing a book would be "a fun little side project"—ha—good one.

IF YOU'VE MADE IT THIS FAR, THANK YOU. TRULY.

Walking alongside Lumira through blood, ruin, and beautifully controlled chaos means more than you know.

If her story left a mark, the best way to help others find it is by leaving a quick review—on Amazon, Goodreads, or wherever you share your reads. Your words matter. And they help keep the chaos alive.

And if you think the story ends here-don't worry. Book Two, When Shadows Burn Steel, is coming Fall 2026.

New enemies. Old betrayals.
And a girl who won't be caged.

Pre-order now and be the first to return to the chaos.

www.ingramcontent.com/pod-product-compliance
Lightning Source LLC
Chambersburg PA
CBHW020012120726
47903CB00004B/1244